I0600753

The Obsidian Gates

Heart of the Warrior
Book Two

By

C.R. Richards

Copyright © 2017 C.R. Richards
All rights reserved.

Book layout by www.ebooklaunch.com

For my Ninja Roadie, Brent. Thanks for being a loyal fan and an even better friend.

Chapter One

SILVER RIBBONS from a lonely moon fell in tatters through the fog about the docks. Their thin fabric touched the surface of dark water as it slapped against rotting wood. Nature's other voices had been silenced this night, as if Erthe was holding its breath. Julian D'Antoiné wrapped his cloak tighter about his body against the chill of an islander autumn night. He too felt the horrible anticipation as he waited for the heavy axe of war to fall.

A lone pillar stood broken amongst the cold waves. It was a testament of simpler times before airships and industry had come to these little islands. He gritted his teeth as another bit of metal from the abandoned dock struck the wood with a hollow thump. Storming toward his personal albatross, he gripped the man's arm as he was about to throw another noisy projectile.

"We're trying to avoid detection, Marcellus, not announce our presence to these Grey Cliff Islander bumpkins."

"We wait in the darkness for a filthy thief with no honor." Marcellus De Costa turned incredulous eyes upon him. "Why trust this mercenary scum, my lord prince? You have loyal men who could see the job done."

He raised a hand again to toss the bit of metal, noticed Julian's glare and then placed it carefully atop a pillar. The deep, ill-formed indentation in his cheek paled to a sickening gray under the moonlight. Marcellus was a rabid dog. His own father had tried to put him down. Julian, at the Sarcion's wish, had saved him from public stoning. It was Marcellus' thirst for power, rather than gratitude, which kept him by Julian's side.

"Our friend can't resist the smell of money."

"And what of Valdeon? The people need their prince to lead them when the storms of war come."

Julian slammed a fist against the rotting wood of the railing. "The Lion Ring is the key to Valdeon's salvation."

His Akutarian allies had come to Andara's shores promising Julian aid in taking the throne. Their lust for the continent's resources and wealth hadn't become clear until their Emperor had sent his general to oversee Valdeon's conquest. Lord Gorman was impatient to spill Andarian blood. If Julian didn't find the whelp who bore their father's ring soon, it would be Gorman upon the throne.

Hatred tightened around his heart in a painful embrace as he thought of the half-breed boy. A child of two ancient enemies, he was an abomination. No one would embrace his reign. Rather, he'd be given a painful death by an angry mob. It would be a kindness on Julian's part to kill the boy quickly, instead.

"You have left your ship against Lord Gorman's orders, Andarian."

Two Jackal warriors stepped from the ruins of an abandoned boathouse. Julian took an involuntary step away from their gruesome visages. Blood encrusted braids fell across battle worn armor. The odor of their unwashed bodies drowned the stench of discarded fish entrails and stale brine. Teeth, yellow with age and neglect, escaped the confines of cracked lips as they grinned.

One of the Jackal warriors, a man with an empty left eye socket, stepped forward. He extended his hand palm up and began tapping the tips of his fingers together. Julian understood their culture well enough to know that they reserved the gesture for calling wayward harlots in their brothels.

"Why do you linger here? Guilt? No. I think not."

"My vessel is in need of minor repairs. I have no interest in hovering over the crew as they perform menial tasks."

"No doubt they were happy to be rid of you." He turned toward his comrade. "Go. Inform Lord Gorman our wayward dog likes to roam when he's off leash. I will stay with the Andarian's ship until he reaches San Leonora."

Obeying with surprising discipline for a barbarian, he left them as soundlessly as he'd arrived. Wrapped in armor and weapons, the Jackal warriors were infamous for their stealth and lust for blood. They were brutal killers who took joy in violence. Working in packs like their namesake, the Jackal were expert predators.

Though he refused to tolerate their disgusting taunts, Julian took great care not to push them too far.

"Lord Gorman knew you'd try to go back on your word, *prince of nothing.* He told me to watch you like I would a cornered beast hiding in the darkness. Murdering your own kin for a trinket. I would say you were more of a vulture who should have its neck snapped."

Then the man's remaining eye went wide. Blood dribbled from his open mouth. He dropped to filthy knees and onto the gray boards of the dock. Marcellus stood over the body, knife steaming with the man's blood.

"You should have listened to your lord." He spat atop the body.

The mad fool had just signed his own death warrant. Lord Gorman had a disturbing way of knowing the desires in a man's heart. One glare into Marcellus' crazed eyes and the Jackal General would see what he'd done. Watching the euphoria upon his murderous companion's face, Julian wondered if exposing the deed would be of benefit. Lord Gorman would most certainly kill him, leaving Julian with one less burden.

"What foul stench plagues us? It turns the stomach."

Light burst from a lantern, removing their blanket of secrecy. Its owner leaned against the remains of a boathouse with arms folded and an amused look upon his face. The devil only knew how long he'd been watching them. Short blond hair bristled atop a sunburned scalp. Bronze pierced his ears in long rows of loops. A dull brown cloak hung over his loose-fitting trousers. Its filthy hem brushed at the rim of worn leather boots.

Known for stealth almost as much as for greed, mercenaries were the nomads of Andara. They held no allegiance to anything except wealth. His impertinence was no surprise.

"You're late, Cutter." Julian stepped around the filthy body to join him at the edge of the light. "I should think you'd be on time for the large sum I'm paying you."

Cutter shrugged and rubbed at the dirty blond stubble on his scarred chin. "You said you were interested in the boy. If you'd rather I come to hold hands with you in the dark, so be it."

"You know where he is?"

"He escaped Marianna on a cargo airship. They'll land here on Larkspur soon. I have men waiting on the docks." Cutter let the greedy smile cross his face. "So many men to feed and arm. It may take a few extra coins to see the job done."

"Do you think I care about the cost?" Julian shoved a dagger under his chin. "Listen well. Find the boy. He has a ring I want. Cut it off his hand if necessary once you've killed him. Bring the ring to me in Valdeon within three days' time or I'll send my new friends to fetch you."

Julian waved his hand toward the shadows. A shroud broke away from the darkness and floated toward them. The Dirge hovered beside the corpse. Lowering its head like a hungry animal, it sniffed and grunted toward the abandoned flesh. Gray-skinned fingers wagged anxiously toward its bloodied prize.

"My Dirge is going to accompany you to find the boy. It will keep you true to your word." Julian grinned as Cutter paled and took a step away from the creature. "If I may offer a word of advice? Don't come between it and a meal."

Julian nodded at the Dirge and turned away when it pounced upon the body. Chewing flesh and bone, the creature began to devour its feast. Raw, frenzied hunger drove the Dirge to near madness as it ate. They were difficult to control at the best of times. Bloodshed turned them feral.

"You'd better hurry, Cutter. This body should sate its hunger for a few days, but I can't promise the creature won't turn feral if you're delayed."

"You've made your point," Cutter said, disgust upon his face. "I think I've been properly motivated to kill this boy of yours."

Julian pushed past Cutter, leaving him to stare unabashedly at the feasting Dirge. Money was an excellent motivator for most, but no one could stand against the fear of certain death. He took a happier pace across the rotting docks. The Lion Ring would soon be upon his finger. Lord Gorman hadn't secured the throne of Valdeon quite yet.

Chapter Two

SETH MCCLOUD STRETCHED atop a bundle of woolie wool to make use of the delicious fresh air washing over his face. He breathed in the salty fragrance of the ocean passing beneath their airship. A small patch of starry sky peeked through the crack between hatch and cargo hold. His amber flecked eyes stared up at the cold stars. They'd witnessed a great many things from their perch above the world of man. His mother's murder, the raid on his island home, and the assassination of his father were shared memories between them.

Shifting his gaze to the Lion Ring upon his finger, he waited for a sign. Its power had come to him a few hours before as he protected the people of his island home from raiders. The ancient spirit living within the heart crystal had readily given him its wisdom then. Now the lion head seemed content to float quietly in the center of its stony belly as Seth's blood rose and fell about its mane. He slapped the ring's silver band against his thigh with an impatient sigh.

Riley Logan thrust his nose into the thin patch of air, gulping in the sea breeze and releasing it again with grateful sighs. "I'll have angry words for my brother Tom. *Hide in the cargo hold,* he says. Never mentioned how foul it would be down here."

Massive bundles of woolie wool, produced by Riley's family and other farmers on Marianna, filled the hold. Known as the finest wool in Andara, it could only be found on their little island home. In the rush to escape, the crew had left barrels of salted lamb and some sort of smoked fish stashed among the bundles. The mix of odors was nauseating.

Boots clomped on deck, stopping a few feet from the tiny opening. Seth pushed Riley into the bundles of wool and leapt after him. They waded through the itchy material toward the shadows of the hold. A larger patch of indigo sky opened above their heads.

"You there. The hatch has come open. Would you have miles of woolie wool wasted upon the waves? Go stow the cargo!"

"Aye, Captain!"

Two sailors dropped gingerly onto the topmost bundles. The youngest, a thin towheaded man with a ragged red cap, gave a quick nod. Waiting for the Captain's back to disappear, he scurried down among the bundles. His companion, a bulky bald man with a rough beard and squinting eyes, reluctantly followed.

Light burst into the hold as he activated the crystal lantern. Seth and Riley ducked their heads down behind the barrels of smoked fish as the beam from the lantern penetrated the darkness beside them. Resisting the need to scratch, Seth kept his body perfectly still.

"Look there, Artie," the thin sailor said. "Someone's gone and squashed a bundle."

"You think stowaways maybe, Nate?" Artie wiped at his large runny nose. "Captain don't like stowaways.

Threw the last one overboard right in the middle of the straights."

Seth gripped the hilt of his sword. He didn't want to fight. It had been a night of killings. He willed the bloody memories from his thoughts. Their survival depended on Seth staying strong. Grief and fear must wait until they were certain their hunters were no longer following them.

"It weren't no stowaway. The rope's come untied," Nate grumbled. "You was supposed to tie down those bundles."

"Get off it! How can you expect me to do the job with all those killings in Haven Bay? I've never seen raiders so keen to take a town in my life. They've gone barmy if you ask me. Hurry on, Nate." Artie sneezed and brought a filthy linen to his nose. "Why don't we tell the Captain the job's done and go to the galley?"

"Aye," Nate said with a snort. "Warm rum at the table is better than playing tickle the bundle with you in this here hold. I need to steady my nerves."

The two sailors tumbled back to the deck, slamming the hatch closed after them. Seth lifted his eyes, but the indigo sky and all its stars disappeared. A sharp click echoed in the belly of the hold as the latch shoved home, locking the hatch firmly in place.

"The last of the fresh air," Riley murmured, flipping on the small crystal lantern his brother had given them.

"It's a short flight to Larkspur."

Fabric brushed irritably against fabric as Riley made himself comfortable among the bundles. Seth left his friend to his thoughts. They'd both seen horrors in this night of madness neither would soon forget. He leaned against a barrel and closed his eyes. They were safe for the time being.

How odd his life had become. A week ago, he had been living the simple life of a Grey Cliff Islander. Tonight, he was hiding from savage creatures who were bent on killing him for the Lion Ring upon his finger. All the horror and killing over the past few days had been born of one chance meeting seventeen years before. His mother, Anne McCloud, had fallen in love with a man who'd borne the blood of her family's greatest enemy. Trying to hide her son from the world, she'd brought them to a small, remote island well off the coast of Andara.

It wasn't until their enemies had found his mother at last did the truth come to light. Her murder brought his father, Edmund D'Antoiné, to Marianna. He'd told Seth of the truth behind his mother's well-intended lies. He'd also given to Seth an awesome responsibility passed from father to son. Edmund the Leo had been a famous ranger in the Jalora Legion on the mainland of Andara. He'd named Seth his heir and placed the Lion Ring upon his finger. Through an unspeakable act of treachery, his father's past caught up with him. Edmund had died in Seth's arms.

He smoothed at the iridescent stone encased in silver. The ring had been put on his finger less than a day ago, yet it seemed they'd been together for much longer. The lion head turned within the stone to regard him and then looked back out into the nothingness. Still it remained silent with no offer of direction for its bearer.

The airship's thrusters roared. He threw an arm out trying to steady his body. The ship was sinking faster now, taking Seth's stomach with it.

"Great gulls!" Riley cried.

"They'll be down to unload the cargo in a moment," Seth told him, switching off the lantern. "We'll wait for our opportunity and hide on one of the lifts going to the docks."

The ship shuttered one last time and was still. Shouts and stomping boots headed toward the cargo hold. Predawn sky opened above their heads and suddenly the hold became a flurry of activity. Sailors with nets and ropes began rolling the bundles of wool into the waiting rigging. It wouldn't be as easy catching a lift as he'd hoped. They missed two loads before they found their opening as one of the sailors paused for a drink of water. They dove on top of the bundles and twisted down inside until they could not be seen from the top or the bottom of the net.

"Hoist away!"

Their net was lifted with jerking pulls into the air. He heard Riley yelp something about the height and chose not to look down as they swung across the emptiness. The moment the bundles touched the docks of Larkspur Port, Seth and Riley bolted into the crates of another shipment.

Seth peered carefully over the top of a nearby crate, scanning the docks. Men and mules pulled at the cargo ropes in the dim torch lights. Their movements cast shadows upon the nearby water while the rest of Larkspur was hidden under the blanket of darkness. Labored grunts as rope rubbed upon pulleys made the dull music of the docks. Try as he might, Seth couldn't hear anything over the rhythm.

Then a jab of apprehension struck his stomach and ran up his spine. Across the docks, well hidden among the shadows, floated a figure shrouded entirely in black. Grey skin stretched over a thin jaw. Its gaping maw sucked in hungry gulps of empty air. Seth held his breath as terror crawled along the walls of his heart. The hideous creature, known as the Dirge, had struck down his father. Then their hunger had turned toward the new Bearer of the Lion Ring. If not for Wolf, another powerful Valdeonian ranger, Seth would have joined his father in death.

These insatiable hounds had been clever enough to suspect their prey had stowed away onboard the airship. The Dirge's stare remained fixed upon the laboring men as they unloaded the last of their cargo. Lifting its hooded head in strange jerking movements, the creature suddenly turned away from the docks and melted into the shadows.

"The Dirge are here. We'll try to avoid them by staying in the center of the crowd. Ready?"

Riley nodded, lifting a small crate of wooden stake nails to his shoulder. The crate hid his face and copper curls well enough to get them through the crowd. Seth picked up his own crate and moved behind Riley. Following the dock workers to the warehouse, they quickly put down their loads.

Leaning against the tower of crates, Riley groaned and clutched at his side. Seth helped his friend to stand upright. Trembling and more pale than usual, Riley didn't look well. His friend pushed firmly away to stand upon his own strength. Seth's hand came away bloodied when he released him. Turning his squire around, he examined Riley's torso. A nasty looking gash ran along his side. He'd come between Seth and the assassin Pavel Sandor as they'd made their escape from Marianna's airship port.

"You need a healer."

"What we need is a ship to the mainland, Seth."

A stubborn glint he well recognized filled Riley's eyes. The Logan temper was up again. Seth supported his friend as they hurried on through the rows of cargo. He'd have to hide Riley somewhere close to the ships until he could find one headed to Eastland Isle. He'd seen two vessels moored at the docks on either side of their airship as they'd hurried from their hiding place among the woolie wool. Fewer choices meant fewer places to hide.

Passing between two warehouses, Seth helped Riley to sit upon a crate. He didn't like the thought of leaving his injured friend alone, but it would be quicker and less conspicuous if he ventured to the ships on his own.

"I've found you at last, boy," a man called from the shadows.

The Lion Ring's magic surged up his arm in a frantic wave to flood his eyes with power. Then he saw it in tendrils of green. The ring's power showed him the true nature of people and their emotions. Greed. Instinctively, he knew its ugliness. It penetrated the darkness, reaching across the distance toward Seth with grasping fingers. Despite his best efforts, their hunters had found them.

Chapter Three

TENDRILS OF GREED swirled in frenzied ribbons around the pale mercenary. Short blonde hair clung to his scar-lined skull. Bronze loops caught the light of a nearby torch as they grasped tightly to weather-worn ears. This hunter of two-legged prey was well armed and clearly practiced in battle. Easy strides brought him across the distance, ever closer to his prize.

"You escaped those bumbling Amity Raiders on Marianna. Tslavians are too cheap to pay for real talent. The rich Valdeonian buffoon, on the other hand, knows good money pays for good men."

Julian.

The name burned in fiery letters upon his heart. His father's squire, Dante, had warned Seth against this villain. His half-brother arranged Leo's murder just as he'd struck down their other siblings. Julian's hunger for the Lion Ring hadn't sated, though their father's blood was on his hands.

Blades pulled free from their scabbards all about him. Running wasn't an option. They'd been trapped.

"Force me to give chase and it will be all the worse for you," the mercenary warned.

"Then you leave me little choice."

Seth stepped away from Riley and pulled his sword. More men came out of the darkness. They began to circle as they slapped ropes against their thighs and rattled chains meant to break bone.

Nervous sweat formed along his palm, making the hilt slick under his grasp. He'd been confident and strong in battle back on Marianna when the raiders had attacked. The bravado he'd embraced back home had faded in the winds of change. Riley groaned behind him. Confident or no, he wouldn't let them strike at his helpless friend.

Forcing his body to remain still in the First Stance of the ranger's Dance of Death, he made ready for their advance. They came at him en masse, circling slowly to gauge his skill. Moving in tandem as one, the men he faced now were battle-hardened and used to fighting together.

The first came at him in a rush. Steel slammed against his blade with the force of a runaway wagon. The foul odor of stale sweat and drink engulfed the space between them as his attacker pressed hard to gain the advantage. Seth dug his feet in and pushed hard at the man's body. The height he'd inherited from his Valdeonian father gave him added leverage, but he was still losing ground. Why wasn't the Lion Ring's magic working?

He gave the ring a good shake as a new wave of men rushed toward him. "If you're going to do something to help me, it better be now!"

Then energy from the spirit of the Lion Ring flooded his veins. Seth breathed in the ancient power reaching down from the heavens to cover his face in a mask of solid silver. His father had called it a Death Mask. For the ranger who bore it, a sense of absolute peace and oneness with nature's energy provided confidence and courage. Enemies of the Jalora, however, fled in terror rather than face a ranger's mask. Its horrible power burned the moment and manner of death into the mind of any who gazed into the silvery depths.

Seth and the ancient power regarded the foul vermin coming toward them. "There will be no mercy."

The mortal creatures scuttled upon the wooden dock like cockroaches fleeing from the light. Moving forward at a relentless pace, Seth followed them. The prey had become the predator. Eternal power scanned the shadow to find the vermin. Warily striking at his blade, some managed to fight their terror. This enemy valued money rather than their own skin.

Examining the mortals with the cold indifference, Seth pounced. His blade sliced through flesh and bone. A savage pleasure burned brighter inside him with each swing of his weapon. It was a feral hunger, anxious for more blood.

Steel clashed with steel behind him. Others had joined the fray. Then a powerful swordsman pressed against Seth as they fought back to back. His unexpected ally was skilled with a blade. He seemed to have no trouble keeping pace with Seth's strikes.

The mystery of his unknown ally's identity faded from Seth's thoughts as the ancient power commanded his attention. A handful of the mercenaries were escaping. It turned Seth's full focus back to the mortals fleeing before them. Striking without pause, Seth's blade was a deadly unyielding force. The tip finally came to rest before the toe of his boot as the last man fell at his feet.

He took a breath, slowing the exhilaration coursing through his veins. The Death Mask's magic attacked indiscriminatingly those who gazed within its surface. He mustn't allow it to unleash its power upon the stranger who'd helped him. Taking deep breaths, he let the power fade. Soon the chilly breeze of midnight struck his face. Only then did he turn to face the man and his companion.

They stood a few inches shorter than Seth. Both were dressed in Mainlander garb. Tan tunic tucked neatly into brown trousers gave them the appearance of militiamen or officers. Sea blue cloaks fell to the top of their boots, completing their uniformity of dress. Clearly, they weren't from the Grey Cliff Isles. He supposed it was inconsequential where they came from. Fate had been kind to bring visitors to the darkened docks of Larkspur in his moment of need.

"My thanks to you," Seth said, sheathing his sword.

"It appears we happened by just in time." The younger of the two men grinned. "Jason Elder from Netherton."

Tight brown curls fell in a perfect frame around his good-humored face. Sparkling green eyes failed to conceal his constant state of amusement as he extended his hand. Seth took it, not missing the mischievous grin upon his face. He suspected it was a permanent fixture.

"Seth McCloud from Marianna."

He snapped his mouth shut with a frustrated grunt. The Jalora wouldn't allow its rangers to lie. Complete honesty would be yet another difficult challenge while he and Riley were on the run. The truth in the wrong hands would see him dead.

"Please forgive my rushing away, but we have a ship to catch."

"Oh? Where do you travel?"

"Eastland Isle." Seth slapped a hand over his mouth as the words escaped his lips.

"Amazing. Isn't it, Boyd?" Jason slapped a hand on his friend's shoulder. "We're headed to Port City."

"Quite the coincidence, I'd say." The other man chuckled. "You don't mind traveling companions, do you?"

"Good! Let's fetch your friend. We don't have much time. Our ship is pulling in its gangplank." Jason turned to his traveling companion. "Boyd, go fetch our package. Seth and I will hold the ship."

Seth bit his lip hard as Jason took his arm and guided him into the crates where Riley was waiting. He couldn't see any ill intentions surrounding the two men. They appeared trustworthy on the surface, but strangers of any type were best avoided.

The copper curls atop Riley's head fell in an untidy veil across a nearby crate. Seth shook his friend's arm, but got no response. The assassin's blade had cut deeper than Riley would admit. Jason gently eased past Seth and threw Riley over his shoulder like a rag doll. It was a blessing his best friend was unconscious for the trip across the docks. He was overly sensitive about his height and wouldn't like a stranger carrying him as if he were a child. Helpless, and resigned to follow their new traveling companion, Seth snatched up Riley's pack.

Jason was already running for the ship when he cleared the warehouses. Seth followed, staying close until they reached their vessel. It was a small cargo ship from Portsmeth. Judging from its hovering height above the docks, the ship had delivered its cargo and was going back empty. Strange. Most captains wanted to have payment for both trips. Since the Grey Cliff Isles were a fair distance from the coast of the mainland, they were usually paid handsomely to carry back woolie wool.

"Captain!" Jason called as they raced up the gang-plank. "You will hold this ship until my friend arrives."

"Now see here!" The Captain, a rotund man with a shaggy beard and mustache, turned bright crimson as he struggled to keep up with the fast-moving Jason. "I have cargo to pick up in Port City. You assured me we would make my schedule."

Jason ignored the sputtering captain and put Riley's unconscious form down upon a tarp beside the railing. Seth propped his squire's head atop one of their packs. He needed a doctor to see to the wound at his side.

"I'm sorry, Riley." Seth slammed a fist upon the deck. "You made the wrong choice in following me."

A sharp stab of apprehension pierced Seth's stomach. He hurried to his feet and stared across the docks toward the warehouses. A shrouded figure leaned over the dead bodies of their enemies. Violent yanks rocked the lifeless corpses as it fed. Sensing his gaze, the Dirge lifted its shroud-covered head to return the stare. Torn flesh hung from its chewing jaws as a grating song began to pass across its lips.

Struggling with the words, the unhuman mouth sang, "Kill. Lion. Eat."

Any remaining courage he possessed shattered at the twisted song of the Dirge. Its unrelenting hunger would drive the creature onward, never sleeping, never stopping until it had completed its mission. Kill the Lion. Imagining the sensation of those boney gray fingers touching his flesh made his skin crawl.

"By all that's decent in the world, what is it?" the Captain asked at Seth's shoulder.

"We need to leave right now," Seth told Jason, who'd joined them at the railing.

"Yes, I think you're right. They're coming now," Jason said.

Boyd stormed up the gangplank, leading a man clapped in irons. The prisoner, a surly looking brute with wild hair and massive fists, glared at Jason as they approached. Hatred glistened in his eyes as they bore through every man upon deck. Seth had no doubt this villain would murder the entire crew if the opportunity to escape appeared.

"Are you a constable, Jason?" Seth asked, keeping his eyes upon the prisoner as Boyd pulled him below deck.

"I bring criminals to justice."

Jason folded his arms with a grin. He regarded Seth with a slight tilt of his head as if he were waiting for some sort of reaction. Seth, growing uncomfortable under his amused gaze, ran his fingers over the Lion Ring. It had given him the ability to see emotions swirling around the mercenaries as he fought them.

Perhaps using the same power with Jason would give him a better idea of the man's intentions?

He concentrated upon the ring, ignoring the chilly air as their ship lifted away from Larkspur Isle. Setting all his will to the task, he called to the power with his mind. The moments passed by and Jason's grin grew wider. Nothing happened. The Lion Ring remained still.

"Who the devil are you?" Riley snarled from the tarp. "Where are we?"

"We're headed to Port City on Eastland Isle." Seth kneeled beside his friend and adjusted the pack underneath his head. "This is Jason. He's a constable."

"Jason?" Riley grumbled. "It sounds like you're awfully chummy. How do you know you can trust him? Honestly!"

"Your friend has uncommon sense, Seth." Jason chuckled. "I assure you, young man. I mean you no harm."

"The prisoner's secure." Boyd came to stand at Jason's shoulder and stared down at Riley. "Well, awake, are we? Let me have a look at you, Squire."

Seth regarded Jason's companion with new interest as he pulled a healer's bag from beneath his cloak. Boyd pushed through them to kneel beside Riley. Seth stood away as he began rummaging through the bag and silently placing small vials of liquid upon the tarp.

"You're a healer as well as a constable?" Seth asked.

Boyd exchanged a quick glance with Jason. "Of sorts, sir."

"Come. Boyd knows what to do." Jason gripped Seth's shoulder and guided him away. "It appears you and your squire have seen some trouble this night, Lion."

He cast a sharp look at the constable, but the likeable face revealed nothing. Lion. How had he guessed which ring was upon Seth's finger? He'd consciously kept his hand hidden and didn't recall the mercenaries naming him as Leo's heir.

"It is comforting to be traveling with a ranger." Jason winked at him. "Much safer."

"You seemed skilled enough with a blade."

"One must be skilled with the sword if he is to travel to dangerous places like the Grey Cliff Isles. And perhaps a bit more careful with secrets." He pointed to Seth's left hand. "Nothing on Erthe or Heaven glows like the Lion Ring when the Jalora's power flows. It attracts attention, for good or bad."

Seth leaned heavily against the railing, his curls whipping wildly about his ears. Jason was right. He'd have a hard time hiding from his hunters with such a powerful talisman fixed upon his finger. They must be more careful. If not for Jason, the Dirge would be feasting upon their bones. Even with his new skill, Seth was no match for the creature. Riley, in his state, couldn't defend himself at all.

Heat burned at the tender skin on the back of his neck. Wood thumped against wood as a water barrel began to rumble next to him. Seth closed his eyes, sinking to his knees. The power was trying to take control again. He'd agreed to be Bearer of the Lion Ring, praying its touch would keep his temper and the power it brandished in check.

"Why did I allow Riley to get mixed up in this?" He clutched tightly at the thick strands of sweat-drenched hair. "If only I had insisted he go home instead of into danger with me."

"I'm not sure what ordeal you've been through tonight, but you're safe now. Boyd and I watch over you."

Seth stretched out his hands before him. They were shaking violently. He couldn't stop them. Gulping in deep breaths, he desperately tried to follow his father's teachings. He must calm his anger or the power would escape. It would strike those upon the deck without caring who was friend or foe. In his desperation, he summoned images of home. Memories of Leo and the grief he hadn't faced yet brought a darker inner storm. The power was escaping. It threw Seth face down upon the deck as he struggled against it.

"No, Boyd!" Jason cried. "Stay back! His power will kill you. Listen to me, Lion. I'm here to watch over you. No one is going to harm you or your squire on my watch. I swear it."

Great glowing claws of power burst out of the Lion Ring like a lightning bolt. Their sharp tips lashed at Jason, brutally tearing his left arm. He screamed and staggered away. The animal within the stone smelled blood. It hung over the deck, sniffing hungrily in the direction of its wounded prey.

"Help me!" Seth screamed, gritting his teeth as he held the massive lion back.

A tan dog whimpered as it sat upon the deck, licking its wounded leg. Sinking its head down in submission, the dog kept its sharp eyes upon him. Then a reassuring hand came to rest over his. It was Jason. The gloved hand was drenched in hot blood. A steady stream of red gushed from three vicious claw marks along his left forearm. They'd both been lucky. The beast living within the Lion Ring had been ready to spill more innocent blood in its fury.

"I'm sorry," Seth whispered, resting his forehead against the wooden deck. "I can't control it."

"You never need to be sorry for marking me, Lion. This binds us in ways you will come to understand in time. Rest now." Jason kept his hand upon Seth. "They'll need blankets, Boyd. It's best if you and the crew stay below deck for a time."

"Why do you help me, Jason?" Seth asked, his teeth chattering. "You can see I'm dangerous."

"It is the duty of every person on Andara to help a ranger. They are, after all, the servants of good."

"Sometimes, they serve evil."

The mysterious Valdeonian ranger who'd kept Seth's existence a secret was no servant of good. He'd betrayed Seth's father and formed an alliance with the assassin, Pavel Sandor, instead. Though this ranger's identity was still unknown, his intent was clear. He'd wanted to take Seth for his own reasons.

A soft touch brushed against his mind. It was taken away as quickly as it appeared. Jason squeezed Seth's hand until he couldn't ignore the constant pressure.

"Did a ranger try to hurt you, Seth?" Jason asked at last.

The world about him began to spin, disappearing into a patchwork of gray and black. Jason, the ship and its crew fell away. His body faded into the nothingness. Seth's mind was left alone to marvel at the vast emptiness of eternity.

The chill of an autumn wind touched his neck and face. Slowly, his body began to feel again. He opened his eyes. Jason was gone. Strange. His life force, however, was a tangible presence below decks. The sensation was oddly reassuring.

"Bad dream?" Riley asked, tugging his blanket up to his chin.

Seth lifted his body slowly to a sitting position and clutched at his own blanket. "How's Jason?"

"He can use the arm well enough," Riley said. "Those will be nasty scars."

"And the dog? The poor creature must be terrified."

"What dog?" Riley shook his head. "You must have imagined it. They don't let dogs on these cargo ships. Don't want them wetting on the woolie wool."

"I supposed I must have been mistaken." Seth smoothed at the blanket. "Imaginary dogs are the least of our worries. We need to find some answers."

"Aye. Where do we start?"

Seth set his mind on the future. Looking up at the pink clouds of dawn rushing by overhead, he was suddenly reminded of the wharf floating by Marianna. He'd hidden his childhood treasures inside. Now they were burned along with the wharf. His mother's letters from the mysterious "C" were among them.

"We head for the Isle of Carlotta," Seth said at last. "Perhaps my mother's friend can give us the aid we need."

He prayed Wolf could find him in such a distant place. Now more than ever, he needed the sage advice of an ally he could trust.

Chapter Four

Xavier De Vincente, Bearer of the Wolf Ring, reached out with his senses in the entry way of the McCloud home. Austere furnishings with cheerless color seemed to shrink away from the vibrant power of the Jalora. Touches of love remained here and there, but the overwhelming residue of hate was strongest in this house. It seemed the last place anyone would raise a Lion and the next Jalora Master. Known as "Red Hearts," these masters were the very essence of passion.

He touched the wall along the staircase leading up to the family's small bed chambers. Remnants of the young Lion's great power still vibrated from the walls. He would be a strong lord. Seth hadn't learned to control his abilities yet. The destructive force behind the Lion's power was a danger to anyone around the boy. Xavier had sent him away from the island to escape his hunters. He must join him soon, before the power escaped.

The Dirge, creatures of evil who fed upon human flesh, had sabotaged his ship. Crafted for mindless killing, the foul beings had no understanding of crystal-powered engines. They'd managed to delay them by a day rather than cripple his ship completely. Repairs were underway, but he had no patience for waiting.

A sudden wave of warning along his spine brought Wolf's mind back to the cold little house on a miserable little island at the most remote part of Andara. It had been a practical hiding place to keep the bloodthirsty away from a helpless babe, but it was no place to raise the future King of Valdeon.

"Throw your dagger at me, Emma Sandor, and the Jalora's punishment will be fierce."

Wolf turned his gaze to the darkened doorway of a small study. Mistrust. Hatred. Anger. They swirled about the woman in violent bursts of red and black. He descended the stairs slowly, approaching her with absolute calm.

"You can plainly see my face, woman. I do not hide under masks or cloaks." He held the Wolf Ring out for her to see. "This other ranger you were waiting to attack. Tell me of him."

Her worn features changed from suspicion to relief. An odd reaction for a Tslavic assassin who faced a Valdeonian ranger alone in the darkness. He'd sworn to bring such criminals to justice. The fact she was a servant to his country's ancient enemy made his fingers long to grasp the hilt of his sword.

"He is Valdeonian as best as I could tell. Leo tried to discover his identity, but hadn't any luck either. He was known to us simply as the Dark Ranger. I first met him when he came to Marianna a few days after Seth was born. Vowing to protect the boy, the ranger kept us all safe for many years. I did as he ordered for Anne and Seth's sake, but I never fully trusted him. The Dark

Ranger had his own plans for Seth. I'm not sure what they were."

Hiding the boy away from his people was one thing. He was a half-breed and not likely to be accepted as the heir. Keeping Seth away from the Lords of Valdeon, however, was inexcusable. This Dark Ranger had much to answer for in his treachery.

Time was against Wolf. He had to rejoin Seth and get him to safety before news spread of his existence. It would be impossible to keep quiet. The Orb, a massive sphere of crystal, was tied to the Bear of the Lion Ring's life force. For weeks, it had been black with death at the Leo's passing. Seth's acceptance by the Lion Ring had brought the Orb back to life. It glowed among the other talisman of the Altar of Providence like a vibrant beacon of hope. Each—the throne, the crown, and the orb—waited impatiently for their new king to take his rightful place.

He'd seen the Jalora's power flow in frenzied pulses among the altar when it had called him as Right-Hand to the Master. Second only to the Lion, he was bound by honor to protect their king. The Right-Hand's station, while one of amazing abilities and afforded respect, came with a horrible price.

Emma let her hands fall before her. "I promised to erase all trace of Seth and his mother on Marianna. I've finished burning the documents from Pavel's personal safe. No one will be able to trace Seth's escape."

Go to the Police Station across the square.

The urgent tone in the Jalora's command drew him closer to the door. Had more killers come to Haven Bay? The streets were already stained with blood. It would grieve the young Lion if more of his friends and neighbors fell victim to those who hunted him. He must put an end to the bang tail mischief if only to put Seth's mind at ease. Keeping the boy calm was of utmost importance.

"One more thing, Wolf," she said. "A small Valdeonian vessel baring the royal crest was moored in the fields outside Haven Bay last night. I saw it while I was tracking Pavel after he escaped jail. I fear the D'Antoiné family knows of Edmund's son."

Indeed, they did. Julian, the bastard prince, was the reason the Jalora had sent Wolf to Marianna with such urgency. The D'Antoiné family had vehemently opposed Edmund's marriage to his Tslavic princess. Anne's family shared their revulsion for such a union. Would her son be spared when his mother had not? Unlikely.

Emma Sandor, despite the dangers, stayed with Anne and her son all these years. Worry. Fear. Hope. They circled about Emma as her memories showed him images of Seth's childhood. She loved the boy. Wolf could guess the question she was trying hard not to ask him.

"I serve the Lion," he said with a slight nod and turned from her to walk out the door.

Shouts and fists striking flesh permeated the windows of the police station. Wolf pulled the door open, striding across the hall and down into the cells. A group of Marianna farmers circled around a raider tied to a chair. One of the farmers, a tight-jawed redhead, landed his fist upon the raider's face. Blood gushed from his broken nose to splatter across the black tattoos upon his cheeks.

"Tell me why you're so interested in Seth McCloud," he said, leaning close to the raider.

"You can't frighten me, woolie farmer." The raider spat in his face and laughed. "I'll not tell you anything."

Brilliant red burst up from the farmer's collar to cover his cheeks. Blue eyes flashed in murderous fury. Wolf examined the man more closely. Honor. Steadiness. Unwavering honesty. He'd been Seth's protector and a guiding force in the young Lion's youth. The little woolie farmer was in danger of becoming a murderer if Wolf didn't intervene.

"These men are the least of your worries," Wolf said, enjoying the terror creeping into the raider's eyes. "You will tell me or I'll take the knowledge from you."

The woolie farmer turned wide eyes upon Wolf as he approached. Fury drained from his face to be replaced by awe. He backed away, stumbling over his friends who'd gathered in a tight group behind him. It appeared the redheaded woolie farmer was what remained of their leadership upon the little isle.

Wolf grasped the rope binding the raider to the chair. He lifted the man to his eye level. The raider struggled helplessly against the biting rope. It was useless to resist. The Jalora's power would penetrate his ugly thoughts. Extending his power to probe the man's mind, Wolf saw images of the villain's memories. Mental pictures streaked across Wolf's consciousness in a whirl of colors until he found the information he needed. Growling with disgust, he dropped the man.

The chair, suddenly bearing the raider's weight, creaked in alarm.

"Mercenary scum! Why bring them into the mix? Didn't Julian feel you were enough?"

"We were paid by Pavel Sandor. Those mercenaries came to the isle on someone else's purse." The raider let an insolent smile cross his face. "Them D'Antoinés has it in for Leo's half-breed piglet. Both sides of his family are hunting him now. Soon he'll be roasting on a spit with an apple in his mouth."

Fury, powerful and quick, burst from Wolf's body without warning. He pulled his sword and brought it down on the top of the man's head. The blade's descent was an unstoppable force until it reached the floor board beneath. Time resumed with gruesome results. The raider's body fell in two pieces along with the split sides of the chair.

Wolf steadied his breath, coaxing the fury out of his body. He'd never experienced such intensity of emotion. The power of the Right-Hand. He'd heard the legends of the famous temper with its unyielding power used to defend the Lion's honor.

"Great gulls!" one of the islanders cried, cowering with the rest against the wall. "What has come among us?"

The redheaded farmer pushed away from his friends and came to stand before Wolf. "You're the ranger from the fields last night. The one who saved my boys."

"Yes," Wolf said, sensing the father's worry for his youngest. "Your son has gone off with the Lion as his squire. If you still have sway over your boy, I urge you to summon him back home. He has no idea of the danger waiting for them both on the mainland."

"Aye," he said. "I don't like leaving Seth on his own. You'll look after him then?"

"It is my duty to do so." Wolf made for the door, stopping to look over his shoulder at the little farmer. "The Jalora's blessing I give to you for your kindness to the Lion, Thomas Logan."

"Here now. How does he know your name?"

The whispers fell away as Wolf left them. Faithful Basilio raced toward him upon the row, breathless from his run. He'd been ordered to remain on the ship and oversee repairs. His squire must have good news to leave the duties his lord had given him.

"They've finished then?"

"We have enough power in the engines for flight, my lord, but not great speed."

Wolf nodded. They must catch up with the young Lion. More hunters were on his trail than Wolf first supposed. These new soldiers he'd fought in the fields when saving the woolie farmers were a mystery. He wanted to know their interest in the Lion.

"Tell the captain to sail directly for Eastland Isle."

"Yes, my lord. What of Julian, the bastard prince?" Basilio asked.

"He has murdered his other brothers. Julian won't hesitate to kill the Lion in his attempts to take the throne." Grim decision took hold of Wolf's heart. "The dark-hearted creature's hours upon the Erthe are dwindling. Once I find him, nothing will stay my hand."

Chapter Five

Sunlight danced along the waters beneath the hull of their airship. Seth closed his eyes and breathed in the briny air. Fabric snapped against the steady wind as it tugged about the sails above him. Their journey from Larkspur to the coast of Eastland Isle had taken over a full day. He'd spent most of his leisure time in Jason's company. His new friend was a lively storyteller. Most of his tales were filled with humor, offering a much-needed escape from the terrors awaiting them on the mainland.

A great yawn from the deck announced Riley had awakened at last. Boyd had kept him sedated after they realized the little woolie farmer's stomach didn't take well to air travel. The hours of forced sleep had brought the healthy color back to his cheeks.

"Feeling better?" Seth extended his hand, helping Riley to his feet.

Riley nodded with a grunt. "Where are we?"

"Close to Eastland Isle. Look. You can see Port City in the distance."

Airships and seafaring vessels circled about the island in steady streams. Flags from many different nations waved above their sails in colorful displays. Their vibrant hues were a sharp contrast to the rolling green hills rambling up from the shore. Seth's eyes followed the stream of traffic over the green toward the center of the isle. A massive circular stone structure stood as tall as it was wide. Dozens of airships descended and ascended from its belly in a colorful wave of activity.

"Welcome to Port City. Amazing, isn't it?" Jason said behind them. "Vessels from every country on Andara visit this port. They'll take you back with them for the right price. If you escape Port City with your money."

"Here now. What do you mean?" Riley asked.

"The streets are full of people who welcome you with outstretched arms. I mean they're overly ready to take your money, Squire."

Jason laughed when Riley's hand flew to the patch of cloth covering their purse. "We've docked. Come on. There's a place I know where you can hide until Boyd and I've finished turning our prisoner in to the local authorities."

They followed Jason down the gangplank and onto the docks. A world bright and abuzz with activity blossomed before them. Vendors selling fresh fruit and dried meats lined the entrance to the port. Jason prodded Seth onward when he stopped to examine some of the strange looking dishes.

"I think it best to keep your curiosity in check." Jason placed a hand upon Seth's shoulder as they entered the airship port. "We don't want to arouse interest in the wrong people."

Completely round, the walls of the port encompassed a space larger than Haven Bay. Several familiar languages and some indistinguishable ones echoed within the building's hollow belly. Travelers from all over the continent hurried to board their next flight. Seth and Riley stayed close to the wall as they passed countless dock entrances and ticket offices. Above their heads, a large piece of fabric covered most of the sky visible from within the port. The thin cover enhanced the outdoor feel while keeping bad weather out and the fresh air in.

Overhead, signs in immense letters denoted the various destinations for Port City's visitors. Passage to Portsmeth, Tslavia, and Valdeon could be found to their right. Destinations less traveled had been grouped together in a small dock to their immediate left. Carlotta and the Azure Isles were among them. Seth noted the location of the dock. He and Riley would have to make their way back after they parted company with their new comrades.

Exiting the airship port, they were engulfed by a large crowd of travelers and vendors. Each person was intent upon their own journey. Seth pulled Riley out of the way as a large cart came barreling down the center of the crowd. Quieting his friend's angry shouts, Seth looked at the disinterested faces. No one else seemed astonished by the bustle. Moving forward with a lurch, the crowd carried them away from the busier rows around the port and into a large square. Several rows jutted out from the open area like spokes on a wagon wheel.

Jason tugged at his arm as they hurried out of the stream of bodies and into a boot maker's shop. The aroma of fine leather was thick upon the air. Seth smoothed fingertips along a beautiful set of boots. Intricate designs stretched across the polished surface.

"Great gulls," Riley said, yanking Seth's fingers away. "Look at the price! Better you don't touch them. We can't afford anything so grand."

Puffs of smoke drifted across the counter to lazily disperse over the rich leather goods. The proprietor, a thin man with gray hair and keen eyes, watched them without comment as they wandered through the store.

"Rawlings," Jason said, tossing a small bundle to him. "Tobacco from Lea, as promised."

He opened the bundle, sniffed, and nodded to Jason. Rawlings reached under the counter and pulled upward. A section of shelves popped open. It swung slowly away from the rest of the wall. Jason beckoned them into the empty space beyond. Following him, Seth walked inside. Stale air was as thick as the darkness. Then a small light flashed on overhead. Low buzzing from the glass echoed within the windowless room.

"By the green, green fields. What is this contraption? I don't see any flame," Riley said, toggling the switch up and down until Jason put a hand over his fingers.

"You've never seen a crystal lamp before? Where'd you pick these two bumpkins up? A hog pen?"

Their prisoner, who'd had the good sense to remain quiet for most of the trip, spat upon the floor. His laughter was cut short by Jason's swift jab to his midsection.

"The police station is close by. Boyd and I'll be back soon. Stay put. The less people who see you the better."

"What do we do now?" Riley asked, peeking out through the crack in the wall after they'd gone. "Your new friend isn't going to let us go to Carlotta."

Seth joined Riley at the opening. "Jason means well. We wouldn't have escaped those assassins in Larkspur without his help." He rubbed a hand over his tired eyes. "All the same. He doesn't understand the risk if we stay together."

"So, what do we do?"

Their new friends would be no match for the Dirge. Seth couldn't draw more innocent people into his troubles. Jason did have a point about remaining hidden though. He picked up one of the clean rags on the crate and wrapped it around his left hand. Seth hoped the Lion spirit understood.

"I think it best if we leave for the ticket office. I saw the departures board. A ship called the *Bronze Maiden* sails for Carlotta at dusk. It seems to be the only vessel to do so."

"We have trouble headed our way," Riley said, shutting off the overhead light.

Three men had entered the shop. Two of them went to the counter and grabbed Rawlings while the third began knocking over goods from the counter. Muffled behind the fake wall, their words were low and brutal. It wasn't a mystery who they were after.

Seth pushed open the wall and flew at the men. Silently sweeping up behind the mercenary who was brandishing a fist before Rawlings' face, he brought the hilt of his sword down hard upon the villain's skull. The second man turned, aiming his dagger at Seth's torso.

Twisting his body, Seth knocked the man's hand away and brought a fist to his nose.

"Watch your back, Ranger," Rawlings pointed behind him.

The third came at him with sword drawn. His eyes suddenly widened and he stopped abruptly. Letting his arms drop to his side, the mercenary's weapon clattered to the floor. Riley stood behind him with a blade at the man's back. Grinning at Seth, he pushed his prisoner through the ruined leather.

"Did Julian D'Antoiné hire you to kill me?"

"And what will you do if I don't answer? I don't fear you, boy." The mercenary laughed and pulled his knife. "Nightmares walk among us now. You'll join your father in death soon enough."

His knife arched up in a brutal strike, stabbing down toward Seth's chest. Another blade flew past him to plunge deep into the mercenary's throat. Wet gurgles of laughter bubbled from his bleeding mouth. Then the mercenary dropped to the floor in a dead heap. His lifeless eyes remained fixed upon Seth.

"Your hunters are persistent." Jason came up behind them, wrenching the knife from the dead man's throat. "Come. We'll go out the backway. Rawlings, I owe you another bag of tobacco."

They hurried past the counter of Rawlings' store and out the back door leading to an alley. It was filled with empty crates and castaway garbage from the shops. Boyd's head popped up from behind one of the piles as they drew near.

"Lots of foreign faces, Jason." Boyd twisted around to a thin opening between shops.

Colorful ribbons danced upon the air above a thick crowd lining the row. Performers twirled past, their flutes and drums filling the city with music. Merrily dressed dancers carried the poles holding their ribbons. They moved the fabric along to the beat until the ribbons appeared to be one with their bodies.

The jovial merrymakers danced past the opening, heading further into the city. Their parting left behind some unwelcome company among their numbers. A few unfriendly faces suspiciously scanned the crowd. More mercenaries.

"I know a place we can hold up until I find a way to get you to the mainland," Jason said. "It has decent food."

"Good," Riley said. "My stomach has a hole in it."

"I'll cover our path." Boyd shook his head with a frown at Riley. "I'd ask you to help, Squire, but you stick out like a carrot in a box of green beans."

Seth took a tight hold on his rising irritation. The afternoon was waning toward evening. It would be dusk soon and they had an airship to catch. Jason wouldn't be easy to shake off now. A momentary twinge of guilt softened his mood. The constable had willingly jumped into harm's way once again to help them. He'd be the worst sort of person to brush aside such courage.

They turned and doubled back until Seth lost sight of the Port. The minutes stretched into an hour as they followed Jason deeper into the city. He had no idea where they were or how to get back to the ticket offices. Every instinct he had told Seth that Jason was a friend. He remembered the dog he'd seen cowering upon the deck of the ship after his power had wounded Jason. Was it a dog or was it something else?

The first time he met Wolf, the animal spirits in their rings greeted one another. Could the dog have been another animal spirit from a Heart of the Warrior Ring? His eyes dropped down to Jason's gloved left hand. He'd kept the hand covered even after blood had soaked the fabric.

"Here we are," Jason said.

A tavern with broken shutters affixed to a rundown building stood across the row. Cracked windows hung inside a crooked frame. Its rustic appearance suited the rough neighborhood.

"This is as good a place as any around this part of the city," Jason said, keeping his hand firmly on Seth's shoulder.

Boyd hurried out of an alleyway to join them. Speckles of blood dotted the back of his right hand. He nodded at them and held open the door. Several suspicious faces watched them as they made their way to a corner table.

"I've seen friendlier faces during an Amity Island raid." Riley ran a hand along the sheath of his sword.

"They don't get many strangers out here." Boyd waved the innkeeper over. "The stew's passable."

Seth and Riley took him at his word. They ordered stew, bread, and cheese with a tankard of ale. The stew was tasteless and the bread hard, but Seth ate every drop. He turned his attention to the common room. Paddy's Inn, back home on Marianna, had never been this sullen. The patrons drank their ale in silence. A few conversations, whispered low, were many times followed with pointed looks directed at their table. He'd always enjoyed the atmosphere of cheery Marianna pubs. This establishment, by comparison, was uncomfortable and tense.

Lifting his ale to take a sip, Seth stopped inches from his lips. A ripple of warning raced along his spine as he looked out across the other patrons again. Sitting in a close group at the opposite end of the common room, several men in hooded cloaks stared at him. Their own drinks were left untouched.

"Careful, Ranger," Jason warned in a low whisper. "You draw attention to yourself."

Seth nodded slightly and turned his eyes back to his empty bowl. Moving his hand slowly under the table, he slapped a quick knuckle upon Riley's leg. He motioned carefully toward the group of men.

"What's got them so curious?" Riley asked, resting his own tankard upon the table.

The men suddenly stood as one and formed a line to march out of the common room. Everyone else watched as they disappeared out the door. Whoever the men might be, they took the sullenness with them. Cheery conversation circled about the tables as someone brought out a guitar and began to play a lively tune.

"I don't like the looks of those men. Boyd and I will circle behind them to make sure they don't pursue their interest in you," Jason said low. "Stay here and don't wander off. This is a dangerous part of town, especially now as darkness is coming upon us."

"Have a care. Something's not right."

Jason gave him an uneasy smile and hurried out the door with Boyd following close behind. They moved to the window, peering out into the row. Watching his new friends follow the cloaked men sent the warning ripples along his spine again. He couldn't identify specifically what was behind his sensation of foreboding. It was a nagging, persistent ache in his stomach.

Then he saw them. Three cloaked men had broken away from the departing group. They stepped out of the forming shadows to follow Jason and Boyd. Their weapons, elegant steel blades, were drawn.

"We have to warn them," he told Riley.

"He said to stay put, Seth. I agree with him this time."

"Jason's saved our lives twice now. I can't let him be cut down by those men."

Riley grabbed his arm and spun him around. "Think Seth. Why should someone we hardly know make himself our - or should I say *your* - protector?"

"His reasons don't matter right now. We can't let them be harmed." Seth clucked his tongue irritably when Riley rolled his eyes.

The sun was disappearing behind the buildings when they hurried out of the common room. Seth moved toward the alley he'd seen Jason and Boyd enter moments before. Boots pounded toward them upon the row. Riley was suddenly bumped from behind sending him sprawling to the ground.

"My thanks to you, Gents!" A young hoodlum called as he ran up an alley in the opposite direction.

"Our money!" Riley slapped at his empty pockets. "Come back here you sneak thief!"

Riley rolled to his feet, face red and curls bouncing. The Logan temper was up. Nothing would sway him from following with hound-like fervor. Seth cast an anxious glance down the path Jason had chosen. He turned away and hurried after his squire.

Chapter Six

WANING LIGHT from the setting sun fell across Seth's path. Riley's boots pounded up ahead of him, their soles echoing against the shop walls. Keeping to his foolhardy pace, he was plunging deeper into the maze of a city. Then Riley's urgent racing suddenly stopped. Silence crept into the alleyways as if the walls were preparing for violence.

Seth pushed ahead faster. He flew around a pile of overturned crates and slid to a stop. Riley stood at the mouth of a small junction. His red curls swayed as he strained to see down three alleyways sprouting in different directions before them.

"Seth! Can you make out which way the rascal has gone?" Riley pointed a finger at his left hand. "Quick! Use the ring."

Biting down a few angry words he'd had in mind for his squire, Seth lifted his left hand. The animal spirit had been violent and savage the last time it had made an appearance. He couldn't keep it from attacking Jason. Would he be able to control it now?

He pulled the fabric away from its crystal belly. The Lion's head remained motionless. Nothing happened. Seth slammed his fist against the wall with a growl. They must retrieve their belongings and make the ship to Carlotta by dusk. Its departure time was drawing dangerously near.

Be calm, Lion. The paths before you join at a square.

The voice was neither male or female. He'd first heard it when his father had put the Lion Ring upon his finger. It had come to him again in Haven Bay, warning him to escape the island. He couldn't be certain who or what the voice was, but he had no doubt it was a friend.

Breathing in slowly to calm his mind, Seth knelt to take a closer look at the head of the first alley. Rational thought and a calm heart were needed to follow this sneak thief in his own backyard.

"You take the alley to the right. I'll take the left. Keep running until you come to an open square. And Riley," Seth said, gripping his cloak to hold him, "have a care. It could be dangerous."

Riley let his eyes fall to the Lion Ring. Calm determination had replaced anger when he met Seth's gaze again. He nodded and took a more careful pace when Seth released his grip. Riley was quickly learning to trust Seth's new gifts. Perhaps more quickly than his ranger.

Leaping to his feet, he dove into the left alley to match Riley's pace. Echoes bounced off the cobblestone as three sets of boots filled the small space. Their unnatural sounds struck at Seth's nerves in sharp beats. They weren't alone. Someone had been waiting for them.

The last dim fingers of a fading sun hung over the square ahead. Ignoring the involuntary shiver, he burst into the square a few seconds ahead of the thief. Keen eyes set in a dirtied face took Seth in with an appraising look. Those eyes, though young, had seen hard times. He wouldn't easily part with his new-found prize.

Then the thief dropped to the stone. Riley stood over him, fists raised.

"You are caught," Seth said. "Give us back our money and we'll let you go."

"Think I'm on my own, do you?"

Another young man jumped out of the alley behind them. "Hello again, Mate!"

He shook a heavy pipe toward Riley and wagged his eyebrows. The two thieves laughed when the bright red came to his cheeks in a rush. Clearly, these hooligans had lured many a foolhardy traveler into their snare.

Seth's chest tightened as the fury pushed against his control. "We're in a great hurry. Give us our money back and we'll leave. No harm will come to you."

"You think you two bumpkins can do us harm?" The young thief with the dirty face laughed. "I think I'll slit your throat first."

Riley stepped between Seth and the thieves. He pulled his sword and made ready to strike. The thieves stopped laughing, their mocking words wilting away. Seth hurried forward, but Riley threw an arm out to block his path. Taken aback by the grim look in his friend's eyes, he stepped back. In this moment, Seth understood his childhood friend had become more than a traveling companion when he took the oath back in Haven Bay. He'd become Seth's squire and like any squire, he'd kill to protect his ranger.

"Steady on, Mate. No need for your fancy sword," the young thief said, raising his hands. "Go on. Give them back their purse."

The thief who'd pickpocketed Riley reached slowly into his tunic. He pulled out the stolen purse and tossed it to Seth. Hurriedly opening the fastens, he ran his fingertips through the coins. They were all there.

"Come on, Riley. We have a ship to catch."

The young thief's eyes went wide, a strangled grunt escaping quivering lips. His knees gave way and he fell forward onto the stone. Buried to the hilt, a dagger jutted from his back. The pickpocket screamed a curse at his dead friend's body. He flew wildly toward the nearest alley. A dagger halted the young thief's escape. His dead eyes stared up at Seth in confusion.

"What goes on here?" Riley stammered.

Seth scanned the high walls. "Our hunters have found us. Run!"

"Here, kitty, kitty."

They came from every direction. Each of the mercenary hunters brandished an arsenal of weapons. Hate mixed with greed this time in the colors twisting about their bodies. Their first attack had been strictly for money on the docks of Larkspur. This time they sought revenge.

Their leader, cut and bruised, hadn't fared well when they'd last crossed swords. Somehow, he'd managed to escape the gruesome fate of his men, but not with a whole body. One of his ears had been ripped in half. His cheek and neck had bite marks. The Dirge was a wild, untamed predator. These mercenaries didn't hold control over it. Perhaps no one truly did.

One of his comrades kicked the lifeless thief before him, grinning at their leader. "Saved us a few coins, Cutter. Pity though. We could have recruited these lads into the trade. Lead the Lion on a merry chase they did."

"Instead, you murdered them in cold blood." Seth pulled his sword. "My friend and I won't be as easy to kill."

"Temper now," Cutter said, pulling his own weapons. "Your warrior friend isn't here to help you this time and my lord the Wolf is still awash in woolie dung."

A chilling song rose above the men and buildings. It grated against the stone, casting terror before its harsh notes. A dark shadow pushed through the mercenaries, propelling them out of its path. The Dirge had found them.

"Hold, devil!" Cutter moved between it and Seth. "I've been paid to get the ring from his finger. Fat load of good it will do me in your stomach."

The Dirge threw Cutter against the wall with one thrust of its skeletal arm. It moved toward Seth and Riley with unimaginable speed. He readied his sword as the nightmarish thing flew toward them. Its death song grew louder, threatening to burst their ears. Chaos broke in the square as the mercenaries scrambled to get away from the ravenous Dirge.

Gray skeletal fingers stabbed toward Seth like jagged blades. He swept upward with his sword, knocking them away. The Dirge floated backward like a wisp of black smoke on the wind. Lifting its head, the creature howled in an ear-shattering wail. The tattered cowl fell from its head, revealing sickly gray skin stretched across a brittle human skull. Strands of long colorless hair hung lifelessly across its shoulders.

"May the Heavens preserve us from this unholy creature of death," Riley cried.

The Dirge's maw opened to an unnatural width. Two rows of jagged teeth, meant for ripping and chewing human flesh, were stained yellow and brown. It ran a long tongue across the first row and flew at Seth without warning. He swung in a downward strike. This time the creature caught it, twisting his blade in boney hands. Cold dead fingers wrapped around Seth's throat and began to squeeze.

"We need the boy. A thousand credits to the man who kills that thing," Cutter growled.

White dots formed before Seth's eyes as he struggled to breathe. Fear. Dread. Disgust. Those were the Dirge's greatest weapons. He was being overwhelmed by its power until he couldn't move.

Suddenly the boney fingers released him and he collapsed onto the ground. Riley dragged him away from the black shroud as several mercenaries struck at the creature as one. Its frantic song pierced through the sounds of battle, sending dread deep into Seth's soul.

Riley helped him to his feet. "All right, Seth?"

"The *Bronze Maiden* will be sailing soon. We must make the ship or we won't be leaving this island alive."

Riley nodded and put his arm under Seth's shoulders. They hurried into the nearest alley away from the fighting. He had no idea where they were or how to get to the port. Darkness was full on now. Stumbling about with no light would take them much longer to find their way.

Someone grabbed Seth and Riley, pulling them behind a large stack of crates. A hand of iron covered Seth's mouth until he stopped fighting. He pushed away when the grip finally released him. Spinning to face his captor, he reached for his sword. A man wrapped in ash gray stood calmly before him. He was tall like Leo. Though the man kept his head and face hooded, the Valdeonian couldn't disguise his height.

"You are Edmund D'Antoiné's heir." It was a statement rather than a question.

"Who are you and why do you hold us?"

"I've come to protect you, young one. The creature who chases you is not a common thief."

"I know what it is better than anyone, sir. Others like it murdered my father."

The Valdeonian remained silent and still. He gave no indication the news of Leo's death grieved or gladdened him. Indifference had no color. Indeed, the only sign of life about the Valdeonian was the slight shimmer of ambition.

"I will dispatch the creature and its handlers," he said at last. "You are to wait here for my return. We journey to the Obsidian Citadel tonight."

His words were spoken with unshakable confidence. He was a man used to giving orders and having them obeyed without question. His lack of feeling gave Seth pause. Clearly, he'd known Leo. Had this Valdeonian been a friend or a rival?

"How do I know we can trust you?"

The Valdeonian swept his cloak open. The strange design within the ash hue confused Seth's vision. He was unable to focus upon the pattern. Then he caught a glimpse of color upon the man's chest. A mighty golden sword laid over a bright star. Letters spelling, *Jalora Legion*, ran in a crimson circle around the gold. This Valdeonian was a ranger.

Thrusting out his left hand, he waited as Seth dropped his gaze. A Heart of the Warrior Ring shimmered purple upon his left middle finger. It gripped the ranger's finger just as the Lion Ring held tightly upon his own digit. A mighty hawk flew within the belly of the crystal. The predator bird seemed to struggle in its crystal prison and then went still.

A prickling of suspicion came to Seth's mind in the words of warning from the killer, Pavel Sandor. He'd told Seth the rangers would want him. They'd have their own plans for the Lion. Pavel had sworn those plans would be worse than any enemy could bestow.

"I am Esteban D'Antoiné, the Hawk. Edmund was my brother."

Here was the second half of the legendary D'Antoiné brothers who'd joined the Jalora Legion together. He thought back on Leo's great skill. Was this brother as powerful? He certainly lacked Leo's charismatic charm and warmth. Thinking back to the precious days he'd spent with his father, Seth didn't recall Leo ever mentioning his brother. Perhaps they'd had a falling out and had traveled opposite paths? It was entirely possible this was the Valdeonian ranger who'd kept Seth away from his father all those years.

In a gust of wind, Hawk was gone. Shrieks of pain and terror filled the square behind them. He was a powerful ranger. The battle wouldn't last long. Mere minutes remained for an escape.

Seth grabbed Riley and pulled him through a small space between buildings. The lights of the airship port were close now. They would have to run hard to make their voyage.

"We're not waiting for your uncle?"

"You and Wolf are the only ones I trust. I can't afford to accept help from strangers. Not even Jason. Meeting Hawk made me realize I don't know who my father counted as friend or enemy. Come on. We have to reach the *Bronze Maiden* before she sails without us."

Chapter Seven

WOLF PACED the length of his chambers, his evening meal unheeded upon the table. Despite evil's best attempts, his ship hadn't quite been crippled. It sailed across dark skies between the tiny speckles of land at a steady pace. Perhaps not with the same speed it once had, but certainly with the same determination.

Calm your mind. Use the power I gave you. The Right-Hand will always find the Master.

He stopped before the port hole and closed his eyes. Allowing the power of the Right-Hand loose, he became one with wind and sky. The power bounded across the icy waters like a bloodhound on the trail of a buck. Undaunted by time or distance, it sniffed out Seth's heartbeat and latched upon the scent with strong jaws.

"I've found him. He's anxious. His mind is racing." Wolf opened his eyes and gripped the lip of the port hole. "How is it I can feel what he is feeling? We are miles apart."

The bond between you is strong, Xavier the Wolf, but not strong enough. The Lion and his Right-Hand must join.

The Jalora's presence surged from the Wolf Ring in a wave of warmth. It engulfed his body, holding him in its embrace. Tingling sensations touched his head and face like a parent comforting a troubled child.

You were schooled in the legends and have trained for this day.

Yes, he'd been trained to serve the Jalora Master as had his ancestors before him. Never had he imagined himself worthy to be bonded to the special Lion born once in a hundred years. No childhood nightmare or vision could have prepared him to be named the Master's Right-Hand. The horrible honor traditionally fell to the Bearer of the Hawk Ring. What this meant for his family he couldn't say.

He moved to the wardrobe and tugged gently at the tip of a burgundy ribbon caught in the door. It was one of his wife, Dulcina's, hair ribbons. He stroked his thumb across the satin. Some treacherous snake had pinned another of her hair ribbons to their bed chamber door in San Leonora. It was an unthinkable threat. Though she'd tried to ease his mind by discounting the gesture, Xavier had taken the threat seriously. He'd sent her and their two small sons home to San Rudalfo. The rest of the De Vincente family was protecting them during the unrest in Valdeon. Though they were a strong military force on Andara, he couldn't trust in their protection once word of the Lion's return escaped. It was best to have Fausto bring Dulcina and the children to San Lucida. He'd meet them once Wolf collected the Lion and brought him to the safety of Cesar Santiago's home.

A respectful knock brought him back to the business at hand. Wolf tucked the ribbon inside his uniform and turned toward the anxious face of his squire. Basilio frowned at the untouched meal, but made no mention of it.

"We have begun our descent into Port City, my lord."

"Very well," Wolf said. "Make certain all markings and flags have been stowed. We must be as discreet as possible. Tell the crew to have the cannons loaded. They are to remain armed and at the ready." Wolf held his squire's gaze. "And Basilio, tell the captain if anyone tries to follow us once the Lion is onboard, I want them knocked out of the sky."

Wolf checked his weapons again as he made for the ship's railing. The sun had fallen, casting a dark net over Port City. He'd be going ashore alone. Seth's heartbeat was frantic, panicked. He wouldn't be able to control his power in such a state. The animal spirit of the ring would act out of an instinct to protect. A wrong look or move could unleash Seth's fury. It was best Wolf approach him alone. He could hide his own fear, but he wasn't certain about other anxious nerves.

He slid down the mooring lines before the crew had a chance to secure the gang plank. Ignoring their movements to prepare the ship, Wolf pulled on his hood. A ranger's cloak was made from rare material given to the Legion by the Luminawni. Woven with magic, it played with the eyes, seemingly causing its ranger to disappear. If the young Lion's enemies were in pursuit, Wolf would see them first.

Drifting into a darkened doorway of the port, he scanned the crowd. Travelers from all parts of Andara sleepily shuffled along the rounded walls of the port.

Each tired and eager for a place to rest their heads, they paid no heed to his hiding place.

A sudden stab of electric pain struck his heart. Wolf staggered against the wall. Recovering quickly, he set his full concentration upon the young Lion. Seth was running from something or someone. The boy's terror surged through their shared connection like a cannon ball, though this new Lion tried to suppress it. Fury. It reached out to Wolf as well. The Lion Ring was ready to lash out. He had to find the boy before the innocent souls within these walls became prey to the Lion's fury.

Seth's tag-along was slowing him down. Xavier shook his head. What was Edmund thinking? Trusting the Lion's care to a bumpkin squire was folly. Beef-headed foolishness. The boy's father, Thomas Logan, had protected Seth on many occasions. Wolf owed the woolie farmer a debt. Sending his youngest home in one piece would be a first step in repaying Logan's deeds.

The tug of the young Lion's heartbeat pulled sharply toward the east. Compelled by the power of the Right-Hand, Wolf was an invisible shadow against the rounded walls. Blank faces and muttered conversations dwindled as his will came into sharp focus. Find the Lion. Wolf gulped down the stifling urgency of his quest. Was this his life now? Bound above all else - home, family, his own needs - to a boy he'd just met?

A ripple in their connection flooded his consciousness. Relief. Seth had reached a place he considered safe. Then their connection began to weaken as the Lion's heartbeat grew distant. Wolf pounded a fist against the wall. He'd been too slow. Seth had boarded a ship.

He followed the residual energy to an empty dock. A ship made its slow ascension into the night sky. She drifted south, picking up speed. He threw the hood off his head and came to stand at the edge of the dock. Calling to him the sight, his vision sharpened on the letters upon the ship's stern. *Bronze Maiden.*

"Edmund, you ever were a brash fool."

Wolf spat with distaste. Rather than summoning the Sacred Guard, Edmund had sent the boy off to Carlotta - to *her.* He turned back toward the crowded port, pulling the hood on once more. Edmund's foolish choices continued to threaten their country from beyond the grave.

"Not this time, Leo."

He would kill those following the Lion first, then surprise the boy on Carlotta. If he hurried, Wolf could meet them there. They'd see the bumpkin squire back to his father's farm, then make their way to San Lucida.

A shiver of apprehension warned him of an unexpected and unwelcome presence. Cloaked and hooded, Esteban the Hawk pushed through the crowd of unsuspecting travelers. Decades had passed since the Hawk Prince left Valdeon to hide from his brother's wrath. It had been Wolf's ill luck to meet the blackguard twice within a week's span.

He'd seen images from Seth's past. A Valdeonian ranger had visited the island before Edmund knew of his son. Wolf thought back to his time as a boy visiting San Leonora. He remembered Esteban arguing impatiently with his brother, the king, for a chance at power. Perhaps Hawk saw an opportunity in Seth. The young

Lion's innocent heart may just believe Esteban's tales out of fondness for Leo's memory.

A rush of fury summoned forth the power of the Right-Hand once more. Speeding around the circular walls, Wolf stepped out to block Esteban's path before he discovered Seth's destination. Cold eyes peering out from an emotionless face glared at Wolf as he removed his hood.

"Have you lost something, Hawk Prince?"

"My Lord De Vincente," Hawk said, rubbing at the pale scar across his cheek. "I think we look for the same thing."

The light touch of Hawk's power brushed tentatively against Wolf's mind. His block lifted in response, slapping away the touch. The power of the Right-Hand had come to him without thought. Protective in its intensity, this new presence within him confirmed the distrust he felt for Hawk.

Esteban's jaw tightened. A cold glint came into his eyes as he fixed his gaze upon Wolf. The next touch was more insistent, almost surgical. Pushing harder with his power, Hawk tried to stab his way into Wolf's mind.

Endurance. The De Vincente family maxim had kept him alive on more than one occasion. Much more was at stake this time. Though his head was splitting and nausea filled his stomach, Wolf kept to the lessons his father had taught him. He must endure. The Lion's safety was at stake.

Hawk straightened with a grunt as he withdrew his power. Short of breath and sweating, Esteban turned away from Wolf with poorly disguised hatred. He'd been beaten. A bishop-level ranger should have easily been able to take a deacon ranger's memories. Would Esteban's massive ego allow him to consider Wolf's selection as the Right-Hand? Most likely not.

"I will leave you to your searching," Hawk said at last.

"You were once a member of the Sacred Guard, Hawk Prince. Do we still serve the same purpose?"

Hawk spun away from him and stalked through the crowd toward the main entrance. Wolf waited until he was satisfied Esteban had left the port, before returning to his own ship. It was pointless to hide now. The Hawk prince certainly had helpers following him already. He couldn't go after the boy quite yet. It was best if the Lion stayed hidden for a while longer.

"Captain, we're being followed," he told the man as he walked up the gangplank. "It's imperative you take a normal, steady pace toward Valdeon. Make for San Lucida."

He must return to the Palace of Kings for further guidance from the Orb. A stop in San Lucida on the way was in order. Cesar Santiago would be expecting Leo's heir. He'd be disappointed. Seth was best left on the distant Isle of Carlotta until Wolf had made the necessary arrangements for his safety. Cesar, however, would insist upon going with Wolf to fetch the young Lion. His old friend and mentor was difficult to sway once his mind took hold of a decision. Many, no doubt, would be anxious to help. How many would offer, seeking the young Lion's favor?

Wolf sighed. Endurance. It had served him in battle. Now it must see him through more political maneuvering.

Chapter Eight

Jorge Pacarro bent low to grasp a stray weed from the base of one of his vines. Some had scoffed when he'd planted the first seedling twenty years past. No crop, the naysayers had told him, could survive on the rocky base of Lucida Ridge. Patience and a strong stubborn streak helped nature along. Now his estate was the largest wine producer in western Valdeon. He absently threw the weed, dangling from his hand, into the nearby plains grass. Many things needed tending. Let them get out of order and raw iron must be used to clean them up again.

He lifted the rust-colored beaded braids from his neck and wiped away the sweat. Such hot weather for late fall was unusual, but no doubt the breezes from the ocean would soon cool the land. Jorge walked slowly toward his villa. He looked upon it and smiled, knowing he was the envy of every man in San Lucida. He'd been rewarded with this stretch of land for services to the throne of Valdeon. It was an honor to be chosen as squire to a member of the Sacred Guard, but he was secretly happy when his lord, Cesar Santiago the Ferret, had retired. Jorge was ready to settle down at last and work his land rather than leaving it to his hired hands.

A sudden burning along the skin of his torso almost brought Jorge to his knees. He'd first felt the sensation when he'd hidden the Regent Medallion from Julian D'Antoiné's men. They'd tried to steal it for their dark-hearted prince to help him rise to the throne. Any who bore the medallion would rule in the Lion's absence. Its angry power would have forced Valdeon to kneel before its bearer. Jorge had snatched it first, ruining their plans. He'd paid the price for his good-intended sacrilege. The medallion's magic had left him with odd spells of burning. He'd hoped time at home would somehow dissipate the magic's energy.

The burning grew more intense and shot up along his spine. He winced and turned his head to the left in a quick jerk. A figure stood in the empty fields past his vines. Its black shroud floated in the breeze among the tips of the plains grass. A gust of wind caught the cowl covering the figure's head. Gray skin pulled taut over thin cheek bones. Tar orbs glared at him from where its eyes should have been. Jagged rows of teeth flashed under the sun's rays as it snapped hungrily. What unholy creature of evil was haunting his daydreams?

Jorge sputtered an ancient Pacarro Tribe prayer to the Erthe Mother. Meant to protect and comfort, it would do little of either. He'd left the villa without weapon or company. This hellish nightmare had not advanced yet. It seemed to be weighing options.

"Father!"

His son Duarto's call broke the spell cast over the afternoon. The creature flew toward the safety of the rocks, leaving the grass undisturbed and Jorge wondering if he'd imagined the hideous being.

Squawking hens and loud bangs of metal announced Duarto's arrival as he cleared the corner of the barn. His rust-colored hair, cut short for military service, glistened under the sheen of scented hair tonic. Twenty years old with a good strong form, Duarto wasn't immune to the latest fashions from San Angelica. Jorge hid his smile as his son stumbled through the corral, knocking over a stray bucket. He waved at his father urgently.

"Father, My Lord Santiago has returned from San Leonora and is here to see you. He says his news is important. Mother has sent me to fetch you." Duarto, free of the bucket, gave him a slight frown. "He's brought us three cases of rum."

Cesar was convinced he could make rum to rival the southlands of Valdeon. It had become his mission upon retirement to build a new rum empire. His efforts had transformed the city into a popular vacation spot for wealthy Valdeonian travelers. Most of them came not to drink the rum. Rather they were curious to see the great copper vats standing like beacons beside the shores of San Lucida Lake. Poor Cesar. His dream of a great rum empire was never fully realized. He usually ended up giving the nasty-tasting rum away, long before anyone could be fooled into buying it.

"Come. Let us join him while we may." Jorge gripped Duarto's shoulder, guiding him back in the direction of the villa. "Perhaps there is still time to sway him from opening his kerosene concoction."

Lady Donna Pacarro stood upon the side patio of their villa. His wife's plain brown dress had been hurriedly replaced with a cream-colored floral nonsense. Long dark braids showing signs of age had been whirled up atop her head. Speckles of polish dotted her hands, firmly planted upon her hips. Cesar had caught her at cleaning the silver.

"My lord approaches at last!" She pinched Jorge's arm and gave him a long-suffering sigh. "Lord Santiago has been waiting for nearly half an hour. He has unpacked a case of rum."

"Peace, Wife." Jorge kissed Donna's cheek despite her effort to avoid him.

"Go wash yourself, farmer." She pushed him toward the rain barrel with a laugh.

Jorge dunked the cloth his wife had set out for him into the rain barrel. He hurriedly washed his face and neck. Dirt stubbornly resisted the washing and remained under his fingernails. He hated appearing before his lord untidied. Once a squire, always a squire. Well, there was no help for it. Something urgent must have brought Cesar back home. He wouldn't willingly have left Wolf on his own.

The glass doors leading out to the veranda were open wide. Sunlight and the aroma of wild prairie flowers swept over Jorge. He would never tire of the sensation. Today, a new odor greeted him among the flowers. The sour smell of distilled alcohol and some indefinable ingredient assaulted his nose. Cesar hadn't been idle as he waited for them on the veranda. Gurgling rum fell into three generously filled tankards. Cesar slammed the empty jug upon the table when he saw Jorge. A flame was burning in those old eyes.

"Forgive my delay, my lord."

"Forget the formalities, Jorge. Come have some rum! I have much to tell you. And you too Duarto!"

The old ranger grabbed Duarto by his arm, thrusting a tall glass in his hand.

The news Cesar brought back from San Leonora must be of the utmost importance. His lord still wore the shiny black boots practical only in the halls of the Palace. His tunic was rumpled and he was missing his belt. Cesar, it appeared, had come to Jorge straight from his ship.

Jorge held a chair out for his lord and took his own seat. Duarto sat beside them, peering uncomfortably into the tankard of kerosene-flavored drink. He kicked at his son's leg in warning, motioning him to set the drink down upon the table.

"Something has happened, hasn't it? You wouldn't willingly leave Wolf alone in San Leonora." Jorge cleared his throat after managing to swallow a sip of rum. "Is there news?"

"Indeed! Amazing things are happening, Jorge." Cesar edged forward on his chair. "The orb pulses with life once more."

Hope. He hadn't held much for many months. Their king, Edmund the Leo, had died and the Lion Ring lost. Jorge had journeyed with Cesar and the other western lords to San Leonora and the Palace of Kings. They'd hoped to grieve before the Altar of Providence, but the Jalora had shut and sealed the golden doors of the throne room. Perhaps its reasons had just come to light. The Orb of Valdeon tied the land and the Bearer of the Lion Ring to the spiritual body of heaven. If he understood the legends correctly, the bond between ranger and orb also tied the Jalora's protective power to Andara. Now new life pulsed within the orb. It could mean only one thing. Edmund D'Antoiné's heir had been chosen and the Jalora had accepted him.

"Where is the young Lion, my lord?" Jorge gripped his tankard with shaking hands.

"Many plan to search for him."

"Including Julian, no doubt." Jorge's fingers reached for his hatchet, gripping empty fabric instead. "We must find the Lion first and take him to safety."

"Is he in Valdeon, then?" Duarto asked.

Cesar shook his head. "No, Edmund was a rash man, but never was he a fool. The boy is in hiding."

Duarto looked eagerly at his father, then back to Cesar. "How are we to find him, my lord?"

"A fine question. If I can't trust my squire who can I trust?" He slammed the tankard down upon the table with a little more force than was warranted. "A few nights ago, I was summoned to the throne room. Xavier the Wolf stood before the Orb, staring into its depths. The Chancellor was beside him, stunned into silence."

Cesar leaned in closer, speaking low across the table. "Wolf told me the Jalora has commanded he go to the young Lion and bring him here to the safety of my home."

The Heir to the Lion Ring, his future king, was coming here? Such a thing had never happened to his recollection of the Lion's ancestry. Of course, there had never been a need.

"Why were the other members of the Sacred Guard not with him?" Jorge sipped some of the rum absently. Stopping the reflex to spit out the burning liquid, he forced it down.

"Dragon cannot send the Legion into Valdeon, but he can have the Sacred Guard and the other Valdeonian rangers investigate unofficially. They are home except my Lucio. He was ordered to the Buells."

"The Chancellor didn't object? He finally sees Julian for what he is then?" Jorge asked.

Cesar shrugged with a frown. They'd dealt with Julian's many indiscretions in the past. It was widely known the West did not respect his claim to rule as Regent of Valdeon. All the Western Lords refused to follow him and shunned him from their lands. All of them, except the money loving Cristiano of San Angelica. The man refused to stand against Julian for the sake of the steady supply of coins into his own pocket. The treacherous fool had already tried to drive his own son, Rafael the Fox, from his house. Shunning a member of the Sacred Guard was proof of the man's lack of honor. Only the merchants within his city did not see it in the light of truth.

Heat sparked under Jorge's shirt, prompting his memory back to the incident a few moments ago. The strange creature watching him hadn't been a figment of his imagination. If Wolf's friends knew of his plan to bring the Lion to San Lucida, it was conceivable his enemies knew as well. Perhaps they'd sent the fowl creature to spy on Wolf's allies?

"My lord, I had an unwelcome visitor this morning among my vines," Jorge said. "It was a creature, shrouded in black. The fowl thing's skin was gray. It stared at me with tar-colored eyes. Everything about it felt wrong somehow. I don't think it's coincidence the thing of evil arrived this morning."

"Wolf spoke to me of such creatures. He called them 'The Dirge.' They hunt the flesh of men, but it is unclear who holds their leash." Cesar rubbed a hand across his balding head. "This is troubling news. I'll ask Wolf to summon the Sacred Guard to San Lucida. Perhaps he should send word to Dragon as well? The young Lion must be protected for all our sakes."

Indeed, he must. Jorge thought back to the night in the palace gardens when he'd found Wolf wrapped in the Jalora's power. The ranger had been in a dream state. He'd called to someone named Seth, swearing to protect him. Could this young man be the new Lion? If he was, danger had already found him.

"I must return home to prepare for his coming," Cesar said at last. "Can I count on your support?"

Jorge came around the table to kneel before his lord. He took up Cesar's left hand where the Ferret Ring - now worn by his son - had once clung to its bearer. Jorge put the red oval skin to his lips.

"I serve the Lion."

He released his lord's hand and stepped away. Duarto took his place without hesitation. He'd received many honors in his years of service as squire. None of them compared to this moment. His greatest achievement, his only son, had courage enough to follow his father into service to the Lion.

"So too, do I swear, my lord." Duarto kissed their lord's finger.

Cesar rested a hand on Duarto's shoulder. "I am as proud of you as I am of my own Lucio, young Duarto Pacarro! You, I have no doubt, will become a great man like your father before you."

Duarto shot Jorge a pleased grin as they helped Cesar up from his chair. He swayed a bit as they headed down the path toward the courtyard. Two of his guardsmen were waiting. The old ranger waved them away when they tried to help him mount his horse. He jumped into the saddle with remarkable agility for his age and alcohol content.

"We will see an end to civil unrest in Valdeon!" Cesar shouted and spurred his mount toward the city.

Jorge put an arm around his son's shoulder. "Come, pride of my heart. Let us go into supper."

Warmth grew around the skin of his torso. The medallion's magic flared and then faded into a soft pulse. It too felt the grip of fate ready to descend upon them.

Chapter Nine

A GENTLE BREEZE greeted Seth as he stepped upon the gang plank of the *Bronze Maiden*. Warm and inviting, it beckoned him onto the tiny docks of Carlotta. Absent was the harsh slapping of angry waves upon rock, typical of their isle home. This sea rolled slowly about them, shimmering with sun-capped crystal waves. Brilliant blue waters - unimaginably clear - tumbled lazily against white sands. Stretching out across the clear blue sky, palm leaves shaded patches of white along the isle's empty beaches. Sniffing again at the fragrant breeze, he let the aromas of spice and flowers wash over him. Carlotta was paradise.

"Look what's coming our way." Riley elbowed Seth in the ribs.

Young women with dark hair and tanned skin hurried toward the ships. Their arms carried baskets full of fruit and flowers. Brilliant white blouses ended at the top of skirts decorated in vibrant colors and designs. Lose waist-length hair swayed as they came at Seth and Riley in a rush. Surrounding them with their beauty, the young women lifted wreaths of flowers around their necks. Lips brushed against Seth's cheek, sending a pleasant shiver through his body.

Then they were gone, already surrounding the crew with their baskets and smiles. A snort of laughter from the deck sent Seth into a blush. One of the crew, an older man with sparkling eyes set in a weather-worn face, grinned as he set a flame to his pipe.

"I envy you, my fine young gentlemen," he said, puffing at the pipe. "Many aboard this vessel would pay dearly to see the beauties of Carlotta."

"Why can't you?" Riley asked.

"Carlotta may be a small island in the middle of nowhere, but it has a queen just the same. An iron lady she is too. I remember our first run a few years ago. The captain was summoned to the queen's presence. He came back less than an hour later, pale as you please. I swear he'd had the fear of death put into him that day. No member of this crew has been allowed to set foot upon shore since. Not even the captain."

He lowered his pipe and gave them a hard look. "I hope you have the queen's permission to be on Carlotta, lads. Heaven help you if you don't. The *Bronze Maiden* is the only way on or off this island. Well. For regular folk."

Resentment and fear. They radiated around the sailor briefly, then faded. Carlotta had secrets it would seem. Seth scanned the little docks with a quick turn of his head. No other vessels were moored, not even fishing boats. If other ships did visit the island, then they weren't showing their sails during the *Bronze Maiden's* visit.

"We're docked here until we can unload the cargo and then we must leave by the Iron Lady's command.

You have an hour to do your business. Hurry back if you need a lift."

"Come on," Seth said, heading down the dock. "We'd better find my mother's friend quickly. It sounds as if the Queen of Carlotta isn't agreeable to visitors."

"Aye, but where are we to go after we leave Carlotta?"

"I don't know. Let us hope my mother's friend can give us the answers we need."

Sandaled feet rushed down the wooden docks behind them. Having sold their wares, the young Carlotta women hurried past Seth and Riley on their way to the village. Fish darted out from beneath the dock as they passed. Their colorful bodies moved in rapid zigzags just beneath the surface.

A village perched at the rim of a low hill. White stone houses looked out over the blue ocean. Topping each little house was a domed roof as blue as their lovely sea. Following their beautiful guides, they entered the town square. Tiny store fronts painted with accents of orange, yellow, and blue, lined the inland edge of the space. Fish, fruit, and flowers hung from wooden arbors beside them.

"What do you suppose it is?" Riley asked, pointing at a gigantic wooden tub in the center of the square.

The massive container stood at chest height. Bound with steel, the wooden tub looked like a giant barrel cut in half. Five people could easily stand within its belly. Whatever the purpose of the tub, it seemed to be of great value to the village. Someone had taken great care to keep the wood clean and oiled.

"Do you know anything about this place?" Riley asked.

"I understand it's a short distance off the coast of Valdeon," Seth said, taking in the vibrant colors of the square. "I wonder how my mother came to know anyone here."

"Look, a tavern." Riley pointed to their right. "Let's ask for directions."

The Three Palms Cantina rested at the edge of the square. It was a small, comfortable establishment which seemed to be the center of Carlotta society. Remnants of some sort of celebration hung from the arbor covering its outdoor dining area. The Cantina's single patron sat amongst the fallen decorations, oblivious to the fading joy about him. He leaned his elbows upon the table and stared lazily toward the beach.

A man of middle years leaned inside the doorway of the Cantina, watching them draw nearer to his establishment. He wore light linen clothes and thin sandals that clicked as he wagged his foot. Dark, watchful eyes examined Seth under thick eyebrows. His intense gaze drifted across their swords and rested upon Seth's left hand. The Lion Ring had worked its way out from under the fabric he'd wrapped around his fingers.

"Welcome, my young friends, to the Isle of Carlotta." The innkeeper's rich baritone held a merriment his eyes did not share. "The Sunset Children greet you with well wishes. I am Roderigo. How may I be of assistance?"

"We're looking for the Cottage on the Cliff. Can you help us?"

The innkeeper frowned under his busy mustache. "Do you have permission to be on the island, my young friend? I hope you do."

"We're meeting someone there," Riley interjected quickly. "You do know where the cottage is?"

He looked at Seth's left hand again. "Yes. This address is familiar to me."

Lifting a finger, he pointed up the row leading away from the sea. Seth gave him a nod of thanks and headed across the square. Riley joined him, throwing glances back toward the inn.

"I don't think we're welcome here," Seth said, quickening his pace to escape the eyes still staring at their backs. "Let's find my mother's friend before the *Bronze Maiden* sets sail."

Palm trees lined the slow ambling path uphill. Small white houses peaked through the glossy green of strange plants and their aromatic tropical flowers. The green walls thickened until even the sunlight struggled to peek through the leaves. Soon their view ahead mirrored the path they'd just walked. It was suffocating. Clearly no one bothered to cut back the jungle trying to consume their single row.

"I hope we don't end up at the other side of the island." Riley tilted his neck upward, eyes lifting to the bright blue above.

The row curved lazily back toward the sea. Seth wiped at the sweat bubbling at the back of his neck. Had the innkeeper sent them on a nature walk for his own amusement?

Then the path's gentle journey was abruptly blocked by a tall iron rod gate firmly closed across the row. The cold iron, out of place in the warmth of Carlotta, disappeared into the thick green landscape.

Riley tapped him on the arm and pointed to a sign affixed to the gate.

Cottage on The Cliff.

"Hello," Seth called through the bars. "Is anyone there?"

He placed his hands on the gate, hoping to lean his head through. They swung open with a steady creak of protest. The iron was polished and kept, but high humidity was the enemy of metal. Seth had seen many an airship port pulley ruined in the harsh Marianna weather.

"Come on," he said, stepping through the opening. "We have to find my mother's friend. I'm not leaving Carlotta until I do."

They followed the path as it wandered through a manicured lawn much out of character with the rest of the island. Shrubs, expertly shaped into images of horses and swans, stood vigil in perfectly symmetrical rows.

Rising against the clear sky like a mythical temple was the grandest building Seth had ever imagined. Brilliant white, the mansion was straight out of a fairy story book he'd read as a child. Polished marble covered the short staircase leading toward an elaborately carved wooden door. Ornate columns stood beside the entrance like sentinels.

"Doesn't look like a cottage to me," Riley said, brushing at his dirtied shirt.

No indeed it didn't. This had to be a mistake. Seth tightened his fist, trying to banish his uncertainty. He had no time for second guessing his decision. The *Bronze Maiden* would be leaving soon without them. He mustered his courage and knocked.

The door handle, molded into a golden swan's neck, tilted toward the ceiling. The bird's head swung inside as the wooden door swept open. A man dressed in crisp white stood in the gap, blocking their view of the house within. Silver hair framed pale cheeks. Hard green eyes examined the intruders with a cold glare.

"The tradesmen's entrance is to the left," he said.

Harsh Tslavic vowels emphasized the disapproval in his words. Seth took a step back to escape them. His mother's killer had forever embedded their sound in his nightmares. He had no idea what they would find on Carlotta, but Tslavians were the last thing he'd expected.

"Forgive the intrusion," Seth said. "We're looking for the Cottage on the Cliff."

"Are you?" The Tslavian lifted his eyebrow slightly and frowned. "What is your business here?"

Tap. Tap. Tap.

Straightening his uniform, the Tslavic man stepped to the side and bowed low. An elderly woman dressed entirely in light blue lace stormed down the hall toward them. Slapping her walking stick one last time on the marble tile beside the door, she lifted her chin and stared at them with a frosty glare.

"Strangers, Majesty," he said. "They're armed."

This was the Iron Lady, Queen of Carlotta, the sailor had warned them about. Age had frosted the white hair expertly swirled atop her head. Two perfectly formed ringlets dangled along her rigid neck, defying the humid climate. Her face, devoid of emotion, revealed nothing. Standing in her presence, Seth understood his intimidation. She was a fortress of stern dignity.

"Forgive me, My Lady. I mean, Majesty. We were looking for someone at this address. Someone who may know Anne McCloud. I am Seth McCloud."

The Queen of Carlotta raised her chin, regarding Seth as if he were an unpleasant smelling piece of discarded fruit. "And what proof do you offer, young man?"

Seth exchanged a look with Riley. Awestruck, his squire shrugged and turned back to stare at the Iron Lady. Neither one of them had met anyone so grand. He'd certainly not expected his mother's friend to be royalty. Having his identity questioned was an unexpected challenge too. He had no papers to prove who he was, after all.

Lifting the heart crystal necklace from his neck, he handed it to her. The priceless crystal had been a present from his father, Edmund to the woman he'd loved. He'd found it hidden among her other precious mementos back in Haven Bay.

"A trinket like this is easily stolen by clever thieves," she said at last, still gripping the necklace tightly in her fist. "Though I've faced more formidable enemies in my day than two penniless wanderers."

"I offer you undeniable proof I am her son." Ripping away the cloth covering his left hand, he held the Lion Ring before her.

She stared at it, motionless and deep in thought. "Come closer, boy."

He took a small step forward, towering over her with his height. Fingers, still strong despite their advanced years, gripped Seth's face tightly. The frosty steel softened in her eyes.

"Yes, you are the very image of Edmund D'Antoiné. I had to be sure."

"You knew my father, Majesty?"

She lifted her hand over Seth's and let his mother's necklace dangle between them. He took the chain, lifting it over his head. Her eyes watched the heart crystal as it fell onto his chest. Private memories swam in their depths. Something akin to a smile of fondness crossed her firm lips.

"Of course, boy. I was at Anne and Edmund's wedding. In fact, they honeymooned here. I am your Grandaunt Charlotte."

Chapter Ten

AUNT CHARLOTTE MARCHED down the tiled hall, folds of silver-blue linen and widow's lace trailing behind her. *Tap. Tap. Tap.* The steady rhythm of her ebony walking stick struck the stone in time to the swish of expensive linen.

Tymon frowned at their immobile forms and shook his head. Remembering his manners, Seth hurried to take Aunt Charlotte's arm. He chanced a look at the woman beside him again. Her body may have been old and somewhat frail, but the spirit contained within her was fierce.

The Cottage on the Cliff was much grander than its humble name suggested. Decorated in the soft and warm architecture of the island, it put visitors immediately at ease. Touches of splendor, like the large glass dome above the main hall, added a feel of elegance to the home. Bright morning sun streamed in through its glass, lighting the rest of the house. Woven curtains were folded at the base of the dome, ready to shade the hall if the sun grew too warm.

Two servants rushed to open double glass doors standing at the rear of the hall. The aroma of flowers and sweet brine mixed upon the breeze. Seth breathed deeply as he stepped upon the massive marbled patio.

White stone, surrounded by a sea of neatly trimmed lawn, stretched toward the land's horizon. Azure waters seemed to rise to kiss the stone.

"This patio is my favorite place in all of Andara," Aunt Charlotte told them. "Of course, the flora of the island is threatening to suffocate us now that my August is not here to tend the gardens."

Walking farther toward the center of the patio, Seth saw the edge of the white stone ending at the top of a staircase. It appeared to lead down toward a beach a short hike below. A large neglected terraced garden rolled down the cliff on either side of the stairs. Heavy, gnarled vines and weeds strangled dozens of rose bushes as they grew closer to the patio's edge.

His aunt stopped beside a garden table at the center of the patio. Plates of fruit and cheese had been set out for them. Charlotte's gray eyes stared past the edge of the patio. She made no move to sit down. Taking the hint, Seth hurried to pull a chair out for her. Aunt Charlotte lowered herself into the chair like a swan coming to rest upon its nest.

Seth and Riley took their seats with much less grace. Both winced as their chairs scraped against the stone. Riley, fidgeting nervously, examined the multitude of utensils before him. Seth's fingers hesitated over his own set. His mother had taught him proper table manners, but never had her meals been this complicated.

"Where is your father? Edmund would not allow his son and heir to travel alone."

Those gray eyes examined Seth's face, searching out his secrets and exposing his frailties. All the while, her aging hands expertly dissected the fruit. Its juice dripped into a puddle at the bottom of her bowl, while Seth's sprayed across his tunic.

"Edmund sat in the very same chair and swore an oath he would never be parted from you again. The Leo is a man of his word."

"He was here?"

"I sent for him as soon as I received Emma's letter telling me of Anne's murder." Aunt Charlotte allowed her face to soften slightly. "Poor Edmund never understood why your mother chose to hide from him. I think he forgave her the moment I showed him the portraits she drew of her beloved son. You were the treasure of her heart."

Anne's love for her son had fated her to die alone in the bitter cold of Haven Bay. He rested a fingertip upon the Lion Ring. Leo had loved Anne and had come to care for Seth in the short time they were together. It was the future of the Lion Ring he'd been so desperate to protect. His father had cut off his own finger to ensure its safety.

"Leo's enemies found him on Marianna."

Aunt Charlotte's face paled. Her fork twisted ruthlessly into the fruit, sending juice gushing across the table linen. She seemed not to notice as she forced a piece of flesh into her mouth. They sat in silence for a moment, listening to the sea rush upon the sand.

"He was a good man and a noble ranger. Andara has lost an honorable heart." Patting her lips with fine linen, she looked out across the sea again. "Edmund is with his Anne now in a place where surnames mean nothing. D'Antoiné or Von Wolkhurst, neither name matters."

Von Wolkhurst. He recognized the name all too well. They were the ruling family of Tslavia, Valdeon's greatest enemy. Someone from the family line had hired Pavel Sandor to murder Seth. He'd found a golden coin with the image of a Gargoyle - the crest of the Von Wolkhurst family - embedded in the gold. It lay in the field where he'd been ambushed by Amity Raiders the night of his mother's murder.

"No one's explained who you are, Nephew?"

Aunt Charlotte lifted from her chair with surprising dexterity for her age. Lace and linen flew across the patio in a direct line toward the mansion. Seth and Riley hurried from their chairs, jogging to keep up with her. Echoes of the tip of her walking stick upon marble filled the yard.

She didn't slow her pace as she led them through the bright halls of the mansion. Tymon waited for them patiently beside a set of double doors. He bowed as Aunt Charlotte drew near. Pushing the doors open, he waited respectfully for her to pass through. Tymon looked none too pleased to do the same for Seth and Riley.

Charlotte stopped in the center of her parlor. Unlike the rest of the house, it was painted in a warm meadow green. Rich dark wood covered the floor. Shelves, filled with books, lined all the walls except one. A large fireplace stood empty in the center of the far wall. Above its mantle hung a massive painting. A plump older man - bearing a striking resemblance to Aunt Charlotte - sat upon a thrown. Dressed in robes of amethyst, he wore a golden bejeweled crown upon his bald head.

Several children circled about their king, forever captured in paint. They ranged in age from full grown men dressed in uniforms to a tiny baby leaning against his mother's shoulder. Close to the king stood a slender dark haired young woman wearing a small crown. Seth recognized the curve of her smile and those gentle eyes. It was his mother, Anne.

"She let me think her people came from Horner Island."

"I can imagine she wished the lie were true." Her stern lips turned upward into a fond smile. "Your mother met Edmund D'Antoiné on Horner Island while accompanying August and I on holiday. My little Anne was so happy the day they married. Edmund was like a young man again. He had been miserable in his other marriages. Finally, he married for love."

"Dante said I had brothers."

"Edmund's first wife came from an arranged marriage. The poor woman died giving birth to their only son. His second wife was…a mistake. Edmund married his third wife out of obligation. Silly weak little creature that she was. Sickness took her a few years later. They had one son together. He shared his mother's weak health."

Aunt Charlotte shook her head and smiled at Anne's picture. "Your father did his best to honor all of them, but love didn't strike him until he met Anne Von Wolkhurst.

Seth ran his hand through his messy curls. "What of Julian, my half-brother? Dante said he was a disappointment to my father."

"That creature is best forgotten." Aunt Charlotte tapped the Lion Ring. "The son who matters is here now."

"What happened, Aunt Charlotte?" he asked, taking her hands. "Who forced my mother into hiding?"

Her proud shoulders drooped slightly as if the memory still weighed heavily upon her heart. Seth helped her to sit down in one of the overstuffed chairs. She took a linen out of her sleeve and pressed it against her chest.

"Your grandfather found out his daughter was in love with a Valdeonian and called together a rare meeting between the Von Wolkhursts and the D'Antoinés. Both families were complicit in their hatred. Edmund was called back to duty. Anne came here to stay with me while he was away." She gripped his hand again. "Evil uses hatred as a weapon as surely as you use your sword. My brother, the King of Tslavia, brought his men and members of the D'Antoiné family into this very room. August and I tried to stand against them, but we were outnumbered. My brother gave me the choice of betraying Anne or losing my status as Princess of Tslavia. You can imagine what I told him to do with his crown. He sent Anne into hiding and banished August and I from Tslavia forever."

"Your brother is the King of Tslavia?" Riley whistled low and dropped into a chair. "And Seth is his Grandson?"

"It's no small wonder why Pavel Sandor tried to kill me."

Seth sat in the chair next to Aunt Charlotte. He was the child of two hated rival nations. Both sides wanted him dead and now he understood why.

"What became of the mad dog, Sandor?" Aunt Charlotte asked.

"Seth sent him to the bottom of the ocean."

"Riley," Seth warned. "I don't think Aunt Charlotte needs to know the details."

"I am Queen of Carlotta and a Princess of Tslavia. I've stitched more wounds together than I care to recall. These hands have struck down invaders who tried to kill my kin within the walls of our ancestral home. I don't need my delicate sensibilities protected."

She turned her gaze up at the painting once more. "You've avenged your mother. Never apologize to anyone for doing so, Nephew."

"How did you come to be Queen here of all places, Majesty?" Riley asked. "Seems to me someone like you would rule a larger country on the mainland. If you don't mind me saying so."

Aunt Charlotte took a portrait of a man dressed in a Jalora Legion uniform from the little table beside her. "My August once bore the Gargoyle Ring. Tymon was his squire."

The Gargoyle was a ranger? Seth placed a hand over the golden coin. It had been used to pay mercenaries and raiders for killing. The Lion and the Gargoyle were held to different standards of honor it would seem.

She smiled as she handed the portrait to Seth. "My August found this island and bought it for me. The people were near starvation and gladly took the money.

August was a financial genius and helped the people market their nuts and sun fruit." She gave him a proud smile. "They were so grateful to August, they made him their King. So, here is how you find me, Queen Charlotte Von Bohdan of Carlotta."

Seth handed the portrait back to her. Aunt Charlotte wiped at the glass with a small piece of linen and carefully placed it back upon the table.

"Anne was my heir. Her passing makes you the Crown Prince of Carlotta. Long may you rule - after I'm gone of course."

He looked from her determined face to the oil images in the painting. Ruling an island was out of the question. Aunt Charlotte and her August had forgotten their bigotry for Edmund, but the rest of his mother's people had not. How long would it be before the Von Wolkhursts discovered he was hiding in her home? They would come for him and this time Aunt Charlotte may not escape their wrath. He smoothed at the Lion Ring. Wolf would find him. Then they'd travel to a place of safety for Seth's training. He had to keep a tight hold upon his fury until then, for Aunt Charlotte's sake.

Chapter Eleven

BLOOD ORANGE SAILS dotted the skies above Valdeon like a pox upon the poor. Julian gripped the railing of his airship and looked down upon the silent towns drifting by beneath them. The threat of war hung over the houses, waiting with its hungry maw to devour his homeland.

"The Jackal are in position to strike, my lord prince," Marcellus said beside him. "Lord Gorman's armada stretches the entire mass of Valdeon."

Gorman. He tensed with loathing at the name. The insufferable man had been sent to aid Julian in seizing the throne, not to invade as its conqueror. Despite his contract with the Akutarian Emperor, Lord Gorman's forces had taken a threatening position while he'd been out of the country on his own errand.

His father was dead, struck down by those loyal to their true prince. He stroked the wood of the railing with a gloved hand. According to the reports, his father had suffered. He'd taken the news with an odd sense of indifference. Perhaps it made him yet another monster in such times. No matter. Other worries occupied his mind. Chief among them was eradicating these invaders from Valdeon's shores. Lord Gorman was strong, perhaps more powerful than even the strongest ranger in the Legion. Only one thing could stop him now - the Lion Ring, conduit of the Jalora's power on Andara.

Cutter, his new mercenary ally, would find the half-breed who bore their father's ring. His competence was not in question. It was his loyalty. Would his greed outweigh the fear of death once the Lion Ring was taken from the boy's severed finger? Time would tell.

"We're approaching San Leonora, my lord prince," Captain Nunez told him. "Will your…friends allow us passage through their barricade?"

Dozens of armor-plated airships hovered over the capital city in the fading light of a dusk sky. They formed a perfect circle around the wall. Ruined Valdeonian warships smoldered in pieces upon the ground beneath them. Only the army and the city's defenses were left to keep the Jackal horde out.

"Set us down well outside their circle, Captain," Julian said. "I want you hidden in the event we must make a quick escape. Marcellus and I will take a dinghy and journey into the city. It is time I take my proper place as Valdeon's Regent."

Marcellus guided the small dinghy into the shadows of the wreckage. Keeping low to the ground, they came within walking distance to the gates without being seen. They covered their dinghy with torn sail and broken branches, and then set off on foot toward the city. Moans of the dying lingered upon the deserted road. Marcellus kept a nervous pace beside him, his eyes darting from one side of the road to the other. Julian refused to gaze into the wreckage. His focus was reserved for those who hadn't failed their lord.

The Great Inland Wall vaulted into the sky before them. Stone lion heads, a thousand strong, roared in silent warning toward the burning ships. The wall had not been breached for hundreds of years. San Leonora's citizens would put their trust and hope behind its strength. Unfortunately for them, Lord Gorman wouldn't be coming through the gates. He'd come from the skies like a deadly firestorm.

Two arrows pierced the ground at their feet. A pathetic warning from the city's defenders hidden among the roaring jaws of the stone lions.

He threw off his hood and lifted his face. "I am Julian D'Antoiné, Prince of Valdeon! Allow me entry immediately."

"In a pig's eye, you are!" A voice yelled down from the mid-section of the wall.

"Quiet you. It is the prince," another voice said as a small stream of light from a crystal lantern struck them.

An older man with a balding head and tired eyes stepped out of the shadows. He was one of the nameless subservient aides to Chancellor Benito. An odd choice to stand the watch at such a time. He allowed them entry through a small opening hidden within the wall by the gate.

"Chancellor Benito will be relieved to see you, Prince Julian," he said. "He's assembled the court in the Great Hall for an emergency session. I would take you there, but my orders are to watch for the Sacred Guard or other rangers arriving to aid the city."

"I will find my own way." Julian nodded curtly and headed into the streets with Marcellus following close behind.

They'd have a long wait for help from the Jalora Legion. No communications were leaving or entering Valdeon. And as for the Sacred Guard, Gorman's forces were positioned to silence the meddlesome rangers in the heart of their own lands.

Chaos. It was the only way to describe the scene he found in his city. Men and women raced along the streets, carrying what they could to fortify their meager homes. Wooden benches and anything else they could be used to barricade doors or windows had been ripped from its place.

"It is as if the Jackal has already entered the streets," Marcellus murmured.

"I have to get to the palace. The chancellor must name me regent before it's too late," Julian said. "He must agree before more blood is shed."

A small projectile struck the back of his head. Cursing, he rubbed at the spot. Sudden movement from a narrow alley drew his attention to a beckoning gloved hand. Dangling from its fingers was a linen with the crest of the king upon it. No one without access to Leo's chambers could have snatched such an item.

"Check the way ahead," he ordered.

Waiting for Marcellus to disappear amongst the crowd, he approached the shadows at a careful pace. The hand snapped out to grab the front of his shirt and pulled Julian into the darkness. Black gloves and a heavy cowl concealed his features, but the presence of infuriating mystery announced his identity at once. Here was the very same stranger who bypassed the palace guards and entered his chambers without detection. He'd given Julian Leo's location and disappeared again without a trace.

"You are a disappointment to me, boy," he hissed, slamming Julian against the side of the building. "I give you Leo and his heir, while they are vulnerable. It was a foolproof plan I'd spent years concocting and you make a blundering mess of things! Now the Lion Ring is out of our reach and the Regent Medallion is hidden."

"How dare you! I'm a prince of Valdeon."

The hand slammed against Julian's face with a painful whack. "Be silent. You'll do as you're told. Now, you must go and dispose of Chancellor Benito. He is Xavier the Wolf's man. No amount of argument will sway him now that he knows about the Bearer of the Lion Ring. The chancellor must die by your hand or Lord Gorman will seize the throne and take control of Valdeon.

"You are well informed," Julian said, suspicion bitter upon his tongue. "Who are you and how do you know of Lord Gorman?"

"Hasten to the palace. You have until midnight to convince the court to name you regent," the stranger said. "When the last stroke of midnight sounds, I will give entry to the Akutar by a long-forgotten gate. Then any hope you have of wearing the crown dies."

Horrible silence lingered from the shadows. The stranger was gone, leaving Julian feeling the fool. Lord Gorman had another ally on Andara. Who this stranger was, or his reasons for aiding Julian as well, were hidden in mystery. One thing was obvious. He'd been manipulated by both men. The only way for Julian to survive was to kill the chancellor.

Chapter Twelve

A MASSIVE IRON ROD fence stood sentry before them, cutting off access to the peninsula in which the Palace of Kings and its grounds encompassed. Double gates, firmly closed and bolted, were well-guarded by the Valdeonian Army. Impressive though the iron gates were, they couldn't keep out the coming storm. Julian had seen the Jackal and the Dirge in battle. They were invincible.

"Halt!"

A palace guard glared at them between the bars. His expression shifted from alert sternness to contempt. He made them wait far too long before summoning another man to help lift the heavy bar sealing the gate.

Julian lifted his chin as he walked into the grounds. Whispers and dark looks were already making their way through the army. They'd feared him once. He'd give them reason to fear him again. If they survived the night.

"Take me to the duty officer at once," Julian commanded.

"Yes, Sir," the guard murmured, turning to go without waiting for Julian or Marcellus to follow.

"Show some respect. You speak to a Prince of Valdeon," Marcellus snapped.

"A bastard prince more like it," someone said behind them.

Julian grabbed Marcellus' arm, propelling him forward. The time for childish fights had passed. They must find Chancellor Benito in the palace. No easy task with the entire San Leonora Army blocking their path. The duty officer was the only one who could grant them entry in times of attack. They wouldn't make the courtyard without his permission.

An organized chaos whirled about them as the army prepared for battle. Barricades atop the roof of the barracks had been constructed and were now being stocked with supplies. Horses and men filled the courtyard, each busy with their own tasks.

Julian was grateful to escape the thundering noise of the courtyard as they entered Army Headquarters. His relief was short lived. The same quiet halls he'd walked through a month ago were now filled with volunteers clamoring for weapons and ammunition. Their anxious faces fell upon one man. Though Julian had forgotten his name, he recognized the hard features and stoic eyes. He was one of Leo's countless Lion Friends.

"Prince Julian and his companion, Sir." Their guard saluted the Duty Officer.

"Your return to San Leonora is poorly timed, Prince Julian." Those cold eyes reflected his sentiment more artfully then his words ever could. "I've no time to pander to diplomats or anyone else. The palace is in jeopardy."

"I will excuse your rude and disrespectful tone, Commander," Julian said. "We've come to seek admittance to the palace. I must speak with Chancellor Benito."

"You make no offer to help defend the city? I don't recognize Edmund the Leo in you. More's the pity. I'm sure his heir will set a great many things right." The commander turned to their escort. "Take the prince and his companion to the atrium. Then come back immediately. I need brave men at the gates."

The guard saluted. Casting a disgruntled look at Julian, he hurried through the ranks of soldiers and out into the yard. The smell of animal droppings and discarded meals was horrific. Leaping over muck and trash, Julian join the irritated guard at the base of the palace steps.

"Go take your place with my compliments, guard. Fate will soon see you get your just rewards."

They took a reckless pace up the mosaic tiled steps of the palace. Angry shadows stabbed at the massive glass walls of the atrium. Designed as a peaceful place to welcome guests, this night the atrium was a terrifying kaleidoscope of impending violence. He forced his attention forward as they ran toward the most sacred ground in all Andara, the throne room housing the Altar of Providence.

The golden doors protecting the throne room had closed weeks ago upon the king's death. Tonight, they stood open, exposing the stronghold of the Jalora's power. The Sarcion Ring upon his finger stirred in anticipation. Hungry vengeance for its hated rival prickled along the skin of Julian's hand.

A crowd stood chattering in the entrance. Julian pushed through them, ignoring the disrespectful whispers as he passed. He stopped before their talisman of hope, his gaze instantly drawn to the massive golden lion head making up the throne of Valdeon. Gigantic golden paws made up the legs and arm rests. Precious diamonds sparkled within the mane as it stretched up to touch the ceiling of white stone. The Crown of Sorrows, an unimpressive piece of lead when parted from its lion, was still gripped in the golden jaw. Beside the striking seat, glowing like a small moon, was the Orb of Valdeon. Bonding the Bearer of the Lion Ring's life force with land and the spiritual body of heaven, it pulsed in time with the half-breed boy's heartbeat.

Chancellor Benito pranced before the Orb, waving his arms like a gigantic purple bird in his ridiculous robes of office. His captive audience listened intently to Benito's boastful gushing. Spotting Julian over the new Lion's devotees, he waved.

"Prince Julian! The Heir has been chosen and the ring has awakened once more."

Forcing a look of delighted astonishment, he gripped the chancellor's hand. "This is the miracle Valdeon has been praying for, Benito. Where is he?"

Benito leaned closer and said low, "Lord De Vincente has gone to find the young Lion and bring him back to Valdeon."

It would indeed be a miracle if Wolf escaped is woolie dung prison and found the boy before the Dirge did. Of course, Wolf had a talent for doing the unexpected. It was best to have their whole plan.

"Will the Wolf bring him here, my lord?" Julian asked, frowning as the old man shook his head. "Oh, come now, Benito. I am his brother. He will need family around him now."

"You're right, of course." Benito smiled and patted Julian's arm as if he were a small boy or a feckless old woman. "Wolf was commanded to take the Lion to San Lucida to keep him safe. I believe once Wolf hears of the attack on San Leonora, he will summon the Lords of Valdeon from their homes. They will bring the Lion here to lead our forces."

It was unlikely. Wolf would do as he must to keep the Lion safe, even if it meant San Leonora would burn. And who else but Wolf's old mentor would he entrust with the Lion? Curse that meddlesome Cesar Santiago. All the western land owners followed him. If the half-breed Lion reached San Lucida, it would be impossible to take the throne by force. The west must be broken.

"Strange the other members of the Sacred Guard don't know about the young Lion," Julian said. "You haven't sent word to them then?"

"Naturally, everyone in the palace knows. And My Lord Santiago, of course. I'm certain Wolf will gather his men to him soon."

One of Benito's many aids hurried toward them, black robes dragging across the golden emblem embedded in the floor. He lifted his nose and frowned, avoiding any acknowledgement a Prince of Valdeon stood before him.

"My lord chancellor," he said, bowing stiffly. "The others have gathered in the great hall to discuss the defense of the city."

"Yes, yes." Benito waved impatiently. "You must excuse me. Wolf has left careful instructions for the defense of the city. I must attend to them."

The stranger had been right. Benito was Wolf's man. He wouldn't listen to reason or pleadings. It was Wolf who ruled Valdeon, not the old fool before him. Fire and Frost. They grew within Julian's heart, twisting and converging until his will had been forged into iron.

He rested a hand upon Benito's arm. "I must speak with you about a private matter."

The chancellor's aid stiffened. "They are waiting, my lord."

A thundering beat pulsed against Julian's temple. His hands began to shake. Time was running out. He must do the deed. Murder wasn't new to him. He'd killed his own kin to seek the throne. One more death for the good of Valdeon.

"Please, Benito. It will only take a moment." Julian gave him his best look of distress.

"Tell them I'll be there in a moment," Benito told his aid.

The throne room began to clear of the Lion's worshippers. *Boom. Boom. Boom.* The pulsing in Julian's temples grew stronger. Sweat soaked through his tunic. Still he didn't move.

Then they were alone. Julian, Benito, and Marcellus stood in the overpowering presence of the Lion. Golden eyes watched his hand as he reached for the hilt of his sword. Thrusting the blade deep into the old man, his right hand felt separate from the rest of his body. Surprise spread across the wrinkled face. Benito sank to his knees, fingers reaching out toward Julian. Within the cold iron of his will, he had no remorse to give.

"Betrayer! Murderer! Abomination!" A voice thundered against the white marbled walls of the throne room. *"You dare spill innocent blood in my temple. I curse you to live with the truth you've run away from for so many years."*

Power latched on to Julian's right hand. Brilliant burning light crept up his forearm. Unbearable pain threw him to his knees as he cried out. Laughter, low and contemptuous, replaced the anger. The Jalora had finished its strike and had now gone back inside its golden hiding place.

An ugly rash was forming quickly from his finger tips to his elbow. Red and raw, his skin had never experience so much pain. He'd escaped death, but was this better?

Marcellus stood pale-faced and shaken beside the chancellor's body. His eyes remained fixed upon Julian. Was the mad dog judging him? Julian hurried to his feet, keeping his arm curled against his body. No man had the right to judge his actions. He'd done what he had to do for Valdeon's sake.

"I go to take my rightful place."

"Your rightful place is at the end of a rope, murderer!"

The captain of the guard, a burly man with dark bushy eye brows and hands like a bear paw, marched toward them. Several of his men followed with weapons drawn. They circled around Benito's body.

Horror etched deep lines upon their faces. They were almost comical in a holy place meant to inspire peace.

"You don't understand, dullards. I must be made Regent or more Valdeonian blood will be spilled this night!"

"An empty threat, Usurper." The captain grabbed his arm and flinched away when he noticed the angry red sores making their way up Julian's right arm. "A cell is where you belong, and may the Lion Heir throw the key away."

Hard stares surrounded him. A few of the mob waved their swords, anxious to see more blood spilled. He would find no rational ears among them. Julian turned an anxious glance to Marcellus. He looked away. Very well. Let him join this mob of the walking dead. The fools had signed Valdeon's death warrant in their misplaced loyalty to a Lion who would never come.

"You must listen to me, Captain. I've encountered these men who hold San Leonora in their web. Let me try to broker peace with them. They'll listen to me." Julian pulled hard against the man's grip. "The Jackal will only speak to the ruler of Valdeon. Make me Regent and I can ensure peace will return to San Leonora."

"Valdeon needs no Regent, bastard prince. The Lion has been named. It is he who will save us from these invaders, not a slithering murderous snake like you." He spat on the floor beside Marcellus' knee. "You and your mad dog are of no use to Valdeon."

"What goes on here?"

Leo's Lion Friend, the duty officer, approached them. Strange the man had come to the throne room.

He'd seemed adamant about seeing to the defense of the gates. The duty officer tilted his head slightly and stared curiously at Julian. Black flooded over the whites of the officer's eyes. The tar hue lingered for a moment then was gone. Julian blinked. Had he imagined it?

"Your warning came too late, I'm afraid," the captain said, keeping a tight grip on Julian's arm. "We weren't in time to save Chancellor Benito, but we have captured his killer."

"Justice will be done," he said, with a nearly imperceptible grin at Julian. "Take them to the dungeons and make certain the lock is sturdy. We don't want such dangerous villains running lose. The Lion can deal with them when he returns."

Julian cast a strained look over his shoulders as he was dragged out of the throne room. Something wasn't right. Then he saw two fangs bite playfully upon the duty officer's lips. A Changeling! Lord Gorman had outwitted him again. Valdeon would be lost and there wasn't a soul who would help him.

Their guards shoved them down the ancient steps toward the damp of the cells. Julian's shoulder slammed hard against the wall. Their captors pushed him again, clearly unconcerned if he made it to the bottom with or without a broken neck.

They walked past a dozen or more open iron doors. Leo had been lenient with debtors and thieves. Things would be different when he was king. Every cell would be full of those who'd been traitor to Valdeon. Perhaps one of these cells would be Xavier the Wolf's permanent quarters.

"Inside you go, traitor prince." One of the guards pushed him inside the last door to his left. "And may the Lion throw away the key."

Marcellus came tumbling in after him. He spun to the left, avoiding Julian's gaze, and sank down to the stone floor. The heavy iron door slammed shut with finality. Murmuring voices struck the walls outside with curses. Finally, their heavy footsteps retreated, heading back to the free air above. Julian and his silent companion were left with dull light from a distant torch.

"You didn't protect me," Julian screamed at the Sarcion.

He kicked savagely at the door and fell against it in a heap. Cold iron touched his wounded skin. He hissed in agony and rolled away to lean against the stone. Marcellus was watching him with his back pressed against the opposite wall. No doubt the fool thought Julian was talking to him rather than the dark presence living inside the ring.

It wasn't I who stained the Jalora's floor with blood this day. Though violence will come soon enough. You must bear the burden of your own impatience.

Julian held out his burning right arm. Sores oozed with white puss and blood. A foul smell had begun to waft up in the dull air. He dropped it to his side and covered the offending limb with his cloak.

Then the screaming began. Faintly at first. The chorus of terror and pain rose toward a crescendo. Panicked cries grew closer as muskets fired. Julian let his chin sink to his chest. The Jackal had entered the city.

Chapter Thirteen

JORGE SMOOTHED a fingertip along the ridge of paper, carefully turning the page of his book. He'd borrowed it from the great San Leonora Library with every intention of seeing it safely returned. Circumstances had forced him to borrow the book a bit longer than he'd expected. Sniffing in the unique odor of ink upon paper, he began reading the next page.

"Come along, Duarto. Night is upon us. These eyes can't see details in the darkness. The light is better in your father's study," Donna said, pulling her reluctant son inside.

"Yes, it certainly is." Jorge lifted his eyes from the pages.

Many merchants had come calling, selling fabrics and other festive bobbles to celebrate the arrival of Wolf. His wife, unfortunately, had been an eager buyer. Jorge shook his head, wondering what the town would do when they saw the young Lion with him.

Donna handed their daughter, Inez, what was left of the two bolts of crimson fabric she'd purchased for the occasion. Golden thread sparkled in spiraling patterns within the material. Assuming she'd planned to make a dress with the hideous cloth, he'd remained silent. The truth was much more disturbing.

"Ouch! Mother, must you skewer my flesh!" Duarto jumped under her fast-paced fingers.

"You are supposed to be a soldier in the San Lucida Brigade, brave one," Jorge said with a grin. "What will happen when you taste the sword?"

"Silence your tongue with such evil talk," his wife chided.

"Father is quite right. You'll have to toughen your tender skin if you are to serve with men like my Franco." Inez rested her hands upon Jorge's shoulders.

Their daughter had her mother's dark hair and pleasant, Valdeonian features. Inez, however, had been gifted with Jorge's sense of humor. Blessed with a gentle heart, she'd been much sought after by those young men brave enough to risk her father's hatchet.

"And you'd know all about the brigade without serving a day, I suppose." Duarto rolled his eyes. "Ouch! Mother, have a care."

"If ever you give birth, my brave son, then you'll know real pain." Donna tugged at the fabric of his sleeve. "Now be still. I won't have you walking the streets of San Lucida with crooked arms."

Leaving his son to Donna's will, Jorge took Inez' hand and kissed it. He gently pulled her around to stand before him and placed a hand upon her growing stomach. This was his first grandchild. Soon he'd have another reason to stay home. A grandchild was a blessing he'd longed for since his own children outgrew their toys.

"If you were my wife, I would not be dallying in San Lucida on such an evening."

Inez kissed his forehead. "My Franco must see to the safety of the docks before his lordship arrives."

"Franco just wants a try at those new muskets from Heidelbrecht," Duarto told her. "Wolf is a Jalora ranger. He can see to his own safety."

It came without warning. The sharp stab of power burned in his torso, throwing him down upon his knees. He dropped Inez' hand and clutched at the pain inside his body. This warning had come with a stronger intensity then when he'd seen the hideous Dirge standing upon his lands.

"What is it? What's wrong?" Donna dropped her sewing and came to him.

Hurrying to his feet, Jorge held up his hand to silence her. The storms of violence were coming. His warrior instinct told him so. A stillness had fallen over his land. The night music of cicadas and other insects had fallen silent. Then a horse's hooves thundered frantically upon the drive.

"Take Inez into the back room."

He took his hatchet from the cabinet and pulled his sword from the sheath hanging beside his old squire's cloak. They were remnants from an old life he'd thought he'd exchanged for retirement. Peace, it would seem, was a fickle companion.

Moving through the villa on silent feet, he shooed their cook and the house boy toward the back. Duarto rushed out of his chambers behind him, sword drawn and still wearing the partially sown shirt.

Together they made their way to the door to the courtyard. Jorge readied his hand on the handle and nodded to his son. Duarto flattened himself behind the door, ready to pounce. Heavy steps thundered upon the tiles. Jorge gripped the handle of his hatchet as they grew closer. Would his strike even hit home? The Dirge seemed made of air and midnight.

He threw open the door with a fierce battle cry. A young soldier from the brigade staggered toward him. Bright red blood soaked his shoulder. Gashes and sweat covered his face and head. Bewildered, he looked from Jorge to Duarto.

"Take his other arm," Jorge said, gripping the young man before he could fall.

They helped him to a chair in the parlor. Duarto stuck flame to candle and sat it down on the table beside the chair.

"It is Juan Marico from the brigade," Duarto said.

Jorge ripped open the bloodied tunic. He could see the wound much more clearly in the dim light. The blade piercing his body had been jagged, brutal. No Valdeonian swordsman would use such a barbaric weapon. Young Marico had been lucky. He would live, but the wound must be sewn.

His eyes flew open. "Duke Pacarro, Hell has come to San Lucida!"

Jorge put a restraining hand on the man's shoulder. "Calm yourself. Tell me what happened."

"They hid themselves in the shadows of the canyon, my lord. The strangers dressed in blood-caked armor came out of the very walls! They couldn't be stopped! We stood against them with every weapon in our arsenal. Nothing worked. It was as if they weren't human." Marico's eyes stared at the tiny flame of the candle. "Then the ships came."

"Ships?"

Jorge turned knowing eyes upon his son. Ships could not come over the mountain range from Tslavia. Map makers had branded them the Border Mountains, but those who lived at their feet knew the true nature of those cliffs. The winds were too dangerous to fly over. Experienced climbers refused to risk their lives upon the unforgiving rock. The mountains were cursed, though the Legion tried to deny it. Those who knew their true nature called them, the Forbidden Mountains.

"They came from the northeast," Marico said. "The sails bore the insignia of flesh eating Jackal."

Invaders in San Lucida? He rubbed at the heat throbbing in his torso. The Dirge hadn't simply been curious. It had been a scout. He should have paid more attention to the omen of evil. The medallion's power had warned him before, but this time Jorge hadn't wanted to believe such violence could once again visit his home. He'd been a fool.

"We must have a look, Duarto."

"Yes, you must. Cesar will need help," Donna said, sweeping toward them in a rush.

She had their hunting clothes draped over her arm. Silently handing them to Jorge, Donna took the box of bandages from Inez. She pinched her daughter's arm, snapping Inez out of her state of shock. Marico, Jorge well knew, was in her Franco's troop.

"I've sent Neto to gather the other hands. They'll meet you in the courtyard. I'll see to this young man," Donna told them.

Jorge smooth a hand across his well-worn tunic. It was the color of the plains grass. Good for hunting and remaining hidden, it had seen him through many a year. He tossed Duarto's hunting clothes to him and began to change.

"Have a care, husband." Donna caught Jorge's arm when he'd finished dressing. "You're a farmer now, not a Legion squire."

"Even farmers fight when they must," he said, kissing her cheek. "Don't open the door for anyone. I'll leave someone to stand watch over the Villa."

"Find Franco for me, Father," Inez called to him.

Jorge didn't turn. He couldn't bear to see her pleading eyes.

They stepped into the courtyard. Lanterns positioned along the perimeter of the yard did their best to lend cheer to the darkness. If enemy ships had fired upon San Lucida, his home would be a tantalizing target. Neto, his land manager, had apparently come to the same conclusion. He and his men began dousing the lights of the crystal lanterns.

Dressed in hunting gear, Neto came to silently stand before Jorge. Face etched by the harsh Valdeonian summer sun, his age was impossible to guess. He'd first met Neto during a battle in the southern border of the Buells. Jorge had saved his life, earning his respect and loyalty. He had no idea which country Neto had originally hailed from, but he was a long-time San Lucida fixture now.

Five other men waited nervously behind Neto. They were local hands who made a living hunting for the various ranches outside the city. One night a week, they met in Jorge's barn to drink and swap hunting stories. It had been Jorge's good fortune to catch them before the bottles had been passed around.

"Keep your eyes and ears sharp," Jorge told them. "I'm not sure what we'll find."

Jorge took a steady run down his drive. The others followed, their boots crunching upon the gravel. Sound would travel on such a night. He turned sharply off the road and into the plains grass as they passed the last row of his vines. Tall grass whipped at their legs as they ran toward the steep incline of Lucida Ridge.

Plains grass may have covered the outer surface, but inside the terrain was much different. Shaped like a large bowl, Lucida Ridge surrounded the city. Solid rock made smooth by an ancient ocean made it impossible to climb down inside. A narrow canyon was the only passage in or out other than air flight. While Lucida Ridge was the city's greatest protection, its rim left the city vulnerable to curious spies. It would be the perfect place for Jorge and his men to see the facts of the attack for themselves.

His breath came in hungry gulps. Legs once used to running with warriors, were growing tired. Jorge gritted his teeth. He'd grown sluggish, puttering about his vineyard. Peace, it would seem, had left Valdeon. The time for warriors had come again.

"Do you think these attackers are still inside the city, Father?" Duarto asked, breathing hard as they ran up the steep hillside.

"We shall see, my son. It's best if we're prepared for any violence these men of evil have concocted."

An angry orange glow pulsed from the top of the ridge. Familiar constellations, normally visible on such a clear night, had been blocked by a heavy cover of blackness. It could only mean one thing. San Lucida was on fire. Bursting toward the edge of the deserted rim, Jorge stared helpless down on the ruins. The enemy ships were gone. No soldiers or sounds of battle remained. Their noise had been replaced with the song of sorrow. It was a refrain he'd hoped to never hear again.

"What nightmare has fallen upon us?" Duarto asked, his young eyes reflecting the horrors below.

"My Lord Santiago will need our help searching for survivors in the city." Jorge looked upon the grim faces alight in the glow of the flames. "Keep your eyes and ears open. Death waits in the shadows."

A horse trail, worn smooth by the San Lucida Brigade on their daily patrols, wandered through the plains grass close to the lip of the ridge. Heading east toward the entrance to the canyon, Jorge kept a sharp watch upon the horizon. They were easy targets, silhouetted against the backdrop of fiery light coming from within the bowl. The need for haste, however, outweighed his instinct for stealth.

One remaining torch, hanging precariously on its side, made a small circle of light at the canyon's mouth. Staying close to the rock wall, Jorge crept closer to the torchlight. He stopped at its edge to examine the ground. Many boots had entered the canyon recently. None of them were of Valdeonian make. Jorge pulled his hatchet. The canyon was a good half mile long with many places to hide. They could be walking into an ambush.

"Neto, bring up the rear and watch the shadows behind us."

Jorge gripped his hatchet tighter and stepped into the darkness of the canyon. Ears trained to hear the slightest noise registered the shallow, frightened breathing of his companions. He kept them moving forward, past the dark crevices and wayward boulders. Nothing. Even the nocturnal creatures who crept along the canyon floor seemed to have abandoned their homes. Jorge and his companions were the only life remaining in the canyon.

Then darkness and rock fell away. Before them was a hellish scene of devastation. Every structure in the once great city had been toppled by cannon fire. Ravenous flames continued to feast upon ruined homes at the edge of San Lucida Lake. Rubble, close to the canyon, smoldered in the aftermath of the strike. Ash covered the ground before them. The invaders had struck here first.

"No!" Duarto rushed forward, ash flying up in gray clouds as he passed.

Jorge hurried after him. It was a short sprint to the ruined headquarters of the San Lucida Brigade. The dead littered the ground about them. Most had been partially covered in ash and debris. Uniforms torn and bodies scorched, the San Lucida Brigade had met their end at their own headquarters. His son-in-law, Franco was among them. How would he find the words to tell Inez?

These invaders had struck without warning and the city defenders hadn't had time to pull a single weapon. He'd faced many an enemy in his time with the Legion, but never one who possessed the strength and skill to defeat a stronghold of the Jalora. A new enemy had come among them. The Legion had to be warned.

Duarto waded into the bodies of his comrades. "I should have been here. I should have stood with them."

Jorge pulled his son's face to his own. "Listen to me. The Jalora has spared you for a reason. Do not wish for death."

Duarto nodded slowly. Jorge released him. His words meant very little in the moment. It would take his son a long time to be relieved of the guilt. If indeed it did fade.

"We must find Lord Santiago," Jorge said.

Ignoring the ash and blood beneath his feet, he waded through the remains of the brigade. His boots struck the stone of the main row leading into the city. It, miraculously, seemed intact though covered with debris. Crawling over chunks of stone and shards of glass, they headed toward what he hoped was south.

The Santiago estate had stood upon the southern shores of San Lucida for centuries. It was there, Cesar would have gathered his forces. Jorge covered his face as they drew closer to the belly of the fire. The intense heat pushed them off the row and behind the protection of a large pile of rubble. He soon wished he'd endured the flames.

Bodies - men, women, and children alike - were scattered about the piles of stone and charred wood. They'd had no chance to escape the storm of cannon fire. No armored strangers were among them. These invaders either hadn't been touched or their comrades had taken the bodies with them.

Then a figure ran wildly through the rubble toward them. It was Mario, Cesar's house steward. His bald head was covered in soot and blood. His clothes, normally meticulous in their tidiness, were ripped and filthy.

"Duke Pacarro, the worst has happened!" Mario fell against Jorge, gripping his tunic. "The house of Santiago has fallen."

Cesar. He couldn't be gone. The numbing ache in Jorge's soul began to grow. He'd seen his ranger best a troop of men and walk away from the fight unscathed. Though Cesar had grown old, the Jalora's power had stayed with him. Who would dare to strike at a member of the Sacred Guard?

"Did you hear me, Duke Pacarro?" Mario trotted before him on anxious feet. "The house is this way."

Jorge nodded and followed Mario's panicked pace. He could see it now, the iconic statue of a ferret wrapped around a swan's neck. It had stood in the courtyard of the Santiago Estate since the time of Cesar's grandfather and continued to keep watch over the lake. The villa hadn't shared the fountain's good fortune.

Flattened beyond recognition, the house had obviously been the main target. Charred traces of cannon fire clung to the ruined stone. Bits and pieces of the Santiago family's memories were scattered among the rubble.

"My lord!" He called into the ruins. "Cesar Santiago!"

"There are no survivors in this rubble, Jorge Pacarro," a voice said behind them.

Xavier the Wolf, burning with the fury of the Jalora's power, stood at the entrance of the estate. His sword pointed toward them, ready to spill blood. Those penetrating eyes were fixed upon Jorge.

"Wolf," he said numbly. "It was an attack in the night. Ships, bearing the symbol of a Jackal, aided their treachery."

The ranger's stare intensified. He was reading Jorge and the others to make certain they were telling the truth. Then the unpredictable Wolf sheathed his sword and closed his eyes. They waited breathlessly for the Lord of San Rudalfo to move again.

Wolf's eyes flew open. He turned his head and started to run toward the rocky beach of the lake. A shadow followed him. Basilio, Wolf's squire, darted after his ranger. The disagreeable man shot a glare over his shoulder at Jorge. His look was full of judgement and dislike.

"Come," Jorge said. "We follow the Wolf."

Cesar Santiago lay upon the rock-encrusted beach, inches from the water. Wolf gently turned him over, exposing several dark red holes in his tunic. The old ranger managed a smile as he looked upon the aura of power surrounding Wolf.

"Xavier, you've come." Cesar wiped at the blood bubbling through his lips. "Julian's army of assassins descended upon us. The bastard prince stood in my courtyard and demanded our surrender."

"He will pay for what he has done, Cesar. This I swear."

Pain clouded Cesar's eyes as he looked upon Wolf again. "I sent Lucio a letter, pleading with him to come home and guard the heir."

Wolf shook his head. "A foolish choice, my old friend. Julian must have attacked because he knew you would help the Lion."

"Swear to me you will keep Lucio from Valdeon until it is time, Wolf. Swear it!"

The Lord of San Rudalfo put a hand on the cheek of his old friend. "I swear it, Cesar."

Then Cesar's pained face turned to Jorge. He held a shaking and bloodied hand toward him. Jorge hurried forward and took it. He knelt beside his ranger and wept.

"I call you to service, Jorge Pacarro." Cesar's fingers gripped his hand weakly. "Our people must have a leader. They will need you in such times. Promise me, Jorge. You mustn't fail them. Take care of our people until the Lion returns."

"I swear it, my lord."

They watched together as the old ranger's eyes closed in death. Silence descended upon the beach. The raging fire and the moans of the dying faded. Jorge gently lowered his lord's hand and placed it upon his chest. A light had left the world. Nothing would be the same again.

Wolf stood and lifted his eyes to the rest of the city. "I must go to San Rudalfo and ready my fleet. Julian will pay dearly for this treachery."

"What of the heir?"

"He is safe enough away from here. I must see to San Rudalfo and my people." Wolf held Jorge's gaze for a moment. "Remember your duty, Jorge Pacarro."

Then he left them in a burst of speed. Jorge's eyes turned to the frightened people of San Lucida gathered at the edge of the beach. They too watched Wolf disappear into the ash-filled night. The Lords of Valdeon couldn't save them this time.

He put a hand over the patch of skin were the Regent Medallion had once touched and let the hard determination come once more. He had a promise to keep.

"People of San Lucida," he said, lifting his voice above the moans of despair. "I want all able-bodied men and women to form a group at my left. We must comb the ruins for survivors. Those who can stand, I will need your help in setting up a medical station for the injured."

"Get moving!" Duarto shouted, pushing at some of the stunned survivors. "You heard Duke Pacarro. We go to search for the missing."

Others, bruised and bleeding, crawled toward him. Absolute trust was in their eyes. They'd found their leader and a haven among the chaos. Jorge wished he could share their confidence.

Chapter Fourteen

THE CREW WAS SOLEMN as the ship set sail again. San Lucida still glowed behind them, its body slowly dying. Impotent Anger. Confusion. Hatred. They pulsed about the crew in brilliant colors of mourning. Wolf understood their grief well. He'd lost his teacher and a dear friend. Gone too was his hope to save Valdeon.

San Lucida's fall brings deep sorrow to my heart, Right-Hand, the Jalora said, its grief joining with his sorrow. *The people's disobedience has allowed evil to enter Valdeon like an infestation. Vermin outnumber the rat catchers. Look you to my failing strongholds.*

Then the bustling crew on the deck faded away. In their place were many scenes of fire and destruction. Wolf recognized the cities Evil's armada attacked. They were the homes of the Lords of Valdeon. Death and destruction were everywhere.

"Is there nothing we can do, Holiness?"

My power has faded. Evil knows this and will do anything to keep me from growing strong again. The Lion must be protected. He is the only one who can restore Valdeon and through it, Andara.

"And San Rudalfo? What of my home? I don't see it among the others."

Evil strikes at the Lion's greatest allies.

It said no more. Wolf staggered a step forward as it released him from the vision. He'd seen his worst fears and his private hell in those images. Nothing he did would save Valdeon, but he still had to try.

"Captain!" Wolf pounded up the stairs to the bridge. "Get us to San Rudalfo in all haste."

The captain's haggard face struggled to hide his frustration. He and the crew had been sleeping in two-hour shifts for the past seventy-two hours. Their nerves were worn and their bodies tired. Wolf was asking the captain to drive his men at an even more brutal pace.

"Forgive me, my lord, but if we push these engines any harder they will fail."

"Listen to me, all of you." He brought forth his full power, capturing every ear. "The Jalora has shown me a vision. Valdeon is under attack. Every stronghold ruled by the Sacred Guard has or is about to fall, including San Rudalfo. We must reach the armada and rally the rest of the military."

Exhausted faces, once dull with shock, stirred in lines of hate and fury. San Lucida's fate had shown what awaited them in their own home city. Hurrying back to their stations, they no longer worked to serve their lord. These men would drive their own bodies into the ground for the sake of their families.

"Get those engines to full power!" the captain growled. "I don't care if we explode. Get us home."

One man stayed in the center of the deck, still watching Wolf with desperate eyes. Basilio, his squire, had been in the ruins of San Lucida as well. He'd seen firsthand what carnage and destruction these Jackal had brought to their homeland. Women and children were as worthless to them as rodents. Wolf turned away from the worry he saw surrounding his squire's body. His courage would fail him if he allowed the worry to invade his own mind.

The long hours stretched past midnight as they flew. He wrapped his cloak tighter about his body. They kept to the clouds as high as they dared to go to hide the ship. The air had grown thin and frigid. No one was willing to leave the deck for the sake of a little warmth.

Flames were spotted the ground beneath them. It seemed all Valdeon was on fire. Each passing mile etched another chasm of worry for his family upon Wolf's heart. His overwhelming anxiousness kept him from landing in Varianne at the house of his best friend, Fausto De Qunitaro. Dulcina wasn't one for panic. He knew she'd keep her head and go to safety, but still the dread pounded against his thinning nerves.

Their ship descended tentatively out of the clouds as the distinct shape of the ancient Moonstone Temple came into view. Once the stronghold of the Jalora Legion before the Obsidian Citadel was created in Lea, on this night of evil it had become a tall shadow against the backdrop of fire.

"We're too late." Basilio slammed a fist upon the railing.

The city lay in waste. Cannon fire had flattened most of the buildings Wolf had known since he was a babe. The beautiful orchards of orange trees were burning in a sea of flames. And his villa - he couldn't see it through the smoke and ash. He may be too late to save the city, but was he too late to save his family?

"The fleet!" one of the crew shouted.

Vessels from his crippled armada crashed to the ground, crushing the houses beneath their fiery bulk. Standing within the red sails, leering down at their kill like predators were a pack of Jackals. The strange ships darted in and out of the strike zone. They were easily outmatching the San Rudalfo vessels.

"Incoming!"

They'd been seen. Red sails slapped at the wind as the Jackal pack turned to engage his vessel. Metallic hulls skimmed the thick smoke settling over San Rudalfo. They came at his crippled ship like predators who've trapped a wounded deer.

His time had run out. The Jalora Legion must be warned about the conquerors who'd taken Valdeon in a single night. Turning from the oncoming vessel, Wolf hurried to one of the emergency launches. Terrified eyes stared at him from behind the water barrel. It was the ship's cabin boy. Wolf took him by the back of his small tunic and lifted him up to eye level. The boy was no more than ten years old. His wide eyes stared at Wolf. He was almost as terrified of his lord as he was of the oncoming ship.

Wolf put him in the launch as Basilio unfastened the hooks and mooring rope. The little vessel hovered above the deck like a fragile bubble of hope.

"Can you fly this boat, boy? Listen to me, I call you to service. You will go to the Obsidian Citadel and report what you have seen this night to the Dragon. Do you understand?"

"The Citadel, my lord? You want me to go all the way to Lea alone?" Tears were beginning to form in his huge brown eyes.

"I command you to a blood oath, boy. You will not rest until you reach the Dragon. And you will not fail me or Valdeon." Wolf held his face firmly. "Swear it to me! No matter what happens, you will not stop until you've seen Dragon personally."

"Yes, my lord." The little voice grew stronger. "I swear the blood oath."

"Good lad, I am most pleased." Wolf pushed the launch over the railing. "The Jalora's blessing goes with you."

The little thrusters headed toward the north and Lea. With luck, the boy would make it out of Valdeon and over the Border Mountains. It would be a rough trip, but their hope for aid was resting on his small shoulders.

"We can do no more aboard this vessel, my lord." Basilio tugged at the mooring ropes of another launch. "Those ships are coming up fast on our starboard. We must see you safely to the ground."

Cannon fire boomed in a deafening chorus, striking his vessel full-on. Wood and bodies tumbled across the deck. The ship tilted wildly, throwing Wolf off-balance. He flew over the side of the dying ship, plummeting toward the hungry arms of fire.

Chapter Fifteen

Wind ripped at Wolf's hair and clothes, striking his skin with stinging fingers. Above him the ship's hull exploded in flames. Moaning its death cry, the vessel split at the center. Fiery bits of wood and engine plummeted toward him, matching his speed. He was going to die. Crushed upon the ground, his body would burn into nothingness.

Call the wind to you, Right-Hand! The Jalora wrapped about his body, holding him in its power. *You must survive!*

Wolf calmed his panic and let the Jalora take control. An enormous surge of power burst from the Erthe to meet the brutal wind. Their energy struck his body at the same moment, knocking the air from his lungs. Wolf gulped in new breath, gasping as cold and hot penetrated his skin. New sensations filled his awareness as his body seemed to fade away. It was as if he'd joined with the elements.

Slow.

A single thought altered the wind's direction and stayed the Erthe's gravity. Wolf's momentum slowed until he floated upon the ashes showering from his burning ship. He rested the toe of his boot upon a plank. Frozen in place, the wood felt firm under his foot. He pushed off again and the plank resumed its spinning fall toward the flames.

The wind, flighty imp by nature, wiped away the thick smoke beneath him. Staying on his present course, Wolf was moments away from dropping onto a burning house. Its roof had been eaten away, exposing thick ceiling beams. Heat burned at the soles of his feet. He wouldn't survive the inferno long.

Sending his will for a final push from the wind, Wolf's foot struck the top of one of the smoldering beams. He pushed away from the crumbling roof. Hitting the ground hard, he ran as the fiery death from the sky fell toward him. Wood, fabric, and steel smashed the burning house under its weight.

Thrown onto the main row by the force of the impact, Wolf sat in the dirt, dazed by the horrors he saw before him. Places he'd played as a child were gone, burned to the ground or shattered by cannon fire. People he'd known his entire life now lay lifeless upon the ground. Butchered and burned. He'd been too late to save them. Their lord had failed in his sacred duty.

He wiped away the wet stinging from his eyes. The devastation and loss must wait until he had Dulcina and the children safely out of Valdeon. Wolf came to his feet and headed west toward his home. It couldn't be far. He wasn't sure. So much devastation and death. He was drowning in it.

A familiar landmark, untouched by the night's violence, lined the road. The wooden-rail fence marked the edge of his estate. Had his herd of Thunder Stallions been spared? Wolf leapt over the railing when he heard screaming from inside the fence. Large clumps of black and blood filled the fields. His once beautiful herd had been butchered down to the last colt. One of the mares was still screaming, waiting for death as she bled out. Thrusting his blade into her neck, he quickly ended her suffering.

Still carrying his exposed blade, he ran through the gruesome fields toward his ancestral home. The brilliant glow of fire tumbled over a hill parting the herd from his orange orchards. Flames ravaged the trees all around a great pile of bricks. The home he'd known all his life, where he'd been married and raised his children, was completely gone. Another gash ripped through his heart. Wolf shook his head. No. Wood and brick didn't make a home. His family was his heart. They would endure. He would rebuild the estate when peace returned to Valdeon. Yes. They would return. Dulcina was gifted with design. He would give her a bigger villa with more room for the children. Anything she wanted.

He staggered around the foundations of the ruined house, looking for signs of his family. Toys were scattered across the ruined patio. Crushed and burning, they'd been abandoned by the little boys who loved them. One, a large wooden horse Leo had given Danel, had been twisted from its rockers. Unease crept into the last sane place within his mind. No. He had to keep hope. The safety of his family was the only thing of consequence right now. He'd find a way out of Valdeon whether it be the inhospitable mountains to their north or the sea to their south.

"Dulcina! Children! Where are you?" Wolf screamed into the orchards. "Papa is here! Come to me!"

Then he saw it. Dulcina's burgundy shawl lay in a pile at the entrance to their orchard. He knelt beside it without touching the torn fabric. Wolf couldn't face what his power would tell him about her fate. Broken twigs and trampled grass gave him the truth regardless. Several men had been through this entrance. Lifting his sword to part the branches, he held his fists before him and pushed through the broken limbs to follow their path.

Row upon row of trees, some blackened and some burning, blocked his path as he ran. He tore through them, twisting and breaking branches with his bare hands. Wolf called their names again and again until his throat was raw with the strain. No answer. No sound except the popping of hot sap as it exploded in the heat. Following like a bloodhound, he kept his eyes to the ground. The smoke and ash were too thick to penetrate the air, even with Ranger Sight.

Breaking through the last row of burning limbs, he stumbled into a makeshift clearing. The trees had been cut down and pulled aside to form a large circle. In the center stood an old growth tree. Its leaves and fruit had been stripped away, leaving the larger branches bare. Three shapes, two smaller than the first, hung from its branches. They swayed slowly back and forth like gruesome paper lanterns.

The last piece of his sanity slipped away. Wolf, neither feeling heat or pain, walked through the flames and fell to his knees at the feet of his family. The fiery maw circled about him, ready to devour. He kept his eyes upon the once beautiful face of his wife. Failed. He'd failed them all.

Chapter Sixteen

Fire. It surrounded Seth, but his skin felt no heat. He was in a burning orchard covering rolling hills. Screams of the dying echoed above the roaring fire. Confused, he turned his head to the right and then to the left. The movement was slow, dream-like. This place held no memory for him, yet it seemed familiar.

Standing in his bedclothes, Seth reached a hand into the flames. They parted at his touch like a veil over a dirtied window. His eyes were drawn to the blurred image before him. Three pairs of bare and bloodied feet swayed in the heat of the raging fire. Two young boys and their mother had been hanged in a large orchard. They'd been savagely beaten from the looks of their faces. Seth covered his nose and mouth against the phantom stench as the flames licked their bodies.

A man he recognized knelt beneath them. Wolf! The ill-used victims had been his family. Seth remembered now. The long dark hair of his lovely wife Wolf had tenderly stroked. The tiny arms of his sons as they'd once wrapped around their father's neck. He'd seen them in Wolf's memories when they'd first touched rings.

Hungry flames pounced upon the grass beside the ranger. They were coming dangerously close to his boots. Still Wolf remained where he was, frozen beneath his family. He would join them in death soon if he didn't move.

"Wolf! Get up!"

Wolf turned his head slowly and twisted around to gaze toward Seth. Dull eyes filled with hopelessness no longer seemed to recognize him. His face was marked with pain and despair. Tears chiseled channels through the soot caking his cheeks. Wolf turned back to his family, embracing the silent vigil he held for their sake.

Another intelligence, ancient and powerful, came to join Seth's consciousness within his mind. Its presence, filled with urgent impatience, gripped Seth's body in a flood of energy. They looked together at the grieving father devoid of hope.

"I call you to me. Do not forget your oath, Right-Hand!"

Wolf, eyes burning with brilliant light, struggled to his feet. Stretching out his arms toward Seth, he plunged them into the flames. Reaching with his own arms toward the man who had saved his life, Seth called to him. Too late. The flames, the orchard, and Wolf had disappeared into the misty haze.

"The others must survive as well, Lion."

A dirt row stretched beneath his bare feet and ran in a slow curve away from a harbor. Its path took travelers into the center of a seaside town not much larger than Haven Bay. Lying in the middle of the road was the still form of a young man. Hurrying toward him, Seth knelt and turned him over onto his back. Several oozing wounds covered his body. The youthful face was bruised and swollen. This man, barely out of boyhood, had been savagely tortured.

Explosions and violent chaos thundered from the other end of the burning town. Armored men, like those he'd seen on Marianna when violence visited his home, were burning the last of the buildings. They'd be coming for this young man soon.

A brilliant glow pulsed at Seth's side from beneath the blood and muck. It was coming from the young man's bloodied left hand. Lifting the injured flesh gently, he turned the hand over.

A Heart of the Warrior Ring clung to his middle finger. He wiped away the filth covering the green crystal. An animal jumped out of the depths of the stony belly to follow his touch. It was a rabbit.

"The Lion, the Wolf, the Hawk and now the Rabbit." Seth smiled when the tiny creature tried to jump toward the Lion Ring. "We must be connected somehow."

The young ranger stirred and opened swollen eyes. His left hand pulled away and grabbed at Seth's nightshirt. He tried to lift his body, but the wounds were too many. Escape would be impossible on his own. Seth lifted his shoulders and began to drag him toward the harbor. Strange the invaders had left the docks untouched. They'd unwittingly given this young man a means of escape.

Reaching the warm waves as they rolled against the rocky shore, Seth continued to pull the young ranger into the water. He cradled the Rabbit's head above the waves and waded in waist deep towards a dinghy. Hefting the ranger into the boat, he dragged the vessel out farther into the waves by its mooring line.

Then the dinghy and its ranger disappeared. He spun about in the waters. No. He had to help Rabbit. The ranger couldn't defend himself. Either was Wolf. He couldn't just leave them.

The ancient presence gripped his body again and lifted him out of the sea. Standing upon the waves, Seth and the ancient power turned toward the shore. Seven silhouettes stood waiting for him upon a grassy knoll. Their eyes burned with the power of the Jalora.

"Listen well, Sacred Guard!" Seth shouted to them. "Leave these shores and wait for the appointed time. Hide yourselves. You must survive for my sake!"

The roar of a mighty lion thundered through the night sky. It shook the foundations of the dream-like world. Seth held his *hands to his ears, trying to block out the terrible roar. The misty world shattered like chards of glass about him. He began to fall.*

Sweat drenched bedclothes clung to his body. Shapes and patterns came into sharper focus as candlelight flickered wildly in the room. He was sitting up in bed at the center of an unfamiliar chamber. The gentle sea breeze rolled across the railings of the balcony and through a gigantic hole where a glass door had once been. Its remnants lay scattered across the floor.

One of the tiny flames moved closer to his left. Curly strands crushed with sleep framed a familiar face. Riley, dressed in his bedclothes, held the arm of an elderly woman clutching her dressing gown. Beyond them, Tymon stood in the doorway. A few of the household servants cowered behind him, giving Seth frightened looks. He was back at his Aunt Charlotte's home on the Isle of Carlotta. He fell back against the pillow. The men, the stench of burning bodies, and the roar of the great beast were gone. Safe. He was safe, but what of Wolf and the other rangers?

Riley moved tentatively toward him, his hastily pulled-on boots crunching the glass. "You were having a nightmare."

"It wasn't a dream, Riley." Aunt Charlotte joined him at Seth's bedside. "No soul in Andara could mistake the Lion's Roar. The Jalora has given us warning this night. We mustn't take it lightly. Tymon, cancel our shipments to Valdeon. Those shores are no longer safe."

"Lion's Roar? Do you mean to say such a terrible noise came from me?" He looked again at the destruction of her beautiful room. "And I caused this damage? I'm sorry, Aunt."

Such a weapon could bring down buildings. He had no idea how to control it. What if the power escaped again and hurt someone?

"The hinges made a ghastly noise. I'd meant to replace them soon. We'll put you in your parents' chambers. It has a better view of the sea."

Giving him a slight smile, she turned and made her way back toward the door to Tymon's waiting arm. The servants followed them, giving tentative looks over their shoulders at Seth.

"Well, you know how to rouse a house," Riley said. "I was shaken out of bed by your terrible roar. The others were already outside the door when I got here. We heard you yelling in Valic." He kicked at the rubble at his feet. "I've never seen glass shatter so completely."

"More than warning ships from Valdeon was behind the roar. I think I had a vision."

He recounted finding Wolf in the orchards and helping Rabbit at the seaside town. Riley whistled low when Seth told him about seeing the seven rangers standing upon the knoll.

"Who do you think they are?" Riley asked, handing Seth a glass of water from the pitcher at his bedside.

"I called them the Sacred Guard. They certainly behaved as if they knew me."

Riley shook his head and patted Seth's shoulder as he stood up. "One more reason not to go to Valdeon. Try to get some sleep. You'll feel better with a bit of rest."

"Sleep?" Seth clutched at his blanket. "What is happening to me? First I start hearing voices. Now I have visions? What if I'm going mad?"

"You aren't going mad, Seth. We all heard the Lion's Roar."

Seth twisted the blanket in his grip, trying to hold back the panic threatening to overwhelm him. Sleep. How could he sleep when his dreams were filled with hellish visions? What if his nightmares turned violent and the Lion's Roar escaped again? Would it seek out his aunt or other innocents inside the house? He'd had no idea the kind of power his father had put upon Seth's finger. It was no wonder to him now why so many sought the Lion Ring.

"I wish my father had explained. I wish he was here with me."

"Leo's gone," Riley said quietly. "Please, Seth. Let's go to the rangers. They could help you...."

Seth shook his head and fell back into the pillow once again. Would the rangers help him or would they use the gift his father had spoken of for their own benefit?

"If you are quite recovered, Squire, her majesty commands we prepare for refugees who come to our shores for aid."

Tymon stood in the doorway, fully dressed and looking as polished as he had when they'd first met. The thinly veiled mockery behind the title "Squire" communicated his anger more than blunt insults could.

He lifted his eyebrow and frowned at Riley. "I assume you've had at least a little training on healing salves and making bandages. You may be of some assistance."

Turning without waiting for Riley, Tymon headed down the stairs toward the hall. The hues of anger and fear trailed after him in streamers.

"Send word if you need me, Seth." The Logan temper burned across his squire's face as he hurried out of the room after the Tslavian.

Seth couldn't fault Tymon's anger and fear. He'd brought danger with him to the home of his aunt. His hunters had conquered Valdeon in a single night. Finding a fledgling ranger and his squire wouldn't be much of a challenge. They'd come looking and hurt any who'd given him aid. He must leave soon. Waiting for Wolf was no longer an option.

Chapter Seventeen

DIMMING PATTERNS of torch light struck the floor of Julian's cell. He'd spent the immeasurable hours watching them fade as the torches hissed out one by one. Breaking through the bars of the small opening in the door, the thin rays of light served as a reminder life hadn't ceased altogether. The death cries of his city had faded hours ago. A deafening silence had settled over San Leonora and the Palace of Kings.

Plunging his right hand into the nearest beam of light, he took stock of the Jalora's handiwork. Weeping sores had invaded the skin from fingertips to wrist. A sick smell of rotting flesh emanated from his appendage. Forcing himself to touch the hot skin, he withdrew his finger sharply when one of the sores burst at his touch. Thick ooze ran down his fingers to drip upon the floor. It did wonders in calming a hungry belly.

Marcellus gagged from the corner and quickly turned away. How disgusting must his grotesque plague be if it sickened his mad cell mate? Here was a vicious dog who'd dissected his victims for curiosity's sake. Each one of his experiments had been alive and conscious for the ordeal. Mad or no, he must be placated.

"Come now, Marcellus. The Chancellor of Valdeon must have a strong stomach."

Adopting the appropriate amount of patriotic fervor, he stretched out his good hand toward his cell mate. Marcellus abandoned his brooding for a moment. Twitching eyes stared at the outstretched hand.

"Valdeon will be great once more with you beside me, Chancellor De Costa. Soon Andara will bow to Valdeon just as it was in the old days. I will be king, perhaps even Emperor of Andara."

"How inspirational. I might be moved to tears at any moment."

The iron door slammed open. His Changeling nanny stood in the doorway, the keys twirling on his extended gray finger. Black orbs sparkled with laughter as the sharp features took them in.

"Come along, mighty prince. Lord Gorman longs for your presence."

"You!" Julian hurried to his feet and came at the creature. "If I had but two good hands—"

"But you don't." Thin black lips stretched across sharp teeth. "I see the Jalora's curse has started its chewing of your flesh. What a foul stench. Perhaps we should have you sleep with the Dirge from now on. I know they would find the odor pleasant."

The Changeling stepped aside, holding the door open wider. "Come along. Lord Gorman isn't a patient man. And no mischief." It snapped sharp teeth close to Marcellus' arm. "My body isn't limited to fragile human forms."

Climbing the steps, Julian headed back to the world of the living. He squinted and lifted his face toward the sun's rays as it struck the Atrium's glass surface. Invaders couldn't stifle the feeling of warmth it gave. They could, however, take away any sense of dignity the Palace of Kings once possessed. The great works of art and many of the tapestries had been pulled from the walls. Furniture lay broken and scattered upon the crumbled tile floors. Blood was everywhere. The bodies of the palace defenders - most of them loyal to Leo - covered the ground.

Standing along the interior wall of the Atrium cowered several men of the Valdeonian court. Julian's followers. They lifted their eyes to him with desperate hope as he entered. Moving to join them, Julian stepped over the corpse of a palace guard.

"The conqueror of this land commands I place you in the center of the Grand Atrium, Julian Bastard Prince." The Changeling pointed a gray finger toward an uncluttered section of floor. "He has planned some entertainment for his guests."

As if choreographed as part of an elaborate spectacle, Gorman's personal guard marched into the atrium. Blood-caked braids banged against their armor. Boots struck marble in perfect unison. Taking up position around the length of the Atrium, the Jackal soldiers drew their swords. Metal banged against metal as they beat their chests with the hilts. The sound grated against Julian's nerves, quickening the blood rush to his ears.

Then a nightmare entered his ancestral home. Iron, formed to make a hideous skull, completely covered the head of Valdeon's conqueror. Pristine and polished black armor encased his brawny form. Blades jutted from the metal covering the back of his hands. They offered no hope for tenderness from their ruthless owner. Rather his fingers were accustomed to holding the enormous sword hanging at his hip.

Lord Gorman, giving the bodies of the dead and the living no notice, kicked at a stray piece of statuary. "Have I not made it clear this palace is to remain untouched? It is mine and I won't have my possessions ransacked."

"Yours?" Julian glared into his metal-encased face. "This is my palace and my throne."

"Is it, prince of nothing?"

Gorman stretched his arm across the atrium. Towering over Julian, the Akutar Lord's arm cleared the top of his head by at least a foot. Bright blue eyes sparkled with hidden laughter from behind the mesh of their prison. They were the only hint a man of flesh and blood lived beneath the mask.

Reluctantly turning, Julian faced the golden doors of the throne room. They were sealed once more. Even the handles had sunk back into their golden depths. Several broken wooden beams had been abandoned at the throne room's threshold. It would appear the Jalora had no more appreciation for those usurpers than it did for an actual prince of the D'Antoiné blood.

"All your plotting and scheming to steal the throne as gotten you nothing." Lord Gorman pointed a metal finger at Julian's rotting hand. "The Jalora has already condemned you for spilling innocent blood upon its sacred ground. I'd say those closed doors are your final answer as to whether you'll ever sit upon the throne of Valdeon or remain the prince of nothing."

"Betrayer! Murderer!"

Orryo picked up a piece of broken glass and threw it at Julian. The projectile fell pathetically short. Once one of his most ardent suitors for power, Orryo had become the voice of the disappointed. His protests of shock and revulsion were joined by the angry cries of the crowd.

Julian turned his back on them, ignoring the whimpering of toothless dogs. Their hands were dirtied with treason as well. Pretending they'd been wronged to an emotionless head of metal would see them dragged away in chains.

"Look upon your faithful, Julian Bastard Prince. Only now do they realize the treacherous depths to which you'd go to seize the throne. Murdering your brothers and killing your sire to clear a path to the Lion's Seat. Making an alliance with conquerors from across the sea. Then ultimately handing them Andara just to see your obsessions realized. You are the worst kind of traitor."

"I am a patriot. I can't help it if you don't have the wit to understand."

Lord Gorman's hand flew to the hilt of his sword. He squeezed it until the metal covering his fingers scraped together. The sound made Julian's teeth ache. Let the blowhard bluster. He was still on someone's leash. Julian would be dead otherwise.

"I was almost disappointed you didn't run to the Wolf when you had the opportunity. He would have helped bring Andara's protector to the throne, for only the Lion could have saved Valdeon and Andara. Greed stayed your rotting hand. Now the die has been cast.

You are nothing but a puppet whose presence I must endure."

"We had a contract. Don't pretend you didn't readily agree to follow my plans in exchange for Andara's resources."

"Winning without honor is no victory." Lord Gorman pushed Julian out of the way with a heavy hand. "I take no pleasure in winning Valdeon by deceit."

Standing at full height, Lord Gorman faced the remaining members of the Valdeonian court. They cowered before him, casting uncertain glances at their dead countrymen.

"You have been spared in exchange for your part in the fall of this city," Lord Gorman said. "I can give you more power than you could possibly imagine. Agree to serve me and I will make you members of an elite group of warriors, even more powerful than the pathetic Sacred Guard who once roamed these halls."

Hunger was back in their eyes. This time it was directed at a new master. Fools. Lord Gorman had a horrible fate waiting for them. These men had no idea the hell they were being offered. He'd seen a Dirge in its early stages onboard ship. Half man and half monster, it was mad with hunger for human flesh. Sanity and shame had been eradicated from its failing mind. If not for the bars between them, the Dirge would have attacked his handlers. They knew no loyalties, but to their own terrible hunger.

"Take them to my ship and show my new comrades every courtesy," Lord Gorman said with a wave toward the anxious Valdeonians. "And you Marcellus De Costa.

What of you? Would you have this power also? I could use such a warrior."

Marcellus cast a quick look to Julian. "I have sworn allegiance to Prince Julian and would stay by his side, Lord Gorman."

"Very well. I suppose even a puppet must have a lackey."

Lord Gorman marched past the golden doors of the throne room. He turned into a short corridor leading to the various offices of the chancellor's Legion of administrators. This route also passed by an important relic of the old order. The Great Hall was another symbol of the Sacred Guard. They used the room to passed judgement on the guilty. Gorman's steps were sure as he entered. Julian's anger flared again. It was as if Gorman had visited the palace before. Or, more likely, someone had given him a detailed map. Someone like the Changeling, or the traitor stranger who'd pretended to help Julian.

A massive map of Andara had already been nailed to the ancient stone. The historic tapestry, once hanging in its place, was torn and punctured from several clumsy attempts. Julian regarded the tatters of ancient fabric. It was one more relic gone to dust under the boot of these invaders.

"Valdeon fell in one night. Our friend assures us Andara is no less fragile." Lord Gorman stepped closer to the map.

Several iron markers connected with red string decorated the map along the coastline of the mainland. They were each located in thinly populated or wilderness areas. Someone who knew Andara and the

Jalora Legion had chosen tactical locations with little or no patrols. Gorman had help in his planning. It was obvious such research had taken years, and not days. Julian glared at the back of his metal head. He had a new goal now. Revenge.

Then a brilliant light burst into the room. Julian lifted his hand to block the glare until his eyes adjusted. The light swirled in multiple hues finally stopping a few feet before Lord Gorman. Julian, despite his hatred of the man, stood behind his large body and peered carefully into the oval floating before them.

A man's form appeared within the frame. Muscular bulk filled the massive angular throne set within solid rock. Large powerful hands gripped the iron arm rests. Hard dark eyes glared at them from a cruel face. Scowling, his attention finally rested upon Lord Gorman.

"All hail, Uther, Emperor of Akutar," Gorman said with a slight note of annoyance.

"Where is the Lion? You promised to bring the Jalora's plaything to me." Uther's body shifted upon the throne. "You disappoint me again!"

"I've handed you Valdeon in a single night. I should think you'd be pleased to have one more corner of the Jalora's territory," Gorman said evenly.

"A land of little consequence without its Altar of Providence. You grow too bold, Gorman. Do you covet my throne so much you'd risk your father's anger?" Uther reached through the portal, stabbing a finger inches away from Gorman's metal mask. "My arm is still strong, whelp."

Gorman bowed his head in strained respect. "Long may you reign, Father. If this conquest doesn't please you, send me to take a kingdom worthy of the challenge."

Julian moved away to lean against the stone wall, watching father and son. How many times had he exchanged angry words with Leo? It would appear Gorman and he had something in common. They both hated their fathers. Hope brightened in is heart as he observed Gorman's tension and repressed fury. Julian had just been given a golden opportunity to find a way through his impenetrable armor.

"Just like your mother. Pretty words designed to appease me. I never know when she's lying either." Uther leaned back in his throne. "The Sarcion values this land. You can't be trusted to do what's best on its behalf or mine. I've sent someone to represent my interests."

A bulbous head and wisps of white flew through the portal. Whisper, Uther's emissary to Andara, floated gleefully beside Gorman's leg. Julian resisted his urge to fly at the little creature. It had made all the arrangements for Julian's contract with Akutar. Whisper had been the voice of their emperor, promising lies and then abandoning him while he rotted in the dungeon.

"Greetings my emperor and many happy returns, my lord prince," Whisper said.

Gorman kicked the little creature away with disgust. "Speak to me again, foul vermin, and I'll rip you into pieces."

"Enough!" Uther growled, silencing the room. "Win me Andara. And Gorman, bring the Lion whole and in irons to me or don't come back. It is I who must defeat him, not my underling."

The portal closed with a loud pop, leaving them in strained silence. Gorman's men were watching their lord and trying hard to be invisible. They had sense enough to avoid his anger. Whisper didn't share their wisdom. It tittered at the Akutarian Prince's back. Power prickled along Julian's arms as the Sarcion's presence filled the room. Gorman spun around and caught Whisper by its throat.

"Let me go, Prince of Akutar! I will tell your father. He already contemplates letting me have you for sport."

Gorman squeezed a little harder, laughing as the eyes bulged. "There are many dangers on the battlefield, Whisper. I can't ensure your safety. You may end up in the gullet of a Dirge. I'm sure my father will survive your loss."

He threw Whisper toward the wall and it floated through the air, narrowly missing the stone. Hissing, the little creature vanished into the shadows. Good riddance to the foul thing. It shared culpability in the Jackal deception. They'd made a fool of him, shutting down his grand plan to take the throne. Julian was determined they would all shared in his revenge.

"Have the Armada strike at a few of the coastal towns north and east of Valdeon's borders. I want to capitalize upon the rumors and fears this country's fall have induced."

Gorman took one of the iron markers laying upon the table before him and threw it at the map. It stuck to the hilt in the ancient wall. Shuttering with the impact, the marker rested upon the line of Valdeon's northern border.

"Have our ships prepared for the main force of the United Realms and Legion Armadas," he said. "They will try to take back Valdeon and the Jalora's sacred place of power. It will mark the beginning of their end."

"Are you mad? The Legion's armada is undefeated. They have the Jalora's power—" Julian began.

"A diminished power," Gorman said, leaning his hideous metal skull across the space between them. "Their defeat will spark fear among the nations of the United Realms. No one will send men and arms to their aid. They will be much too concerned with invaders at their own doors. The Jalora Legion will fall and Andara will be easily taken."

Shouts and a scream of fury sounded at the door. One of the Jackal backed into the room dragging Zoya behind him. Her long dark hair flew wildly about them as she fought. Small in frame, his half-sister was no less dangerous. Julian grinned with brotherly pride when he saw a long gash across the warrior's cheek. Underestimating Zoya was a death sentence.

Pulling away from her captor, Zoya made her way with a seductive cantor toward Lord Gorman. Julian moved to stop her, but the tip of a sword came to touch his throat. If Zoya noticed her brother, she gave no sign. Ignoring everyone else in the room completely, she focused on the new object of her obsessive interest.

"If you would have me, mighty conqueror, then come yourself. Don't send lap dogs." She ran her hand along Gorman's armored chest.

"Zoya!" Julian barked.

"Your lord calls for you."

"He is a fallen lord. You are of more interest to me, Lord Gorman."

His hand flew out to grip Zoya by the throat. "Do you think I would lust for a filthy mongrel? My bed is reserved for the royalty of Andara."

Gorman threw her to his men. Zoya's keeper, the soldier she'd marked, ruthlessly twisted her arm. She glared at the soldier over her shoulder. Julian recognized the murder in her look. The unlucky Jackal soldier wouldn't survive the night.

"No! I won't be taken. Brother! Save me."

Zoya's betrayal wasn't a surprise. She was a creature of opportunity. He'd known her nature when he'd taken her in. She, however, had miscalculated his true heart. They may have shared a mother, but he wasn't the forgiving sort. Turning his back to the little bird who'd held as much of his love as he was capable of giving, Julian put a restraining hand upon Marcellus' arm. She too had cast him aside for a more powerful toy. Let the fates have her. Zoya was one less millstone around his neck on the path to the throne.

"Sibling tenderness is a stranger to you, isn't it, Julian?" Gorman folded his arms. "You have shown me how fortunate I am to be an only child. See the Prince of Valdeon to his bed chambers. If I have any more need of Andarian wisdom, I'll seek council from a stray pig."

Julian shook the hands away and stormed out of the Great hall with Marcellus close behind. Stray pigs. Gorman would soon learn not to underestimate a prince of Valdeon. He stopped abruptly as a chill of air brushed against his leg.

"What are you doing here, Whisper?" Julian swung his fist at the little imp, but it backed away out of his reach. "You have betrayed me!"

"No, Julian, not I," Whisper insisted. "It's Gorman. He's a mad dog. None of his warriors dare to oppose him and I, well, I am too weak to do anything against him." Whisper floated closer to Julian, wringing its hands. "You see how he treats me! I, an emissary of the emperor himself, is swatted like an insect."

"Your emperor broke our treaty. He wants Valdeon and Andara for himself." Julian leaned his shoulder against the golden doors of the throne room.

"Uther and Gorman have conquered many lands. I am not strong enough to resist their will." Whisper came to hover close to Julian. "Perhaps you and I can work together."

Julian stood away from the door. "Work together? To what end?"

"If you can take the Lion Ring back and sit upon the Altar of Providence, then not even Gorman will be powerful enough to stop you."

The little imp twirled with expectant glee. A plan was beginning to form. Gorman thought he had won Valdeon and had counted Julian out. It would be his greatest mistake.

"You work for me now, Whisper."

"Of course, my lord prince," Whisper said. "Where do we begin?"

"The half-breed boy still has my ring. With your abilities, we can find him."

Julian ran his fingers along the golden surface of the throne room doors. No power in heaven or hell could keep him from the Altar of Providence once he possessed the Lion Ring. Nothing. Certainly, not the half-breed who didn't understand he was dead already.

Chapter Eighteen

The moans of the injured and dying filled their makeshift tent. These vicious monsters from other shores had known where to strike. Jorge ran his fingers along the last of their small supply of ointments and bandages. Any medical supplies from San Lucida's hospital had been destroyed along with the building and its healers. He, trained as a squire, was among a handful left in the city possessing the knowledge to heal the wounded.

Bram stood beside him, making bandages from stray bits of cloth. The retired Framburg Healer had come to San Lucida for the temperate climate and leisurely pace of life. Now the work was harder and more taxing on old bones. Jorge stretched his sore muscles. He understood well the aches of weariness. How long had he been combing for survivors in the rubble? Hours? Days?

"I have more bandages and healing ointments at my villa," Jorge said.

"We can see to the wounded until you return, my lord." Bram nodded his snowy head toward the handful of nurses and midwives who'd answered the call.

Jorge gave him a nod of thanks and pushed out of the tent. It was affixed to the ruins of a grand house along the main row. Several eyes lifted as he stepped out into the open air of a hazy afternoon. Some gazes were full of fear or anger. Others remained blank and in shock. They all parted as Duarto and their hands raced to meet him.

"I've posted men upon the ridge, Father," Duarto told him. "Still no sign of Wolf's fleet."

Jorge nodded slowly, noting many ears were listening to their conversation. "My lord the Wolf is powerful and his fleet captains are skilled. Even they cannot push back the invaders from Valdeon in such a short time. We must be patient. Come. I have to gather medical supplies from home."

"You aren't leaving us, My Lord Pacarro?" A woman ran at him, gripping his arm.

He gently dislodged her trembling fingers. Smoothing at the baby's cheek she held in her other arm, he forced a reassuring smile. More women and children gathered closer to him. Jorge remained in their circle, letting his calm dispel their fears. Cesar was dead. He was their protector now.

"Would you abandon us too? Where is the young Ferret? Why isn't he here protecting his people?" Men, fueled by fear and impotent anger, joined their number.

"You dare question a member of the Sacred Guard?" Duarto pulled his sword with an angry growl.

His son had remained disciplined and patient for Jorge's sake, but even he was beginning to show the strain. Neto and the other hands formed a half circle behind Duarto. They were ready to strike at the men they'd sworn to protect. Jorge rested a hand atop his son's fist.

"My young lord obeyed his orders. I will not have him questioned."

Jorge's voice rose above the angry shouts. A new strength burned behind his words. He held their eyes until the crowd quieted, settling back around their circles of comfort. Many times, he'd seen fear take over a gathering. Mobs were formed when no one stood against the raw emotion.

"I will return shortly with more medical supplies for the wounded. Guards have been placed upon the ridge. No more invaders will enter this city. I promise you."

Jorge walked toward the canyon without another word. Duarto and their hands followed him silently as they passed through the rubble of their homeland. He kept his eyes straight ahead. Seeing the damage in daylight brought more heartache. He needed his courage for the people he protected. Grief must wait until he was in a place of quiet and shadow.

"Do you think Wolf has gone after the Heir, Father?" Duarto came to walk beside him. "Only the Lion can stop Julian and return order to Valdeon."

"Wolf is a wise man. It was he who kept Valdeon from civil war after our king disappeared. He'll know the best way to proceed." Jorge examined the exhausted faces of his men. "Come, let us go home. People may be fleeing to our villa for safety. Your mother will need us."

The walk back to his vineyard was a three-mile hike from the canyon's mouth. It was a trek he'd easily done many a morning. Today, the journey seemed to take a lifetime. He hadn't been this drained and exhausted since the last time he'd gone into battle with his ranger.

His weariness subsided a bit as they climbed the last hill leading to his vineyard. Sunlight struck his tired eyes as he took the top. Lifting a hand to block its rays, he let out an involuntary curse. Floods of people covered his land, smashing the tender vines.

"Where have they come from?" Duarto asked. "How are we to care for them all?"

It was an excellent question for which Jorge had no answer. They left the fields and made their way to the row leading through the gates of his property. Two men stepped out from behind the pillars to block their path. One was dressed in the uniform of a Fort L'Azure guard from Valdeon's central coast. The other was from a town on the western side of the Constantina River.

"State your name and your business, stranger."

"I am Duke Jorge Pacarro and this is my land, soldier." Jorge smoothed at the skin of his torso as the burning power came again. "San Lucida has fallen. Why have you brought these refugees here rather than San Marimosa or one of the other strongholds?"

"We were given orders to find the Regent of Valdeon," one of them said.

He was a man of middle years with thinning hair and cheeks roughened by the sea air. The dark blue of his uniform had been dyed black in places by dirt and blood. Battle hardened eyes took in Jorge and his men, calculating their threat.

"You are from Fort L'Azure," Jorge said. "Is Tulio the Rabbit with you?"

He shook his head, casting troubled eyes to the ground. "I saw My Lord Cristobal fall."

A member of the Sacred Guard dead? By the Erthe Mother, this was devastating news to be sure. The young rabbit hadn't left his teen years. He remembered the curly-haired youth visiting San Lucida with his mother. Tulio had been a quiet boy, completely in awe of Cesar.

"I guided as many refugees as I could up the shores of the Constantina." The guard cast a look over his shoulder at the people waiting for safety. "Not many of us were left."

"We found them a bit later," his companion said. "A handful of rangers had gathered survivors along the Constantina. They were leading us toward San Marimosa, but those Jackal devils found our trail. The rangers formed a defensive line to cover our escape. They ordered us to take the people to the Pacarro land outside of San Lucida."

"Why here?" Jorge asked.

"Our orders were to seek out the Regent of Valdeon. We aren't the only ones who are leading our people to this spot, Duke Pacarro. Word has spread all over the west. The Regent will offer us safety and shelter."

"The western strongholds have fallen then?" Duarto asked, his words barely above a whisper.

"Yes, though we don't know San Marimosa's fate. These Jackal devils were too thick in the region. We kept well away from them by skirting Mendoza land."

The western strongholds had fallen, which meant their neighbors to the east must be under attack as well. Wolf hadn't returned, because he couldn't. They were on their own. The weight of the Regent Medallion burned inside his body. The medallion's magic hadn't hidden there as it sought the next Regent. It had chosen him already.

"Have you seen the Regent, my lord? Is he in the city?"

Jorge let out a slow breath. "I have a feeling he'll be joining us soon. Get the people ready to move into the city. They're too exposed here in the open. The canyon walls of San Lucida are our best defense."

"Yes, my lord. You make good sense considering what has happened to your villa."

Duarto grabbed the man by his shoulders. "What about the villa?"

Jorge had already sprinted forward as fast as his exhausted body could manage. He weaved in between the lost people of Valdeon toward home. The shattered voice of Duarto calling for his mother and Inez joined the throbbing of panic in his ears. Only the moans of the suffering replied.

Then he reached the crumbled remains of the villa he'd built with his own hands. Roof tiles and bits of wall were strewn across the ruined courtyard and beyond. A great explosion had taken out the villa's structure. Nothing was left. His home and stables, even his vineyard had been flattened by cannon fire.

"Mother! Inez!" Duarto called into the mass of debris.

Jorge pulled his son away from the rubble and held his face in his hands. "They are gone, my son."

His battle-trained eyes had seen what Duarto did not. Beyond the rubble, a group of men performed their gruesome duty beside a mass grave. The bodies of Jorge's wife and daughter rolled into the hole as he watched, joining the nameless dead who hadn't survived their trip north. No gravestone would mark their passing.

Cradling Duarto's forehead against his chest, he waited for his son's sobs to subside. Jorge's grief wouldn't come. The burning of the medallion's magic flooded his body, steeling his heart against the tragedies which filled his life. A sea of frightened faces stared at him, waiting. He'd made a promise to be a rock for them until the Lion Heir found his way home to his destiny. Turning away from all he had loved, Jorge moved to the center of the row. He was the last full-blood son of the Pacarro tribe. His heart knew well what it was to walk the Erthe without home and hearth.

"Help gather the people," he said. "We have a long walk to the canyon entrance."

Chapter Nineteen

WOLF CRADLED his arms against his chest as he stumbled over the clumps of wild grass. He had no idea how much time had passed since he'd left the orchard. Gone too were the memories of his escape from the fiery death he so richly deserved. The sun's rays attacked his stinging eyes and dug hot nails into his blistered skin. The great power filling his being was beginning to fade, leaving him weak and shaken.

Dropping down upon the grassy plain, he examined the burns and blisters covering his forearms. The skin on his hands and wrists remained undamaged. Forcing his exhausted mind to focus, he remembered reaching through the fire toward the young Lion. His fingertips had touched Seth's night shirt. Then the fabric dissolved back into the nothingness before Wolf could grab hold.

Lifting his hand to block the sun's glare, he scanned the land about him. The power had brought Wolf to the low foothills of Elena Plateau. Named for a tragic young woman whose lover abandoned her to death upon the rocks, it was the halfway mark between San Rudalfo and Varianne. The tale was one of his wife's favorites. Had Dulcina's own lover not abandoned her to death as well? He rested his forehead in his hands and began to weep once more. They were gone. He had failed his family and his people.

"I should have been here to rally San Rudalfo's armada."

Many of my servants stood against the Sarcion's forces. They fought bravely and died. You would have joined them in death had you been in Valdeon. Your family and friends would still be gone. Do not forget. I have a higher purpose for you.

Yes. He did have a higher purpose now. One person was responsible for the fall of Valdeon. Julian the bastard prince had loosed this enemy upon them. It was he who'd killed the people of San Lucida and San Rudalfo. It was he who'd pay dearly for it.

"I swear a sacred oath upon this land. You will die by my hand, Julian Traitor Prince!" Wolf howled an impotent cry of grief into the vast, empty sky.

"An empty threat from a wounded pig."

A shadow fell across the dirt before him. Holding up his hand to block the sun, Wolf strained to see the intruder. Blood-soaked braids and filthy armor seemed to be the uniform for the invaders from other shores. He'd first fought them in a field on the little isle of Marianna. Now the scavengers had come to feast upon the dying body of his homeland.

"Is this the mighty Lord of San Rudalfo we were warned to take care against? I just see a pathetic coward groveling in the dirt."

The would-be assassin yanked the jagged blade from its sheath and came to stand over him. Wolf reached for his hilt, but the sheath was empty. He'd left his father's sword upon the ground at the feet of his family. His Legion dagger. Wolf's fingers struggled to grasp ahold of the small weapon on his belt.

Bellowing a fierce battle cry, the Jackal warrior swung the jagged blade toward Wolf's head. Raw energy crackled in the air about them as another blade blocked the strike. Brilliant white light surrounded Wolf's defender. The Jalora's power pulsed about him in a fury. He knocked away the deadly blade. Two more swift strikes dropped the Jackal devil in a bloodied heap at the ranger's feet.

"Wolf?"

Fingers gripped his chin and held it firm. Owl, one of the twenty-two Valdeonian who followed the Sacred Guard, knelt before him. Dirt and deep scratches covered his face. His uniform was ripped and crumpled.

"Fuenton has fallen. I hurried to San Rudalfo for aid, but found it too had been destroyed," Owl said, still holding his chin. "Wolf? Can you hear me?"

"All the strongholds have fallen."

"Listen to me. I found your sword and tracked you from San Rudalfo. Your trail wasn't hard to follow." He spat at the filthy armor beside them. "This man was a scout. Enemy soldiers aren't far behind. We must leave this open country and reach the woods of Varianne.

"These wounds look bad." Owl let his finger drop and touched lightly at Wolf's arms. "My squire was killed and I have no healing knowledge. Where is Basilio?"

Wolf shook his head. He didn't remember. Basilio had been with him on the ship. Hadn't he?

"Come. I'll help you to my horse. We have to move." Owl gripped Wolf's upper arm and pulled him to his feet.

The ranger helped Wolf onto the horse's back. Shifting on the saddle, he left space for Owl in front of him. The animal stomped anxiously as its ranger mounted the saddle. Owl smoothed at its neck offering what little comfort he could. He prodded his horse toward the north where the distant tree line of Varianne stood like a fortress wall of green.

The forest may have remained untouched, but Wolf had seen Fausto's ancestral home under attack. It was a strong fortress forged out of the side of a mountain. Long-dead invaders had found it impossible to breach the parapets. Its strength, however, was also its weakness. Once the gates were closed there was no way in and no easy way out.

"We have company." Owl pointed toward the east.

A horse and rider appeared on the horizon at the base of Elena Plateau. Racing toward them at full speed, he swayed unsteadily in the saddle. It was the Griffin, another of the twenty-two Valdeonian rangers. He'd been bloodied. A deep wound in his left torso covered his uniform in dark blood. His right leg was twisted at an awkward angle below the knee.

"Thank the Jalora! I found you alive." Griffin pulled his horse to a stop before them. "The Jackal has spread like locusts along the grasslands. They hunt you, Wolf."

His square face blurred in Wolf's vision. Closing his eyes against the nausea, Wolf focused on the swaying motion of the horses. Hunted. Yes, he was hunted by relentless scavengers. If not for the two rangers with him, he'd be completely at their mercy.

"Wolf's injuries are bad," Owl whispered as they rode. "I don't know how to bring down his fever."

The ground exploded a few wagon-lengths to their left, spraying dirt and grass in great clouds of dust. Their horses reared with panicked screams. The rangers struggled to get them under control as more whistles descended from the sky.

"Cannon fire!" Owl spurred his horse forward with jolting speed.

New stabs of pain shook Wolf's muddled mind out of his haze. He looked to the skies just behind them. A massive airship cut through the Valdeonian afternoon. The steel hull and blood-orange sails filled the sky like the blistering rash along Wolf's arms.

Clouds of smoke puffed along the ship's deck as the crew fired their cannons at will. Wolf and his companions couldn't last much longer under the barrage. Their horses were already showing signs of exhaustion. He hated pushing them farther, but they must reach the cover of the tree line.

Another strike hit the ground, spraying them with dirt and grass. Their hunters' aim was improving. Wolf scanned the horizon. Not a rock or tree between them or the green border of Varianne. Their fate rested on the speed of their horses.

I have given you the power of the Right-Hand. Use it to save yourself and your comrades.

The Jalora's power burned within his body, pushing away the pain and fatigue. Wolf jumped off the back of the horse and twisted his body to land upon his feet.

Pulling his sword free, he centered all his power into the blade. Pointing the tip before him, he sliced at the air between his body and the Jackal ship with a growl of defiance.

Waves of energy rushed toward the ship with the speed of a hungry tidal wave. Smashing against the ship's blood-orange sails, the power ripped through them like a child's paper kite. Groans of collapsing iron and snapping wood echoed down from the deck of the wounded ship. It was crippled.

Wolf called the power back to him and prepared to send it out again. This time he aimed for the steel hull. The sour taste of rage and hatred filled his mouth until he wanted to vomit. He didn't care. Hell, curse them for what they'd done. The Jackal must be crushed beneath his feet down to the last man.

I will not lose you to your own vengeance, Right-Hand. Enough.

The power drained from his body abruptly, taking the last of his strength with it. Wolf collapsed into the dirt again, panting with exertion and the intense pain of his burned skin. Shaking uncontrollably, he gripped at the empty air. It was no use. The Jalora was gone and had taken its avenging power with it.

Chapter Twenty

WOLF DRIFTED in and out of consciousness as the lolling gallop of the horse edged him toward sleep. Low murmurs hummed in his ears. The words were lost in the steady beating of hooves. Time moved in swirls along his senses. The only sensation that seemed real was the burning along his arms.

"Wolf, they come!" A hand slapped his face hard.

Griffin's blurred countenance filled his field of vision. The ranger was on his own mount, bumping against Owl's horse. Wolf tried to push upright, but something was holding him in place. He'd been strapped to the ranger's back with a leather strap.

"What bang tail mischief is this?"

"The Jackal comes!" Griffin slapped him again. "You must escape. Owl and I will lead them away from you."

"No. We stay together. I won't have you killed for my sake."

"We are the last of the Altar Guard," Griffin told him. "It is our greatest honor to protect the Right-Hand."

Altar Guard. It was a title of honor used for the twenty-two Valdeonian rangers when a Jalora Master walked upon the Erthe. They were soul bound to protect the Sacred Guard, so in turn Wolf and the others could protect the Lion.

Electric sensations raced up his spine in a sudden warning. The stench of decay soured sweet pine sap in the trunks about them. Shrouds moved through the trees like a deadly fog. The Dirge had join their braided comrades in the hunt.

Wolf sliced through the leather strap with his dagger and swung down off the horse. His knees buckled as he hit the ground. Forcing his body upright, he stood to face death incarnate. The two Dirge drifted a few feet apart, their fingers clutched at the air with hungry anticipation.

Have a care, Xavier the Wolf. A strong body and mind is needed to control the power of the Right-Hand. I fear you have neither in this moment.

"Kill their handlers," Wolf ordered the rangers. "I will see to these spawns of evil."

Pulling his sword, Wolf took the first stance. Phantom fire burned the skin on his arms once more. Endurance. His father, Bearer of the Wolf Ring before him, had drilled its meaning into his mind with the fevered consistency of a zealot. Those lessons were never more important to him than this moment. Here he stood, burned and exhausted from grief, waiting to strike down the evil responsible for taking his entire world. He couldn't fail. Not here. Not now.

Then the Dirge began to sway in perfect synchronization as death's song filled the forest. Reports from battle survivors claimed the Dirge Song left men frozen with terror. Wolf wasn't moved by their song. He no longer feared death. He welcomed it.

Springing at them with a fierce cry of fury, Wolf's blade struck the first Dirge. His steel cut through the dark fabric with ease. Then he struck bone. Sending power into his own song of death, Wolf pushed the blade harder. The Dirge fell into two pieces, its fingers still grasping in unending hunger.

Teeth bit into his exposed arm and began to rip. Wolf screamed as the blinding pain grasped his body. Burning fury exploded from the depths of his very soul. It burst from his mouth in one terrifying word.

"Die!"

The Dirge released his arm and staggered backward. Its shroud, bones, and what little blood was left in its rotting veins exploded into countless pieces. His power had destroyed these two creatures, but were others hunting the innocent of Valdeon?

Backing away from the gruesome jumble, Wolf bumped against Griffin's horse. Both ranger and animal had taken hits in the fight. Griffin gave him a nod. He was in pain, but there would be no relief for any of them today.

"There'll be more of them," Owl kicked at one of the Jackal bodies. "May they rot in their own juices."

"Yes. It would seem they've sent a great many men to strike at Varianne." Griffin frowned toward the northeast, in the direction of Fausto's home.

Three wounded rangers against a large army and their deadly comrades. It wasn't a risk Wolf was willing to take. He had to reach Temple Cave and meet the others. Fausto and his family were beyond Wolf's aid. Jalora willing, young Raven had remembered his oath and had escaped before the army cut off Varianne entirely.

A bullet struck the dirt by his foot. Twisting his body, Wolf darted behind a nearby tree trunk. Reaching his powers out into the forest, he saw them. Warriors - numbering in the hundreds - were finished with their part in the assault on the halls of the De Quintaro home and had come to join their comrades to hunt for Wolf. They had to move fast before the Jackal surrounded them.

Owl's horse screamed as a bullet pierced its neck. A moment later, Griffin's horse shared its fate with a bullet to the eye. The animal went down, trapping its ranger underneath. Griffin screamed as the heavy bulk landed on his ruined leg. He grasped at the dirt and pine needles, struggling to pull himself free. Wolf shifted his body, preparing to run toward his trapped companion. An arm slammed against his chest.

"Don't." Owl pushed him back behind the safety of the trunk. "The journey ends for Griffin and me. You must go on. Andara's fate rests with the Lords of Valdeon."

Owl darted to his fallen horse and pulled his musket from the saddle. He crawled over to join Griffin. Propping his comrade up with rotting logs and a bed roll, Owl handed him the musket. Taking cover behind the corpse of the animals, he turned his eye to the tree line.

"What are you waiting for? Run, Wolf!" Griffin cried through gritted teeth. "You must survive!"

Reluctantly pushing through the pine boughs, he ran north. The two rangers had given their lives for his.

He'd never forget their courage and sacrifice. Swearing a promise to their memories, he'd survive to earn the absolute faith they'd had in him.

A pine bough scratched against Wolf's blistered forearm. He cried out, angrily twisting away from its sticky needles. The pain in his arms was growing worse. He lifted them up and turned his nose away. The blisters had grown angry as they wept. He gritted his teeth and kept going.

The last time they were together, Wolf had made the young Lords of Valdeon swear they'd meet him at Temple Cave should trouble arise. If any still lived, they would be there. Staggering from pain and exhaustion, he forced his legs to keep moving. The banks of the Constantina couldn't be far now. If he kept to the thick trees, then his passing would be hidden from the Jackal roaming the forest.

Endurance.

"Find the one thing you value most and hold onto it in your very soul," his father had often said. "How much would you endure to keep this treasure near to your heart?"

His most valued treasure, his family, was gone from the world. Others must take their place. The Sacred Guard was under his command. They were all so young. None of them deserved such loss. He'd keep those who'd survived safe long enough to see Valdeon free again.

A twig snapped to his right. He was being followed. Pulling the hood of his cloak over his head, Wolf brought the power to him. The cloak, made from material given to them by the Ancients, allowed its ranger to refract light. It provided the illusion of invisibility. He took a step back into the sharp needles of a clump of pines and waited. He steadied his breath, letting go of the pain of his arms.

Three of the foul-smelling soldiers came out of the trees with weapons drawn, scanning the ground for any signs of foot prints. The thick covering of dead pine needles and dried leaves hid his footprints. A blessing since he hadn't had time to erase his passing from the ground. The men stopped on the trail directly in front of him.

Moving his fingers to the handle of his dagger, Wolf tried to grasp it and failed. The strength in his limbs was failing. He was no longer able to defend himself. Bringing his hand against his chest once more, he waited. Stealth was his best and only defense.

His pursuers exchanged a few unintelligible words and fanned out to cover the forest heading north. Temple Cave was at the northern most point of Valdeon, at the head of the Constantina River. He hadn't wanted to traverse the rough rocks along its banks, but there was no longer a choice.

The sweet smell of water drifted upon the gentle breeze. Wolf pushed through the trees to his left. Desperate with thirst, he stumbled down the sharp bank holding the rushing waters of the Constantina. He fell to his knees and gulped gratefully at the cool water.

Rambling slowly through the center of Valdeon, the Constantina River was the lifeblood of commerce. Merchant and fishermen made their livings upon its waters. Many took for granted its gentle nature. Few could see its origins. Only a member of the Sacred

Guard could approach the cave entrance and pass the seal's magical barrier. All others would only see solid rock before the river took their lives.

Seven rivers ran down from northern Andara to twist and wind through the Forbidden Mountains. They joined in a massive waterfall plunging from a misty mouth. Water flowed seemingly out of midair. Its breathtaking beauty was stunning. The Jalora had sealed the canyon to protect the fabled Temple Cave. It was beneath this mist and flowing water he must go to find the entrance.

He kept to the banks as the river's fury grew. Strong currents pulled at dead trunks and boulders along the edge. He was getting close now. The thunder of water striking rock and river greeted him as he edged along a curve. Tears joined mist upon his cheeks as the mighty waterfall tumbled down to Erthe.

Climbing up the rocks along the ridge, his boots slipped upon the wet surface. He called to his power, but it was too late. His strength was gone. Splashing into the roaring river, Wolf kicked desperately toward the shore. It was pointless. He was too weak to make the rocks. The climb to the sealed entrance may as well have been a thousand miles away.

Then a fist grabbed the back of his collar. The Jackal had found him. He'd failed again. Kicking and flailing his burned arms against the water, he tried in vain to pull away. Finally, the river and his unrelenting pain took him toward darkness.

Chapter Twenty-One

Seth rolled over on the bed. Rubbing away the groggy haze, he blinked irritably at the light striking the mirror in his new chambers. Peace remained a stranger. His fitful dreams about Valdeon had finally ceased in the still hours just before dawn. An uneasy sleep had taken him.

He turned his face toward the brilliant sun bursting through the open patio doors. It must be close to noon day. He'd never lazed about in bed this late in his life. Sitting up, he reached for the stack of letters Aunt Charlotte had given to him. They remained how he'd left them, bound and unread. Grief for the loss of his mother, and perhaps a little fear, had kept them in their satin prison. He'd come to Carlotta for answers, hadn't he? It was senseless to pretend he wasn't curious about his mother's words from the past.

Hesitant fingers tugged at the ribbon. He let it fall to the floor and then opened the first letter. Reading through her familiar handwriting, he devoured the words with voracious curiosity. His mother's loneliness and pain echoed within the ink. She'd kept a brave face for him for many years, but the truth she shared freely with Charlotte.

Finishing the bundle, he set two letters aside and read them several more times. The first one was dated seventeen years earlier.

Charlotte,

I need the counsel of my wisest friend. My little Seth grows stronger each day. He is a precious gift to Andara, but how do I make certain this gift is used for good? How will I ever know the right thing to do? Shall I risk everything and take him to the Jalora Legion? Or keep him hidden in a life of mediocrity for his own safety?

Seth eased off the bed and moved toward the patio doors. He looked out across the waters with growing frustration. Would this be his life? Find one answer and receive a thousand questions along with it? He picked up the second letter, written a few months before her death.

Dearest Charlotte,

What we have feared has finally happened. Pavel has threatened Seth's life. Each day, my boy becomes more like his father. He has Edmund's quick wit and keen mind. I see a power about him too. It has threatened Pavel into action. I managed to sway him this time, but I must take Seth away very soon or Pavel will take his life. He is certain Seth is a threat to Andara, though I cannot see his reasoning. I fear Pavel has gone mad. Can we come to you, my Aunt? I must keep Seth safe and there is no one else I trust. Even Edmund would take our son to his doom.

Seth added the two letters to the bundle with shaking hands. His fingers struggled with the ribbon and finally he put them back on the nightstand. Another dead end. He was out of ideas and had no more clues except the ones he had given his word not to follow.

Dressing in the linen trousers and shirt Tymon had left for him, he opened his chamber door. The corridor was quiet as he stepped out onto the marble floor. Riley's door stood open, drawing the breeze from the ocean. As expected, his room was empty. Tymon had recruited Riley to help with making healing ointments and bandages in anticipation of Valdeon's refugees. His best friend had readily agreed. He wouldn't stop until he matched Tymon bandage per bandage.

Everyone, except Seth, had a job to do. His aunt Charlotte was busy managing the island's preparations for possible refugees as well as unwanted guests. In the few hours of spare time left to her, she'd made it her personal mission to teach Seth and Riley the fine art of polite dining. The rest of Seth's hours were spent in useless wanderings.

Tap. Tap. Tap. Aunt Charlotte was headed in a quick pace toward the center of the hall. Seth crept on quiet feet to the railing for a look. She wasn't alone. The café owner who'd given Seth directions when they'd first arrived followed respectfully behind his queen.

"Nothing?" She stopped to stare into his round face. "Are you absolutely certain, Rodrigo? You couldn't see a single ship along the entire coastline?"

"No, Majesty. The towns along the southwest coast have been reduced to rubble with no signs of life. It is as if every soul in Valdeon has disappeared." Rodrigo made a *poof* gesture with his hands.

"Perhaps they can't reach us and have gone inland," Seth said, walking down the stairs to join them. "I'll lead a search party a few miles into Valdeon's countryside for a look."

"Rodrigo, this is my nephew and the Crown Prince of Carlotta," Aunt Charlotte said, lifting her chin. "He seems to have forgotten the promise he made to his father."

Rodrigo bowed to Seth, but his eyes were busy taking measure. Remaining silent, he straightened and turned his attention back to the Queen of Carlotta.

"Allow me to protect the boats then." Seth slapped a fist upon his thigh, trying to quiet his rising temper. "You refuse to let me search for refugees or aid in planning against attack. I can help build things or…I don't know. You must allow me to do something besides fiddling with dinner forks and linens. Please, let me help."

"No, Seth, I forbid it." Aunt Charlotte tapped her walking stick in sharp emphasis. "You must remain hidden for all our sakes. Swear to me you won't leave this island to go searching for trouble on Valdeon."

"Very well, Aunt. I promise."

Gulping in angry breaths, he turned from them and stomped across the marbled floor toward the front entrance. Several servants scurried away from him, their terrified whispers echoing against the walls. Each word pushed his temper closer to escape.

Seth flew out the front door and onto the tidy grounds. Smothering in his uselessness, he couldn't escape his guilt. Seth was a prisoner in luxury while Wolf and the other rangers faced certain death. He slapped aside one of the delicate arms hanging from an unlucky piece of statuary. No. This was no place to calm his temper. It was too kept and controlled. The jungle outside the gates suited his present mood.

The gates stood closed at the end of the drive, blocking his path to the trees. He gripped the handle and twisted hard. Metal groaned under his touch. Lock and handle fell in pieces upon the ground at his feet. The power was escaping again. It shimmered around his hands in excited pulses of red and white.

Wood creaked as something heavy fell against the guard station door. It was the crumpled keeper of the gates. Wide eyes stared at Seth. He staggered back inside the little building and slammed the door closed. It was the liveliest he'd seen the man since their arrival on Carlotta.

Crossing the road at a run, he pushed through the thick leaves off the main row. He was close to losing control of his temper. The power was best released into the trees along with his frustration. A northwest path should keep him well away from the village. Anxious to be alone, he quickened his pace.

One last push through the thick leaves dropped him into the center of a group of resting fruit pickers. Women and children huddled together against the massive trunks of the Sunfruit trees. He took a tight grip upon his anger and managed a quick nod to them. The women curtseyed and the children clung tighter to their mothers. The look of fear in the children's eyes added fresh fuel to his guilt. Word of his dangerous power had spread to the village it would seem.

"May the day bless you," he blurted in their dialect.

Not waiting for awkward responses, Seth hurried into the jungle on the other side of the orchard. A long walk at a quick pace soon brought him to the white sandy beaches on the other side of the island. Nature was untamed here with fewer humans to bother the habitat. He sat down upon the warm sand and stared out over the waters. Distant lines upon the horizon came into view. Valdeon and its empty shores.

"Who am I? What am I?" Seth growled at the waters separating him from his destiny.

You are my servant.

Seth sprang up and spun around. Grabbing for the hilt of his sword, he realized too late he'd left it behind. His arm fell limp at his side. No one waited on the sand or at the edge of the jungle. He was alone.

"Show yourself!"

Playful laughter filled the beach. Bright green leaves shook violently directly before him. Then a massive cat jumped out of the bushes and onto the sand. Its ethereal green eyes flared with power as it faced Seth. The Spirit of the Lion Ring. He stood still and quiet upon the sand, watching as the beast sniffed the ocean breeze. It had first appeared to him in the tiny kitchen of his father's farm. The Lion had called to him, wanting him to be its new bearer.

"Who are you?" Seth asked, his eyes still searching the bushes. "I know you're not the Lion Spirit."

Indeed, I am not! The beast serves me for I am truth. I am justice. You will not find me in a bush, Seth D'Antoiné, no matter how hard you look.

Something pushed at Seth's back sending him face first into the sand. He rolled to his knees, ready to lunge if the invisible force attacked again. Was he going mad or could this be the same voice guiding him in Marianna and Eastland Isle? He looked down at the Lion Ring, contemplating its depths. The blood in his veins coursed through the ring as well. They were joined, relying on each other for life.

The Lion Ring is just an object. I am what it represents. I am the Jalora and we are one. Your mind and heart are open to me while my direction is available to you. Serve me, for the Will I follow is of the light.

Seth smoothed at the ring fused to his finger. They were connected until death broke them apart.

Chaos has overcome you, Child. It swirls like a vicious wind, casting you at its whim. Obey me and I will guide you through the storm. Serve me and purpose will fill your life just as it did for all your ancestors. Know your father. Know yourself.

Then the great cat roared, shaking Erthe and water. It pounced at Seth, passing into his body. The thick green leaves, palms, and sea disappeared. Thick mist formed about him, clinging to his skin and clothes. Delicate ferns - like those he'd seen in picture books from the northern countries - covered the ground. Somehow, the beast had taken him to another land. Carlotta must be a continent away.

"Where are we?"

This is the Realm of Dreams and Mist. It is a place which exists between dream and reality. Time cannot reach you here.

Then smoke and battle cries took their place as a man stood alone with a farm tool in his hand.

Mikel D'Antoiné. I made the covenant with him over eight hundred years ago. He was the first Lion. Mikel bonded his descendants to uphold our covenant for as long as a D'Antoiné bears the Lion Ring. You, Seth D'Antoiné, are the last of his direct line.

Other men came to stand behind Mikel. Their resemblance to the original sire was striking. Each shared the same features and those fiery amber eyes. The faces of countless women and children pleaded at their feet. Each Lion stood with firm resolve between those who were helpless and the evil reaching for them from the darkness.

Protect the innocent. Punish the guilty. The covenant has been broken. A new one must be forged. You are the bearer. It is your time, Seth.

"What would you have me do?"

Many will not accept your mixed blood, Lion. Though I have caused this miracle to come about, there are those who will not be ready for what your birth will mean. You must become invincible to survive.

"Those men, the Lions who came before me, were mighty warriors. How am I to ever be great like they were?"

The Lions of old began to fade into the mists surrounding him. Their numbers diminished until one face remained. He was a man of middle years. The muscle and sinew had not left his body with age. Amber-flecked eyes bore through Seth as if the memory of the man could see him.

Then he moved. Seth scrambled to his feet as the old Lion came at him in a rush. His rock-hard torso slammed into Seth, sending him flying into the misty air. He landed on his back and immediately rolled to the side before his attacker could bring a foot down upon his head.

"What goes on here?" Seth asked, taking the first stance.

"You've run off without your sword, whelp." His attacker grinned through a thick beard. "I was told you were clever."

"Why are you doing this?"

"I am Ignacio, tenth descendent of Mikel the original Lion. You are to be blessed by my teachings." He feigned a lunge at Seth and laughed when the bait was taken. "Be a little grateful to your distant grandpapa. I was the only one in your long line of ancestors willing to teach you. They too object to your father, Edmund's disgrace."

"My father and mother were legally married! He had no disgrace in which to be ashamed."

"Only you."

Fury burst out of Seth in great waves of power. He lunged at Ignacio and immediately found himself on his back. Blinking up at the dome of mist hanging above them, Seth choked and tried to catch his breath. Ignacio's booming laughter echoed over the mist covered ferns. He circled around Seth slowly as if he hadn't a care in the world.

"Surprised?" Ignacio asked with a playful little whistle. "I was a Lion for twenty years before death took me. Many a warrior I faced. Most with more skill than you."

Seth found his breath at last and got to his feet. "We'll see how skilled I am."

Then a sharp pain sliced along his back. Hot blood soaked through the borrowed linen shirt. He cried out and turned to face his new attacker. It was another Lion. This one wore clothing more suited to Seth's time. His clean-shaven face and neat hair exposed the elegant features of the D'Antoiné family. Hate too was plainly visible upon his countenance.

"Ah, Hugo, there you are," Ignacio said, folding his arms. "What? I said I was the only one willing to teach you. Others have been strongly encouraged."

"Why strike at my back?" Seth gritted his teeth. "Don't you have the courage to face me directly?"

"And what do you think you'll do, half-breed? You can't change the past." Hugo let a cold smile come to his lips. "The past, however, can hurt."

He lunged again, bringing the hilt of his sword down hard upon Seth's head. Crumbling to the ground, his eyes filled with spots of light and dark.

Enough. Save your strikes for when you next spar.

Ignacio and Hugo bowed low, their bodies slowly dissolving into the mists.

"Bring your sword next time, half-breed." Hugo's translucent amber eyes sparked with hate.

"Count on it."

Seth stood up straight, trying to hide how much the strike along his back pained him. They'd see he wasn't Leo's disgrace. Seth had been chosen to be the

Bearer of the Lion Ring. The Jalora thought he had potential. It saw him as more than just a half-breed.

Calm your anger. We have much to discuss. A new covenant must be forged between you and I. Swear to serve me and bind your very soul to the people of Andara. If you make this oath, I will restore my power and protection to the land. Decline, and my power will fade forever from Andara. Evil will take control.

His very soul was to be bound to Andara? Seth wasn't sure what it meant or if he could do it. Then he remembered the horrors in his dreams of Valdeon. How soon would they be visited upon the rest of Andara?

"Very well," he said. "I swear upon my very soul to serve you."

The mist grew thicker until he couldn't see. A bolt of white light pierced the mists and struck the Lion Ring. The crystal upon his finger glowed through the thick wall of gray like a beacon of hope.

It is done. Our covenant has been forged. Soon you will journey to the Obsidian Citadel and seek out the Book of Ancients. Only then can our new covenant begin. Learn well the teachings of your ancestors. Evil will try to stop you from fulfilling this destiny.

"The citadel is a massive fortress. Where do I look for the book?"

The world about him began to spin, disappearing into a patchwork of gray and black. His body faded into the nothingness. Seth's mind was left alone to marvel at the vast emptiness of eternity. Then something flew toward him in the muted stillness of space. It was a book bound in ancient leather. Elaborate symbols of constellations and land masses decorated the surface. Golden clasps locked the great cover closed.

Open the Book of Ancients, Lion. It awaits you behind the Obsidian Gates.

Seth, compelled by the voice's command, struggled to reach the book. Phantom fingers grasped in vain at the thick pages. Wind struck the book, sending it flying into the distant emptiness. He cried out, but the book and its secrets were gone. He was alone once more.

Seek the book beyond the Obsidian Gates. Patience, Lion. You have much to do in the here and now. Come to me in this place at sunrise. You have much to learn and very little time to learn it.

The mist faded away, pulling its fingers from the sand about him. Bright stars twinkled above him in an early morning sky. How long had he been gone? It seemed as if mere minutes had passed. Seth pushed through the thick jungle toward the cottage. He'd have just enough time to take a meal and grab his sword before returning to the beach. His reluctant ancestor might not be so bold when Seth had a weapon in his hand.

Chapter Twenty-Two

THREE CARLOTTA SUNRISES had come and gone as Seth trained. He'd enter the Realm of Dreams and Mist just as the sun's rays fell upon the ocean. Darkness covered the island when he returned to the real world again. Time, however, held no meaning in the Realm. Skills that would have taken him months to learn he mastered in a single excursion into the mists.

Aunt Charlotte made certain a meal was waiting for him in his chambers. She never questioned where he spent his time. Riley, on the other hand, couldn't contain his curiosity. He'd tried to follow once, but the Jalora hid Seth's passing among the trees.

He wouldn't know where to begin explaining his experiences within the realm. The Jalora showed Seth possibilities his human mind hadn't or couldn't consider before putting the Lion Ring upon his finger: bending light with a thought, or changing the nature of simple objects and turning them into something else. The Jalora had called this "science," but to Seth it was remarkable magic.

Sometimes Ignacio would train him one-on-one. Other times, Hugo would join them. Those lessons always ended bloody. Seth had yet to land a strike upon either Lion. His body, in contrast, looked like a leather checkerboard of bruises.

His two heavy-handed teachers hadn't appeared as he'd trained with the Jalora today. Satisfied with Seth's performance, it had parted the mists and taken them back to reality. The afternoon sun unexpectedly found Seth's skin again as he stood upon the solid ground of Carlotta. Grateful for time to heal, he hadn't complained.

He pushed through the bright green leaves and stood staring at the breathtaking blue waters. Breathing deeply, his nose caught the faint smells of flowers and Sunfruit. Interesting though The Realm of Dreams and Mist may be, he preferred the reality of his own world.

Moving to the water's edge, he sat down upon the warm white sand. The Azure Ocean glistened in sparkling diamonds as it struck the beach with a steady rush. His eye looked to the northeast, just making out the distant shores of Valdeon. Though sleep came readily to him after his intense training with the Jalora, the nightmares hadn't stopped entirely. He'd dreamed of those shores again. A red Jackal was marching across Valdeon, eating everything in sight. Nothing could stop it or frighten it away. All the while the beast ate, a large black shadow hovered behind its shoulder. Cruel eyes stared at him from the depths. Those orbs had frightened Seth more than anything in the dream.

Sleep still alludes you.

"I have so many questions, so much uncertainty."

The Jalora wrapped around him, gently soothing the tension in his shoulders and chest. He rested his head upon his knee once more, sighing as the touch eased him.

You are not ready for the answers you seek. They will come to you in their own time. Remember, if you remain a faithful servant to me I will not abandon you even in death. My council and guidance is always available to you no matter the hour.

Seth rubbed his cheek against his knee. "What about the Valdeonian men in my vision?"

The vision I gave to you, The Jalora said, drawing circles in the sand with an invisible digit. *You know who they are.*

"The Lords of Valdeon," Seth said. "And Wolf? What will happen to him?"

I will see to the Wolf. Come. I have a new lesson for you today. Rise and take your sword.

Seth jumped to his feet and drew the sword his father had given him. He waited patiently in the first stance.

Do you feel the wind on your face, smell the sea breeze upon the air? Join with them as I've shown you in the Realm. Use their power and their grace in your own movements.

He swept through the breeze, moving his sword through the streams of air. His movements grew faster and more elegant as he focused on the wind rather than his arm. Sweat began to drip from his hair as he pushed his body onward.

Be gentle with your feet, Lion. A ranger must move in absolute silence. His enemy should not mark his coming.

Seth brushed lightly against the sand, aware of how hard he pressed down with his boot.

Excellent. Soon, this will be second nature to you. Look upon the sand.

Seth stopped and took the first stance. He was several yards from where he had started, sweating hard with the effort. Seth looked down upon the white sand. He had managed to dance through the movements without making any imprint at all.

"How is this possible?"

We did this thing together, Lion. We are one. You are guided by my wisdom and power. I bond with your body, using it to dispense justice. Now go to the docks. Another lesson waits for you there.

Seth picked up his shirt and began to run along the beach. White shore wrapped around the full circumference of the island. It would be his quickest route to the docks. Water and sand flew by beneath him, with no prints left to mark his passing. He allowed himself a satisfied grin.

The Jalora had unlocked something within him. Its mentoring had drawn out new speed and fighting skills he'd never thought possible. The transformation should have been unnerving, but his trust in the Jalora overcame the doubts within his mind.

Seth stopped his run beside a pillar beneath the docks. He took deep breaths, sucking in the salty air. Several Carlotta dock workers were unloading the cargo as young women from the village sold small cakes from baskets. The familiar sights and sounds of life in a harbor town.

Make for the crates on the dock. Hide yourself.

Crouching low, he lifted his torso onto the wood and crept across the dock without being seen. He crouched behind large crates newly deposited by a group of sailors from a recently docked ship.

"I thought the *Bronze Maiden* was the only ship allowed to journey to Carlotta."

The Queen of this island nation is a wise business woman. She has found a way to circumvent commerce rules set down by the United Realms and has made trade agreements with several nations. Yet another reason she has the respect of Andarian heads of state.

"I had no idea."

Come now. Time for your lesson. Look at the sailor in the blue cap. Concentrate upon him. Reach out to the man with your senses and tell me what you see.

Seth focused on his weather worn face. Nothing happened. "I don't understand."

The Jalora came to him, wrapping around his body and entering his skin. They stretched out their joined senses across the distance to the sailor. Images of the man standing in a forest of tall trees crossed Seth's vision. A woman and two small children were beside the sailor.

"He is from Portsmeth and has a family there." Seth gripped at the shirt still wadded in his fist. "How is it I can see inside his mind?"

It is called probing. Try another. Remember, we must do this thing together.

Seth nodded and scanned the group of men. He picked an older sailor this time. Memories from the man's youth immediately came to life. Several images of surf and sail were foremost on his mind. Here was a soul meant for the sea. Sailing upon the air currents, on the other hand, held no pleasure for him. He held many regrets for days long past of a simpler time.

Movement among the crates caught his attention. Three men crouched behind a crate, looking across the docks. Their behavior seemed rather odd. He stretched his mind out, catching one of them. Dead bodies were scattered across a phantom floor. Women screamed within his mind. These men were murderers. They'd escaped from a Hesperian jail and stowed away onboard the first vessel they ran across.

Punish the guilty!

The three killers waited until the dock workers turned their backs to haul another load. Springing out from behind the crates, they ran across the docks toward the village. Seth moved like a ghost toward them. He stepped out into the center of the ramp, blocking their path.

"Hold, killers," Seth shouted, sending the strength of his voice to strike them. "You'll not set foot upon this island."

Desperation. Hate. Anger. They radiated from the men in a hideous mix of hues. Each of them had tasted blood before and wouldn't hesitate to kill again. Hard eyes stared at him from faces lacking any remorse. Anxious hands smoothed at ill-fitting clothes snatched off the bodies of their victims.

"Out of the way, boy. We've smashed bigger and better bugs than you."

Their leader, a large man with the build of a boulder, waved the tip of his stolen sword at Seth. His rough, ugly laugh barreled across the docks. The other two convicts shook with nervous titters. Their darting eyes looked from their leader to the waiting treasures of the island. Seth was the only thing standing between them and the paradise they were eager to plunder.

"Justice waits for you. Murder won't go unpunished." Seth drew his sword. "Protect the Innocent. Punish the Guilty."

"Look at his hand," one of the men cried. "Ranger!"

Their leader leapt away from his men and grabbed one of the islander women walking past. She dropped her basket of goods with a terrified cry. Her fear struck Seth like a tidal wave. The ancient power surged from the Erthe and crashed down upon him from the heavens. Crossing the distance on the wave of power, he thrust his sword through the man's throat. Dead hands slipped down the woman's frozen body. She screamed as he hit the dock.

"Turn away," Seth and the Jalora's joined voices told her.

Then the Death Mask formed its horrible reflective surface upon his face. Seth and the ancient power turned as one toward the two remaining killers. The ugliness of their souls cowered away as he looked upon them. They were vermin, ruled by animal appetites. Any humanity in their shriveled souls and been extinguished by a life of violence and avarice.

"Mercy!" they screamed, clawing at each other to escape him.

Seth moved with the wind as it swept onto the dock. His blade cut through flesh and bone, never wavering until the killers were dead upon the boards. Standing among the gruesome pieces, he took deep breaths until the Death Mask lowered from his face.

He'd waste no remorse on their execution. Death had come too quickly for them.

Sobs shattered the tranquility of the Carlotta afternoon. Women cowered at the edge of the dock, watching him. Clutching at the innocent he'd saved, their horrified tears spilled onto her loose hair. No. They mustn't be afraid. The Lion was their protector. He must make them understand.

"Come, my ladies," Seth said, bringing all the gentleness he could muster into his words. "No harm will come to you now."

Spellbound and tears abandoned, they stood. Fear faded from the colors surrounding their bodies. Rapt attention and awe replaced it as they beheld him. It was as if they believed his word alone would keep them alive. Circling about him, their soft hands gripped his arm.

He led them down the ramp toward a crowd from the village. Men, women, and children stood upon the white sands, curiously regarding him. They were surprisingly composed about the violence. Strange. Perhaps this little isle wasn't the peaceful haven he'd believed it to be.

Red curls bobbed up and down among the crowd. Riley Logan pushed through the linen-covered bodies. Trails of unfinished bandages peeked out of the stained apron hanging about his neck. He must have been with Tymon making ointments again.

"Seth!" Riley cried, gripping his sword in hand as he ran. "I heard you call me. What have you been up to?"

"Called? Do you mean to say you heard my voice?"

The crowd parted as Rodrigo marched toward them. His dark, expressive eyes took in the women upon Seth's arm. Then he took a few steps up the ramp with Riley at his elbow. A long whistle escaped from under Rodrigo's mustache.

"Killers came to our shores," Seth said. "They were looking for a safe place to hide with no law to keep them in line. These innocents got in their way."

"I would say they made a poor choice in destinations, my Prince." Rodrigo beckoned to the women clinging on Seth's arms and shooed them into the crowd. "I will have someone see to the mess."

Seth lifted a bucket from beside a water barrel and dipped it in. He dumped the entire contents over his head, washing the blood from his bare chest and hands. Rodrigo came back down the ramp and beckoned them to follow him into the village. Riley fell into pace close beside Seth. Frown firmly in place, his friend was trying hard not to speak. Seth stretched his mind out to Riley and was surprised to see images of himself as a boy, then as a young man.

"You are worried for me," Seth said at last.

Riley's head snapped up and he gave Seth a long look. "Aye, Seth, I am. Ever since you put the ring on, you've been changing. I heard the crowd talking. You moved through those men like they were straw. Look at you, Seth. You were covered with blood, yet I've never seen you so calm."

"I brought justice to those men. They were criminals who killed several guards breaking out of prison. They would have hurt someone on the island, perhaps even Aunt Charlotte."

Riley stared at him open mouth. "They confessed to you?"

"No."

Rodrigo waved to them. "Will you come to the café? Killing is thirsty work."

They followed him into the village. The children surrounded Seth curiously. One small girl handed Seth a cloth to dry off with. Thanking her, he sat down at one of the tables under the arbor. He gazed into the innocent faces of the children as they gathered around him. The Lion was their protector. This was his destiny - to defend them from evil. He'd never imagined he'd be doing anything so important.

"My name is Seth," he said in Valic.

One boy caught sight of his ring. His little fingertip touched the crystal lightly. The Lion head twirled in the stone belly, following his movements. Laughing with delight, he called to his timid friends. Soon the other children joined him. The Jalora's pleasure pulsed from the ring as the happiness of the little children circled them.

Rodrigo handed Seth and Riley a tankard of sweet ale. "So, Carlotta finally has a Prince, eh? Our good King and Queen brought us prosperity. What will you bring us I wonder?" Rodrigo pointed at the Lion Ring. "Honor and glory, perhaps?"

Seth took a sip and shrugged. "I don't seek either, Sir."

The man nodded his head slowly. "Something tells me you'll soon have both, my young prince. Good. The Queen's name keeps our people safe, perhaps one day yours shall too."

Rodrigo raised his arms to the crowd. "Come, let us have music and drink! Our Prince has come home."

Drums, guitars, and fiddles chased the sleepy afternoon out of the village. Soon the breeze filled with grilling meats and sweet fruit. Merriment filled the square. Seth and Riley sat in the center of it all, enjoying the fun. It seemed an eternity since he'd laughed or relaxed.

"What are we to do now?" Riley asked, tearing off a bite of meat from the stick it had cooked upon.

"We wait here until I'm…given further instructions," Seth said.

"Good. I like it here."

Seth nodded and leaned back against the stone of the café. Carlotta had become his home. It was comfortable here, safe. Stripping the last piece of meat off the stick, he chewed slowly. The threat from Valdeon's shores seemed far away now, but could he keep it away? Could he protect his new people from the horrors he'd seen in his visions? Time would tell.

Chapter Twenty-Three

FINGERS PRESSED LIGHTLY against Wolf's arms just above the elbows. His mind slowly began to emerge from the depths of his watery dreams. The Constantina River and its angry currents were gone. Warmth surrounded his body. Had the Jackal taken him captive? He opened his eyes, reaching his free hand for the dagger at his side.

"You're safe in the Temple Cave, my lord."

The Valdeonian man leaned over him. Upon his collar was the symbol of a bird. Its brass claw clung tightly to the fabric. Raven's squire. Common sense was catching up to him again. Only a member of the Sacred Guard could pass through the first seal of the Temple Cave. His squire could go in and out at his lord's leave.

"I'm grateful you slept through the cleansing of your burns," the squire said. "Your blisters had become infected. These ointments and bandages will help you to recover."

"Raven?" Wolf asked, biting his lip against the stinging sensation.

"He sleeps."

The squire nodded to Wolf's left. Several blazing orange crystals jutted from the cave floor. Forming a perfect circle, their surface gave off heat and light.

Ernesto the Raven lay upon his blankets, arm's length from their pulsing glow. His sword rested upon the ground next to his right arm. Ernesto's body appeared to be free of bandages or cuts.

"He honored his promise to you, my lord. We left the fortress when the first wave of Jackal landed in Varianne. My Lord De Quintaro made us swear not to return, no matter what we saw or heard."

The squire let his words fade against the cave walls. What was left unsaid hung heaviest in the silence. Fausto, his wife and children, and most of their people were gone or scattered amongst the trees.

"The Jalora has aided in our escape," Wolf said. "It was wise of you to bring supplies, Squire."

"I found at least a month's worth of dried food, my lord. It appears someone has camped here within the last several months. They left the ointment I used on your arms as well." He dropped his eyes uncomfortably. "I believe it must have been Dante, the Lion's Squire."

A little alcove rested just outside the warm glow of the crystals. It was stacked with bandages, dried herbs, and other medicines. Tightly wrapped bundles rested on top of the other supplies. The Lion's Squire had indeed been tucking away goods. He'd been hiding with his ranger in the cave all the while Wolf searched for them. Curse them both! Some things never changed. His uncle had disobeyed the wishes of the De Vincente family to become Leo's squire. Now he'd shown as much disrespect to Wolf by remaining hidden without so much as a word.

"Dante did save our lives, my lord. I may not have been able to heal you without his ointments."

"I forbid you to tell Dante," Wolf said with a grunt. "My uncle takes too much pleasure in vexing me."

A sudden flicker of golden light sparked a few feet to the left of the alcove. Wolf's heart thundered in his chest as he looked upon the mighty lion's head suspended in its circle of gold. The second seal. None but the Jalora Master and his Lion's Guard could cross into the sacred space. Hidden for a hundred years, the golden seal was the last piece of proof a Red Heart was among them. Wolf and his young guardsmen were destined to serve their special Lion born once in a hundred years.

Other things had changed in the massive cave. Cold wet stone and brilliant multi-colored crystals had covered the cave walls the last time he'd entered. Dull in comparison, the old cave had been transformed. White marble, reminiscent of the throne room in the Palace of Kings, covered every surface. Ribbons of gold accented seats carved into the walls. Twenty-two seats to be precise. The exact number of the Altar Guard.

"I'm glad to hear your voice," Ernesto said, sitting up. "You've been unconscious for a long time."

"I count myself lucky to be here at all. If not for your squire, I would be at the bottom of the Constantina."

Raven's squire gave him a sad grin and moved toward the supplies. He returned shortly with a bundle of dried meats and fruits. Placing it on the blanket between Wolf and Raven, he busied himself with making a healing pack from Dante's supplies.

"What are we to do now, Wolf?" Ernesto asked, sniffing at the meat.

He dropped it on the blanket and got up to pace about the cave. Impatience. Anxiety. Grief. Anger. They competed for dominance around his young guardsmen's body.

"We wait for the others. When we're all together, we make our way through the Forbidden Mountains to the Obsidian Citadel. Dragon will give us aid."

Ernesto moved to the second seal and rubbed his hand along its surface. "Beyond this seal waits the holy chambers of the next Jalora Master. Never had I imagined I'd be standing in the Guardsmen's Antechamber. We are walking in the halls of legend."

"May we return with the Master in happier times."

Ernesto nodded and began his pacing again. Wolf understood the helpless anger within his young comrade. He shared it, but the years had taught him patience. The past few days had shown him his own mortality. Each step they took in the future must be carefully planned. One mistake would be catastrophic to Andara's future.

Wolf sniffed at the piece of dried meat hanging between his fingers. The gamey smell of plain venison wasn't appetizing. Apparently, Dante hadn't taken the effort to add seasoning before drying the meat. Perhaps he couldn't. He'd followed his ranger, Leo, into hiding. They'd been on the run from Julian and his new allies for many months before Leo had cut the Lion Ring off his own hand to escape.

Oath Breaker.

Leo had called him an oath breaker when he'd come to Wolf's home for aid. They'd argued over Leo's erratic behavior. Neither of them understood what the division in their ranks would mean to Valdeon. No one could have predicted their once great nation would fall.

He bit into the piece of dried flesh, ripping its tough mass with his teeth. The Temple Cave was a place of renewal and refuge. It wasn't, however, the most comfortable spot on Andara. He rubbed a hand across his face with a slow sigh. Comfort was a luxury he may never experience again.

Rock pounded against rock by the entrance of the cave. Ernesto threw another stone at the bottom of the cave's rough natural arch. Leaning against the solid rock blocking the opening to the outside world, he muttered sullenly. His young face was more solemn than usual. It was to be expected. He'd lost his entire way of life in a night.

"The Jalora has taken great care to spare our lives, Ernesto. Let us not repay its mercy by abusing sacred ground," Wolf said, holding out a piece of meat to him. "Come. Eat while we still may."

"How can I eat when we don't know what has happened to the others?" He sunk down on the rock across from Wolf. "It's been three days. Why haven't they come?"

Three days? How long had he been wandering the plains? And how much time had passed while he slept in the cave? He had no idea if day had turned to night. It was impossible to tell within the cave's belly. Three days. Well, the Western lords had farther to journey. Wolf had seen firsthand the deadly chaos they must pass through to reach the headwaters of the Constantina. Three days did seem overlong after the fall of Valdeon. Showing his worry and doubt, however, wouldn't help young Raven's spirits.

"They will come. The Jalora spared us and it will spare them as well."

"Part of me wishes I hadn't left Varianne with the breath still in me."

How many times had he wished the same thing in the past few days? Putting aside his own hypocrisy, Wolf pulled the full power of a Jalora Deacon about him and unleashed it upon his young comrade.

"Would you dishonor yourself, your father, and all those loyal Lords of Valdeon who came before you, boy? Did you not stand upon the shores in the Realm of Dream and Mist with me? Were your ears deafened when the Jalora spoke through its young Lion? We must survive. We must take up our duties."

Ernesto lowered his eyes. "Forgive my lack of faith, Wolf. What would you have me do? Name it and I shall fulfill my duty."

Wolf softened his voice as he let the power withdraw. "Stand the watch with me. We will not abandon our comrades if it takes them a month to come to this place."

Ernesto nodded and bit into his dried meat. Standing up slowly, he took up his post by the entrance. Shaming had worked this time to keep Raven faithful, but what must he do when the days stretched into months? How would he keep the young Lords of Valdeon from succumbing to despair?

You must take care of them, Right-Hand. They must serve the Lion. Only the Sacred Guard can help Seth fulfill his destiny, The Jalora whispered in his mind. *You are their leader, protector, mentor, and father. See them to the safety of the Obsidian Citadel.*

"It will be as you say," Wolf whispered, running dirty fingers through his hair. He would not make the same mistakes Edmund D'Antoiné had made.

Stone scraped against stone as sunlight suddenly pierced the dim within the cave. Ernesto jumped backward away from the arch. He pulled his sword and stood at the ready. Young Yuli the Otter burst inside, skidding to a stop inches before impaling his body on Ernesto's blade.

"And a warm hello to you too!" Yuli grinned, pushing down Raven's blade with his fingertip. "What's happened in here? I don't remember the Temple Cave looking as grand as this."

Wolf came to his feet. Every movement was an excruciating effort. Grabbing Otter by the shoulders, he held him firm. Yuli's uniform was torn and dirtied, but Wolf didn't see any blood. He let out a slow breath of relief.

"The others? Are they all alive?"

Otter nodded, but a glimmer of sorrow came to his eyes. "Tulio is hurt. It's bad. You must come to the *Wind Chaser*. We were followed. Fox is holding them off."

Wolf lifted the last possession he had left in the world, his sword. "We must get to the ship. Be ready for a fight."

He stood within the sunlight in the opening with the two rangers and Raven's squire behind him. Taking a deep breath, Wolf closed his eyes in a final farewell to the land of his fathers. Then he willed his body forward back into the fray. Cannon fire peppered the banks of the Constantina below them. They'd stepped into the center of a battlefield.

Above their heads, the *Wind Chaser* darted between volleys of cannon fire. It was a sparrow in a hurricane. Fox had designed and built the ship for leisure. Quick and agile, the small schooner wasn't designed for battle. It had no weapons to speak of and was kept from being blown out of the sky only by the cleverness of its captain.

Yuli hurried to a large clump of branches and leaves where he'd hidden a small launch. Ernesto helped him pull the vessel out into the open. Jumping inside, they held on tightly to the side of the launch while Yuli pushed the thrusters for a rapid ascent.

The launch was a mere speck upon the breeze in comparison to the massive metal hulls of the Jackal ships. Wolf's hopes of flying unobserved in the little vessel were quickly dashed. Their presence was noticed at once. Cannon fire struck the air on either side of their small vessel, sending the little launch rocking wildly.

"I hope the boastful accounts of your flying prowess are true, Otter," Ernesto shouted above the booms.

Yuli yanked on the rudder, tossing them to the floor of the launch. Wolf fell on his bandaged arms. Crying out in a pained growl, he struggled to his knees.

Another cannon burst scraped the side of the bow. Yuli pitched the launch again and dove under one of the massive hulls.

"Never doubt my flying skills, Grandmamma Raven." He grinned at Ernesto and pushed on toward the *Wind Chaser*.

Wolf leaned forward, watching as Fox darted between two Jackal ships. They'd tried to trap him, but Fox had the advantage of a more streamline vessel. Though the Jackal ships could outmaneuver any Andarian vessel Wolf had knowledge of, they were no match for the sleek *Wind Chaser*.

Otter set their launch in a head-on course with the ship. Devouring the space between them, the *Wind Chaser* showed no signs of slowing. The slender tip of the bowsprit came inches from impaling their launch. Yuli lifted the nose in a sharp ascent, taking the small vessel over the deck. He cut the crystal engines. The launch dropped to a landing with a jarring thud.

"You better not have scratched my ship, Otter!" Rafael the Fox growled from the bridge.

"Nothing you won't make me buff out later." Otter rolled his eyes with a grin.

Berto the Jaguar, Rafael the Fox, Ernesto the Raven, and Yuli the Otter. They were all onboard. Two faces were missing. Lucio the Ferret was safe in the Buells for now. Tulio the Rabbit, however, was not on deck.

Wolf made for the bridge in a rush to join Fox. "Where's Tulio?"

"We found him with his squire in a small boat off the coast of Fort L'Azure." Fox gave Wolf's burned arms a quick look. "The squires took him to my bed chambers. He needs a hospital. You both do."

"I'll see to him shortly. We need to lose these rabid dogs first. Take us over the Temple Canyon."

Fox turned his sweat-streaked face to Wolf once more. Terror etched ugly lines upon his handsome face. Then another cannon ball struck feet from their stern. He leaned hard upon the wheel, turning away from their hunters.

"May I remind you, Wolf, the peaks over the Temple Cave are impossible to traverse. The wind shears alone will shake this ship apart."

The turbulent winds weren't nature's creation. They been gusting by the Jalora's magic for centuries to protect the secrets of the Temple Cave. Wolf gritted his teeth and swallowed his last doubt. The Jalora had commanded them to leave Valdeon. It had saved its Sacred Guard from their Jackal invaders. He had faith it would help them now.

"You must trust me, Fox. It's the only way out." Wolf leaned over the rail overlooking the deck. "Tie yourselves in!"

Eyes glared at him from the deck and riggings. Fear, grief, and grim determination greeted his words. They began to gather rope and moved toward the masts. The Sacred Guard still trusted his word it would seem. Their faith was a blessing in their new world of banishment.

Wolf braced himself as the *Wind Chaser* drew nearer to the mountain peaks. Shaking violently, the vessel groaned under the strain. Intense blue light grabbed the ship in its brilliant power and pulled them along at a faster pace. They'd crossed over the sacred seal.

"I don't think the mountains want us here, Wolf!" Fox cried, struggling with the wheel.

"Let go and step back, Rafael," Wolf said, untying his safety rope.

Fox took his hands away and stood back. The wild angry wind died down as the blue hue released their vessel. Gentle streams of air filled the sails. The Wind Chaser steadied. Fox let his arms drop to his side. He turned his questioning, awestruck eyes to Wolf.

"The Jackal! They've followed," Berto the Jaguar yelled.

Red beasts barked from the snapping sails of the Jackal ships. They were taking a reckless pace over the mountain peaks. Caught in the fury of the guardian winds, their riggings shook violently against their metal masts. This time the light of the seal exploded in a red fury, engulfing the ships in its power. The brilliance was blinding. Wolf turned away covering his eyes with his arm. Metallic groans covered the peaks. Then were suddenly silenced. The ships were gone when he turned back.

"By hoof and tail!" Jaguar came to stand behind him.

"I must see to Tulio." He descended from the bridge and headed below decks.

"Wait, Wolf," Rafael called. "What now? Aren't you going to explain?"

"The Jalora commands us to head for the Obsidian Citadel," Wolf said. "Set a course."

Chapter Twenty-Four

THE *WIND CHASER'S* GALLEY looked like a raider's pub after a fight. Plates and cups covered the floor. Flour, dried fruit, and other supplies had tumbled from their barrels during the ship's frantic escape. Their solemn squires - the ones who'd survived - busied themselves with cleaning up the ruins.

Wolf passed by them without a word. He knew where he was going. Tulio's feverish moans drew him onward along the short hall. An opening to his left contained a much neater space. Bunks for the crew were secured with hooks. Blankets and other essentials had been held in place by a net tied to the walls. Rafael's tastes favored the elaborate, but on his ship, he insisted upon practicality.

He pushed open the door to Fox's chamber and saw the unthinkable. Tulio Cristobal lay on the bed, beaten almost beyond recognition. Moans of pain and fever filled the chamber. Mixed among them were the haunting calls of a son for his dead mother.

Rabbit's squire slumped in a chair at Tulio's bedside. His head was wrapped in a bandage. Dark blood seeped through the cloth just above his right ear. Clutching at the sling holding his left arm, he struggled to stand as Wolf entered.

"Sit down, Squire. How is he?"

Moving to the bedside, he gently lifted the sheets. Tulio's torso was scored with whip marks until his rib bones were exposed to the air. Wolf's eyes riveted on the symbol carved deeply into the skin of his chest. Jagged cuts formed the disgusting shape of an emasculated ram. It was the sign of cowardice.

Tulio's eyes opened and he began to weep. "Don't show the others, Wolf. Promise me. Don't let anyone else see!"

Wolf let the sheet fall and rested his hand gently upon Tulio's forearm. It seemed to be the only spot on his body not bleeding. These Jackal reveled in brutality. If the strongholds had drawn their full attention the night Valdeon fell, he couldn't imagine what unspeakable horrors the rest of his people were enduring now.

"You have my word. No one else will see."

Tulio's eyes fluttered close once more. The fitful sleep returned. Wolf took his hand away slowly. They'd almost lost their youngest. Rabbit hadn't been ready to be left on his own. Another mistake in Wolf's leadership. Cardinal Dragon sent orders a few days before the fall of Valdeon. All Valdeonian rangers, including the Sacred Guard, were to return to their lands. Wolf's suspicions were raised when Dragon's messenger revealed his identity. Esteban the Hawk Prince of Valdeon reappeared to deliver the orders after decades in hiding. Wolf readily disobeyed out of instinct. Staying with Chancellor Benito had been the right thing to do. Why hadn't he kept the Sacred Guard close as well?

"My Lord Cristobal and I fought the Jackal with the other men of the Fort." Rabbit's squire smoothed at his bandaged forehead. "I was knocked unconscious shortly after they came. Night was upon us when next I opened my eyes. The town was ablaze and everyone in it slaughtered."

He turned his face away and began to weep. Grief. Anger. Hatred. They were becoming constant companions to the refugees of Valdeon. Waiting for the squire to compose himself, he gently probed the man's memories. Fire. Smoke. Screams. Confusion. Panic. Those memories would take a life time to fade.

"I searched the city for my young lord, but couldn't find him."

"You feared he'd been taken by the Jackal."

"Yes," he said, guilt hanging heavy in his voice. "I staggered to the beach, unsure what to do next. Then I saw a curly haired man pushing a dinghy out into the waves." The squire's eyes turned distant. "He just disappeared. I was convinced it was my head wound playing tricks on me. The little boat seemed like a good idea, so I swam out to it. Lord Cristobal was inside as you see him."

A curly haired young man in the water? The Lion had saved Tulio somehow just as he'd saved Wolf. Seth would be a mighty lord one day, if they all survived until his naming.

"We go to Lea and the Citadel. Tulio will get the help he needs soon."

"I will stay with him, my lord." The squire nodded and managed a troubled smile.

Berto the Jaguar, his second, waited for him outside the chamber door. "How is he?"

Wolf shook his head. "Tulio needs healing we cannot give him."

Berto frowned, his jaw tightening with teeth-crushing severity. Jaguar was a horse lord from the fabled fortress of San Marimosa. Used to hard work and honest speaking, he hadn't much patience for the politics of court. Blunt by nature, his frustration was painted upon his face. Soon the anger would be unleashed. Wolf wouldn't stop it. He deserved brutal words by men who had the right to speak them.

"The others are waiting in the galley, Sir. Our squires man the vessel."

The Sacred Guard stood as he entered. They surrounded a long table clear of debris by their patient squires. Each of them bore the signs of war. Gone were their pristine uniforms and confident air. Standing before him were four men, beaten and chased from their own lands.

"Tell me of the West." Wolf lifted an overturned chair and sat down at the table. "How did you escape?"

Fox leaned against the table, ignoring the scrapes and clatter of chairs as the other guardsmen found their seats. Rafael was a creature of elegant comfort. He owned the finest art collection and wine cellar in Andara. Famous for his San Angelica lace, he always found subtle ways to add it to his immaculate attire. Hidden behind the lace and class, however, was one of the deadliest warriors on the continent.

"I anchored on the docks of Fort La Val after my father had publicly disowned me, stripped me of my title, and had me thrown out of the city. His bravado should have been a warning." A dangerous spark of fury flashed in Rafael's eyes.

"Otter and his family were kind enough to take me in after my crew abandoned me." He backed away from the table as if the words he spoke were poisoned. "Yuli and I agreed it would be best to warn other Western lords about my father's actions. We were too late. San Marimosa was under attack when we arrived. Juanta and the surrounding towns had already fallen."

"San Marimosa pushed back the armada. They weren't expecting our cannon fire to puncture those metal hulls." Berto pounded a fist on the table for emphasis. "I saw the *Wind Chaser* and remembered my promise to you, Wolf. We sailed to the Temple Cave as soon as we could."

"And Tulio? How did you find him?" Wolf asked.

"We flew to Fort L'Azure to make certain Rabbit wasn't trying to reach us. I was sickened to see it burned to the ground. Bodies were everywhere." Fox turned his keen, penetrating eyes to Wolf. "The Jalora guided us to the small boat floating aimlessly in the waves. If Tulio had not managed to escape in the dinghy, those monsters would have ended him. One might say it was a miracle."

His intense gaze bore into Wolf. It was heavy with expectation and accusation. Forcing his eyes to remain on Rafael's face, he waited for the question.

"Odd. Berto, Yuli, and I all shared the same vision right before we reached Tulio."

"You had the vision too?" Raven leaned across the table anxiously. "The second seal has emerged in the Temple Cave. A Red Heart has come among us."

Expectant silence fell over the galley. One by one, their young faces turned to Wolf. Questions swam in their eyes. Pleadings for reassurance blazed in the colors about their bodies. He was their leader. Troubling though it may be, he owed them the truth.

"Yes. He has been chosen. His name is Seth D'Antoiné. He is Leo's son by Princess Anne Von Wolkhurst of Tslavia." Wolf ignored the cries of surprise and disbelief. "I've met him in the place where his mother had kept him hidden all these long years. The young Lion is being hunted by the same killers who murdered Leo."

He began his account of being summoned by the Lion Spirit of the Ring and taken to the Altar of Providence to see the Orb pulse with the young Lion's heartbeat. He told them everything he could remember, except one secret. His secret. Being called as Right-Hand to the Master was a duty he must bear alone.

The young Lords of Valdeon had been beaten. They'd lost everything. Soon they would be asked to be bound by their very souls to serve this new Jalora Master. Each of them well knew the legends and lived with the possibility their service would be as members of the Lion's Guard. This elite group was the personal bodyguard to the Jalora Master. They were no longer bound by the Legion's code. They took orders only from the Right-Hand. The Lion's Guard was honored and revered, but they were also pitied. Never in the history of Andara had a guardsman's service ended in anything but a horrible death. It came by the hand of the very master they served.

"I don't care who his birth mother is," Berto said. "He was chosen by the Jalora and joined with the Altar of Providence. We must find him. He's our only hope to free Valdeon."

This was met with affirmations and fist-pounding upon the table. Wolf shook his head as their voices grew louder. Impatient youth and its misguided anger would see them throw their lives away.

"San Lucida, Fort L'Azure, Varianne, and…San Rudalfo all destroyed." Wolf thundered over their voice, pausing as they quieted down again. "The Jalora has been weakened. It will grow stronger as the Lion grows stronger. We aren't ready to go back yet." He waited as they fidgeted in their seats. "The Jalora commands we seek asylum in the Obsidian Citadel. It promises we will find protection there."

"How long must we stay away from Valdeon, Wolf?" Otter asked, fiddling nervously with a splinter from the table. "How long before we can return home?"

"We must be patient, Yuli," Wolf told him, gripping the young ranger's shoulder. "Trust the Jalora. It will keep us alive. One day we will return. Justice will be served upon Julian for what he has done."

"But, Tulio." Otter sunk down into his chair. "And my family. I left my house without saying good-bye. What will my father think? I must get word to him."

"I'm sorry, Yuli. Any contact with our families could mean their deaths. We must keep ourselves hidden." Wolf sighed. It would be easier said than done. "We are each other's family now, yes? And don't worry about Tulio. He is under my protection."

Boots pounded down the steps and through the hall toward them. It was Fox's squire. The careful emotionless calm usually frozen upon his face was gone. Excitement and hope had replaced it.

"The Legion Armada approaches!"

They hurried up to the deck in time to see a sky full of white sails capturing the sun. The Jalora Legion's emblem blazed defiantly up their flags. Wolf cheered with the rest. Valdeon hadn't been abandoned to its fate.

"Do we join them?" Fox asked with a grin.

Wolf shook his head. "We have our orders and Tulio needs a proper hospital. Remain on course for the citadel."

Chapter Twenty-Five

SUNSHINE HUNG LAZILY over the beach of Carlotta, languidly drying the ocean's touch on Riley's skin. A short snore from the sand beside him drew his attention away from the cloudless sky. Seth's eyes were drifting shut and his breathing was growing steady. Good. His ranger needed sleep. In truth, a lazy afternoon was a welcome surprise. He'd spent most of his time in the kitchens working on healing ointments with Tymon. Seth, well he'd been off training heaven only knew where. Riley tried to follow once without much success. Tymon had warned him not to follow again, pointing out the Jalora's presence on Carlotta. It wasn't easy curbing his curiosity. Seth woke before the household and came back when they were headed down for the night. His torso was covered with bruises and scratches, as if he'd been fighting for his life.

Today was a new day. After nearly a week of eating on his own, Seth had joined Riley for breakfast. He'd explained the Jalora had instructed him to be ready for an important task. It gave no hints as to the nature of the undertaking. Hours had passed without event. They'd taken Aunt Charlotte's advice to head to the beach and enjoy the rest of the day.

Riley rolled his head lazily back toward the horizon. Aunt Charlotte's cottage faced the southern beaches of Carlotta. Several smaller islands, known as the Azure Isles, stretched across the waters to finally disappear in the horizon. Most of them were uncharted and uninhabited. Rodrigo refused to send any of Carlotta's ships to trade in the south. He feared the raiders who frequented the area. Riley agreed with him there. Raiders had terrorized Marianna for years. They were a cruel lot and not to be trusted.

Quick, efficient footsteps made their way down the stairs to the beach. Crisp white linen glistened under the afternoon sun. Riley grimaced. Tymon, the last person he wanted to see today, led a small procession of household staff toward them. The Tslavian carried two sets of clothing, while the others brought fresh fruit and luncheon.

"I'd hoped to see the last of him for a while." Riley nudged Seth. "All the time we spent making ointments and bandages, he groused about me not trying hard enough. Said I would never make a proper squire. Now look. All our work and not a refugee to be seen."

Luncheon was served in a small parade of dishes. Riley took a bit of each one. Aunt Charlotte certainly wasn't holding back on the beach-side picnic. Tymon gave him his sourest face as he ate. Riley turned his back on the fussy Tslavian and took a long drink of Sunfruit punch. He wasn't about to let Tymon spoil the afternoon.

"Her Majesty encourages you to enjoy the afternoon relaxing on the beach," Tymon said, handing Seth a plate. "She feels it would be best for your health."

Riley touched the piece of Sunfruit to his lips. Tingles danced along his arms, tickling the tiny hairs. Seth was using his powers again. Tymon recognized the touch too. The corners of his eye twitched slightly, cracking his cold reserve.

"Is there a reason her Majesty wants me to stay on the beach this morning, Tymon?" Seth asked quietly.

The Tslavian stood rigid in the sand, struggling to remain calm. Riley had grown to know Tymon a bit better as they worked in close quarters. He hadn't like Seth coming to Carlotta and putting his queen in danger. Anger often simmered beneath his exterior, occasionally coming out in jabs at Riley's fitness as squire to the Lion. This time his demeanor was different. He seemed frightened.

"She has visitors," Seth said at last. "Very well. Riley and I will stay out of the way."

"Very good, Sir," Tymon said, relaxing visibly. "Is there anything else you require?"

"No, thank you."

Riley wiggled his toes until they were hidden under the sand. Aunt Charlotte wasn't one to be anxious. Despite the threat of Valdeon's invaders possibly pounding on her door, she'd organized preparations for refugees with absolute command. Aunt Charlotte had earned Riley's respect and his gratitude. They came to her as strangers. Rather than bounce them off the island and save herself worries of invasion, Aunt Charlotte had taken them in. Maybe she had her own troubles today?

"How did you know Aunt Charlotte had visitors?" Riley asked with a mouthful of food.

Seth swallowed his bite of apple. "The same way I knew those men at the docks were criminals."

"The ring again, eh? Your new little trick will come in handy."

Full dishes emptied quickly under the care of two hungry young men. Riley leaned back in the sand as the servants took their plates away. Closing his eyes, he let his mind drift over the waves. Marianna seemed a world away. He thought about Mum. Riley hadn't had time to tell her he was leaving home. A sliver of guilt wormed its way into his heart. No matter. His brother Tom knew well enough what happened and why Riley had to accompany Seth. She'd fret of course. Mum always said worrying was the biggest part of her day.

Another face ran along his memories. Honey Bea. He'd not had time to say good-bye to her either. She'd understand. He hoped. Beatrice, Seth, and he had grown up together in Haven Bay. She'd developed a bit of a pesky crush on Riley over the past year. Following him into town on the Farm Row. Teasing him relentlessly. He'd kissed her once. Only because he'd had to, of course. The scent of her body and taste of her lips were uncomfortably pleasant memories.

"Why don't you write her?" Seth asked.

"I wouldn't know what to say." Riley sat up and glared at him. "Doing your magic on me is rude."

Seth chuckled and slapped at his arm. "Come on. I think we've had enough leisure for today. Let's wash the sea and sand off."

Slipping his sandals on, Riley followed Seth across the sand and onto the steps. They took a quiet pace. It wouldn't do to disturb Aunt Charlotte and her guests.

They needn't have worried. The patio was empty when they reached the top. Odd Aunt Charlotte wouldn't entertain her guests outside on such a fine day. She adored the patio.

"Do you think Aunt Charlotte's visitors have gone?" Riley asked, stretching with a yawn.

"You can't want another nap? We've lazed about all afternoon."

Riley shrugged and stepped under the freshwater spray at the edge of the patio. It was a contraption Seth had thrown together during one of the dull days before he'd started disappearing to train. He ran fingers through his copper curls to get the sand out. Handy invention.

"Considering the troubles waiting for us on the mainland, I'd say we should get rest while we can," Riley said, pulling on the clothes Tymon had left for them.

Seth quietly pulled open the patio door. Their bare feet tiptoed over the cool tile toward the main staircase. Riley reached the first stair and turned to give Seth a grin of triumph. His friend hadn't followed. Seth stood in the center of the tiles. His body was rigid as he stared at the parlor door. Then Riley heard it too. The subtle, but distinct sound of fear. Aunt Charlotte, the Iron Queen, was afraid.

"Where are you going?" Riley hissed as he moved toward the closed door. "Aunt Charlotte doesn't want to be disturbed."

Seth crept to the door with a speed only gifted to rangers. Putting his sandals on the step, Riley begrudgingly joined him. Seth had made up his mind.

Heaven itself couldn't change it again. He held up a warning finger when Riley shoved his shoulder.

The door was opened a crack. Riley could make out Aunt Charlotte seated in her favorite chair by the window. Tymon was standing just behind her. They both looked upset. Aunt Charlotte wasn't one for panic, but today she looked on the verge of it.

"You've always been most generous with your goods and your kindness, Majesty," a man said from the other side of the room. "Our long friendship is precious to me. I've come to warn you and to plead for your aid."

His accent was unmistakably Valdeonian. He spoke with fancy words like Leo used. The man must be gentry if he knew Aunt Charlotte. Whoever he was, the Valdeonian had brought trouble with him. Riley held his breath, waiting for him to go on.

"Have all the cities fallen? San Rudalfo as well?" Aunt Charlotte asked. Her fingers squeezed the delicate handkerchief in her hand.

"Yes, Majesty. Valdeon has fallen to the Jackal. Our king is dead and the Lion Ring lost. We have no hope left."

Seth's body straightened beside him. He lifted the Lion Ring and stared deeply into the crystal. Riley fancied he saw tiny pulses of light within its depths. Blinking a few times, Riley shook his head. He'd seen Seth do amazing thing since putting the ring upon his finger. Its ability to glow shouldn't be a surprise.

"It will be as you say." Seth took a deep breath and stretched his hand out to open the door.

"Great gulls," Riley hissed low, grabbing his arm again. "We don't know who they are, Seth."

"I must give hope to the hopeless, Squire. This man was once my servant and has remained loyal to me. I can put his mind at ease about the Lion Ring at least."

Riley let go of his arm and stepped back. Seth's voice sounded strange, as if there was someone else speaking through him. Whoever it may be, they knew Aunt Charlotte's visitor. Riley rubbed the back of his neck irritably as Seth pushed open the door. He'd no choice but to go with him and make sure the stranger inside wasn't another hunter in disguise.

They were positioned on the settee across from Aunt Charlotte. A Valdeonian man of middle years sat with his back to the door. He stretched his arm across the settee to reach for his wife's hand. Both parents held their two daughters close, helpless to stop their tears of loss and fear. Riley rubbed the back of his neck. He'd spent days preparing ointments and bandages for Valdeonian refugees. No ointment could heal the heart from such a wound.

A young man, close to Riley's age, stood in the corner of the room with his shoulder leaning against the wall. His finger moved sullenly up and down one of Aunt Charlotte's picture frames. It didn't take Seth's ranger powers to see the young man's frustrated anger.

Then their father suddenly stiffened on the cushions. He turned slowly toward the door. Wonder mixed with confusion on his face. The Valdeonian pushed away from the settee, struggling to stand on a crippled leg.

"Edmund?"

Seth lifted his left hand and held it out toward him. The Lion Ring suddenly came to life, glistening brighter than a thousand lanterns under a Marianna sky. Excited cries pierced the dazzling light. Seth's ring certainly had a way of stirring people up.

The Lion Ring's magic disappeared into the crystal, leaving Riley disoriented. Aunt Charlotte was out of her chair, marching toward them. The Valdeonian woman pressed her body against the far wall, clutching at her children. Father and angry son, however, stood dangerously close to Seth.

"No, Nephew." Aunt Charlotte hurried to take Seth's arm. "Leave us!"

"You know this ring, Sir?" Seth asked the Valdeonian. "And my father, Edmund?"

"Of course, Lion. I am Fausto De Quintaro. I was the Raven before my son bore the ring." He touched the ring's crystal surface with reverent fingertips. "Where are the others, Lion? They should be here with you."

Others? What in the green, green fields was the man talking about? Unless he meant Wolf, the ranger who'd saved them in Haven Bay. Shivers ran along Riley's spine as he recalled Seth's account of his dream their first night on Carlotta. He'd said seven men stood upon the shores of Valdeon. Perhaps they were real then and not nightmare ghosties from Seth's imagination?

"They've abandoned us too, Father! When will you accept the truth? Ernesto ran away like the coward he is at the first sign of attack. The Lords of Valdeon have fallen." The young man thrusted a finger at Seth. "And the Lion. Why should this half-breed be any different than his kin? The D'Antoiné family has abandoned its sacred duty."

"Here now," Riley said, stepping closer. "You shut your foul mouth or I'll shut it for you."

"Can't your lord speak for himself, woolie farmer?"

The young man came at Seth fist first. Riley jumped between them, ready to throw his own punch at the Valdeonian's hateful mouth. Then a ribbon of color smacked across the young man's shoulders. Fabric spun in the flurry of arms and legs. Time slowed to its normal pace. Riley was swinging at empty air. The young man was sprawled on the ground with his father standing over him.

"You dare attack the Lion, Arturo? If the Sacred Guard were present, you'd be a dead man right now and rightly so."

Arturo wiped at the blood on his lip. "Forever the Raven, eh, Father? Even above your own blood."

"Stop this!" Lady De Quintaro cried. "I've lost my home, most of my kin, and my country. Losing one of you at the other's hand would see me to my grave."

Seth rested a hand on Riley's shoulder. "Stand down, Squire."

He eased past Riley, briefly meeting his gaze. Seth wasn't angry or frightened. His eyes held the same sorrow he'd had when they found Tom Gunn and the other Marianna Militiamen dead. Riley slapped his fists on his legs. Though Seth had never said a word, Riley suspected he blamed himself for their deaths. Here he was again about to do the same for people he'd never met.

"Tell me, Lion." Arturo came to his feet, shaking with rage. "Where were you when my home was being destroyed? Where were you when your people were dying?"

"Don't you listen to him, Seth." Riley came to stand between them again. "You aren't responsible for any of this."

"You're wrong. I'm the Lion Protector. It is for me to make things right."

"You can never make this right." Arturo's voice broke and he burst into impotent sobs.

Seth rested a hand on his shoulder when the young man sunk to his knees. Then something strange happened. A presence filled the room, touching Riley and everyone else around him. It was warm and loving, recalling the times his mother had held him as a child. She'd wrapped him in his favorite blanket. Was this the Jalora then? He'd seen its wrath, but hadn't considered it could also be kind. As he looked upon Seth's peaceful face, he knew. No other family on Marianna was kindlier than Anne McCloud and her son. Could it be Seth's heart they were feeling now? Perhaps this Jalora magnified its ranger's nature? Whatever the presence, the Jalora or Seth's nature, it was having a soothing effect on Arturo. He grabbed the Lion Ring and pressed it to his lips.

"By the Jalora's grace, we have met this day," Lord De Quintaro said. "We must see you to Valdeon—"

"No! He'll be killed before he takes two steps. I won't allow it." Charlotte pushed away from Tymon's protective arm. "Seth is the Crown Prince of Carlotta. My blood. Not yours. Mark me, My Lord De Quintaro. If you try to take Seth back to Valdeon, I will withdraw my aid to your family. No more aid will be offered to Valdeon and no more protection for its refugees."

"He'll be no safer here, Majesty. The boy is still a selected and cannot defend himself. He needs to be with the others and to take his place."

A steel edge came to the Valdeonian man's voice. His eyes swam with a kind of fever Riley last saw in Pavel Sandor. Aunt Charlotte must have noticed it too, because she came to take Seth's arm.

"Seth doesn't know who he is! He doesn't understand what you ask of him."

Lord De Quintaro regarded Seth curiously. "Edmund would have told him, prepared him."

"Edmund is dead. Seth's mother hid their son away from Andara to protect him. He knows nothing of the Legion or Valdeon. Without the others, he must remain hidden. Make no mistake, I will protect my nephew no matter the costs."

"The others? Do you mean Wolf?" Seth asked, stopping their conversation. "We can trust Wolf, Aunt Charlotte. He's saved my life before and helped us to escape Marianna the night my father was murdered."

"Where is Wolf now?" Lord De Quintaro asked anxiously.

He wasn't sure who Wolf was to these Valdeonians, but the mention of his name started them buzzing again. Riley hadn't seen the ranger's face clearly, but he remembered the power coming off his body. Wolf was deadly, but Seth seemed to have absolute trust in the man.

"We commanded him and the others to go into hiding. I don't know where he is now."

We? Seth was talking about the Jalora as if it were a person. Riley looked around the room, waiting for the awkward questions to come. Nothing. Everyone behaved as if Seth's talk was normal.

"I must think on these things." The Valdeonian lord rubbed hard at his face and paced around the room.

"Won't you stay the night in safety, Sir? Your family is exhausted." Seth put an arm around Aunt Charlotte's shoulder. "Please, Aunt. Lord De Quintaro is a friend and needs our help."

"Very well," Aunt Charlotte said. "They may stay, but I want no more discussion of Valdeon."

"Thank you for your kind offer of hospitality," Lord De Quintaro said. "Our ship may have been followed. It's better if we press on toward our destination. Will you escort us to our ship?"

"Of course." Seth bowed.

"Come, my little ones." Their father held out a hand toward his daughters. "We must go. Thank her Majesty."

Riley followed Aunt Charlotte and Seth as they escorted their guests to the front drive. Lord De Quintaro helped his family board the carriage with a strength not typically seen in a man his age. He'd been a ranger once, but could he still do all the things Seth could do? He'd taken down his son easily enough in the parlor. They'd have a hard time stopping the Valdeonian if he tried to kidnap Seth.

"Fausto De Quintaro is an honorable man, but he is not above his tricks," Aunt Charlotte told them, echoing Riley's thoughts.

Seth hugged her. "I love you, my brave lady. Riley and I will be back soon."

"Your sword, sir." Tymon marched up to them, eyes burning at Riley. "A ranger should never be without his sword."

Seth nodded his thanks and strapped on the sword belt. Tymon's firm hand grabbed Riley and pulled him aside. He released Riley with a shove, sending him into the shrubbery. Tymon thrust his face inches away from Riley's nose.

"Now do you see the dangers, Squire? Your ranger has more betrayal and danger to fear than most. As his squire, you must be ever vigilant. Remember my words and perhaps you'll both live until his naming."

Tymon pushed Riley away and joined Aunt Charlotte on the porch. He guided her back inside the cottage. Casting another ugly look over his shoulder at Riley, Tymon slammed the door shut.

"Aunt Charlotte has a point," Riley grumbled, joining his ranger upon the steps. "That Lord whoever he is looked like he would drag you to Valdeon. Did you understand what he was talking about?"

"No, but he has sent his family ahead in the carriage. Maybe he has more to tell us?"

"Aye," Riley said, hurrying to keep pace with Seth. "Let's hope a talk is all he wants."

Chapter Twenty-Six

LORD DE QUINTARO waited for them at the gate of the cottage. His son stood quietly beside him, looking at Seth in awe. Riley was unnerved by the change in the young man's attitude. They made their way down the road toward the village in silence. Keeping to a slow pace for the sake of Lord De Quintaro's crippled leg, they followed the thick, leaf-lined path. A frown spread across the older man's face, then changed into a smile and back to a frown.

"You plan to return to Valdeon," Seth said suddenly.

"You've learned to probe as a selected? It is rare, Lion."

Probing. Well, at least Riley had a name for Seth's mind reading trick now. They continued to walk in silence. He was glad of the quiet pace. It gave him a better chance to take measure of the Valdeonian under the canopy of leaves. Crippled though his leg may be, Fausto De Quintaro walked without a stick as if defying the injury. Straight hair hung neatly behind his ears. Hi smooth-shaven face held an expression more suited to laughter than pensive thought. Then there were his keen dark eyes and the way they sparkled when he looked at Seth. He was one to watch.

"Your Aunt is a wise woman, Highness," Lord De Quintaro said at last. "Valdeon is a dangerous place, especially for the bearer of the Lion Ring. It would be wise for you to continue to hide yourself here for the time being until other arrangements can be made."

Seth exchanged a look with Riley. "Other arrangements?"

"You must understand, Highness. The Lion Ring is much more than a trinket. It is our covenant with the Jalora and a desperately needed symbol for the people to rally behind. It is my duty to see you trained properly, even if it means I must train you myself. I and others loyal to you will find a place of safety to conduct this training. Then we will gather our forces and march on San Leonora to take back Valdeon."

"Do the others you speak of include Esteban the Hawk?" Seth asked.

Lord De Quintaro stopped on the path. His lips twisted with a distaste akin to someone drinking sour milk. Arturo spit with a curse upon the path, narrowly missing Riley's sandaled foot. Riley pulled his foot away with a hiss. He didn't understand. Hawk was Seth's kin. He was also a ranger. Didn't it mean he could be trusted?

"The Hawk has come out of hiding to prey upon Edmund's son. Mark me, Highness. Beware Esteban D'Antoiné. He was no friend to his brother and will be no friend to you either."

"I don't understand all this," Riley said as they started down the path again. "Hawk is a ranger. Aren't he and Seth on the same side?"

"Once perhaps, Squire, but no more." Lord De Quintaro shook his head. "Esteban will forever be a shame upon the D'Antoiné family line."

Their group walked in thoughtful silence. The gentle sea breeze brushed through the leaves to caress his skin. Its comforting touch was lost upon Riley. Danger had found them again. Tymon was right. He'd been a fool to ignore it.

Riley moved closer to Seth's shoulder as they approached the Valdeonian ship moored upon the docks. This Lord De Quintaro fellow hated Seth's uncle from the sounds of things, but he liked Wolf. So, who were they supposed to trust among all these people pretending to have Seth's best interests at heart?

"I think your squire is afraid I will pull you onboard ship, Highness." Lord De Quintaro chuckled. "I must tell you I had thought of it."

"I knew it," Riley grumbled, reaching for his absent sword.

"You changed your mind. Why?" Seth asked.

"Who says I have?"

Lord De Qunitaro burst into laughter when Riley moved between them.

Let him laugh. Seth wasn't going anywhere with the man. His ranger had a promise to keep to Leo. He was meant to stay away from Valdeon.

"Traitors hide aboard your ship." Seth raced up the gangplank, leaving the three of them to stare after his back.

"Great gulls, Seth! Wait!"

Riley chased after him with the De Qunitaros following close. They reached the deck of the vessel and skidded to a stop. Seth stood in the middle of the deck surrounded by Valdeonian sailors. Many were bandaged from recent fighting. These men had lost their home and their hope. How many would blame Seth and come after him as Arturo had done? Honestly, what had his ranger been thinking?

Then a presence, fierce and hungry, descended upon the deck and came to surround Seth. The Jalora. He was beginning to recognize its feel all too well. Beside him, Lord De Quintaro took a sharp intake of breath. It told Riley what he'd suspected from the moment Seth put the Lion Ring upon his finger. He was different than the other rangers, special in a way neither of them understood. Riley yanked one of the belaying pins from its slot and gripped it with shaking hands. Special or no, he needed someone to watch his back.

"Traitors are aboard this vessel! They plot to deliver the De Quintaro family to their enemies," Seth and his new body mate said. "Know this! The De Quintaros are under my protection. Face me now."

One of the sailors stepped out of the crowd. "Who are you, stranger, to come aboard this ship barking orders?"

"The eyes do not lie. D'Antoiné!" Another sailor smacked at his friend's arm.

They pulled their swords and rushed at Seth with a vicious battle cry. Five other sailors joined his charge. Riley ran across the deck, lifting the belay pin to block a strike at Seth's back. Knocking away the man's body as he stumbled forward, Riley brought the pin down hard upon his skull. Twisting his body around to block another strike, he saw the blurred movements of Seth's body. Those mysterious hours of training hadn't been wasted. His ranger was unimaginably fast.

The death mask engulfed Seth's face, erasing his features and replacing them with a solid silver surface. Riley had gazed into Seth's horrible mask by accident on Marianna. It'd shown him the moment of his death - not a memory he enjoyed reliving. This time the mask remained blank when he stared into it. Their attackers were not as fortunate. They screamed and turned away in terror. The mask had slowed their charge, but hatred drove them on despite their revulsion. Seth met them, sweeping through their numbers.

"The Lion Protector has come. We will allow no acts of violence against our subjects."

Seth and the Jalora threw their joined head back, releasing a terrible roar. Its fury and power shook the ship and the dock. Screams filled the deck. Riley fell to his knees, holding his hands over his ears. Great gulls! The beast was coming for them. He was desperate to escape its horrible jaws.

Releasing the power, Seth lifted his face to the sun. Gentle sea air brushed against his cheeks as the death mask retreated. Riley looked at the warrior standing among the bodies upon deck. The boy he'd grown up with was gone. One day this powerful Lion would be a mighty leader of men. Sheathing his sword, Seth turned to the men who'd fought with him. Fausto De Quintaro, his son, and the remaining crew stood with Riley. They all had their eyes locked upon the Lion. No one dared break the spell of the moment.

"Drop your sword, Lion!"

A man dressed in an officer's uniform stood beside one of the launches. One hand struggled with the knots holding the launch in place. His other bloodied arm was wrapped around the neck of the eldest De Quintaro girl.

"Sara!" her brother cried, moving toward her.

"Don't, Arturo." He pressed the point of his dagger to her throat, halting the young man in his steps.

Riley lowered his weapon with the rest. The villain was going to kill an innocent girl in his hatred for Seth. What kind of a mad world had found them?

"What have you done with my wife and Isabella?" Lord De Quintaro lifted his hands to placate the man.

"Your lady wife will forever be a hellion, Fausto." He lifted his wounded arm a few inches. "Never fear. They live."

Seth took a few steps toward him. "You've been loyal to the De Quintaros for many years. Why betray them now?"

"Your brother's new friends are very generous, Lion. They paid me a kingly treasure for the secret entrances into Varianne." He twisted the dagger's tip deeper into Sara's skin until tiny trickles of blood fell onto her collar. "Imagine what they would pay for news of you!"

"I will give no mercy to a betrayer of children. Close your eyes, Sara, and sleep." Seth and the Jalora told her.

The dark eyes squeezed shut and her limp body fell through her captor's arms to lie upon the deck. It was all the opening Seth needed. One moment he was standing just a few feet in front of Riley, the next he had his sword slicing the villain from head to toe. In all his years upon the Erthe, Riley had never seen anyone move so fast, not even Leo.

The crew sunk to their knees and began murmuring rapid words in Valic. Riley didn't understand a word, but he could guess what they were saying. Seth leaned over and snatched up a piece of brightly colored fabric floating slowly along the deck in the sea breeze.

"Why are they on their knees?" Seth asked in Islic as he wiped his sword clean on the discarded piece of cloth.

Riley stepped through the men and came to join him. "The sooner this ship leaves, the better I'll feel."

He remembered the girl and knelt beside her. Sara didn't open her eyes when Riley touched her shoulder. He put a finger on her neck. The pulse of a healthy young heart beat in a steady rhythm.

"What did you do to her, Seth?"

"The Jalora needed her to sleep."

Riley put the back of his hand under her nose. She was indeed asleep and probably wouldn't wake until Seth told her to. He cast a glance back at the bodies.

"Well, it won't do the girl any good to wake up in blood," Riley said.

Seth picked her up carefully and took the girl to the stairs of the bridge. He placed Sara on the lowest step and leaned her against the railing. The De Quintaros hurried to join them. Seth and Riley stepped aside for her anxious family.

"Take Sara below. See to your mother and sisters," Lord De Quintaro told his son.

"We'll drop the pieces off in deep water." The captain kicked at the dead body. "He was my first mate for five years. This treachery explains how the Jackal knew our location when we tried escaping over the eastern border. It was our good fortune our side trip to Carlotta was unplanned."

"Did he know your destination?" Seth asked.

"Yes." The captain rubbed at his stubbly chin. "We'll take a different route to another island. Make ready to sail!"

"We've just had our invitation to leave, Seth," Riley told him.

Fausto De Quintaro took Seth's arm and pulled him to the railing. Riley followed. He wasn't about to let his ranger be alone with anyone aboard this ship.

"Listen to me, Lion. Be wary of who you trust. I didn't understand before I saw you fight and heard…you must hide yourself. Protect the gift you were given. We must sail quickly to lead any traitors away from Carlotta and you. Soon I'll return. I must protect you in my son's place." Lord De Quintaro gave Seth a sad smile. "Your father was my dear friend. I hope you believe me to be your friend as well. Stay safe, Lion."

"And you, Sir."

Seth insisted they stay upon the docks until the De Quintaro's airship disappeared in the burning orange horizon. They walked silently through the sleepy village and back toward Aunt Charlotte's estate.

"We'll have to leave, won't we?" Riley asked.

"Yes." Seth lifted his eyes to the twinkling stars beginning to appear in the twilight. "I'm going to miss this place."

Riley would miss it too. Carlotta had become a kind of fortress for him where nothing evil could enter. The outside world with all its problems didn't exist. Well, until today. He supposed it was best they were leaving. The thought of anymore violence on the little isle would ruin the last bit of hope he had for a peaceful life. Let it stay exactly as it was.

Aunt Charlotte was waiting for them at the front door when they returned to the cottage. Not waiting for pleasantries, she marched down the tiles toward the parlor. The tip of her walking stick tapped madly with each angry step she took.

"They are safely off." Seth kissed Aunt Charlotte's cheek when she sat down in her chair.

"Yes, so I've heard. You call far too much attention to yourself, Nephew. I'm pleased you saved the De Quintaro family, but everyone on the island must have heard the Lion's Roar. Again. Have you forgotten Valdeon's shores just across the water?"

She was right. They were supposed to be in hiding. It wouldn't be a good idea to keep announcing Seth's presence this close to Valdeon. Riley moved underneath the portrait of Charlotte's family. Casting a few anxious looks at Seth, he began tugging at a wayward string hanging from his trousers. Aunt Charlotte wasn't going to like hearing Seth's plan.

"I must leave Carlotta, Aunt," Seth said quietly. "My enemies have found me. It's no longer safe for you or the people here if I stay."

"Yes, I know." Aunt Charlotte smoothed a linen across her cheek. "It's time for you to enter your father's world. I don't mean breaking your promise about Valdeon. I think it might be time for you to enter the military."

Aunt Charlotte lifted Seth's left hand in her own, showing them the Lion's Ring. Riley came to stand behind her chair, looking over her shoulder. Bursting out of the ring's milky white belly, the Lion's head shook its main of black. Impossible. A few hours before, they'd stood in this very parlor showing the De Quintaro's the Lion Ring and its clear stone. How in the green, green fields had it changed colors?

"Let the spirit of the ring guide you. It grows impatient too." She lifted a hand to Tymon as he entered the room. "We will provide you with money."

Aunt Charlotte waved aside their protests. "It is the duty of every family to support their cadet. Once you're a soldier, your country supports you." She touched Riley's hand resting on the back of her chair. "Mr. Logan, kneel before me. The squire to our Crown Prince must have a title. I'll make you Carlotta's first Earl. Yes, they should accept your qualifications now."

Earl? Great gulls. He'd no idea what she meant, but he did as he was told. Aunt Charlotte understood the new world they were entering. If a man's name and station were what saw him through life on Andara rather than his honesty and hard work, then so be it. He'd certainly not throw his station around like pompous old blowhard, Elder Newcastle back in Haven Bay.

"Do you swear to serve your Liege Lord and your Queen faithfully as Earl of Carlotta?"

"I do, Majesty."

"Rise, Earl Riley Logan of Carlotta."

Their Queen put a hand to her chest and sighed as if her heart were lead. "This day has been too tiring for an old woman. I am for my bed. Tymon can make arrangements for your departure."

They bid her good night and soon made for their own beds. Riley stopped on the stairs and looked up at the stars shining through the glass dome above them. It was a melancholy feeling.

"What is it?" Seth asked.

"I was just thinking this may be the last time we sleep in safety. Who knows what waits for us on the other side of the ocean?"

"Come on, Earl Logan. Let's enjoy this night's sleep."

Chapter Twenty-Seven

NIGHT OVERTOOK DAY as they flew over peaceful meadow grass and thick woods covering the Commonwealth. Forming a nearly perfect circle of land about Lea, it was neutral territory and a safe meeting place for the United Realms.

Rising out of the largest city in Andara, the Obsidian Citadel stood ablaze with lights to greet them. Formed out of a black-stoned mountain by the last Jalora Master, it was home to the Legion and the UR Army. Wolf gripped the railing, dizzy with relief. Soon they would be within its stone belly, safely surrounded by rangers.

Fox maneuvered the *Wind Chaser* past the city's air ship docks nested near the base of the mountain. Taking a slow pace upward, he headed directly toward the top of the mountain fortress. Legion and UR ships were moored upon the mountain's side at mid-level. The Wind Chaser drifted past. A special dock had been built at the top of the citadel for the exclusive use of the Lords of Valdeon.

Others had been allowed entry upon the docks this night. Wolf stretched his powers toward the platform. Cardinal Dragon - leader of the Legion - and his Bishops Council stood stiff at attention. Their squires waited in the shadows, stomping their feet to chase away the cold fingers of an early winter. Concern. Relief. Anxiety. They circled about the group in chaotic flashes of color though the rangers tried to hide their angst.

I have given you discernment and great wisdom, Right-Hand. My rangers are loyal, but faith among the people we protect has been shaken. Many would use the young Lion for their own purposes. Dragon and his council must know of Seth, but it is best to keep his existence secret to only those you trust.

"Bring Tulio." Wolf turned his back to the railing, hiding his words. "Be guarded in what you say about the young Lion. We don't know who we can trust anymore."

Nodding, the rangers followed Berto below decks while Fox and the squires secured the ship. Wolf scanned the waiting crowd all the while. They were all rangers, sworn to follow the Jalora and duty bound to aid the Lords of Valdeon. Yet none of them had sensed the spy within their midst. Had the Jalora's power ebbed so low?

Strands of short white hair wagged in the brisk wind atop Dragon's head. Their frantic dancing was the only sign of the turbulent emotions swirling about his body. The cardinal's neatly trimmed beard remained still as he maintained his carefully prepared expression of calm. His probing began at once as Wolf walked down the gangplank and onto the battlements. He batted the cardinal's touch away irritably. Dragon opened his mouth to speak, thought better of it and extended a hand to call forth their squires with blankets and drink.

"It gives me great relief to see you here safely, Wolf," he said. "We'd feared the worst when your cabin boy arrived to tell us San Lucida had been destroyed." Dragon's piercing gaze bored into him again as confusion cast Wolf into an awkward silence. "You don't remember sending your cabin boy, do you?"

Wolf shook his head slowly. The effort reminded his body of the brutal beating it had taken over the past few days. Fatigue descended upon him. Its weight was unbearable.

"The boy said you sent him off in a launch just before your ship was blown apart beneath you. He also said San Rudalfo was burning."

"Burning, yes…my orchards…my family." Wolf squeezed his eyes shut, forcing away the grief. "We are hunted men now. No place is safe from those demon hounds. Will you help me hide the young Lords of Valdeon, Dragon?"

"Word has already been sent to those we can trust. The Legion will protect the Sacred Guard, never fear."

Burgess the Manitou came forward, resting a hand upon Wolf's shoulder. His round face, in contrast to the Dragon's expression, was open and honest. Wolf saw genuine concern there. Bright green eyes sparkled with the youth hidden inside his aging body. Fast approaching seventy, Burgess was the eldest in the Legion and perhaps the most kind.

"Come, Wolf. We must see to your comfort."

"Thank you, Burgess. We have much to discuss first. Evil has taken Valdeon."

"And the Altar of Providence?" Percival the Swan asked. "Was it taken as well?"

Swan was a lanky man with thinning hair and sharp features. His typically sour face had sunk further into pessimism. Wolf couldn't recall a time when the bishop had said a happy word.

"The altar has its own defenses. I believe the Jalora focuses most of its power within the throne room of the Palace of Kings. It will protect the altar while it still may."

He thought of Seth, wondering if the boy had any idea he was as much a part of the Altar of Providence as any of the other sacred relics.

"Then you believe it is safe," Tad the Falcon asked.

He was new to the council and several years younger than the other bishops. Keen and powerful, Falcon had risen fast into the upper echelon of the Legion. He was plain speaking, and someone Wolf trusted.

"The Altar of Providence will endure if the Jalora's power remains."

Boots descended the gangplank in a slow rhythmic pace. Berto and the other guardsmen carried a makeshift litter. Tulio laid upon it, screaming as the cold air touched his damaged skin. His moans and weak flaying silenced the rangers standing about Wolf.

"May the Jalora watch over Valdeon," Burgess said, resting a hand on Wolf's shoulder. "May it save us all."

Dragon came beside the litter. He rested his hand gently upon Tulio's head. Energy radiated about the cardinal's hand as he stretched his power to the young ranger's mind. Tulio stopped his fevered thrashing and began to breathe steadily in a deep sleep.

"We've prepared a special chamber within the heart of the citadel as per the Jalora's command," Dragon said.

"Why be concerned about our remaining together now?" Berto's anger exploded in ill-timed sparks of red and black. "You are the one who ordered us separated days before the invasion."

"I gave no such order."

Dragon stiffened beside the litter. Burning red tipped the back of his ears. The cardinal was dangerously close to losing his patience. In a rash fit of temper, Berto hadn't simply questioned the leader of the Legion, he'd accused him of subversion. Though the Lords of Valdeon were no longer under Dragon's command, they still needed his aid. It was best to be careful.

Wolf hurried between them. "Hawk has been playing his games again. Yes. The Hawk Prince has reappeared. He searches for...for the Lion Ring."

"But it has been lost. What could he hope to accomplish by disbanding the Sacred Guard?" Bishop Manitou asked.

"The Lion Ring is exactly where it should be, on the finger of Leo's heir." Wolf stopped their questions with a weary gesture of his burned arms. "He is Leo's son born to him by a union with Anne Von Wolkhurst of Tslavia. The young Lion is safe for now. It is imperative his existence remains secret until the Jalora commands he come forward. He is being hunted by relentless hounds."

"He should be brought here to the citadel," Bishop Swan said, his thin cheeks sucking inward as he spoke. "We can keep him safe while he is trained."

"Listen to me," Wolf snapped. "Hawk handed me orders with Dragon's signature on them. They came from inside this fortress. Would you bring the Lion here when there may be spies among us? I think not."

"Agreed. These Jackal can't have infiltrated the citadel without help. Traitors are inside these walls." Bishop Falcon tapped a fingertip against his lips. "We must ask ourselves. Where did the Hawk make his nest all these years? And who aided him?"

"He'll answer for his actions when next we meet," Dragon said. "In the meantime, our forces must retake Valdeon. I'll place the Lion upon the throne myself."

Wolf regarded the distant look in Dragon's eyes. An almost imperceptible smile formed under the neatly trimmed white mustache. Once again, the Jalora's warning was well timed. The cardinal had plans for Seth, but was he truly arrogant enough to believe the young Lion would be his puppet? Or did he hope to remain in control of the Legion despite everything?

Wolf carefully formed his mental block. If Dragon knew Wolf had been named Right-Hand, he would know about Seth's future as the next Jalora Master. The Lords of Valdeon had been beaten and weakened. They couldn't stand against Dragon and his bishops. It was best to play along and take Dragon's aid for now. Seth was hidden and he would remain hidden until Wolf had recovered enough to join him on Carlotta. It would appear his duties as Right-Hand where much more than simply protecting the master's body. He must be protected from those who would use him - friend and foe.

"Don't underestimate the Jackal," Wolf told him. "They cut through our forces and took Valdeon in one night. I've never faced more bloodthirsty killers. Did the Jalora not warn you before commanding its forces into Valdeon?"

Dragon took Wolf's arm and guided him toward the entrance to the citadel. Rangers and squires alike hurried to follow. Worry lines crossed his forehead and sprouted down by his eyes and mouth. The cardinal's calm reserve was beginning to crack.

"The Jalora stopped communicating with us after it alerted me to your pending arrival. I was forced to make the decision without its guidance. Many nations have come to the Commonwealth, begging for aid for the Legion to defend their borders against these invaders. Several of them refuse to send men and weapons to join us in this fight. They have lost confidence in the strength of the Legion. I did what I must to calm tempers. Rest assured, these ships are captained by experienced rangers. The Jalora will be with them."

He released Wolf's arm with a confident nod. Dragon had been blessed with visions given to him by the Jalora. He'd used these insights to govern not just the Legion, but the U.R. Dragon was putting a great deal of faith in his own wisdom. The Jalora - he noted - had not voiced its opinion on Dragon's actions.

The mighty stone walls of the citadel engulfed them. Crystal lanterns illuminated the wide corridors. Their shimmering rays were absorbed by the black walls of the citadel. Fist-sized shafts opened in one-hundred-foot intervals to draw fresh air into the bowels of the fortress. Wolf shivered as a touch of the chilly winter air fell upon his neck.

Resting within the black rock were two sets of double doors. The first was marked with the symbol of the Altar of Providence. Behind those doors were suites belonging to the Lords of Valdeon. None could enter accept by permission of the Sacred Guard.

Two glowing orbs appeared on either side of the doors as they approached. They were guardians formed by ancient magic to protect the Legion from intruders. Spinning anxiously as their magic touched Wolf, they prepared to welcome the Sacred Guard home.

"Not here," Dragon said, moving to the second set of doors several feet away. "The Jalora commands you be guarded in a place where we may treat your wounds."

The orbs immediately moved to block Dragon's path. Their magic ran over his body in fast-moving rays of light. Satisfied he was a member of the Legion, the orbs floated to the side as the rest of them passed through. Wolf allowed the relief to reach his shoulders. They'd entered Legion Headquarters at last. None but those loyal to the Jalora could walk within these halls.

Two rangers - both skilled by reputation - stood guard beside a thick steel door. No doubt they were wondering, as Wolf was, why they were guarding a supply room door in the depths of an impenetrable fortress. Bishop Falcon opened the door and stood aside as Tulio was carried through. Wolf nodded his thanks to the rangers and entered.

Lucio the Ferret came toward the door in a rush as it opened. His perpetually cheerful round face dropped as he stopped to stare at them. Wolf supposed they did look like a shipwreck. Torn and bloodied uniforms barely covered the wounds of war. Most worrisome, perhaps, was the heavy mantle of defeat hanging over them.

"We'll leave you," Dragon said.

His troubled gaze rested briefly upon Lucio. Then he hurried down the hall, leaving them in the awkward silence. His bishops followed behind. Their quiet murmurs of condolence echoed in the massive belly of the fortress. None of them had found the words to tell Lucio of Valdeon's fall.

"Lucio," Wolf called to him. "Come here, son."

He held out his hand. Lucio staggered hesitantly toward him. Trembling with anxiety and fury, his wide eyes drifted across the bandages covering Wolf's arms. Tears pushed against his lashes when the others brought Tulio's litter into the room. They carefully rested his litter on the cot farthest from the door.

"What's happened to Tulio?"

"Valdeon has fallen to Julian and his allies," Wolf said. "They've destroyed the strongholds and taken San Leonora. The Sacred Guard has been marked for death. We would have lost Tulio if not for the Jalora's intervention."

Ferret shook his head vehemently. "No. The Heir has been found and we're going to take him to San Lucida to my father!"

"There's more. It won't be easy for you to hear. San Lucida has been destroyed. Jorge told me they came in the night." Wolf held his face, forcing him to hear the truth. "I was there, standing in the ruins. Your father died in my arms."

"No!" Lucio pulled away from him. "You're wrong, Wolf. I have a letter right here." Lucio pulled a parchment from inside his tunic and threw it at him. He let his unnoticed tears fall across sunken cheeks. Pressing his back to the wall, Lucio sank down to the floor. His sobs of fresh grief filled the room.

"The Heir has been chosen. I saw him…." Lucio's words fell away as his chin sunk to his chest.

"I'm sorry, my friend." Berto knelt beside him. "The Jackal are unstoppable. They show no mercy."

"We must stop them," Lucio growled. "Who else will stop them, if not the Lords of Valdeon?"

Wolf infused the Jalora's power into his words. "We've been ordered from Valdeon for now, Ferret. Never fear, one day the Jalora will call us back. We'll make Julian pay dearly."

Ferret pushed up onto his feet. "Yes. We will."

"You're missing one very important member of the Sacred Guard," a voice said behind them.

Leaning against the far wall was a ranger. His uniform was filthy and his boots covered with mud. Folding his arms across his chest, he regarded them insolently. Curly hair, damp with sweat, hung just above mischievous green eyes. He tapped his Heart of the Warrior Ring against the flesh of his bicep. The head of a canine howled at them from the belly of its green crystal. He was a second level Acolyte. How had he snuck up on a Deacon level ranger?

"Who in blazes are you?" Wolf crossed the distance to stand between him and the wounded Tulio. "How did you get in here?"

"Jason Elder, the Coyote." The ranger bowed with a grin. "And you are the Wolf. I'm both pleased and disappointed."

"Have a care, Ranger." Berto pulled his sword. "Remember whom you address."

"Oh, I remember all right. Thus, the reason I've come," Coyote told them, his grin growing broader. "You see I've just arrived in Lea from Eastland Isle."

Wolf reached for the sword no longer hanging at his side.

He snapped his jaw tight. Eastland Isle and its Port City. He'd lost Seth's trail there. How much did the man know and what did he want for the information?

"I bring news of the young Lion."

Lucio was on him in a moment. "Where is he, Ranger? Did you bring him with you?"

"We became separated. Patience. I'll explain it to you, if you let me tell the tale."

Coyote poured himself a drink of water and swallowed it hard. His hand shook with fatigue. This ranger had been traveling hard.

"I first met Seth on the docks of the little Island of Larkspur in the Grey Cliff Isles. He was fighting off mercenaries. Do you know of these men, my lord the Wolf?"

"Yes. I ran into them as well on Marianna."

"It should please you the Lion cut down his attackers." Coyote shrugged with a chuckle. "I helped a bit, not that he needed it. The boy is a selected and can form the Death mask. He was able to fight to the tenth stance."

Wolf and his guardsmen let silence answer the Coyote's veiled question. None of these accounts of Seth's amazing skill surprised them. They, in fact, expected such miracles. Many more would follow. Coyote lifted an eyebrow and grinned again.

"I accompanied the Lion back to his squire and we all journeyed to Eastland Isle. We became separated in the thieves' district of Port City." Coyote took another long drink and set the glass back down on the table. "Seth has more than thieves and mercenaries chasing him. A traitor ranger is in alliance with Pavel Sandor, the assassin who murdered Seth's mother. The maniac attempted to kill our Lion as well. Seth believes this ranger is Valdeonian."

"And you came here to confront me?" Wolf huffed.

"I came to kill you, sir, if you were this dark ranger." Coyote shrugged in his easy manner. "The traitor, unfortunately, isn't among you. My journey isn't over."

"Why so loyal to a boy you just met?" Fox asked, suspicion swirling about him in waves.

Coyote lifted his left sleeve and winced as the fabric caught on the open scars there. Raw power surged and sparked from the three jagged cuts along the ranger's arm. Sudden images of the young Lion raced across Wolf's vision. Seth was kneeling upon the deck of a ship. Grief, fear, and fury swirled about him like a tornado of emotions. In his moment of need, Jason Coyote had reached out to help him. The Lion Spirit, unchecked by its inexperienced bearer, had lashed out in uncontrolled desperation. Those marks were deep, nearly to the bone. Coyote had suffered when he was marked. He was still suffering, though his pride tried to hide it.

Only the Right-Hand can aid the Lion's First Marked now, the Jalora said.

Wolf's fingers smoothed gently a hairsbreadth over the raw wounds. The Lion's power clung to them. Moving up his digits, the power raced along his skin until it found the blue stone of his Wolf Ring. The skin about his ring grew warm, but the power stayed where it was.

You are the only mortal who can draw the Lion's power safely away from those it would devour. This Citadel was created by the last Jalora Master. It will absorb the Lion's great power and distribute it harmlessly away from my servants. Go to the wall, Right-Hand. Release his power.

Wolf pressed his ring against the wall. Instantly, the Lion's power left him and struck the stone like a tidal wave. The Citadel shook about them as if the Erthe itself had opened. Then the walls began to glow with a sheen of black.

The Citadel has been awakened. It prepares for the coming of the next Jalora Master.

Coyote slowly lifted his eyes and regarded Wolf with an opened mouth. "I am your man, Right-Hand. What would you have me do?"

"Obviously, you are very clever having snuck in here without being seen," Wolf said. "I fear there are spies within the Citadel, and Lea, who would try to conspire against the Lion. Take your squire and hide in the shadows. You report directly to me, Coyote. Not even the Dragon can know of your mission."

"It will be as you say, Right-Hand."

Coyote opened a small hidden door in the stone. It was a dumbwaiter. He gave them a wink and crawled inside. Pressing his legs against his chest, he activated the dumbwaiter and disappeared into the heart of the mountain.

"We are at the top of the citadel. He must be mad." Berto sheathed his sword.

"Before you even begin...." Wolf held up his hand. "We are being watched. The Lion is safer if we stay away from him for the time being."

"There is much you haven't told us, Right-Hand." Fox glared at him, his hurt and resentment were evident.

"I'm sorry, Rafael. You all deserve to know the entire story. I suppose I haven't quite accepted it yet." Wolf sighed. "As you know, I was summoned by the Spirit of the Lion Ring to the Altar. The Orb showed me Leo placing the ring upon his son's finger. Then it named me as Right-Hand. I suppose I didn't want to believe it. The Wolf but serves. Despite our new responsibilities, we remain an easy target for the Jackal to find. Dragon has agreed to hide us among the Legion."

"What?" Berto cried. "Wolf, we are stronger together!"

"Yes, Jaguar. We are. But, we aren't strong enough to take back Valdeon without the Lion. The Jalora has tasked me with protecting you. Please trust me."

Jaguar turned away, but reluctantly nodded his head. Ferret and the others fell silent. Their entire world had come crashing down in one night. Then the power of the Right-Hand came to Wolf. He let it flow across the distance, wrapping around each of their bodies. They stood up straight, unable to break free from the hold of his voice.

"Listen to me. You must come when I call you. No matter what you are doing or how important it seems, it will never outweigh my summons to you." Wolf held their gaze and infused his own commitment into them. "You must swear to send word to me if anything unusual happens or you feel you are in danger. Understood? Swear upon the Jalora you will do as I say."

"We so swear."

"Get some sleep. You leave at first light. Have faith in the Jalora, Rangers. We will see each other again."

He sat upon his cot, staring at the new glow in the black stone. Their lives would be in constant danger now. He must trust the Legion and the Jalora to keep them safe until they were strong again. And somehow, amid all the dangers, he must find a way to reach Seth. The future of Andara rested upon the Lion's ability to harness his power before the Jalora faded from the land.

"One day I will come for you, Julian traitor prince," Wolf murmured. "These hands will put your head on a pig pole."

Chapter Twenty-Eight

THE STENCH OF HUMAN filth and decay covered the streets of San Leonora. Julian did his best to avoid the larger piles, but it was impossible in the dark. The charming street lamps once lending light and decoration to San Leonora neighborhoods were now stumps of jagged iron. Their ornate tops had been taken by the Jackal to replenish ammunition. Sadly, most of the cities statuary had suffered the same indignities.

Marcellus hadn't taken the time to note their absence, banging his shin against a jagged edge. He cursed in hissing obscenities. Julian grabbed at the front of his cloak and hissed his own quiet warning. The streets of his beloved city were no longer safe, especially for a prince of Valdeon. In the time their invaders had taken charge, food and water had been withheld from the people. Brutality and marshal law kept the weaker ones docile, while others had become feral.

This neighborhood was particularly dangerous, welcoming only those who were strong enough or mad enough to enter and survive. Even the Jackal soldiers wouldn't enter this district, except in well-armed troops.

Noises filled the darkened windows of a ruined little house to their right. Guttural shouts from the ugly tongue of a Jackal soldier. The brutal slap of an open hand on a tender cheek. A woman wept as her children screamed and called. Julian turned away unmoved. Let the Jackal have their fun. Such women would keep them occupied while he out flanked their numbers. She and her brood were expendable. Pawns in a greater game.

He moved on toward the edge of the city, Marcellus bumbling along behind him. The weeping faded and they entered another silent street. He stepped into the center and froze. Marching boots were coming toward them fast. He pulled Marcellus into an alley and ducked behind what they hoped were empty barrels. Many had died under the Jackal regime. Their bodies were often stuffed into anything large enough to hold them. Abandoned flesh was left to rot under the sun.

A Jackal troop rounded the corner at the far end of the street. Their appearance may have suggested barbarian rogues, but these were well-practiced and disciplined soldiers. Watchful eyes scanned the street around them. They needn't have bothered. The creature they brought with them would warn of any trouble before it struck. Julian recognized him. It was Orryo. Still dressed in the jacket he - now it - had worn to court, the creature was harnessed and leashed between its keepers. Julian shuddered at his wild eyes and wordless ranting. All of them had been promised immortality and limitless power when they took up the cup. While many kept their sanity, and were let lose upon Andara, all would eventually end up as mindless vultures whose only thought was of feasting upon carrion. The weaker the mind, the faster the monster within would come.

Their new pet sniffed in Julian's direction, sucking air inside its maw in excited gulps. The mad hound had recognized his old master's scent. It pulled against the leash, nonsensical sounds falling over a swollen tongue. The troop stopped, straining to see inside the dark recesses of the alley. Julian pulled Marcellus farther inside as one of the soldiers came to stand next to the barrels. He stared into the darkness for what seemed an eternity. Julian held his breath hoping his erratic heartbeats couldn't be heard.

Then the soldier's eyes dropped to the barrels. He knocked one of the lids off and cursed. Sticking his hand deep inside, he pulled out a severed arm. Rotting skin rolled off the bone. The Jackal cursed in his gruff tongue and threw the dead arm at the Dirge. The creature grabbed at the flesh and began to feast. They pulled Orryo along allowing it to carry the prize. Dead eyes looked over hunched shoulders into the alley toward Julian. A promise was in those soulless orbs. He hoped the thing would end up dead before it could make good.

Julian skirted around the gruesome barrels and made his way back into the center of the street. Marcellus walked quietly beside him, his mad eyes twitching with a new rhythm. Seeing their former ally in such an ungodly state had to be unsettling. Julian was accustomed to the Jackal magic. Though Orryo deserved everything he'd gotten, even he had to admit the sight wasn't pleasant.

They came to a short row at the end of the street. It was a dead end with a house fallen into decay just off the row. The roof and part of the house had caved in decades before. Weeds had taken the garden. Most San Leonorans had forgotten its existence, but war has a way of making discarded things useful again.

Turning his focus back on the night's task, he pushed quietly through the door. Inside the ruined old house were the makings of an army. Men, angry and grieving, were assembled for one cause. Revenge against the men who had taken their freedom. He gritted his teeth against the overwhelming excitement. Those lesser men in court society, the ones who didn't know of Julian's betrayal, were still anxious to serve their prince in the hopes he would free them. He'd sent them out to gather those who sought to free Valdeon. Primed and ready, they would be willing to march against the Jackal this very night. Would they show as much exuberance in following a son of the royal house?

He threw off his hood, waiting as the conversations fell silent and all attention was on him. No respectful bows or cordial greetings were offered from the crowd of stone-faced men. Indeed. He could feel the weight of their accusations. They were right, of course, but nobody except Marcellus or the Jackal could confirm their suspicions. He was betting a great deal on their ignorance of recent events. If Valdeon and the throne were to be won, he needed to sway their hatred firmly toward Lord Gorman. It vexed Julian to need such common folk, but he wasn't strong enough to do this alone. He needed more pawns to fall in battle on his behalf.

"What have you to say, Prince of Valdeon?" One of the men, a rough-handed blacksmith from the looks of his attire, spat upon the dirt floor. "Have you come to explain why you hid away while San Leonora fell and your people were butchered?"

Julian stiffened against his hatred. These men wouldn't listen to empty words. He must try a different tact, emotional manipulation. Without a word, he lifted his sleeve and pulled off the glove with a brutal tug. Puss and blood fell from his hand and arm. The men nearest to him stepped back in disgust.

"You think I was hidden away? Perhaps I was, if you consider being tortured within the walls of my own home as hiding. Lord Gorman is creative with his curses." He lifted the rotting arm a bit higher from the men in the back to capture a full view of his deformity. "The Jackal let me go, believing I was too weak to return to my people. They no longer fear a rebellion by whipped dogs, as they call us."

"And you, Prince of Valdeon, do you believe us to be whipped dogs?" the blacksmith asked.

"By coming here tonight, I believe you to be patriots," Julian told them, covering his arm. "I believe a man with hope can never be defeated, not completely." He was willing to bet their lives upon it.

"What would you have us do, my prince?" Marcellus asked, as if on cue.

"These Jackals don't fear us or the Jalora. Their defenses seem impenetrable and their resolve unshakable. I say to you: no army achieves perfection. A weak spot must exist in their armor. We must find it." Julian eyed them, pleased they were paying attention. "Watch their numbers. Make note of guard changes and lapses in discipline."

"And what of you, Prince of Valdeon?"

"It is for me to take the greatest risk," he said. "I spy on Lord Gorman in his lair. Go. We must chase them from the palace before they can open the golden doors of the throne room. If these monsters can take the Altar of Providence, then all of Andara is lost."

A new sense of urgency hovered over the crowd as they shuffled out of the little house. Julian snorted and shook his head. Well, the Jalora still had faithful dullards left in Valdeon, though it had abandoned them. Fools.

His mood was considerably lighter as they traveled the midnight streets toward home. Hope in such dark times was a precious gem among coal. He'd given the men incentive and they wouldn't disappoint, not with the Altar of Providence at stake.

Marcellus held open the dislodged piece of iron rod meant to block the commoners from the royal gardens. He closed it again when Julian was safely inside. They stepped upon the gravel walk together.

"What mischief have you wrought this night, brother?" Zoya jumped from the ornate shrubbery and onto the gravel walk to block their path.

Her long black hair hung wildly over the armored chest plate the Jackal had awarded to her. Rape may have been their intent, but not even the Jackal had been prepared for the vicious killer trapped in the small form of Julian's little sister. She'd killed two of their number before their commander had ordered her freed. They'd taken her into their troop in a place of honor. The commander's knife had etched two long warrior's lines into her cheek in honor of her kill. She was faithful to them now, not to the brother who had saved her from the streets.

"Creeping in the dark, Julian?" She gave him a hungry grin. "I wonder what Lord Gorman would think about his guest breaking curfew?"

He kept his temper carefully in check. Zoya would make good on her threat. He'd seen her chase after Gorman, trying to win his favor first with seduction. Failing to tempt the Jackal general, she tried to impress him with her talents as a cold-blooded killer. Turning on her brother - someone Gorman obviously hated - would certainly win her the points she so desperately wanted.

Yes. She was a clever girl, but she'd forgotten who taught her those tricks. He had his own game in mind, one that would see both his albatrosses taken care of at once.

"May I speak with you alone, Sister? Will you excuse us for a moment, Marcellus?" He held out his good arm toward her. She stared at it, contemplating the consequences.

His companion, caught staring unabashedly at Zoya's tight-fitting uniform, murmured his apologies and moved to stand beside a bench. A pleased grin curved on her lips. She took Julian's arm as he led her behind a clump of trees out of Marcellus' earshot.

"Well done, sister," he snapped with false impatience. "You almost ruined everything. I've been laying out my plan for days, but here you bumble in making threats. I hope he doesn't decide to leave us now."

"What plans?" Zoya's eyes narrowed. She didn't trust him anymore, but her greed would see her undone.

"Marcellus has agreed to be my chancellor despite our situation," he began.

"You've hinted at his place for quite some time, Julian. Nothing new there."

"Yes, but now he's unsure. I had to offer him some incentive. You, sister, are to be his bride," Julian stood his ground as the venom came to her eyes. "Imagine. Zoya De Costa, the chancellor's lady and most powerful woman in all of Valdeon."

The venom faded as greed overtook it. She twisted a piece of her hair, deep in thought.

"Gorman's intention is to leave Valdeon and head to northern Andara. His emperor has promised me Valdeon. I have to have someone I can trust as Chancellor." Julian's soft laughter caused Zoya to stop twisting her hair. "Marcellus wants you, Zoya. He always has. You can control him with a touch."

She looked down at her armor, contemplating it and the role she'd earned as a warrior. Then her dark eyes moved to Marcellus. She smiled slowly, her predator smile he knew so well.

"Why should I settle for life as a dullard's wife when I can be a warrior queen?"

"Gorman only beds noble blood." Julian let his own smile come. "How can he refuse you when you hold Valdeon in your lovely hands?"

"I'll take your mad fool in hand, Julian, for a time." Her eyes were fierce as she looked upon him once more. "Know this. When Lord Gorman and my Jackal friends leave San Leonora, I will take your stooge's place. We can't have weakness near the throne."

"Agreed, Sister." He kissed her on the cheek. "Perhaps it is time Valdeon became more progressive in its leadership."

Zoya spun away from him with a wicked grin. She moved toward Marcellus like a snake after a rat. Caught in her seductive gaze, Marcellus stood watching as she approached. The poor fool was almost drooling. Julian snorted as she took his arm. The seduction had begun and her rat would fall quickly. They were a match fashioned in hell. Two off-balanced killers with propensity for cruelty.

"I wonder which one will die by the other's hand?" Whisper's tiny voice said at his leg. "Have a care they don't join against you, my prince."

Julian smothered his anger. He'd asked the little creature not to eavesdrop in the past, but it had a mind of its own. Theirs was a fragile friendship built upon the rickety foundations of betrayal. It was best not to offend the little creature. Julian's list of allies had dwindled to a dangerously low number.

"Your news must be of great importance if you found a way to leave Lord Gorman's side, Whisper." Julian forced a smile and bowed his head. "I am grateful to you."

"Allies must look out for one another, Prince Julian. The news I bring has much to do with your intentions for the throne." It floated up to hover at Julian's eye level. "Lord Gorman's men have reported chasing the Lords of Valdeon over the Forbidden Mountains. His spies in Tslavia saw the ranger ship survive the Jalora's magic. Their Jackal pursuers did not. The rangers headed in the direction of Lea back to their ranger headquarters."

Julian slammed a fist against a hapless tree trunk. Wolf! The ranger was a constant burr in his boot. Would nothing kill him? The Dragon would welcome them with open arms, of course. Wolf's report of Julian's part in Leo's death and the fall of Valdeon would turn the UR against him. Well, let them turn against Valdeon. It wouldn't do them any good. Gorman and his Jackal had their own plans for Andara.

"Lord Gorman has sent spies to Lea," Whisper's voice broke in on his dark thoughts. "Their orders are to kill the Wolf and the young Lords of Valdeon. He is sending the new Dirge, the ones who still resemble humans."

"Wolf and his men will be hidden within the walls of the citadel. It is impenetrable."

Whisper let his sharp little teeth show. "The Legion will soon have their hands full elsewhere. The one you call Dragon has sent an Andaraian armada to attack Valdeon. Lord Gorman himself will be on the command ship to meet them."

Julian let out a quiet laugh. Lord Gorman would soon be up to his neck in blood. Andara would be ripe for the plucking. The Jackal would move on soon to more appetizing fare, leaving Valdeon to its rightful ruler.

Chapter Twenty-Nine

JORGE DABBED ointment on the laceration covering most of the tiny child's arm. He tied off the bandage and smiled encouragingly to chase away the little one's tears. His mother pulled the boy close, rocking him in her arms. She'd sustained wounds along most of her body. Jorge pressed a bit more medicine for her pain into the woman's hand.

He'd found them under the rubble of a collapsed house outside the camp. No matter how many times he warned the people not to explore the ruins of San Lucida, new reports came of wounds and death each day. More refugees streamed into the city at all hours. He was running out of safe places to put them.

Jorge parted the tent flaps of the makeshift hospital and stretched deeply. Sunlight peaked over the canyon walls. Another night's sleep lost. Why did these small catastrophes always seem to happen in the middle of the night?

Whistles from the canyon opening told him Duarto and the hunters had returned. His son's dower face communicated the disappointment more than words could. This was the third morning they'd come back without meat. Supplies of dried food were running thin for the people who were already here. Yet more and more refugees came each day to find the Regent of Valdeon. Living with their disappointment was wearing on his patience.

Duarto and the hunters stopped before him. He gave them an understanding nod. His son fell in step behind him as Jorge moved back toward their tent. Hungry, miserable faces looked up at him as they passed. He could do nothing to comfort them. No news or orders had come from Wolf or anyone else since the fall of Valdeon. He was beginning to worry the Sacred Guard had not survived.

Such dire thoughts would not help the people under his care. If he could not provide them enough food and adequate shelter, at least he could give them hope. They must know the Jalora hadn't abandoned Valdeon entirely. A new Lion had been chosen. He would deliver their people from the evil occupying their land. Jorge held firm to his belief as he struggled through the days. It was time to share this little piece of hope with the others.

Pacarro tradition brought all the members of the tribe together for meals. He'd started this practice to make certain everyone was accounted for and felt part of their new, but dismal community. The women and children began to gather as soon as they saw him turn toward the breakfast fires. Jorge jumped up on a large piece of wall and waited for them to settle.

"I have news to share with you. By a promise given before our city fell, I've remained silent. This secret must now be shared, for such news will bring each of us hope." He smiled as even the men fell silent and leaned forward to listen to his word. "The Orb of

Valdeon pulses with the new life of the young Lion. My Lord Cesar Santiago swore it was so days before San Lucida was destroyed. My son and I have sworn to serve our true King. Will you do the same?"

An old woman riddled with age raised her thin hand. "Will he come to us soon, Lord Pacarro?"

"I don't know how long he will be, old mother," Jorge told her. "The Lion will return to the West just as the Jalora has commanded."

She hugged several of the women nearby. Happy tears and proclamations of hope spread quickly around the camp fires. Jorge smiled at the scene. It was a start. Hope, once instilled into a single heart, was difficult to kill.

"How do we know you're telling the truth?" one of the men, a new arrival, shouted. "We were promised the Regent of Valdeon and have yet to see him here."

Duarto was on him in a flash, smashing a fist into his face. "My father is a man of honor! Xavier the Wolf trusted him enough to confirm the Lion's naming the night San Lucida fell. Do you think you're better than a Lord of Valdeon?"

The man looked away when Duarto released him, but Jorge didn't miss the hatred in his eyes. He was a person to watch. Grumblings around the camp were nothing new. Questioning his way of leading. Demands for more food for those who labored at the expense of the helpless. Jorge had thought he'd kept them under control, but it would appear new trouble makers had come among them. It would be interesting to see their true intent. In his time as squire, he'd seen many ruined towns fallen on hard times. The Legion helped them back on their feet. Many were grateful for the aid, but there were always those who tried to benefit from the weakness and hardships of others. The rangers were quick to put these troublemakers in their place, but Jorge was fresh out of rangers. He'd have to trap the wagging tongues on his own without the aid of the Jalora this time.

He called over Mario, an old friend and a man still loyal to the Santiago family. "I must take the hunters to the far canyons tomorrow, my friend. We need meat for the people. I want you to keep an eye on him. He is a stranger to me. I fear they are up to no good."

They'd started off before dawn the next day and traveled most of the morning along the foothills of the Forbidden Mountains. Old superstitions invaded their thoughts as they traveled under the ridged cliffs. Jorge had heard the tales of hauntings and evil creatures since childhood, but hunger outweighed fear. He kept his men moving at a steady pace.

Most of the mountain peaks towered above Andara like jagged teeth. Violent winds rushed from their cliffs to pounce upon the foothills. From coastal rocks to the eastern border with Duhnland, ships found it impossible to enter Valdeon from the north.

One path had been formed through those northern mountains. Known only to the Legion and a few raiders, it rested between San Lucida and the mouth of the Constantina River. No wider than the main row of a large Andarian city, the treacherous path was only taken by experienced trackers. Death waited for the unprepared within the small canyon. This danger was mirrored in the skies. A few experienced captains and crews dared to sail above the path. The wind wasn't quite as wild, but it still made its presence known. Jorge had endured the trip a few times on Leo's ship. Jolting and groaning the entire passage, he'd feared he would never see the other side.

They reached the entrance at midday. Rock walls twisted inward, hiding the canyon's opening from the casual traveler. A searcher must be looking for the optical illusion to find its entrance. Jorge kept his hand upon the rock as he stepped into its mouth. Wind howled down from the ridgetops to strike his face. Ancient roots, long dead, groaned against the constant force. Jorge suspected they were responsible for the many claims of ghosts and evil spirits living in the canyon.

He knelt to examine the ground before them. Animals were abandoning Valdeon, running for the lush green meadows of Tslavia. He couldn't fault their instincts. They were leaving behind withering shrubbery and certain famine. He traced a footprint among the hoof marks. Humans had come this way. Children were among them. Foolish. They'd be taken as spies as soon as they cleared the mountains, if those same mountains didn't kill them on the way.

"What is it, father?"

"Refugees are trying to escape through the canyon," he told his men. "We must go after them. They'll never survive the mountains."

Jorge said a silent prayer to the Erthe Mother and plunged inside the rocky walls of the canyon. The prints were more noticeable in the mud of the wet floor. Thirty people - men, women, and children - had passed this way. Perhaps they were from the east and hadn't heard of the dangers waiting for them among the cliffs?

Thunder crashed above their heads, raining down ear-piercing echoes upon them. No. Not thunder. Cannon fire. He'd never forget the sound. Jorge looked to the sky, trying to see above the great walls. A thin patch of blue stretched above them. Suddenly fiery orange burned across the gap. White sails were aflame over a Jalora Legion ship. Then a steel hull chased after the wounded vessel, hunting it relentlessly. The Jackal was devouring their Legion and last hope.

"By the Erthe Mother!" Jorge cried, letting out a moan of helpless anger.

"Look!" Duarto grabbed his arm. "Another Legion ship! It's going to fall right on top of us. Run!"

Jorge pushed the hunters on faster as they ran. Reaching the canyon opening was their only hope to escape a fiery death. Then the Legion ship crashed into the gap behind them. Fire burst from its belly and filled the canyon with a roar. Jorge ran faster, feeling the heat coming to devour them.

"Jump!" he shouted as they cleared the canyon.

He dove to the side and rolled upon the rough rock just as angry flames burst from the rock. The flaming fingers retreated inside the canyon. They'd been lucky. The scrub brush surrounding the entrance was tinder dry. If the fire had taken hold, the entire hillside would be up in flames.

Jorge pressed his back against the blackened rock. Wincing at the heat radiating through his buckskin, he took a quick look down the blackened canyon. It was filled with rock, ship, and bodies. No one would take this road again. Jalora would help the refugees who'd gone before them. They weren't coming back to Valdeon and no one else was leaving. The Jackal had seen to it.

Chapter Thirty

WOLF DABBED rancid ointment on the jagged cuts running along Tulio's chest. The wounds were angry, seeping with foul-smelling liquid. His fevered moans filled the lonely room with its empty cots. The others had left the citadel one-by-one. Each of them guarded by rangers faithful to their duties. Wolf and Tulio were the last.

"Easy," Wolf murmured, holding him down carefully. "I'm watching over you."

Why had he made such a foolish promise? Now he was honor bound to keep Rabbit's beaten torso hidden from all but his squire. The Legion healers pleaded and argued. Their attempts to sway him remained fruitless. Wolf - though he hated himself for it - would not relent.

Rabbit's body may recover. The hatred and shame, however, had begun to fester in his heart. Wolf understood Tulio better than the young ranger could imagine. Leaning his head back against the cool wall, he closed his eyes. Yes. He understood hatred and shame all too well.

Then heat began to burn against the skin of his arms. Wolf's eyes flew open. He was in San Rudalfo once more. What bang tail mischief was this? Twisting around, he tried to get his bearings. Flames burst suddenly from the ground, blocking his path. Dulcina and the children. He had to find them! Wolf jumped through the fiery wall, falling until his boots made a hollow thud upon a gravel path. The flames dissolved, taking the haze away. He was in the courtyard of his estate at the head of a path his grandfather had built. It ran from his ruined villa toward the orchard.

"Dulcina! Children! Where are you?"

"I'll help you look for them, Wolf," the young Lion said beside him.

Seth was dressed in loose white linen trousers and flimsy sandals. Skin, once paled by the wintry Marianna haze, was now sun-kissed and healthy. Bruises covered his torso. Signs of sleepless nights were upon the young face. Intelligent eyes took Wolf in. Relief. Sadness. And finally, Concern revolved around his being.

"How did you get here, Seth?"

Wolf smoothed at his uniform. It was still intact with no signs of fire damage, exactly as it had been when he and Seth parted in Haven Bay. Neither of them were standing among the flames of Wolf's orchard or anywhere near San Rudalfo. This was a dream. Seth's dream. Somehow, he'd joined with Wolf's subconscious mind.

"I'm not certain." Seth ran a hand through his messy hair. "The Jalora brings me to the Realm of Dreams and Mist. I—"

His fiery amber eyes blazed with sudden fury as he stared into the flames to their left. Seth's body fell into a fighting crouch. The low growl of warning filled the space around them. Wolf's hands began to shake. Seth was already drawing upon his most dangerous weapon, the Lion's Roar. If left to strike freely, it could destroy a city.

"Run, Wolf! They're coming. I'll try to hold them off."

Seth dove into the flames, fists swinging at invisible attackers. Wolf raced toward him. He reached into the fire just as the Lion's body disappeared in the orange heat. Then the Lion's Roar thundered in mighty waves within the dream world. Wolf's uniform burst into flames, engulfing his body. He screamed as a hand grabbed his arm and spun him around. The Lion. He had to keep them away from Seth.

Wolf was drowning in the incredible power. It filled every pore of his body, until he glowed in blazing white. Lifting the attacker over his head, he growled a feral warning at the six cloaked men standing before him. They leapt backward, terror pulsing about their beings. Panting hard, he breathed in great gulps as his vision began to clear.

He was in the citadel at Tulio's beside once more.

"And what will you do with me now you have me in your claws, My Lord De Vincente?"

Cardinal Dragon's body remained perfectly still suspended above Wolf's head. Bands of white light circled about his upper body and legs, effectively binding him. Wolf tossed the cardinal at the band of men as he would a blanket or pack. Staggering back, he placed his hands upon the stone walls of the citadel. The surface vibrated under his touch, drawing the Lion's power from his body.

"What do you want of me?" Wolf pulled away from the stone to fall into his chair.

"We take you to safety, Lord of Valdeon," one of the cloaked men said. "Can the Rabbit travel?"

"If he must."

The Phoenix ring glistened bright blue in the candlelight as Gregory Baldemar, the Crown Prince of Heidelbrecht, pulled back his hood. He was muscular and tall, even compared to his large countrymen. Golden hair framed bright blue eyes and a warm smile. Gregory had been one of Leo's apprentices and a close friend to the Lords of Valdeon. There were few men he trusted more.

The Phoenix and his countrymen of Heidelbrecht were Valdeon's oldest allies. They had sworn aid to the Lords of Valdeon back in the days of Paulo D'Antoiné, Andara's second Jalora Master. In honor of their loyalty, the Jalora gifted the Phoenix ring to Gregory's ancestor. It was the first Heart of the Warrior Ring created after the original nine gifted to the Sacred Guard. The Bearer of the Phoenix Ring had another duty when a Jalora Master walked the Erthe. He was partisan to the master. One who was honor bound to protect the Sacred Guard as they cared for the master during his fits of rage or power.

"Well met, ancient ally." Wolf pressed his hand over his heart and gave the men a bow.

Gregory, ignoring the customary greetings, came to him and rested a hand upon Wolf's shoulder. "Nothing I could say would be enough, Wolf. My countrymen and I will do anything we can to aid you. We'll see you and the Rabbit to safety. I swear it."

"I entrust my life and that of my comrade to your protection." Wolf took his offered hand and stood. "It's good to see you again, Gregory. I wish the circumstances were different. I was glad to hear of your promotion." He pointed to the bright blue stone in the Phoenix Ring denoting him as a Deacon. "Edmund would be proud of you."

"Thank you," Phoenix told him, clearing his throat to hide the pleasure there. "My father awaits us onboard one of our fastest vessels. It's well hidden beyond the trees of the Commonwealth. My men will take you over the darkened city streets to our waiting ship, silent and unseen. We must be quick or the morning light will find us."

Phoenix motioned to the five Heidelbrecht rangers. They brought a litter to Rabbit's bedside. Wolf stood out of the way as they gently lifted him. Moaning softly, Tulio opened his eyes. Wolf came to him and lightly touched his arm in reassurance. It would be a painful jaunt to the ship, but Tulio was strong. He would survive.

"I have a launch hidden upon the battlements," Phoenix whispered at the door.

Hiding his frustration, Wolf stepped aside as they carried Tulio toward the door. He was desperate to join Seth, especially after what they'd just shared. Now wasn't the time. Phoenix was right. They needed time to recover and grow strong again.

"Thank you for your aid, Dragon."

"My protection hasn't ended. You and I will serve together, Phoenix." Dragon gestured into the empty corridor. "Shall we?"

Taking the lead, Phoenix hurried down the still corridor. He stopped in the middle of a long stretch of smooth wall and placed his hand upon the black surface. Stone slid against stone as the wall opened to a hidden stairwell. Crystal lanterns flickered into life, illuminating their way. Stepping aside, he waited until the others had carried Tulio onto the landing and then closed the opening.

It was stuffy, as if the stairwell hadn't touched fresh air for decades. Wolf looked up at the ceiling. No cobwebs or signs of age. Phoenix gripped his arm briefly and then headed soundlessly up the stairs. Wolf stayed close at his back. Chancing a glance toward the empty stairs beneath them, he saw Cardinal Dragon bringing up the rear.

Solid rock blocked their path at the top of the stairs. Phoenix pressed a hand at the wall's center and stood back as it opened. Fresh air flooded the stairwell in a rush. Ignoring the sensation, Wolf looked past Gregory's shoulder. The private air docks of the Sacred Guard stood empty before them. Much had changed since the citadel's awakening. He regarded Phoenix, a thousand questions straining against his lips.

Do I not also command the Partisan? Remember the Lion's warning. Evil still hunts you, Right-Hand. Its eyes watch for you above the streets of Lea. Trust your ancient allies.

"They're waiting for us," Wolf said low.

"Then we'll make it hard for them." Phoenix turned to his countrymen. "I leave Rabbit to your care. Get him to my father's ship at all costs."

He whistled in two short bursts. A man stepped from behind a pile of sealed crates beside the docks. He slowly lifted his right arm up above his head. Phoenix nodded at his countrymen and hurried forward to join their ally in the crates. Wolf followed, staying close to Tulio.

"No sign of trouble?" Phoenix asked him.

One economic shake of his head was all the answer they'd be gifted. Roland, Phoenix's squire, was mute. Somehow, he managed to communicate large amounts of information to his ranger when the occasion warranted it.

"What did he say?" Dragon asked.

"Roland hasn't seen any signs of mischief, Sir. But he suspects trouble is coming."

Blond white hair, cut short against a porcelain face, glistened under the winter sky as Roland turned his head toward the southwest. His smooth, perfect face remained emotionless and serene. The tiny spark of worry in his eyes put Wolf on edge.

"We have to go," he said. "Roland's right. The Jalora is unsettled."

The squire nodded to Wolf and pulled the cloth off what looked to be a pile of crates. Hiding beneath its camouflage, a launch hovered inches above the dock. Wolf smiled. Gregory Baldemar had always been a quick study.

The rangers lowered Tulio carefully into the bottom of the launch. Wolf sat down beside him. Taking up positions around them, the rangers made ready to fight. Phoenix took the helm and waited for Roland to unfasten the mooring lines. He took them slowly into the air as soon as his squire was on board. The little vessel hovered above the battlements for a moment and then streaked across the roof tops of Lea.

Wolf leaned down when Tulio began to struggle against his blankets. "I'm here beside you. Be still now. We aren't out of danger yet."

A sharp prickling sensation raced along his spine, snatching Wolf's attention away from Tulio. He peered into the darkness beneath their hull. Two fast moving launches raced in an upward arc toward them. Driven by armored Jackal, the vessels carried tall figures in their centers. Valdeonians. Some he recognized as criminals by their filthy uniforms. Once safely locked away in the bowels of the San Leonora prison, their new freedom would be wasted seeking revenge upon the men who'd delivered their punishment. Others, cloaked and hooded, were strange when viewed with his power. Their energy contained no emotions or memories. Each had one single-minded thought - satisfying their horrible hunger.

One of the hoods lifted away from its owner's head. He may have been Valdeonian once, but Wolf couldn't say if the thing coming toward them was even human anymore. Dark, soulless eyes stared at him with unfathomable craving. Chapped lips parted, revealing multiple rows of jagged teeth.

The creature and his comrades are fledgling Dirge. They were once members of the Valdeonian court. Hungry for power and willing to risk Jackal Sorcery, these lost souls have struck a bargain with the Sarcion. They have given much in the promise of power and wealth. You've seen the true reward which awaits them, Right-Hand.

Indeed, he had. The Dirge were mindless scavengers who fed upon human flesh. He'd struck down several of the creatures on Marianna when they'd tried to attack Seth. How many more of these grotesque nightmares were wandering about in Andara?

One of the vessels struck hard against their side hull, knocking the rangers off their seats. Anxious fingers grabbed onto their launch, tipping it toward the waiting Dirge. Dragon sliced away the hands as quickly as they reached for the side. The Dirge kept coming, slamming their bloody stumps against the hull.

"Phoenix, get us out of here!" Dragon smashed a boot against one of the stumps and sat back down.

Incited into a frenzy by the smell of their own blood, the Dirge turned on the soldiers in the launch. The unattended vessel tilted and swayed wildly. A ball of flame consumed the launch as it struck the ground with a boom.

The other airboat leveled with their launch feet behind the crystal engines. One solid hit and their little vessel would sink to the streets. Phoenix gripped the rudder hard and shoved it downward. Wolf threw his body across Tulio, holding him in place. The launch groaned and the engines whined under the strain of their fast descent. Then he lifted the rudder and leveled the vessel. Veering sharply to the left, he zoomed through the tight buildings.

They'd lost their hunters for a few moments. Soon the Dirge would sniff them out among the buildings. Wolf looked down at Tulio. He'd sworn to protect the young Lords of Valdeon. Sometimes protecting someone meant staying away from them. He must give the Heidelbrecht rangers enough lead time to escape with Tulio. Bait was needed. And what better temptation for these blood thirsty hounds than the Right-Hand to the Master?

"We must separate, Cardinal." Wolf said. "I can lead these men away from young Rabbit."

Dragon's white mustache dropped downward. "You won't be going alone."

Phoenix dove toward the empty streets beneath them. He leveled the launch a few feet above the stone row and turned sharply into a darkened alley. Slowing the launch to stop in the shadows, Phoenix pulled Roland into his seat at the rudder. His keen blue eyes met the gaze of each of his countrymen.

"Remember your sworn duty. No matter what happens now, you must see the Rabbit to our ship. Roland, don't move until you hear the clash of our swords, then I want you to fly as fast as you can. Tell Tiger to wait for us directly under the ship."

Wolf looked one last time upon Tulio's pained face and then jumped into the row. Dragon and Phoenix landed next to him. They made their way to the mouth of the alley, staying close to the protective cover of the buildings. Wolf stepped out into the row. Now wasn't the time for stealth. He moved to the center with Dragon and Phoenix taking up positions on either side of him. They stood in the First Stance and waited for their quarry.

Their hunters zoomed toward them at full speed. Dragon raced along the ground to meet them. He leapt up on the first launch, stomping heads and hands on his way to the rear. Splitting the rudder and the crystal engine from its vessel, Dragon jumped off the launch. He landed lightly back on the ground as the little ship exploded against a nearby wall.

The crash had dealt with the boat's humans, but it would take more than fire to stop the Dirge. They crawled from the burning wood. The shrouds covering their bodies remained untouched, preserved by hellish magic. Then the song of death rolled toward the rangers. The inhuman sound pounded against Wolf's ears.

Crystal engines roared as the launch carrying Tulio sped away. Wolf readied his body to block their hunters' pursuit of the little vessel. The Dirge didn't move. Their hideous maws opened wide in harsh laughter.

"The boy is an easy kill," one of the creatures said, struggling slightly with the words. "He will wait. We have bigger prey this night…Right-Hand."

Be wary, the Jalora warned, wrapping around him tightly. *A powerful evil surrounds this enemy. You must kill them all before others can be summoned.*

Then he heard the pounding of many boots. Mercenaries poured out of the alleys of Lea. It was a trap and they'd stumbled into it like witless fools. Wolf's grip tightened on his sword. Damaged skin pulled taut across his forearms. He ignored the pain. It would be to the death. The night took a breath and then the mercenary horde charged. Wolf, Dragon, and Phoenix stepped forward to meet them.

Chapter Thirty-One

THE MERCENARIES BANGED chains and slapped blades together. Their battle rhythms thundered against the buildings along the row. Hatred and the lust for revenge pulsed from their numbers. Lanterns glowing inside windows suddenly snuffed out along the length of the street. No aid would come from the citizenry. Lea was a town in the habit of minding its own business unless someone else's benefited it.

Dragon and Phoenix advanced in rapid steps, taking up positions between Wolf and the mercenaries. They drew the full strength of their power as the swarm descended. Pushing the horde back, the rangers kept the first line of attackers away from him. Wolf - for his part - stayed back a few paces. A threat glided at the edge of the battle, unseen by his two allies. The Dirge had its soulless eyes fixed upon Wolf. Its maw salivated in anticipation. Close to frenzied hunger, the creature maintained its position. What was it waiting for?

Then a new line of mercenaries flanked the two rangers. Their numbers stormed at Wolf in a raging stream of steel. His sword met their attack with bone-jarring ferocity. Calling the Jalora's power to his body, he thrust and sliced with an unaccustomed speed. His body went numb as he lost sight of their faces. They became lifeless husks. More and more streamed in, pushing Wolf farther from his two comrades.

A body fell at his back. He stepped sideways and let the mercenary's body fall to the ground. A nasty slit stretched across the villain's throat. Coyote stood at the edge of the battle, sword bloody. Somehow, he'd managed to follow them.

"Rabbit is in danger," Wolf called across the distance. "You must follow him. Make certain he escapes Lea."

"Behind you!"

Coyote's warning came too late. A boney fist struck the back of Wolf's head, sending him reeling to the ground. He rolled over the cobble stones and onto his feet. Shaking off the dizziness, Wolf pointed his blade at the Dirge. Gurgling laughter spewed out of its maw. Any humanity belonging to the man within was slipping away. Standing amid blood and gore, the Dirge's hunger was taking hold.

Steel smashed against steel nearby. Coyote was attempting to reach him. Try as he might, the young ranger would fail. This moment had been carefully planned. The fall of Valdeon, Leo's death, Seth's birth - they were all moves in a larger game. Now it was evil's turn to strike.

"Tell me, My Lord De Vincente," The Dirge asked, slurping between the words. "Your youngest offspring had the breathing disease, yes?"

Wolf's hands began to shake. The Jalora's power slipped away, leaving him weakened. Vulnerable. He was just a man. Another victim of evil. The black soulless eyes stared at him, enjoying his sudden loss of will.

"He proved to be most entertaining. The sounds he made as he struggled for air still make me laugh." Its hideous face contorted into mocking gasps in imitation of Gaspar. "The little creature finally succumbed to death when we hung his brother and mother. Ah, fun ends too quickly."

Wolf flew at the creature with a growl of raw rage. Bringing down his blade upon the cowl of its shroud, he pushed until the rock stopped his strike. Wolf circled back to the vermin who'd killed his family, slashing his blade upon the carcass again and again.

"On the ground, Phoenix!" Dragon shouted over the din.

Wolf pulled his fury, hurt, and grief into the center of his being. The tight ball of hate grew hungry with anticipation. Vengeance. It was all that mattered now. He aimed at the killer's body and let lose the ball of hate pressing against his control. It struck the body with a boom, cracking the ground beneath. He fell to his knees, sobs shaking the strength from his body.

"You are powerful, Jalora plaything." Another Dirge stood over him, it's anxious fingers raised above Wolf's head. "Your death will bring about the end of the Lion."

The Dirge lunged toward him, its rows of teeth dripping with hunger. Then the shroud fluttered in pieces onto the ground. The creature's head bounced along the cobbles stone to disappear among the dead. Phoenix stared down at Wolf with a thousand questions crossing his face.

"They called you, *Right-Hand*," he said at last.

An eerie stillness had descended upon the row. One last death cry sounded in the darkness and then the battle was over. It resonated far away in Wolf's ears as if something from a long-forgotten dream. His body tingled with residual energy. The sensation was all he could feel. It was his only reality.

Dragon came to join Phoenix. His uniform was covered in gore. Blood and sweat ran down the cardinal's cheeks, tinting the ends of his mustache an ugly shade of brown. Wolf began to chuckle. He fell back into the gorge covering the row, helpless as fits of laughter racked his body. Tears of laughter. Sobs of grief. He couldn't tell the difference anymore.

"Sleep, Wolf." Dragon touched a hand to his forehead.

"Your power isn't working on our friend." Phoenix' frightened eyes stared at Wolf. "They called him, *Right-Hand*."

"Indeed, they did, Ranger. We've seen Wolf's power firsthand. If he has been made Right-Hand over the Hawk, it raises some intriguing questions. The most important of which are the young Lion's identity and his whereabouts." Dragon stood away. "Bring Wolf."

Phoenix sheathed his sword. He picked Wolf up and threw him over his shoulder as if he were a child. Wolf didn't resist. He couldn't. Odd. No more sound touched his ears. No more fear filled his heart. He drifted alone in the nothingness.

"Run at full speed," Dragon said. "Don't stop for anything. Wolf's mysterious friend covers our escape."

"Can he be trusted?"

"The Jalora hides his identity from me. Let us hope we can count on his discretion."

Wolf swayed in an awkward angle against Phoenix' back. His concentration waned as they ran. He no longer cared where they were going or if they got there at all. His mind had fixed on imagining his little Gaspar struggling to breathe on the floor of the orchard. The look of terror in his innocent eyes, watching helplessly as his mother…. No. He banished the image back into his fevered mind.

Hands pulled him gently off Phoenix' shoulder. Wood and steel covered the walls as they carried him. Was he on a ship? Phoenix had mentioned something about his father. Then lantern light blazed overhead. He was in a neat infirmary, resting upon a cot. His clothes had been removed and his body washed.

A cry of horror shattered the silence within the room. Wolf rolled his head toward the sound. Tulio was on the cot next to him, breathing evenly in sleep. Roland held a cloth over the Rabbit's chest. His perfect porcelain features warped into a horrified mask. Tulio's dirtied shirt fell to the floor.

"What manner of evil has set itself upon Valdeon?" Phoenix cried.

"Steady yourself," Dragon ordered. "These men have been targeted by evil. It is only by the grace of the Jalora they still live. We must keep them safe."

"Do the others live as well?" Phoenix asked.

Dragon's face struggle to remain placid. Phoenix was an ally, but the Jalora had been quite clear. Secrecy. Wolf tensed against the bedding of his cot. This moment would test the cardinal's loyalty to the Jalora.

Would he keep his promise or would he abandon his word to save face?

"It is enough you know about Rabbit and…and the Wolf. It's far too dangerous for you and the young Lords of Valdeon to say more."

"But, I must aid the Sacred Guard. It is my duty as the Partisan."

"And they will be drawn to you, Phoenix. You must tell me if any contact you."

Wolf didn't miss the arrogant lift of Dragon's chin or the pleasure he saw in the ranger's eyes. Ambition. It would be Francis the Dragon's downfall one day. Wolf relaxed against the pillow. He was in no state to prevent any plans the cardinal may have for Seth or the rest of the Sacred Guard. Healing would take time. The Jalora, in its wisdom, had made certain Seth and the others were safely away from Lea.

Phoenix turned his attention back to Wolf. "I have never seen a ranger with so much power. His skill rivals yours, Sir."

"The Right-Hand is more than a title. If legend holds true, this Wolf will be second only to the Lion."

Rushing boots hurried into the room. Dragon disappeared from Wolf's limited vantage. Urgent words were exchanged just out of earshot. Then Dragon came back to join Phoenix at the base of Wolf's bed.

"What is it, sir?"

"The Legion Armada. It's been destroyed. A few survivors managed to make it back to the Citadel, but most of them are gravely wounded. I must return to HQ before word of our defeat spreads outside the

Commonwealth. See to Wolf and Rabbit. Then return to HQ in all haste, Phoenix. We'll need your sword."

They moved out of the room, leaving Wolf to stare up at the ceiling. He'd been a fool to not send Coyote to look after Seth. The Lion was in danger with no one to protect him. Wolf tried to lift off the pillow, but his strength was gone. A hand slipped under his head. Roland brought a liquid to his lips. Wolf gulped it down. A tingling sensation joined the exotic fruit flavors along his tongue and throat. He was asleep before the last drop drained from the bowl.

Chapter Thirty-Two

A HALF-MOON HUNG over the dark waters surrounding Carlotta. Its silver fingers reached across the sand and into the silent streets of the village. Seth breathed in the perfume of flowers and sweet Sunfruit mixing with the sea air. This would forever be the scent of his personal paradise.

Tymon beckoned he and Riley forward as the last light in the village was snuffed out. Waves rolled upon the silent shore, lulling the inhabitants of the island into a peaceful slumber. They would sleep until nature woke them, safe in their beds. An unaccustomed pang of homesickness filled his soul. He would miss these people - his people.

Their Iron Queen was foremost on his mind as they walked across the docks to a waiting ship. She'd kept her usual stoicism as they parted, but Aunt Charlotte couldn't hide her fear and loneliness from him. Seth had seen her affection in the swirls of dynamic energy about her aging body.

"Welcome aboard the *Sea Angel*, Highness." Rodrigo grinned proudly as he stepped aside to let them board. "She is Carlotta's biggest and fastest ship."

"Where have you been keeping her? Never mind. I don't think I want to know. Are you taking us all the way to the Commonwealth then?" Riley asked.

"No, my lord earl. We take you as far as the coast of Southbay." Rodrigo beckoned them excitedly to the open hold. "Come. I've found you a ship to take you the rest of the way."

An old four-man fishing boat hovered a few feet below deck. Moored tightly inside the hatch, it bounced like a bubble upon the waves. A single white sail wrapped around its thin mast jutting up from the center. Hanging precariously from the boat's rear was an ancient crystal engine.

"You want us to travel across half a continent in this rickety old crate?" Riley shook his head. "I doubt we'll make it to shore."

"You mustn't worry, my lord earl. She's sturdy. My grandfather built her with his own two hands." Rodrigo slapped Riley's back. "Come. I'll show you the route."

He waved to their captain as they walk to the stairs leading below deck. Tymon joined them. He made no effort to leave as the vessel began its ascent into the skies above Carlotta.

"I accompany you as far as the shores of Southbay. Then we must part," Tymon told Seth. "I have my own errand from her majesty."

"What about Aunt Charlotte? I don't like the thought of her being alone."

"Her majesty is occupied with other things."

Tymon gave him a crisp bow and joined Rodrigo as he entered the captain's chambers. It was a large room with a bed on one side and a long table on the other. Bits of gold inlay covered intricate designs carved in the expensive wood. Seth smoothed a fingertip along the door jam. The Sunfruit wine trade couldn't possibly be this lucrative. Carlotta and her mayor still held their secrets close it would seem.

Rodrigo unrolled a large map of the continent, holding the corners in place with small bricks of metal. Andara lay before them, dotted red lines marking the borders of each country. Rodrigo traced his finger along the ocean and stopped at the southern coast of the mainland.

"We've partially loaded the cargo hold with Sunfruit wine to give the appearance we are delivering goods to the continent. Her majesty thought it best in case we're stopped." Rodrigo tapped at the spot on the map. "We'll anchor a few miles off the coast to let you depart unseen."

"Are you sure?" Seth suspected Rodrigo and his men were used to smuggling things in this vessel.

"We are the Sunset People, my Prince. No one sees us come and go."

"You must have a care, Highness," Tymon warned him. "Southbay has a centuries-old border war with Valdeon. They won't hesitate to kill you. Sailing straight through until you reach Netherton would be wise."

"Is there anyone not mad at Valdeon?" Riley asked.

"After Netherton, you'll sail over the wilds of Duhnland. It's best to avoid landing there as well. The tribes don't like unwelcome visitors." Tymon pointed to a small stretch of land on the map between the Commonwealth and the Forbidden Mountain Range.

"Now comes the tricky part. The wind current will try to force your boat over this small patch of Tslavia after you clear the eastern most tip of the Forbidden Mountains. Remember to stay with a true north path. You want to sail over the neutral country of Mandovia. The Commonwealth borders them to the north."

"You see. An easy trip," Rodrigo said with a grin. "We'll reach Southbay before first light. Best to get a few hours' sleep, Highness."

He showed them to a quiet cabin not far from his own chambers and bid them a good sleep. Seth leaned against the port window watching the dark waters pass beneath them. Fate was staring back. He knew this was the right path. The Book of Ancients was hidden within the Obsidian Citadel, waiting for him to open its pages. Where to start looking? The legendary fortress was massive. He needed a plan.

Riley snored on one of the bunks hanging from the ship's wall. His squeamish stomach had been placated by one of Tymon's remedies. Poor Riley. He was a true friend, coming on this insane adventure without question. Seth couldn't let him down.

Several hours later, Rodrigo led them above decks just as the sun was beginning to touch the sky. Hovering inches above wooden floorboards, their little boat shuddered in time to the crystal engine's loud vibration. Seth pushed the hesitant Riley toward their vessel. They boarded, stowing their gear under the seats. Seth took the helm and put the crystal engine in gear. It sputtered for a moment before settling into a steady rhythm.

Tymon shook hands with Rodrigo and joined them in the boat. He sat next to Riley, who had a death grip on the side. Seth waved to Rodrigo. Taking a deep breath, he eased the ship off the deck and over the side. He'd sailed a few small boats on his island home of Marianna, but not enough to classify himself as an expert. Riley's harsh intake of breath as they dropped over the side wasn't helpful in building his confidence.

"Great gulls," Riley hissed. "Have a care, Seth!"

He yanked up on the helm. The little boat shot up into the sky with a gut-wrenching lurch. Steadying the boat's wild swaying, he gently lowered the helm until they were zipping over the dark waters toward land.

Lantern light sparkled along the lines of the port. Seth eased the boat toward the edge of the dock and let the engines slow to a low hum. Reaching with his left hand to grab the dock's railing, Seth's fingers fell under the lantern. Like a burning beacon, the Lion Ring came to life under the beam.

"I'll be recognized before I set foot on shore," Seth whispered to his companions.

Reaching inside his pack, Tymon pulled out a pair of leather gloves and handed them to Seth. The finger tips had been cut off just below the knuckles. Seth pulled on the gloves. The cloth just covered his ring. Well-worn and soft, they'd seen many hours of use by their former owner.

"Many swordsmen wear such gloves. They are allowed as army gear," Tymon told them. "You must hurry. An old comrade of mine sent word the UR Army has put out an emergency call for volunteers to help fight Valdeon's invaders. They'll be signing on new cadets at the Citadel for the next three days. Blend in with the other young men and you should be fine."

"Well, your advice isn't going to help hide Seth's identity," Riley said. "Dante told me only a Lion has those amber flecks."

Your squire speaks the truth. I will help you hide for a short time.

"Great gulls!" Riley cried. "Seth, your eyes. The amber flecks are gone."

Riley dug out a tin from his pack and held it under the lantern light. Seth leaned closer and peered into the tiny piece of round metal. Wide brown eyes stared back at him. He looked like an ordinary Valdeonian man.

"The Jalora takes care of its Lion." Tymon jumped out of the boat. "Be on your guard, Highness. Many will try to hunt you. Take care of your ranger, Squire Logan."

Then he was gone, leaving them to face their unknown future. Seth released his hold, letting the little boat drift away from the docks. He slowly brought them above the rooftops of the sleeping town. Nothing stirred beneath them. If he could keep them away from other towns and villages, they may escape Southbay without incident.

Riley tossed Seth his heavy Marianna cloak. The chilly night air was a rude awakening after the warm breezes of Carlotta. Seth sniffed at the cloth as he wrapped it about his body. It smelled of wool dye and pipe smoke. The evoked memories weren't pleasant.

He'd rid himself of the garment as soon as he could afford to buy another.

Silence fell over the little boat as they flew through the dark. Seth focused on staying true north, while Riley kept watch for the lights of large airships. According to Rodrigo's map, they were skirting the main air route used for journeys south to north.

Southbay passed beneath them through the early morning hours into afternoon. Aching from the lack of physical movement, Seth was ready for a stretch of his legs when they saw a large stretch of Netherton meadow. It was covered with a thin layer of snow. Winter had found them.

He sailed toward the edge of a grove of thick trees and landed. They crawled out of the boat, sinking into the white fluff. Pulling their boat into the trees, they found a dry spot out of the snow. Riley fished a cold meal from his pack and handed a portion to Seth. Dried fish and fruit wasn't the fare they were used to dining upon in Aunt Charlotte's cottage, but the meal filled his stomach.

"A few hours' sleep will be welcome before we press on," Riley said with a yawn.

He put his bedroll on the dry ground. Seth grinned as his friend fell quickly to sleep. He had a good idea there. Seth laid back against a tree trunk and closed his eyes. Netherton. As a child, he'd dreamed of visiting a country so distant from his little island home. Racing toward a massive citadel in the middle of Andara, hunted by killers, wasn't how he'd imagined the trip.

Wet droplets spattered his face. Seth sat up, scanning the gray clouds hanging over the grove. Western wind pushed at the treetops above him. Thunder rumbled in the distance as little flashes of lightening flickered across the sky. The storm was growing stronger.

He shook Riley awake. "We've got a problem."

"Aye. We can't take off during a thunderstorm in this old wreck. It's going to delay our arrival in Lea."

Then another unpleasant sound crossed the snow plain from the southeast. Horses charged through the countryside toward the grove. Metal slapped against leather marking the riders as well armed. Seth slipped through the trunks and knelt in the thick growth at the tree line. A patrol of heavily armed men surged over a distant hill. They were heading at a full charge toward the grove.

"We have to get in the air right now." Seth crashed through the trees and unfastened the mooring lines of their boat.

Riley threw their gear aboard and helped him push the boat out into the open. They jumped inside and scrambled to take their seats. Seth forced the ancient engine into gear and took a sharp angle upward. Rain pattered harder against the hull as they ascended.

Shouts reached them from the ground. Riley yelled an old Islic curse as an arrow narrowly missed his head. Its tip penetrated the mast with a loud thump. Seth prodded the engine faster toward the north. He'd have to outrun them. Shooting at them in a frenzy of arrows, the men gave chase on the snowy ground until the little boat was out of range.

"By the green, green fields!" Riley yanked the arrow from the mast and tossed it over the side. "They were trying awfully hard to bring us down. Surely it can't be a crime to rest under a grove of trees in the middle of nowhere."

"I believe they were searching for someone. We'd better forget any more rest breaks upon the ground until we reach the Commonwealth."

The weather grew worse the farther north they flew. Seth gripped the helm tightly as the wind fought to rip it out of his hands. Rain struck at their bodies, soaking their clothes. Hours passed under the wet skies. Thick trees and wild country stretched beneath them in a blur of green and gray. Duhnland. They were getting closer. He pulled his soaked hood farther down over his face. Despite his concerns, he was seriously considering a stop in Mandovia to dry their things and wait out the storm.

"Look! The Forbidden Mountain Range." Riley pointed at tall peaks and jagged rock to their left. "Is it supposed to be so close?"

"No." Seth slammed a fist upon the seat beside him. "Somehow I've strayed off the true north course. We have to go farther east before we reach the stretch of Tslavia Tymon warned us against."

Thunderous booms struck close to their hull. Gun powder hung in clouds about them. Someone was firing cannons at them from the ground. More shrill whistles cut through the air. A cannon ball struck the base of the crystal engine, narrowly missing Seth. He dove forward, grasping for one of the wooden seats attached to the hull. Their ship plummeted to the ground in a death spiral.

"We need to jump!" Seth screamed at Riley. "Get ready."

The boat skipped across the wet grass like a stone upon the water. They grabbed their gear and rolled over the side just before the boat smashed into a boulder. Seth rolled on the ground away from the crash as fire engulfed the battered boat.

Armed men - thirty in all - walked through the smoke and rain to surround them. Dark green sashes crossed their chests, marking the men as militia. Seth and Riley stood slowly, lifting their hands over their heads.

Fingers itching to take up his sword, Seth took measure of their captors. A handful of experienced soldiers waited patiently among their numbers. The rest of the men fidgeted anxiously. Makeshift weapons and dull blades wagged at Seth. He knew them for what they were - volunteers. It was their obvious excitement that made them much more dangerous than their experienced comrades.

A thin man dressed in a uniform pushed into the circle. Shiny buttons dotted the front of his tunic. He puffed out his chest, making certain all eyes saw the badge upon his breast pocket. *Victorsburg Province Constabulary* was etched in bold letters within the metal. The man was a local constable.

"Another spy. Well done. And a Valdeonian to boot," he said in Tslavic. "Chief Constable Victors will be pleased."

The constable took a few steps toward Seth, close enough to reveal his loathing and far enough away to avoid Seth's weapon. Hatred and fear swirled about his body in chaotic pulses of cowardice. They'd have to step easy. One wrong move and he'd order his men to kill them on the spot.

"You are foolish to fly over Tslavian skies." He spat at Seth's feet. "What can one expect from a Valdeonian pig? Hand over your weapons. You're coming with us."

"He says to take off our swords and come quietly," Seth told Riley. "I suggest we do as he asks. This is Tslavia, not Mandovia."

"Why are we being arrested?" Riley asked in Islic.

"They think we're spies. I'm Valdeonian, remember?"

"But, you're also Tslavian."

"Hatred only sees what it wants to see, Riley."

Bound and stripped of their belongings, Seth and Riley marched south in the center of the militia. Jeers and curses in the harsh tones of Tslavic hate peppered Seth as he walked. Each passing muddy mile wore on his temper. Fighting his fury, he kept a tenuous hold upon the power pushing at his control. He'd learned the cost of striking at an opponent when anger dominated his emotions. The Realm of Dreams and Mist were full of such painful lessons.

Hints of civilization began to appear along their path. Sign posts. Abandoned wheel spokes. Goats roaming the fields along the road. It would've been a peaceful scene reminiscent of Marianna had it not been for the armed men about them.

A stone wall ran lazily across the fields before them. The thatch roofs of a small border town peeked over its top. More spits and cursing greeted them as they walked along the streets. Seth struggled to ignore the jabs as the Lion's Roar grumbled in his throat. Blind hatred and ignorance governed here. Even the children threw stones, though their innocent hearts couldn't understand such ugliness. He must contain the raw power fighting to break free, for their sakes.

Their taunting suddenly stopped when the door to the police station banged open. The townsfolk scattered, leaving the militia to face the man who filled the opening. Chief Constable Victors was a bald man with a great mustache and soldier's gait. Predator eyes locked onto Seth, examining him as if he were a commodity at market.

"If you boys are smart, you won't give the chief any lip. He and his family own the whole province. They are the law here." The constable held up a warning finger to Seth, then turned to greet his master. "We've had a good hunt today, Chief."

The chief constable walked past him and came to stand before Seth. "So, it is true. A Valdeonian spy has come among us."

"Here now. We are no spies!"

A swift punch in Riley's kidney sent him to his knees. Seth reached down with bound hands and helped him up again. His squire's face darkened with anger. Seth squeezed his arm in warning. These men looked the type to kill rather than be bothered by boarding their prisoners.

"Why are you here, Valdeonian dog?"

"My home is the Isle of Carlotta. We were headed for the Commonwealth when your men shot our airboat down. We meant no harm."

The constable hurried to Chief Victors' side and held up the portrait of the Tslavic royal family. "I found it in his pack."

"And this?" Chief Victors asked. "What would a foreigner need with an old portrait of the royal family? It is of no value, unless you are a Valdeonian spy."

"I told you, we're from Carlotta."

"Your sword tells me otherwise." He snatched Seth's sword from the constable's hand, running lustful fingers along the blade. "No matter, I've sent word to an outpost on the Commonwealth border less than half a day's ride from here. Doubtless the Jalora rangers can make you tell the truth. Consider yourselves lucky Andara is at war with invaders from foreign shores. The Jalora Legion has commanded all spies and travelers be questioned by rangers. It is our practice to shoot Valdeonians on sight." He gently put the sword back in its sheath. "I think I will keep this fine weapon as compensation."

"My father gave me my sword, Constable." Seth warned. "Make no mistake. I will have it back."

"You're welcome to try. Take them to a cell."

Chief Victors went inside the station taking Seth's sword with him. Hands grabbed them as soon as the chief was out of site. The militia shoved Seth and Riley down a filthy cell-lined walk. Men from several different countries leaned against the bars, watching as they passed. Many looked as if they'd been severely beaten.

"You get your own cell, Valdeonian." The constable nodded and his men cut their bonds before shoving them inside. "Rest well while you can. I'm certain the rangers will have their own brand of fun for you."

The group of men walked away, throwing final insults into the cell. Their absence was a welcome relief to his aching head. Holding in the Lion's power had taken every ounce of concentration he possessed.

"Constable McTavish would never allow his station to be this filthy." Riley spat on the dirty cell floor. "I don't think I like Tslavia on the whole, Seth. I hope the rangers take us out of here."

He joined Riley on the cot and ran his hands through his hair. Rangers. They would expose him before he could find more information out about his father. Escape was their only option now. He looked around the cells at the other victims of Chief Victors' hospitality. Freedom might not be as easily taken as he'd hoped.

Chapter Thirty-Three

SETH LEANED against the back wall of their cell as far away from the bars as he could get. The stench of unwashed bodies was overpowering. Resting his head against the stone, he concentrated on soothing his temper. It wasn't easy. He was growing more restless with each passing hour. The rangers would be coming soon. Their chance for escape was dwindling. What else could go wrong? Another afternoon lost inside their cage. Tomorrow was the last day the UR was accepting cadets. They had to get out of Tslavia and make it to the Commonwealth before morning.

Shouts and cries for food thundered from the row of cells around them. Their pleas were met with a loud bang of wood on metal. The miserable prisoners quieted down. Sinking back into their own thoughts, the men moved away from the bars.

A guard came to stand before their cell door balancing two trays in his hands. Lumpy mush oozed across the surface. Deceit. Humor. Maliciousness. They filled the colors resting stagnant around the guard's body.

"Feeding spies good food," he grumbled in the common tongue. "Old Dragon must be getting soft-hearted."

He slammed the first tray on the ground outside their bars and kicked it toward them. Tin scraped against rock, spilling food on the floor. Riley sat up with a curse. Seth put a restraining hand on his shoulder. These Tslavians were looking for any excuse to start a fight.

"I think we'll decline the food," Seth said, pushing the tray back through the bars with his foot. "My friend and I don't like the taste of spittle."

Anger. Disappointment. Confusion. They swirled around the guard in waves. He snatched up the tray and headed back down the long rows of cells. Low grumbles and shuffling followed in his wake as the other suspected spies watched him pass.

"Maybe it's best if we are found by the Legion, Seth. They could keep us safe. This is a different world than we've known."

Seth hadn't wanted to believe Pavel Sandor's warning about the rangers and their plans to use him. The villain was a liar and a murderer. He ran a hand through muddy curls. His mother's letter had confirmed the assassin's words. She'd kept many secrets from her son, but he understood her reasons.

"I can't ignore my mother's fear. I trust Wolf, but even he advised me to remain hidden."

Riley did have a good point. They were stuck in Tslavia, surrounded by people who'd rather kill him than listen to reason. The rangers could help them out of their current predicament, but now wasn't the time to turn himself over completely to the Legion's care. Clues may be waiting for them in the Citadel only a lowly soldier could discover. He was determined to continue to hide his identity until then.

Stirring inside the other cell announced trouble was headed in their direction. The prisoners moved away from the bars to huddle together. A frightened hush gripped the jail as the Chief Constable marched along the cells. Several of his men followed behind him. Wicked grins were painted on each face. Seth turned to meet them with Riley standing at his side.

Chief Victors had stripped to the waist. The skin along his torso was checkered with battle scars. In his beefy hand, he held a heavy club with a large knot. It was stained with the blood of many a suspected Valdeonian spy.

"I hear you don't like our food. I should think Valdeonian pigs were used to slop." He sneered as his men laughed. "Maybe we should take you outside. We'll see if you find the hog slop more appetizing. I brought my new pig pokers with me."

He shifted his weapons belt into the light. Seth's sword hung on his right hip and Riley's hung on his left. Fury surged deep within Seth's heart as he looked upon his father's gift swinging irreverently from the villain's belt.

"You've no right to my sword." Seth's rage twisted about his words. "I will have it back."

"Come try and take it, boy."

A fair fight wasn't their plan. It was going to be two unarmed men against a mob. Seth could fight them off with his new skills, but he was already struggling to keep his power in check. One lapse and he'd bring down the entire jail on the men trapped inside the other cells.

"Get out."

The single command stopped their attackers in place outside the cell. The mob parted, scrambling out of the way of the young man standing quietly behind them. Dressed entirely in ash, the only sign of color on his uniform was the golden Jalora Legion emblem. Their ranger interrogator had arrived.

Standing with his hands clasped behind his back, the young man had an air of complete command. Auburn hair fell in short strands against his head. The ranger's neatly trimmed mustache curved upward atop a jovial smile. He stared through the bars, gazing unabashedly into Seth's eyes. Soft probing touched at his mind. Seth easily blocked it. The ranger tilted his head slightly blinking his calm green eyes in surprise.

"We'll need four fresh horses and a little privacy. And constable, you will give their swords and supplies to my squire. I trust nothing is missing."

Chief Victors gritted his teeth. He put the key to their cell into the ranger's outstretched hand with great care. Then he stormed out of the cell area to do as he was told. The ranger gave a small sigh when the constable and his men had at last left the jailhouse.

"I am called, Dragonfly."

He held out his left hand and the Heart of the Warrior Ring toward Seth. The insect fluttered inside the dark green stone. Wolf's crystal had been blue. Seth's was white. The colors were significant somehow.

"I know you are no spy, Hopeful. Why hide when you could have declared your identity and been spared their abuse?"

Seth put his right hand quickly over the Lion Ring hidden under the half glove. "My reasons are my own, Ranger."

Dragonfly unlocked the door and held it open for them. "Not anymore. You are a member of the Legion now. Come, we travel to the Obsidian Citadel in Lea."

Seth hesitated in the cell. If they stayed in the custody of Chief Victors, he had little chance for a fair trial. The ranger would see them safely out of Tslavia, but could they escape his custody once reaching the Commonwealth?

Dragonfly's tolerant smile disappeared. "I wasn't making a request."

Seth nodded to Riley and they joined their new captor outside the bars. The ranger strolled casually along the line of cells. He seemed completely unconcerned his two prisoners stayed several feet behind him.

"Dragonfly? Doesn't sound too frightening," Riley whispered in Islic.

Then the ranger suddenly stopped before one of the cells. He pulled his sword, thrust it through the bars and sheathed it again almost too quickly for Seth's eyes to see. One of the men inside fell lifelessly to the floor.

"I take it back. He's plenty frightening." Riley stepped away, staring at the ranger with wide eyes.

"Tensions are high after Valdeon's fall, Hopeful. Many see spies behind every bush. It's led to killings. We've found a handful of traitors who've crossed the border into Andara. Their purpose is not clear, but we believe they search for something or someone. Shall we?"

Dragonfly held the jailhouse door open. The constable and his men were gathered along the building. Seth tensed under their hateful glares. Out numbering the ranger and his prisoners, the men could easily take their revenge. They remained still. Fear. Respect. Trust. Their faith in the ranger seemed unshakeable.

A young man with auburn curls waited beside the horses. Dragonfly's squire. A brass insect clung to the collar fastened close about his neck. His black uniform was neat, but didn't share the pristine sharpness of his ranger's visage.

Dragonfly's squire handed their packs back to them with a nervous nod. He smiled shyly when Seth took the neck of his guitar. One of the strings had broken, but the instrument appeared otherwise undamaged.

"Our money's all here," Riley said, stuffing the purse back inside his pack. "Plus a few credits extra. We'll consider it payment for the inconvenience."

The young squire choked back a laugh when his ranger frowned at the joke. He handed Riley the reins of one of the horses and took up position by his own mount.

"I've dispensed justice on the spy you seek, Constable." Dragonfly gave him a pointed glare. "Let the rest free and see them on their way."

The ranger motioned Seth and Riley to their horses. His squire jumped up on the mount carrying their weapons. He may have adopted a casual attitude, but Dragonfly was no fool. He wasn't taking any chances. They mounted and waited for the ranger to lead them forward.

"Thank you for your hospitality, Chief Victors," Seth told the seething man. "I'm certain you'll find someone else's sword to steal."

The townsfolk lined the row as they headed east. Hate filled their eyes when they gazed upon Seth, but their reaction to the ranger was completely different. Respect. Trust. Comfort. He gave them hope in a time of fear.

Keeping to a steady pace, they broke free of the town's stone fence and headed into the countryside. Seth's tension began to ease as they put Victorsburg Province in the distance. Plunging into a beautiful wilderness of tall grass and tall trees, peace came back to him.

Dragonfly's squire prodded along, edging unconsciously closer to Seth. Their weapons were tantalizingly close. It was tempting to try and take them, but the ranger would give chase. He was powerful and clearly intelligent. It wouldn't be easy escaping him.

The ranger, perhaps sensing Seth's intent, maneuvered his horse between his squire and his prisoners. The soft probing touch came again on Seth's mind. He turned to the ranger and gave him a sour frown.

"My apologies, Hopeful. You are a mystery on an otherwise dull duty," Dragonfly said jovially. "If you don't feel comfortable sharing your secrets with me, I'm sure there are other rangers you will trust."

A well-worn row crossed their path. *The Commonwealth* was painted in large black letters across a signpost shaped like an arrow. The ranger steered his horse to the north. Hope came alive once more. He was taking them in the right direction.

The row gradually widened until all four travelers rode in a single line. Dragonfly remained close to Seth. Their two squires rode side by side, striking up a friendly conversation. The young squire shared Riley's impatient nature for silence.

"The name's Riley." He extended his hand to the squire.

"Donny." The Dragonfly's young squire grinned. "Have you been to the Obsidian Citadel?" He smiled and warmed to the subject when Riley shook his head. "The Legion is headquartered inside the very center of the mountain. It's amazing. You'll see plenty of it as your ranger trains."

"How many rangers are in the Legion?" Riley asked.

"The Jalora has graced Andara with five hundred Heart of the Warrior Rings, Squire." Dragonfly turned to Seth. "Which one do you hide, I wonder?"

The ranger's eyes were focused upon the road ahead, but his mind was elsewhere. Seth cast a tentative glance over at Dragonfly, not daring to probe with his power. The youthful face was wrinkled in thought. If they stayed with the ranger much longer, he may guess their identity.

"Doesn't Legion mean 'many'?" Riley asked Donny. "Five hundred rangers seem like a handful compared to an army."

Dragonfly pulled up sharply on the reins. He held up an impatient hand to silence their conversation. The Jalora's power wrapped about him, its presence shimmering a brilliant white. Dragonfly extended the power out into the trees. White fingers of light passed through bush and bough as it searched.

Then Seth saw it. Standing in the path before them was a shroud-covered figure. Gray hands pulled off its hood. Though its face was still fleshy with skin intact, the dark eyes and jagged double rows of teeth marked it as a Dirge.

"You dare block our path, creature of evil?" Dragonfly ran anxious fingers over the hilt of his sword.

"I would have what you protect, Jalora plaything."

Dragonfly slid off his horse. He handed the reins to Donny and then began his slow walk to meet the Dirge. Wolf killed several of the creatures to protect Seth. He'd known the Dirge for what they were and he'd known how to kill them. This ranger was walking into a battle with an unfamiliar enemy.

"Have a care, Dragonfly," Seth called. "This creature is powerful. Its kind has struck down many men."

The Dirge opened its maw and started to sing. Harsh notes from its song of death struck the ranger. He took a step backward away from the creature. The white light of the Jalora flickered about his body momentarily then grew strong again. Dragonfly took the First Stance, waiting for the creature to strike first.

"What in all the evils of the world is it?" Donny cried.

"They are flesh eaters called the 'Dirge'." Seth leaned closer to the squire. "Please, you must give me my sword. Your ranger can't fight it alone."

Donny fidgeted nervously with the reins. "I can't. Ronny, I mean Dragonfly, won't like it."

Then the Dirge flew at Dragonfly, thrusting its blade toward the ranger's chest. Dragonfly twisted away and swept his blade upward, knocking the creature off balance. The Dirge feigned a tumble. Striking like a grass snake, it swung at the ranger's ankle. Dragonfly caught the strike with his blade and used the momentum to somersault into the air. He kicked hard at the creature's head. The shroud fell onto the path in a pile of foul smelling fabric.

"I'll admit your ranger's good," Riley said to Donny. "Seth's faster."

"It isn't over yet." Seth pointed to the shroud as it heaved up and down.

Hissing laughter struck their ears. The Dirge floated a few feet above the row. Its body moved within the shroud until it came to an upright stance before the ranger. The creature laughed harder at his surprise.

"Come now, Ranger. I have no quarrels with you. Step aside and be rewarded with your life."

"How dare you suggest I betray my duty and my honor. You'll never have him while I stand."

"So be it."

A lightening thrust stuck deep into the ranger's abdomen. The creature's fevered song rose as Dragonfly fell to one knee. It was impossibly fast. Perhaps too fast even for the Legion to defeat, with the Jalora's power diminished.

"Ronny!" Dragonfly's squire leapt from his horse and caught the ranger up in his arms.

"You've killed my brother."

Donny let a bloodied hand fall to the hilt of his sword. Hate. Terror. Revenge. They circled the squire's body in dark colors. Though it meant his own death, he would protect his ranger. Dragonfly struggled to his feet. He pushed his brother gently to the side and raised his sword toward the Dirge.

"They'll be killed," Seth said, looking at the unattended saddle and their weapons. "I can't let the Dirge strike them down. Not for my sake."

"You can't fight it, Seth. We've seen what the creature can do."

Then Donny's sword rang as he pulled it from his sheath. Dragonfly had left himself open long enough for the Dirge to strike. It plunged its sword into the wounded ranger's left shoulder. Dragonfly sank to his knees. Blood soaked through the cloak at his back. The Dirge slapped Donny's sword away and brought down a vicious fist to his shoulder. He crumbled onto the ground beside his brother.

"Young fools! Your death is meaningless. I will have him anyway." The Dirge circled the injured ranger and lifted its sword to deliver a death blow.

Seth flew at the squire's horse and pulled his sword free. Dancing upon the ribbons of air, he swept between the creature and its prey. His blade smacked upward against the ascending sword, hurling it out of the Dirge's hand.

"Go, creature of evil," Seth said in Valic. "Leave now and we will spare your life."

"Control your temper, half-breed." The Dirge opened its putrid mouth in a nauseating laugh. "You wouldn't want me to develop indigestion. Sour mood. Sour taste."

"Your time upon the Erthe has come to an end."

Ancient power flowed from the heavens as Seth called the death mask to him. Eternal eyes looked upon the creature who'd given up its humanity for power and avarice. Many of the wicked mortals of Valdeon had succumbed to such allures since the Jackal came to their lands.

The Dirge hissed and gnashed its teeth as it backed away from Seth. Pulling the shrouded hood over its head, the creature dove for its sword. It crouched like a wounded animal, swaying in the grass.

"Your magician's tricks won't help you," it said with a menacing hiss. "I will have what you hide."

Then its black hood turned toward the east. Standing at its full height, the creature clutched the shroud against its skeletal body. It swore a Valic curse and then flew for the safety of the tree line.

"I didn't understand what you were saying, but I know you saved our lives." Dragonfly said from the ground. "I owe you a life debt."

"You owe me nothing, Ranger. It was ready to fight us all. Something frightened it."

"I'd like to keep whatever it was close," Riley said, helping Donny up. "We've had enough trouble with those monsters. Here now, Donny. Can you see to your ranger? Never mind. I'll have a look. You've had your head rattled a good one."

"Thank you, Riley." Donny rubbed at his shoulder.

"It sought to disable me," Dragonfly said, trying to sit up. "It could have just as easily struck three inches to the center and taken my life. The question is, why?"

"Aye, you'll live, but not if you keep squirming around." Riley pushed on Dragonfly's good shoulder to keep him still on the ground.

His fingers worked quickly, stitching up the wounds and putting on healing ointments. Donny watched him as he worked. Respect was in his eyes. Seth gently probed the young man. Donny was Dragonfly's second squire and hadn't been long in the job. It was very clear from his memories, young Donny idealized his brother.

"Have patience with your progress, Squire," Seth said, grinning with pride. "Riley was trained by the best in difficult circumstances. It isn't fair to measure yourself against his skill."

"And who trained you, Hopeful?" Dragonfly asked.

"My name is Seth and this is Riley. Mine is a long story," Seth told him. "The creature and others like it give me reason to hide. We'll take you to the nearest village or outpost for medical treatment, but then I must go back into hiding. You understand why we cannot go to the Obsidian Citadel with you now?"

"It's not safe for you to be on your own, Hopeful. The Legion can protect you." Dragonfly pleaded when Seth shook his head. "You're new to these shores and don't know the dangers. I admit you are powerful. Forming the death mask and blocking the probe of a full ranger at your level is rare, but you cannot stand alone!"

Thundering hooves rumbled on the row from the east. Gray cloaks waved on the wind as the riders came toward them at a full gallop. Enormous power pulsed in the air about them. Rangers.

"Now we know why the Dirge ran." Riley thrust his things hurriedly back into his pack.

Unfastening their weapons from the saddle, Seth joined Riley in the wet grass lining the row. They had seconds before the rangers were within probing distance. The thick trees engulfed them as they forced their bodies between the trunks. Seth lifted his block around himself and Riley as they crept silently in the trees. Dragonfly's frantic calls faded among the evergreen boughs.

Eleven rangers rode in close ranks. Stopping in perfect formation, the rangers remained at attention as their leader sprang from his horse. Esteban the Hawk knelt beside Dragonfly. His gestures were angry and impatient. He barked an order to his men. Two rangers dismounted. They helped Dragonfly up onto a horse, mounted their own beasts and led him away with Donny following. The rest of the rangers dismounted. They split up into pairs and began walking toward the trees in multiple directions.

"Time to leave," Seth whispered.

Tree sap and needles stuck to their bodies as they navigated the thick forest. The rangers weren't faring any better in the terrain. He heard branches snapping well behind them. The noise grew more distant as they journeyed toward the south. Satisfied the rangers had fallen far behind, he headed northeast toward the Commonwealth.

Seth!

His body halted suddenly, not responding to his frantic need to keep moving. Cold and commanding, his uncle's unbending resolve was threatening to overpower him.

"No." He put his hands over his ears.

"Seth! Let's go!" Riley pulled at his arm.

It was no use. He couldn't move. His uncle's hold was too strong. Then a firm presence pushed hard upon on his mind. Stunned, Seth fell forward onto the prickly dried needles. The voice fell away. Everything became still.

Chapter Thirty-Four

RILEY SAT crossed-legged on his bedroll watching the morning sun touch the tips of the frost-covered evergreens. Beautiful though the forest was, traveling beneath the heavy green blanket made him long for open skies again. He was beginning to wonder if they'd ever find their way out of the thick forests of the Commonwealth border lands. Well, they'd better find the road to Lea soon, or miss their chance to join the UR Army.

Seth, bundled in his blanket, slept soundly. Riley let him rest. He wasn't convinced Seth had fully recovered from his strange fainting spell yesterday. Riley had managed to drag him into a clump of roots upended by an old fallen tree. Their new hunters, by some miracle, gave up their search and rode to the south. His ranger had been sullen and quiet since. Torturing himself with guilt no doubt for leaving Dragonfly in such a state.

Riley scratched at the fuzz spreading across his chin. He didn't understand Seth's insistence on avoiding all rangers at any cost. He'd trusted Wolf well enough after all. Why not the ranger who'd been willing to lay down his life for them? Well, it didn't make sense to Riley. How were they to find this dusty old book if they hadn't any idea where to look? Seth wasn't willing to ask for any help in finding it either. It'd taken Riley a good hour of constant pestering to persuade him to discuss his quest at all.

He was a squire and a squire's duty was to trust his ranger's word. Despite Tymon's nasty comments about his skills and manners, Riley fully intended to stay true to his duty. Dante hadn't warned him how difficult it would be to hold onto his trust. He wasn't a complete fool. They were lost in this forest country and his ranger wasn't willing to admit it.

Sounds, clinking and clanging, broke through the thick branches to his far left. Riley crept along the forest floor and pushed through the boughs. A steady stream of people walked beside wagons and livestock as they made their way along a well-traveled road toward the north.

"You've found the merchant road to Lea," Seth said close beside him.

"Great gulls! You made me jump out of my skin."

"Sorry." Seth bumped his shoulder. "Come on. Let's pack up quickly. We can slip in among their numbers."

Riley fastened the straps of the pack around his bedroll. Seth waited for him at the edge of camp, packed and ready to travel. They crept through the evergreens and slid down into the ditch by the side of the row. Merchants from the many countries of Andara paraded by them in rainbows of colorful garb. Men, women, and a few children kept peaceful company as they shared the journey. Riley well knew the value of getting along with strangers when you were in business.

He'd seen his dad win over the most stubborn of wool traders.

"Quick," Seth said. "We can sneak in unnoticed between those two wagons."

Scrambling up the incline, they darted in between two clattering wagons full of goods. Pots and metal implements rattled and swung from wooden racks set up inside the bed. Shiny and new, they sparkled brighter than any old pot his mum had in her kitchen.

Hours passed as they walked among the other travelers headed toward Lea. The strangeness of their tongue washed over him. For the first time in his life, Riley understood how small his island home of Marianna was within this strange new world. Seth, in comparison, seemed perfectly at ease among their traveling companions. He had no troubles sharing in easy conversation.

Excited cries and clapping swept through the crowd ahead of them. He rushed to follow Seth, who was jogging up the hill to join the merrymakers. A great city stood at the base of the hill, stretching as far as the eye could see.

"It must be bigger than the entire island of Marianna!"

Seth gave him an excited grin.

The roar of a massive engine rumbled over their heads. Riley ducked down on the road with a hand over his head. A massive ship flying a bright blue flag made its way toward the city. Another one with a green flag followed it.

"Great gulls!" Riley slapped the dust off his trousers. "I've never seen vessels like those."

"Merchant ships headed for the port. Is this your first visit to Lea, young ones?"

A man with thick dark hair stood behind them, staring up at the ships as the glow of their engines lit up the sky. He was dressed in bright purple and green overalls. Red tassels dangled from his shiny black boots. Calloused hands loosely held the reins of his donkey. Riley peered over the beast's rump. Expensive bolts of brightly dyed fabric filled the small cart it pulled.

"I've journeyed from my home in Braumburg to Lea every spring since I was a boy," he told them. "It amazes me each time. Ah, but this is a special trip. I bring supplies for the army. You've come to join the other young men headed for the Obsidian Citadel?"

"Aye," Riley said. "How did you know?"

"You have the look about you." The man laughed and waved to their left.

Several other young men marched down the road. Each was armed with a sword and other weapons. All of them had an air of youthful restlessness. Laughing and talking amongst themselves, they behaved as if they were headed to a fair rather than war.

"Are there always so many?" Seth asked.

The merchant shook his head. "Fear grips the old, while impatience festers in the young. Many believe Valdeon's invasion heralds the fall of the Jalora Legion. Though their parents would have these young men stay and protect their own lands, they answer the Legion's call to arms."

"They're headed in our direction," Riley said. "Saves us some effort in finding it."

"The Obsidian Citadel would be difficult to miss," the merchant told him. "You can see it just there."

Standing in the very center of the city, the Obsidian Citadel blocked the sun. Black towers of rock and steel burst into the sky, dwarfing the structures below. Buildings crawled in its shadows, circling the citadel's entire base.

"The Obsidian Citadel." Seth held his hand up to block the sun. "I mistook it for a mountain."

"So it once was, a hundred years ago. Legend says the last Jalora Master, Gustavo the Lion Claw, wanted his Legion housed at the very center of Andara as a sign of unity for all the nations. It is said he carved the citadel at midnight under a full moon."

The Lion Claw? Riley cast a quick glance at Seth's left hand where the Lion Ring was hidden under the half glove. Had this Jalora Master worn the very same Lion Ring once? Seth's face remained calm, emotionless as the travelers continued their journey toward Lea and its mountain fortress. How much did he know about his ranger ring after the Jalora's visits on Carlotta?

Riley gripped the straps of his pack. Growing up, he could ask his boyhood friend anything and get a genuine answer. Things were different now. Seth wasn't on his own anymore. The presence living inside of him might not like questions.

Crossing over the road like a stone halo, an arch of ancient rock stood alone. It appeared to be the last remnant of a long-forgotten wall standing guard at the entrance of the city. Riley stared up at its smooth surface as it defied gravity. His boots hit stone. Stumbling through the entrance, he cast his eyes downward. Bits of tile formed pictures of horses and ships within the city's main thoroughfare.

"We're falling behind," Seth said, pulling at his arm.

Pushing through thick bands of merchants and their many customers, they hurried to keep up with the other young men journeying to the citadel. The strong and seemingly endless stream of people pulled at their bodies.

"This city makes no sense," Riley shouted above the noise. "Why are we headed south when we need to get to the middle of the city?"

"The roads in Lea are circular. The city appears to be one large market place designed to tempt the money out of your pockets." Seth pointed to a large square lined with booths.

Music and the familiar sounds of commerce roared above the crowd's excited chatter. He was right. Goods of every type and size beckoned. Trinkets of gold and precious jewels glittered from one stand while enticing meat hung from another.

"The others are turning onto a side row. It must be the way to the citadel's entrance."

He stayed close to Seth's back as they pushed through the crowd and onto the row. Large warehouses replaced the bustling activity of commerce. Signs of war filled their open doors. Riley saw it in the faces of the somber men handling bundles of unshapen iron, cannon balls, and muskets. His chest tightened at the reality of what they were about to do. War was coming. Nothing would stop it now.

A chilling shadow fell upon their path. Riley shivered at its touch. They'd arrived at last. The

Obsidian Citadel's enormous rock body loomed over the row before them, dwarfing the long line of young men waiting to join the UR Army. Large panels of wood and steel guarded the citadel's entrance. Great gulls. Three woolie wool wagons could pass through side-by-side.

"I don't understand." Seth stopped in his tracks. "The Jalora said to look behind the Obsidian Gates. These are just ordinary wood."

Riley's stomach sank. Seth had seemed so certain. They'd risked life and limb to follow his guess. Now his ranger seemed more lost than he had in a great while.

"Do you think these black gates it spoke of are somewhere else?"

"I was so sure they'd be here." Seth ran tense fingers through his curly hair. "What a fool I was to think it would be easy. Just find the gates and the book would be waiting on a shelf in plain view."

"You there! Line's moving," a young man called behind them. "Are you two joining up or not?"

Aye. It was a good question. Riley wasn't convinced their plan to join the UR Army would work. Somewhere in the citadel's great stone belly was Legion Headquarters. One slip up and they'd be found by the rangers. Not such a bad thing if anyone had bothered to ask him.

"Remember," Seth whispered, "we are two men from Carlotta. Nothing more."

Riley gave him an impatient glare. No one needed to explain the dangers. He knew well enough.

"Line forms here, Gents!" a commanding voice boomed from the front of the crowd. "Cadets line up here! Quiet in the ranks!"

A soldier dressed in a drab green and black uniform marched down the line of young men toward them. Waving his arms in impatient gestures, he herded the young men into a straight line. Great gulls. Now he knew how the woolies felt on shearing day.

Two young men, twins Riley guessed, pushed into the line before them. Their fur-lined clothing and heavy boots stood out from the normal Andarian garb. Hatchets and daggers hung from leather straps crisscrossing their torsos. They looked dangerous. Riley wasn't the only one to think so. Many of the young men cast inquisitive glances in their direction, but avoided eye contact. A wise approach considering their rough appearance.

Then Seth tapped one of them on the shoulder. Riley cringed and sighed. Great gulls. He was always over friendly with strangers and would never change no matter the dangers. Seth, to his surprise, began speaking in their tongue. The two young men were equally astounded and quickly warmed up to Seth.

"And this is my friend, Riley Logan. He's also from Carlotta." Seth switched to the common tongue. "These are the Claybank brothers, Amery and Aubrey, from North Pointe in the Outpost Territories."

"Pleased to know you," Riley said, not certain whether he meant it or not.

"We are pleased to know you too," Amery said carefully. "I learn common tongue well."

"Step up, Ladies! I'd like to see my bed sometime this week."

Another soldier sat before a thick ledger, quill in hand. Large ink spots covered the weathered table bearing its weight. He banged on its surface with a rough fist. A disgruntled sneer stretched across his face when he took in the Territorysmen.

"You heard the sergeant," their uniformed keeper bellowed. "Step up."

"Do you speak the common tongue?" The sergeant spoke slowly like the gawking idiot he was pretending to be. "Tell me your names?"

Amery put a restraining hand upon his red-faced brother's shoulder. "Claybank."

"Claybank?" The sergeant snorted and slapped his beefy hands upon the ledger. "What kind of a name is Claybank?"

Riley groaned as Seth stepped forward. Though the amber was hidden within his eyes, the fire of his temper was burning like a beacon. He grabbed at Seth's arm, but his ranger shrugged off the grip. Weren't they supposed to be hiding among the crowd? What in the green, green fields could Seth possibly be thinking?

"Their names are Amery and Aubrey Claybank from North Pointe in the Outpost Territories. They've come to help defend their homes."

The sergeant raised his shaggy eyebrows. "Well, well. We have a defender of the people in our midst. You understand these barbarians?"

"I do, and they are no more barbarian than you or I."

"Indeed? And are they citizens of the United Realms? I thought not. It's against UR Army rules to allow non-citizens in our ranks. They could be spies."

Amery tapped Riley on the arm. "What did the fat glob of guts say? He speaks too fast."

Warm brown eyes, open and honest, returned his gaze. Braids of thick dark hair fell in groups down his shoulders. Neither brother seemed to mind the reactions to their odd appearance. Amery certainly had the confidence of a man who knew how to take care of himself. Riley smiled, liking him despite his misgivings.

"He said you're not from a UR country."

"I told you Amery, they would not want to take us!" Aubrey turned to Seth. "But, they must. We have come to fight for our colony like men, not to hide behind soldiers from other lands."

Seth pointed to the arsenal of weapons hanging across his body. "Perhaps if you show him your fighting skills."

Amery and Aubrey smiled in unison. They stepped around the table and headed for the black walls of the fortress. Amery grabbed an apple from one of the soldiers' lunch pails. He leaned against the wall, ready to throw. Aubrey pulled two hatchets from his leather strap. He nodded. Amery tossed the apple into the air. Slicing through the distance, Aubrey's hatchet split the apple. In another lightening moment, he threw again. The fruit split into quarters. Pushing away from the wall, Amery leapt to catch the hatchets before they struck rock.

"I'd say they've earned the right to fight for their homeland, wouldn't you?" Riley said.

The crowd of cadets cheered their agreement. They circled about Aubrey, slapping him on the back. He'd earned his place among them.

The sergeant banged on the table to silence their chatter. "They still have to pay. These barbarians don't look like they have two coins to rub together."

Amery pulled a small purse out of his tunic. "This is all the money we could raise."

"Not enough for the first week."

Bristles of power tickled upon Riley's forearms. The touch was both familiar and foreign. Strange. This didn't feel like Seth's power. Then the crowd of young men parted behind Seth's shoulder. Curly blond hair glided over their heads. Intense blue eyes locked upon Seth and the Claybank twins. Riley didn't need to see the ash uniform to know the man was a ranger. The Jalora's power had heralded his arrival.

Jogging at the ranger's side, a lanky soldier pushed at the cadets in a vain attempt to keep up with the much taller man's gait. Fancy ribbons and shiny metals covered the front of his uniform. Pressed pants, a well-shaven face and clean boots. Aye, he had to be an officer.

"A man has the right to fight for his home." Seth lifted his voice over the crowd. "Both these men have talent. They could make the difference between victory and defeat!"

Cheers thundered from the young men glued to Seth's word. They too seemed oblivious of the ranger coming toward them. Great gulls. He had to get his friend off the street before this strange ranger could nab them.

"We have to go, Seth." Riley stepped between his ranger and the sergeant. "Look what's coming our way."

Then the ranger and his pet officer stepped out of the crowd. Standing a full head taller than everyone among their numbers - including Seth - the ranger stood calmly with arms clasped behind his back. The tingling along Riley's arms raced faster up his skin. This ranger had far more power than the Dragonfly.

"What goes on here, Sergeant?" the officer snapped. "Explain."

The sergeant threw him a quick salute. Pale and trembling, he bowed low to the ranger. Neither gesture received a response from his waiting superiors.

"These Territorysmen think they can join up as cadets without so much as two credits between them, my lord." The sergeant told the ranger. "This hot head insists we allow them in."

"Is this true, young man? Your name?" the ranger asked in a rich baritone.

A Geltic accent laced his words. He was from Heidelbrecht. His people were the main trading partners to the Marianna woolie farmers. Though Riley rarely saw visitors from his country, he'd spoken to a few Heidelbrecht sailors. None of them stood as tall as this giant ranger before him.

"I'm Seth McCloud and this is Riley Logan from the Island of Carlotta. We've also come to join and to pay." He added with a little rebuke. "If money can be raised to allow these men in, will you let them join the army?"

"No. These cadets will need every credit they've brought with them. Let me suggest a wager, instead."

The ranger brought his left hand to rest upon his belt. Brilliant blue glistened from his Heart of the Warrior Ring in the shade of the citadel. Riley blinked his eyes, turning away from the light.

"Spar with someone of my choosing. The one who draws first blood wins. If you are victorious, I will pay for their first year as cadets. If you lose, then you and your carrot-haired friend will come quietly with me."

"Seth, no! It's got to be a trick."

The ranger growled something in Geltic at Riley. Solid silver spread across his face, blurring the ranger's features. Reflecting the terror of the young men caught in its magic, the mask sought Riley out. He well knew the horrors waiting inside the silvery depths. His nightmares were full of them. He'd made the mistake of staring into Seth's mask as they battled raiders on Marianna. Things were different now. He was a squire, protected by the Jalora. This time he didn't cower like the rest of the cadets screaming upon the ground. He stared defiantly into the terrible mask of death. The warmth of a soothing presence surrounded him. He was protected and safe.

"Enough, Ranger," Seth said. "You've made your point. I agree."

"Great gulls, Seth. You know nothing about this man."

The ranger, releasing his death mask, looked at them sharply. He seemed stunned, though his calm face didn't betray it. Lifting his Heart of the Warrior Ring, he extended the bright blue stone for them to see. The image of a bird with flaming wings flew in its belly.

"You don't recognize this ring? I imagined for a moment…." The ranger withdrew his hand. "No matter. I am called the Phoenix. We have a wager, you and I. Prepare yourself for battle."

Chapter Thirty-Five

"THIS IS MADNESS, Seth. You can't fight him."

Riley rolled his eyes to the heavens and snatched the cloak from Seth's hand. His friend's face remained perfectly calm as he slipped off his pack. Grumbling and shaking his head, Riley took the pack and hefted it onto his own shoulder.

"I don't think winning a sword fight is his objective. Look. My opponent has joined us."

A man with blond-white hair and perfect porcelain features moved soundlessly into the circle forming about them. Riley breathed a small sigh of relief. The Heidelbrecht ranger wasn't going to fight Seth after all. He'd chosen an ordinary person. The porcelain man removed his cloak and shoved it into the gaping officer's arms. A familiar insignia clutched at his collar. Seth's opponent was a Legion squire. He'd know how to fight better than most.

Amery gripped Seth's arms. "Why do you do this for us, Seth McCloud?"

"Because he has a great hole in his head," Riley grumbled.

"You have a right to be here as much as I."

Seth drew his sword and walked out to meet the squire. Riley's fingers fidgeted by the hilt of his weapon when Seth stopped a few feet away from his challenger. He was taking measure of the man. Leo had drummed the importance of knowing your opponent into both their skulls during every lesson.

For an endless moment, neither man made a strike. Riley heard rather than saw the blade come at Seth's head. The Valdeonian steel rang as his blade blocked the attack. The porcelain squire backed away and began to circle Seth. His strike came in a viper-like thrust at Seth's torso. Steel rang against steel several more times as the squire pushed his advance. Seth remained on the defense, avoiding the elegant movements of the ranger's Dance of Death.

Riley cursed low. The Phoenix' squire was a talented swordsman. He'd been foolish to assume this match would be an easy win for Seth. Curse that blond-headed ranger. Seth had been right. Phoenix knew exactly what he was doing. Riley could do nothing but stand by and watch his ranger fight.

Then Seth made his move. He feigned a strike to the squire's right shoulder and swept upward at the last moment. The tip of his blade drew a long red line across the porcelain cheek. Riley let out a whoop. Seth's patience had won the day.

"First Blood," Seth called to the ranger.

Phoenix nodded at his squire. Rushing Seth with precision strikes, the squire pushed him backward toward the circle of cadets. Great gulls! Seth had an impossible choice to make. Lose and they were at the ranger's mercy. Win and risk discovery.

His ranger took the First Stance for a flickering moment. Then he attacked. It was over before the crowd realized what they'd seen. Phoenix' squire was sprawled on the ground with Seth's blade at his throat. Gulping in furious breaths, Seth pressed the tip closer to the man's skin. The lion predator in his ring was ready to kill.

"Stop the fight, you blond giant!" Riley shouted. "You've seen what you were after, cheat."

"Well done, Roland," Phoenix said. "We're finished here."

"It's over." Riley carefully pushed Seth's sword hand away. "You won."

Roland didn't move. He was staring intently at Seth. Great gulls. Did the man want to die? Riley offered his hand and pulled the squire to his feet. Roland nodded his thanks and wordlessly left them to stand behind his ranger.

"Sergeant, this will cover their first year." Phoenix threw a purse full of money at the man, nodded to Seth, and walked calmly away.

"Mr. McCloud has earned his place as Troop Leader. See to it, Sergeant." The officer turned stiffly and jogged after the ranger.

Writing with great purpose in his ledger, the sergeant gave murderous glares to Seth, Riley, and the Claybank twins. Wonderful. Riley's brother Tom had described sergeants as the meanest creatures to walk the Erthe. They'd just embarrassed one and from the look upon the sergeant's face, he'd not soon forget.

Prodded and propelled through the enormous entrance of the citadel, Riley went to face his fate with the other young cadets. Black stone jutted from the ground, swallowing them into the innards of the fortress.

"I hope we see sunshine again," Aubrey muttered.

Aye. It was a wish he shared with the Territorysman. Their hopes were soon fulfilled when the shadows of the mountain fell away. A blast of unexpected sunshine barreled down the stone wall, striking them full on. Riley shielded his eyes, turning his head toward the ground until they'd adjusted. Blinking against the glare, he could see the miraculous. The Obsidian Citadel was hollowed out in the very center from bottom to top.

"Imagine the power this Lion Claw fellow must've had to do this to a mountain."

Sand covered the ground of the vast open area. Riley's boot dipped into its shifting surface, but didn't sink. This wasn't like Carlotta sand. Rather than absorbing whatever touched its surface, the sand seemed to adjust to the pressure.

Horses neighed and stomped to his far left. Two stables, each larger than Haven Bay, bustled with frantic activity. The one farthest to the back was much more elegant than its dull green neighbor. It had rich stained wood and bright metal handles upon the doors while its neighbor sported wooden fastens. Armed guards stood before the stables, pointing muskets at a line of shackled men. Valdeonian spies. Their tall bodies sat still but defiant upon the sand.

Wood knocked against wood to his right. Riley saw a familiar sight. Dozens of wooden-sword dummies twisted and spun on their posts. He'd spent many an hour taking hits from the tricky opponent under Leo's watchful instruction. Several young men - likely the cadets who'd arrived before them - smacked their wooden weapons against the stick arms. Yelps and angry curses came from their numbers. Riley chuckled. He knew exactly how they felt.

Seth bumped his shoulder and pointed across the great distance. Large windows covered in elegant fabric kept watch from within the stone of the fortress. Rising from several feet above the sand, the windows stretched to dizzying heights.

Two mammoth black stones stood beneath the windows. Covered in strange markings, the gates had no handles Riley could see. A strange dark feeling came to him as he stared into their black surface.

"Stay away," they seemed to warn.

White orbs floated on either side of the gates, spinning toward the slightest movement upon the sand. Sparks of angry energy erupted along their surface. He had no idea what they were, but the deepest part of his heart warned Riley to avoid the devilish things.

"Those are the Obsidian Gates. You'll never see what secrets they hide, boys," one of their UR keepers told them. "If you want my opinion, Ranger territory is best avoided altogether."

"Those gates are the entrance to the Jalora Legion's Headquarters?" Seth asked.

"That they are, but I warn you. Don't go near them. Hey! You there! Stop!"

Shouts and musket fire echoed against the fortress walls. One of the Valdeonian spies had broken away from the others and was running for the citadel gates. Soldiers streamed out of the black walls. They spread out in a half circle, blocking the Valdeonian's escape.

Out of options and nowhere to run, he stopped and stood to face the soldiers. Then the Valdeonian saw Seth. His dark eyes filled with loathing and disgust. Shouting angry words in Valic, the man spun around and ran at top speed toward the Obsidian Gates.

"What is the mad fool doing?" The UR soldier threw an arm out to stop Seth as he took a step to follow. "Stay in line, Cadet. That's an order."

Riley held Seth's arm, pulling him back in line. The soldiers hadn't followed the mad Valdeonian as he raced toward the black gates. Something wasn't right. Suddenly the white orbs stopped their continuous spinning and locked onto the spy. Two bursts of white light shot from the orbs, striking him in the chest. His agonized scream stopped abruptly as every bit of his body shattered.

"What in the green, green fields?" Riley put a hand to his mouth to keep the bile down. "Did you understand what the mad man said?"

"He was shouting something about joining the rings." Seth closed his eyes for a moment. "Such hatred. How am I to overcome it?"

"Valdeon isn't our problem right now." Riley frowned and bumped Seth's arm. "Sorry. Why don't we figure out this quest of yours first? How are we supposed to get through those gates?"

Seth shook his head. "I don't know."

"Shows over! Step lively!" one of the soldiers called. "We don't have all season."

Thrust back into their own adventure, the cadets shuffled blindly through the sand. A great arch of Obsidian stone waited to devour them. Its feasting came at a snail's pace. Riley groaned when his stomach growled. Great gulls. How long did it take to sign away your life?

"They're breaking us into two groups," Seth said. "Whatever happens we must stay together."

One soldier stood underneath the arch behind a narrow podium. The thick ledger with their names written inside spilled over the sides. He kept his head down and a finger on the page as each cadet murmured his name. Well, it was no wonder they'd been standing upon the sand for what must have been hours. Seth beckoned Riley and the Claybank twins forward when it was their turn.

"Name."

"Seth McCloud and Riley Logan," he said, looking behind him at the twins. "Amery and Aubrey Claybank."

The soldier lifted his head to regard them for a moment. Curiosity made tiny lines about his brow and eyes. Riley held his breath. Had the Phoenix gone back on his word? Great gulls. What would they do then?

"The four of you will proceed to Cadet Beta Three. To your right."

Riley grinned at Aubrey. It was a stroke of luck all four of them had been assigned to the same troop. Maybe the blond giant had spoken a word into the right ear? It didn't matter. Friendship, no matter how new, had suddenly become much dearer to him.

The line moved quicker now as they were propelled through a pair of large double doors. Riley's stomach groaned louder as he jogged up steep stairs with the other sheep. They flooded over the rim of a narrow landing where another soldier stood with his arms crossed.

"Cadet Beta One through Three down the hall to the left. Cadet Beta Four and Five to your right. Move!"

Startled like a herd of woolies, the young men rushed into a large hall carrying Riley with them. Rows of long tables ran down the middle of the hall. Clothing and boots covered their surface. Seth pulled him to the side of the nearest table. Their new friends followed, curiously touching the fabric as they passed.

"Two sets of tunics and pants. One pair of boots. One lock for your trunk."

The bored soldier thrust the pile into Seth's arms. His eyes moving quickly down to the sword at his hip. He let out a whistle, attracting the attention of his fellow keepers. Cracked lips smiled over a few missing teeth.

"So, this is the swordsman, eh? Wish I'd been on gate duty this morning to see you use that fine weapon, Cadet. You'd best keep it locked up tight. The sword is worth a king's ransom."

Riley shoved Seth forward with a little curse. He hoped talk of Seth's fight with the porcelain squire died down quickly. They were supposed to be blending in with the other cadets.

"Beta Three! Form a line. You're with me."

Their sergeant stood at the base of another long staircase. He was short on stature with a lean build and a rough face. Thinning brown hair, mostly taken over by gray, bristled along his scalp. A round patch of skin stretched from his forehead toward the back of his skull. Sharp, battle-hardened eyes regarded them intensely.

"Up those stairs to the right. Move!"

Their newly formed troop hit the steps at a run. Riley skidded across the landing when they hit the top, sliding into the man ahead of him. The cadets crowded in the doorway of a long barracks filled with narrow cots. The cave-like room had no windows or visible means of accepting fresh air. Light radiated from several crystal lamps jutting out of the walls over each tiny bed. Riley groaned. Their Tslavic jail cell had been more inviting.

"Move to your bunks, Cadets!" the sergeant barked.

Riley followed the others until the line stopped and he stood before an open bunk. Seth was to his right and the Claybank twins had the next two cots beside them. Well, at least he'd have company in this hellish room.

"Stand at attention!"

Riley sucked in an anxious breath as the sergeant marched toward them. He stopped before the Claybanks, scanning every inch of their bodies from head to toe. The sergeant didn't look pleased with his new recruits.

Those sharp eyes suddenly shifted to Seth. "McCloud, isn't it?"

"Yes, Sir," Seth said, saluting.

The Sergeant turned on him with a furious growl. "Sir? Do you see me wearing fancy bloomers and smell ladies perfume on my uniform? You will address me as Sergeant, Cadet!"

"Shut your traps," the sergeant growled.

The laughter of the other Cadets abruptly stopped and the room was completely silent. Riley tightened his fists, trying to keep his temper. Great gulls. They hadn't been in the army for twenty minutes and Seth was already in trouble. What had they been thinking, joining the army? They'd knowingly walked into this black prison with no plan for escaping it again once they'd completed Seth's quest.

Riley started forward to give the old windbag a good taste of his own growls, but Seth held up a hand and shook his head in warning. The sergeant gave them both a quick look, but let the matter drop. Strange. He didn't seem the type to allow any nonsense.

"Yes, Sergeant?" Seth asked.

"You're going to be my special helper. I want you to teach these hatchet throwers the common tongue. Until you do, I want you to translate every word I say. Do you understand, Cadet?"

"Yes, Sergeant." Seth moved to stand beside the Claybanks.

"Listen up, Ladies! My name is Sergeant Dancer. I am your whole world. You will run yourselves to death trying to please me. It won't be an easy thing to do, trust me. I don't want to hear one word of complaint or back talk. Your only responses to me when I ask a question should be yes, Sergeant or no, Sergeant."

Seth finished translating as the Sergeant paused to take a breath.

"Tomorrow, we start our time together," Sergeant Dancer told them in an unsettlingly cheery tone. "You have ten minutes to stow your gear and change into your uniforms. We have a little welcome planned for you in the arena."

Riley hurried with the others, throwing his street clothes into the wooden trunk at the foot of his bunk.

He was amazed the old soldier had not only gotten the size of his uniform down, but his new boots as well. His uniform was tan with loose fitting trousers and tunic. It was comfortable enough though the uniform had seen many years of use. The boots, in comparison, were shiny black and hard. Riley suspected he'd have many miles of marching to break them in.

A blonde-headed young man with a cocky grin and bright green eyes sank down into the bunk opposite them.

"That man should be whipped as a horse thief! I'm starving!"

Riley smelled the pungent odor of tobacco weed and looked across the aisle. The blond cadet winked at him with a pipe in his hand. His fast-moving mouth chewed on a chicken leg.

"Where did you get those?" Riley asked, clutching at his own empty belly.

"I can get just about anything, Mate. Name's Tory Dawson, from Lea."

"Riley Logan." He hurried across the distance to take a piece of chicken Tory had extended toward him. "This is my friend, Seth McCloud. Amery and Aubrey Claybank from the Outpost Territory."

"You won't rat me out, will you?" the young man asked.

The Claybank twins in response helped themselves to chicken and sat back down at the foot of their bunks. Amery handed the extra piece to Seth, who struggled for a short second over the stolen meat and then engulfed it in the next.

"We are all culpable now, Tory," Seth said.

"Culpable? Does that mean friendly? I hope so. You're the very devil with a sword, McCloud," Tory told him, with a wide grin. "Lucky the ranger wasn't in a mood to fight you himself."

"Rangers are all good swordsmen, then?"

"Are they good!" Tory slapped a hand upon the bed as he laughed. "He could have split every man in line down the center without breaking a sweat."

Riley frowned. "Do these rangers teach us the sword, then?"

"Where did you say you were from?" Tory asked, shaking his head. "It must be in the middle of the ocean somewhere. How could you not know about rangers?"

"The Isle of Carlotta may not be in the middle of the ocean, but we don't see many rangers in our Sunfruit orchards," Seth said.

"Carlotta? I could have sworn you were Valdeonian. Explains it." Tory stretched, scratching at his back. "The rangers don't teach cadets anything, Mate. They leave us to the UR sergeants. It wouldn't be fitting or possible at any rate. Besides, they've got their hands full, don't they?"

"What do you mean?" Seth asked.

"The head muckety mucks from all over Andara have come to meet with Dragon. He's the leader of the Jalora Legion." Tory, meal devoured, yawned and leaned back on his pillow. "Word has it they are afraid of invasion and won't join in the fight against the Jackal to help Valdeon. Some even say the days of the Jalora Legion are over, because the Lion is gone."

"So, what's the Dragon going to do then?" Riley asked.

He slid his sword into the trunk and locked it just as Sergeant Dancer returned. Seth, he noticed, was dressed and had his gear stowed neatly away before any of them had finished. He was a calm pool in a sea of teeming confusion.

"Times up, Cadets. Single line and follow me."

Forming a single line behind their sergeant, Beta Three marched out onto the landing. Riley followed Seth and the Claybanks as they passed the top of the stairs - the path to freedom in his mind - and turned right down a dark corridor. Their boots echoed in the hollowed-out tunnel. Fearing he was being herded into the belly of the mountain fortress, Riley extended his fingers to touch the rock. The surface was smooth and perfect.

A patch of brilliant sunlight suddenly appeared in the darkness ahead of them. He wanted to cheer. A massive doorway welcomed them back into the world of the living. Riley followed the others down long rows of benches. They hung in tiers along the face of the rock, suspended above the sandy area where they'd waited in line. Strange he hadn't noticed the tiers while they were on the ground.

The rows of tiered benches circled halfway around the citadel. Each end stopped well short of the tall windows of the Legion's headquarters. The benches were filling up quickly with other cadets.

"Where are they?" Seth asked, leaning across the benches toward the sand below. "The Obsidian Gates are gone."

He was right. The great stone gate had disappeared and had taken those dangerous magic orbs with it.

What in the green, green fields? He rubbed hard at the back of his neck. This dusty old book Seth had to find was behind an impenetrable gate guarded by killing magic. It would be tough enough to pass through those orbs, but now they'd have to find the gate again.

"What are we waiting for?" Amery asked, as the sun began to disappear behind the rim of the mountain.

A hush fell over the arena as a group of UR officers made their way onto the center of the sand. Stepping up onto a makeshift platform, their leader stood ramrod straight with his hands behind his back. It was difficult to see his features from this high up, but Riley could make out a well-kept mustache and his impossibly tidy uniform. Impatient movements plagued his upper body as the officer stood waiting for the last of the whispers to die down.

"You men of courage have journeyed from all reaches of Andara to answer the call," he began, pausing as the young men cheered. "Fear has not swayed you from your duty."

Hoots and words shouted in defiance peppered the seats about them. Riley smoothed his sword hand along the top of his trouser leg. This same hand had plunged a blade into the beating heart of another man. He'd done it to save a life, Seth's father in fact, but the good deed didn't erase killing's stain upon his soul. These fools about him had never drawn blood. Would they continue to cheer when their own hand had drained the life out of another?

"A new enemy has arrived on our shores. They've ruthlessly stormed Valdeon and the sacred Altar of

Providence. Our Legion and UR Armadas sailed south to meet them in battle."

Seth tensed beside him, jaw set in an angry growl. His ranger's fury was rising again. Riley could only muster fear. He'd experienced it before on their adventure. Sitting here among hundreds of other young men, its grip upon Riley was strangely intense.

"Word reached the Dragon a few days ago. Our armadas were destroyed, brought down in a single day." Silence met the commander's words. "Only a handful of souls escaped to report back. War is upon us, Cadets. We fight not for honor or glory, but rather for our very lives and the lives of those we've left behind. The Dragon commands our experienced soldiers to guard key strategic points around Andara. Your time as cadets has been reduced from a few weeks to a few days."

Hushed murmurs raced around the crowd of cadets. Some were still excited by the chance for adventure. Other murmurs expressed worry. Seth remained silent as the conversations washed over them. His ranger turned slowly, offering Riley a nod of reassurance. Deep sorrow filled his eyes.

"Cadets!" the commandant shouted over the din. "Welcome to the UR Army."

Chapter Thirty-Six

"I NEVER SEEN a man - if that's what he is under his metal skull - so particular about his linens," the old woman said, wiping at her chapped lips. "I clean the pretty things and then take them down a narrow hall. A box sits against the wall with a fancy grate between me and his room. I take the dirties and put the clean linens inside. They say I'm never to be seen by the Jackal lord or it would be the worst for me."

Blacksmiths, shop owners, and street sweeps filled the old shack. Julian sat begrudgingly among them. They all stared up at her explaining the comings and goings of Lord Gorman's linen. The bastard enjoyed his meals alone, but his dainties had to be delivered by someone and the old crone before them was the gatekeeper. She was his way to get close to the Jackal general when he least expected it. Cut off the head and the rest of the vile snake falls.

"Thank you for a very enlightening report, my lady."

It pained him to deliver upon her a title of respect, but it had the desired effect. The old woman beamed as she sat down amongst the group. Others in the crowd of filthy rats were equally impressed and anxious to show the prince of Valdeon their value.

"The Jackal prepare to move forward into Andara. I've heard their planning, saw their maps for conquest," he began. "They believe San Leonora and Valdeon broken. Soon their forces will leave our lands for a richer prize. This will be our time to strike! A handful of Jackal soldiers can't stand against an army of Valdeonian men."

"You're telling a half-truth, Julian," a man boomed over the low murmurs of excitement. "Lord Gorman does seek to conquer Andara. In fact, that was your bargain, wasn't it? He'd help you take the throne and you'd hand him the rest of the continent."

"How dare you throw such accusations around," Marcellus said, pulling his weapon.

"Things haven't turned out to plan, have they?" Head and face covered under his hood, the man walked down the aisle toward Julian. "More Jackal ships arrive each week while your family home rots in the stench of their vulgar filth."

The sick embrace of uncertainty washed over Julian. This man spoke as if he knew with great authority what Julian had done. The crowd sensed it too. Their murmurs began to turn ugly. Questioning. Even the old shack seemed to groan under the storm of suspicion.

Old hands pushed back the hood covering his grizzled head. Sharp eyes, full of knowing intelligence, glared at Julian with a hatred he hadn't seen outside an audience with Lord Gorman. This old face was well known to him. He'd hoped to never see its features again.

"The Lion's Squire!" Murmurs among the crowd turned from hatred to hope.

"Listen to me!" Dante De Vincente hushed them. "The bastard prince leads you into a deadly fight you cannot win. I've traveled the width of Valdeon, returning our king's body back to the family crypt for a respectful burial. The Jalora's strongholds have all fallen, save one. San Marimosa still stands free, but the others have been used to berth the massive force of Jackal ships arriving to our shores. It is true they prepare to march against Andara, but Julian lies. These villains won't risk leaving Valdeon unoccupied. The Altar of Providence is in danger of being taken. We must keep it from evil's hands."

"And why should we trust you, lackey to a king who abandoned his duty?" Marcellus spat, earning him a dagger in the shoulder.

The old squire's aim was still fierce. He stalked closer toward his prey like a specter of fate. Julian backed away as he approached. Never taking those disapproving eyes from Julian, Dante bent down to retrieve the weapon from Marcellus' still form. The fool's chest rose and fell with life. Pity.

"I should kill you for what you've done, Julian bastard prince, but the honor is not for me to perform." Dante gave him a wicked grin. "Many have sworn to take your head from those weak shoulders. Each stronghold I visited swears to have seen you and your mad dog here leading the charge against their city. I wonder how you could be so many places at one time, Julian? A miracle perhaps?"

He gritted his teeth as the old squire laughed. How had so many people seen him in so many different places at once? The answer was annoyingly obvious. Changelings. Lord Gorman had been clever there.

He'd made it impossible for Julian to leave the relative safety of San Leonora to raise a rebellion against them.

"You've been very quick to place judgment upon me, Lion's Squire. Why, I wonder, have you remained hidden while Valdeon was in danger?"

"I was right where I should have been, beside my ranger as Leo trained his heir." Dante grinned as the crowd's excitement grew. "The Lion Ring isn't lost. It is safely upon the finger of Edmund's true son."

He stepped past Julian and turned to face the room. Dante motioned for quiet. It was granted immediately. Julian slowly lowered his hand toward the hilt of his sword. He'd lost them. Dante De Vincente had snatched their loyalty from his very fingers. No. Not Dante. The boy. This young Lion's death had just become irrefutably necessary.

"There are factions about Valdeon still loyal to the Jalora and the Lion," Dante said. "I plan to join them. Will you follow me into this rebellion? Or are you willing to stay and follow the murderous whelp who had his own father struck down by the Jackal? Decide quickly. This Gorman fellow isn't as foolish as Julian believes. His men are minutes away from surrounding this meeting place."

"Stop!" Julian growled as the traitorous vermin rushed from the little shack.

"The Jalora has cursed you. No cure can help now. It will slowly eat you alive." Dante grabbed Julian's rotting arm above the elbow. "You still have time to make this right. Come with me. We can make our way to the Legion before it's too late."

The familiar scent of spices and herbs wrapped about him, evoking unwanted memories. Dante had seen him from his mother's womb. He'd taken care of the cuts and bruises during his boyhood. The old squire had also been the only one - apart from Xavier the Wolf - who'd recognized young Julian's dark side. He lifted his blade a few inches from its sheath. His hand froze as Dante's dagger tip pressed lightly against his stomach. Some things never changed. The Lion's Squire was no fool.

Julian pulled his arm away. "I would rather rot than help you."

"So be it. I warned Leo against you and the whore of a cow who bore you. He wouldn't listen. Evil pulses in your veins." Dante took a few steps back, well out of Julian's reach. "Know this. I will do everything in my power to stop you and your unholy allies."

Then he was gone along with his followers, leaving Julian standing over Marcellus. His last faithful worshipper. He pulled his sword and swung the tip over Marcellus' chest. It would be so easy to rid himself of this burden. He pushed the blade back into its sheath with a loud clink. The distant howl of Dirge song penetrated the thin walls. Dante hadn't been embellishing. The Dirge were on their way.

"Get up!" He kicked at Marcellus and started for the hole in the wall. "We can't be found here."

Someone had betrayed him. Zoya? Marcellus? Whisper? They all shared a lustful heart for power, but which one had acted upon it? If Dante proved to be right, Gorman had woven an intricate web to keep Julian trapped in San Leonora. He let a cold grin come to his lips. Beasts were most dangerous when trapped. Gorman would soon find the Dirge weren't the only cold-blooded killers in Valdeon.

Chapter Thirty-Seven

WOLF STARED at the raindrops tumbling down the window glass. Their watery bodies obscured Muellerton Outpost's thick walls. Evergreen tops peeked over the rim, surrounding the common area with green. Heidelbrecht was smothering. Wolf missed the warm sun and open country of his homeland.

He ran his finger along the tall glass of mead. Rabbit was at it again. Splashing in the muddy common area, his young body repeatedly moved through the first fifteen stances of the Dance of Death. Relentless in his practice and pace, the young ranger mercilessly drove his body. Rain streamed off his stone face as he concentrated on the movements. Hate swirled about him like a thunderstorm, centering its focus upon the Jackal dagger Tulio had taken as a talisman.

Everyone adapted to loss in different ways. Wolf snorted, gulping down the last of the strong mead. Tulio, at least, was being constructive. He stumbled to the cask and poured himself another glass. The bright yellow liquid splashed across the table and onto the floorboards. He turned from it and plopped back down upon the corner of the bed. Dulcina's burgundy ribbon waited for him. Wolf clutched at it and rubbed the soft fabric against his cheek.

"Dulcina."

Torn between the desire to sleep and the terrifying images haunting his dream, Wolf took solace in the comfort of his glass. He'd always believed turning to drink was a coward's refuge. If not a coward, he certainly was a failure.

"I've spent considerable time and effort to find the legendary Wolf. Instead, I find a drunkard."

She stood in the doorway of his chambers like a phantom from the past. Age may have claimed Charlotte Von Bohdan's body, but fierce intelligence still glowed in those steel gray eyes. Her tongue was no less sharp since their last meeting in the halls of the Obsidian Citadel. She'd stood against her people and the Legion in favor of Anne Von Wolkhurst. No amount of arguments or threats could sway her. She earned the title of Iron Queen that day. Wolf had considered her traitor to Andara. He'd even despised her for standing against the Legion. Now? Meeting Anne's son explained her devotion. His opinion of her, however, had not softened.

"How did you find me?"

"I still have influence in the courts of Andara, My Lord De Vincente, though you, and others like you, tried to discredit me." She moved forward with an annoying *tap, tap, tap* of her walking stick.

Wolf grunted and turned from her to stare out the window once more. "And why have I earned such favor from the Queen of Carlotta?"

"I come on behalf of my nephew. He has been left unprotected far too long."

"I will not be questioned in my duty by such a one as you," Wolf snapped and pushed off the bed to grasp the window ledge. "The boy must remain in hiding on Carlotta. Those were my orders."

"Fausto De Quintaro does not agree with you."

Wolf spun around to regard her. No lie showed in her eyes. Will. Protection. Love. They surrounded her in an impassible wall of resolve. Lifting her chin defiantly, she scanned his face.

"Fausto is alive?"

"He came to seek my aid and found the Lion. Our friend plans to train him while they prowl around Valdeon." Charlotte took a deep breath. "He plans to use my nephew as a symbol for the people."

"And what did the Lion say?"

"The Lion did what he must. He and his squire left for Lea a few days ago disguised as commoners. They are to join the hundreds of cadets in the UR Army."

What bang tail mischief was this! It was too dangerous for Seth to be waltzing about Andara alone. The Dirge were eager hunters and had grown a taste for his flesh. Others, like the Hawk, were no less anxious to find him.

"I have secured a small ship with supplies for your use, my lord the Right-Hand," she said, turning to go. "I realize you won't accept them from me, so I offer them to you on behalf of the Lion. You'll find the ship hidden in a canyon a few miles to the north."

The queen of Carlotta squared her shoulders as she turned to regard him. "I know you are close to Francis the Dragon. Have a care. My August served with him when they were both young. Francis has always shown a taste for power and a willingness to do what he must to get it. Be wary of his intent, Right-Hand. The Lion is young and innocent. He needs the wisdom of someone whose protection goes beyond the physical."

The tapping of her walking stick upon stone faded and Wolf was left alone to contemplate her words. Fausto was alive. Yes. He and a great many others would find hope in Seth, but their desperate hope would see the boy to his grave.

Time is against us, Right-Hand. You must take up your duty and see to the young Lion. A new covenant has been forged between he and I. Even now he searches for the Book of Ancients. You well understand what this means.

Yes. He understood. The moment the boy opened the book and released its ancient magic, the transformation of his body and power would begin. He was to be the next Jalora Master. If he survived. Seth needed the Lords of Valdeon to protect him from those seeking to harm the fledgling master. The Sacred Guard had another duty Wolf didn't like to think about. They were the few who stood between the terrible force of the Lion's power and those innocents caught in the path of his fury.

"I must reach him before he opens the book. It's too dangerous. He must be trained to control his temper."

Indeed. I and others have trained him in the sword and combat, but a master must be more than a soldier.

Wolf nodded slowly. The Jalora rarely explained itself fully. He wondered if Seth understood what the future held. An islander boy from the Grey Cliff Isles would have no understanding of such things. It was up to Wolf to help him become what he must, but how?

You must prepare yourself, Right-Hand. The Lion has already come into his first level of power. Julian and his Dirge forced my hand. You have days, rather than years, to prepare for your mantle.

Smoothing his thumb along Dulcina's ribbon again, he thought of his family and the people of his city. Their father and lord had failed them. Would he remain here drowning in drink while Andara fell to the Jackal? Or could he find the strength of heart to stand with the young Lion against such evil?

Wolf carefully folded the ribbon and tucked it under his pillow. "What would you have me do, Holiness?"

It is a lovely day for a run.

Head spinning from drink, he straightened his clothes. It was best not to look the part of a drunkard. Perhaps Rabbit's squire had hidden his constant intake of mead from the soldiers of Muellerton Outpost? No matter. His days locked away in darkness were over.

You'll not need your sword this day, Right-Hand.

Wolf's fingers hesitated just out of reach of his sword. He didn't like being without a weapon, especially in the wild wood. The uneasy absence of weight upon his hip continued to nag at his nerves as he walked across the common area. He made his way through the rain toward the guard standing at the gatehouse of the outpost.

Wet blond strands dripped down the front of the guard's uniform. Pale eyes fell over Wolf's thin shirt.

Noting his lack of cloak and hood, the guard stood away from the shelter of the gatehouse to let him in.

"Thank you, no," Wolf said. "I'll be taking some exercise."

"You aren't going out in the wild without a weapon, Ranger?" A troubled frown formed upon his face. "These woods are thick with wolves, bears, and other animals not shy around men."

"I dare say they will regret the exchange if they annoy me."

Wolf passed through the small guard's gate within the wall and sprinted off down the mist-covered road. The chilling mist clung to his hair and skin. Soft raindrops splashed upon his eyelids. He wiped them away, trying to focus on keeping his stomach from rebelling.

It is a very slow pace you keep, Right-Hand. I have much to teach you today.

Wolf bit back a curse and sprinted forward at ranger speed. The rain and exertion had sobered him quickly. Nausea replaced the numbness he'd experienced since waking up in Muellerton.

Here is our road.

A steep animal trail to his right ran up the mountain. It followed the curves of a stone cliff stretching up to the sky. Wolf looked dubiously at the rocky path. It didn't appear stable enough to carry the weight of a man. He darted up the path, wrapping the wind about him as he went. His toes skipped across the stones. Sweat began to pour from his body as he climbed. He gave a cry of victory as he burst to the top of the mountain.

Look about you and marvel.

Evergreens circled about a crystal lake. Green meadow grass blanketed the open space around its shores. Beyond the lake, the trees stretched south toward Heidelbrecht's river country. Wolf breathed in the crisp air, listening to the dancing raindrops on the lake's surface. It was beautiful country.

Each bit of life is beautiful in its own way. You must look hard and pay attention to find the mark of purpose upon them. Each creation has its set time to arrive and to leave this world. No creation ever really dies. They pass on to other things. The grass and flowers return to the soil, giving their bodies to the new spring growth. Animals feed upon other animals to take their strength. Your body will return to the earth one day as well, Wolf. But, life has given you something special. It can never die. One day you will join with the others who have left this world. Do you understand what I tell you, Right-Hand?

"Yes, Holiness." Wolf whispered. "I will see my family again one day."

The Jalora wrapped around him, gentle and comforting. *They wait for you on the other side. I have work for you to do in this world before you may see them again. Will you serve me in this life, Right-Hand?*

"Yes, I will serve you for their sake as well as my own. What is your command?"

Keep to this trail until you come to a fork. Then turn toward the river, Right-Hand. The lesson is waiting for you there.

Wolf turned left at the fork, following numerous animal markings upon the trail. His boots were the lone human prints to touch its surface. Water roared above the quiet valley. It ran and jumped wildly down several small waterfalls. Reaching the base of the rocks, the river took a slower pace toward the south.

Then he saw one of nature's greatest warriors. The enormous creature stood in the river's center, swiping at the fish fighting to get upstream. Its brown fur was drenched, revealing the hard muscles beneath.

"A bear! Is it the lesson? Are you asking me to fight the beast with no weapons or hounds?"

Calm yourself. You fear this bear?

"Yes! It could slash a man to ribbons."

The fury and strength of this creature is nothing compared to the power you must subdue, Right-Hand. The Lion will grow too powerful to stand against. You must calm his fury and show your courage to the young Lords of Valdeon. They will not be able to subdue him on their own. Only through you can they stop the Lion's Roar.

Do you remember your escape with the Phoenix in Lea? You broke the stones of the pavement with your voice. We must teach you control. I have given this power to you as a means of calming the Lion. It will protect you when no other weapons are available.

He'd heard tales about the 'Voice' from Valdeonian legends. It was rumored the voice could stop the Lion and pull his body helpless to the ground. The Sacred Guard would then join the Right-Hand to keep their Master under control until his fits of temper passed.

Wolf swallowed hard. He well knew the histories of the Jalora Masters. The last Master, Gustavo D'Antoiné, killed his entire Guard in a fit of rage. The Lion's Roar crushed them to death. It was said Gustavo's Right-Hand - his only brother - failed to calm the Lion. His body had been ripped apart so thoroughly that only the Hawk Ring remained to identify his body.

If Gustavo had killed his own brother, what chance would Wolf have against this boy who knew him only as a stranger? Wolf looked at the bear again. He would gladly join his family in the afterlife, but what of the other rangers? They were too young to die by this boy's fury.

"I don't remember how I summoned the Voice."

In the streets of Lea, you met fury with fury. This is one way to call the power. I warn you. Never meet fury with fury against the Lion. The clash would destroy you both and everything in your path. You must instead tap into the wealth of inner strength living inside your heart. I chose you for your endurance, Xavier De Vincente. Use your endurance to calm him.

"Be steady," his father had lectured. "Ignore the distractions life throws in your path."

Go calm the bear, Right-Hand.

Wolf took a tight hold upon his fear. Stuffing it deep down inside his mind, he stood slowly. His boots moved soundlessly upon the bank until he reached the water's edge close to the great beast.

"The bear doesn't look angry," Wolf whispered.

A bolt of energy shot out of the Wolf Ring and struck the bear's rump. Startled and infuriated by the sudden strike, the beast spun around with a growl. It stood upon two legs, coming to its full height.

Now it is angry.

"Yes, this I can see!"

"Calm yourself, bear." Wolf lifted his hands before the snarling beast. "Calm down. I mean you no harm."

Magic wrapped around the animal in thick bands of light. Iridescent in the beginning, the light became a solid white as Wolf's will and confidence grew stronger.

The bear dropped to all fours. Shaking its large head, the beast sat down in the water at long last. He'd done it. Wolf had calmed the bear. He could almost reach out and pet its fur, so docile was the beast.

Beware, Right-Hand! You are losing focus.

His boot slipped on the moss-covered stone and he fell to his backside in the mud. The bear shook itself and pounced toward him. Slicing through the water at top speed, he bolted from the river bank toward the trees. Grunts and breaking branches followed him as he ran. The bear was angry enough to follow him all the way to the outpost!

Wolf leapt into the nearest evergreen. He shimmied up the tree trunk, stopping near the swaying top. The bear - not wanting to give up on its revenge - pushed at the trunk. The tall tree creaked in protest, threatening to snap at its base.

Focus is very important, Right-Hand. The Jalora roared with laughter. *Have you learned the point of the lesson?*

"Yes. It is burned into my mind," Wolf cried, clutching at the prickly evergreen boughs.

Good! We are finished for today. Enjoy the fresh air.

"Wait! What about the bear?"

It was pointless. The Jalora's presence had parted. He was left alone with his furry companion. The bear, after several long minutes of pushing at the trunk, grew bored. It began pacing around the base of the tree. Wolf found a comfortable branch and sat down to wait. He rested his head against the bark. Eyelids drifting shut, he listened to the rain's steady fall to the forest floor.

"Wolf? Why are you up a tree?"

Tulio stared up at him through the boughs. His young face struggled against the grin trying to break free. It was almost worth being chased up a tree to see him smile again.

Branches snapped violently to Rabbit's right. The clever beast had been hiding to lure him down. Racing toward its new prey, the bear charged through the evergreen boughs like a runaway wagon.

"Rabbit! Climb!"

Eyes wide with terror, he scrambled up the branches to Wolf's perch. They wrapped their arms around the trunk as the enraged bear pushed at the tree again. Their sanctuary moaned, but held firm.

"And now you know why I'm up this tree."

"Do you think the outpost will send soldiers looking for us?" Rabbit asked, clutching at his stomach. "The sun is beginning to set and I didn't pack dried meat."

Wolf thought about the guard at the gate who'd questioned him. He and his friends would have a merry time in the tavern exchanging jests. Not one, but two rangers treed by a bear in one day.

"I most certainly hope not. Stay here."

"What are you doing?" Rabbit cried, grabbing at Wolf's sleeve."

"The impossible."

Wolf climbed down, stopping a few feet from the bear. The beast slammed its claws against the bark, trying to reach his leg. Wolf pulled all his focus into the calm place in his heart. He stared at the bear and brought forth the Voice.

"Calm yourself, bear."

White light wrapped around the beast once more. This time he wouldn't let it fade. The bear fought against the power, thrashing its body to and fro.

"Calm down, bear." Wolf said again.

The bear shook its head in confusion. It staggered backward, pushing away from him as he landed on his feet upon the ground.

"Sleep," he said as the beast rolled to its side.

Rabbit landed soundlessly beside him with wide eyes, mouth gaping in amazement. Wolf took the ranger's arm and pulled him toward the path leading to the cliff's edge.

"It was the 'Voice' wasn't it?"

"Come. We have a ship to find." Wolf dashed down the cliff's edge toward the outpost with Rabbit following close behind.

Chapter Thirty-Eight

SUN AND SKY. Seth had sorely missed them in the confines of the Obsidian Citadel. This was the cadets' first venture outside its great belly since they'd signed on to the UR Army. He lifted his face toward the sun again and breathed deeply. Lea's unique odor - a mixture of cooking meat and old stone - filled the streets as they ran.

The steady beat of boots upon cobblestone lulled his mind into a muted sense of peace. Riley, however, didn't share his enjoyment of the day. Muttering Islic curses and a few he'd picked up from the other cadets, his squire continued to cast accusatory glances Seth's way.

"How are we supposed to find a way through those Obsidian Gates if we spend our time running after the sergeant?" Riley grumbled low. "I thought finding this old book of yours was the most important thing."

"Quiet in the ranks!" Sergeant Dancer bellowed.

Riley did have a point. The Jalora had stressed the urgency of Seth's locating the book. He frowned as the peace of the morning was lost. His first true task as the Lion and he was already falling behind. They'd have to sneak away somehow, but their sergeant wasn't one to let his charges be idle for long.

Sergeant Dancer sat on the back of the wagon, chomping a juicy apple. He seemed in good spirits. Seth suspected he enjoyed prodding his cadets around Lea. He pointed out places they were to avoid and made them repeat his directions for shortcuts back to the citadel. Seth had to admit the instructions were welcome. Anything to take them through the infamous maze of streets.

"I'd get lost in the maze just to escape the monotony of running circles in the arena," Riley grumbled.

"It's best to heed his warnings, Mate," Tory whispered through a ragged breath.

Sergeant Dancer had a multitude of skills. His hearing by far was his greatest gift. Somehow, he managed to hear clandestine card games in the barracks after lights out. Or private conversations during their rare breaks. He was especially good at hearing rumblings in the ranks during their daily exercises.

"Shut your traps and listen! Every year, a foolish cadet or two gets lost in Lea and it takes the rangers to find them. I remember a few years back a young cadet happened into Harrow, the nastiest most thief-ridden place in the UR." Sergeant Dancer shook his head and threw the apple core over his shoulder. "The rangers brought back his bloodied body three days later."

"That's not true, is it?" Riley asked Tory.

"I'll never forget it." Tory shivered, absently hugging his torso. "The rangers used my dad's pub - the Rollicking Rover - as their base. It's close to Harrow. I still see the cadet's body in my nightmares. Never imagined one human being could be so brutal to another."

Murmurs and skeptical whispers spread around the troop of cadets. Seth gently probed Sergeant Dancer and withdrew quickly. He'd been part of the search and had known the young cadet.

The Sergeant's sharp eyes turn to Seth, staring intensely at him. It was almost as if he knew he was being probed. Sergeant Dancer slapped his hand on the side of the wagon, bringing it to a sudden stop.

"McCloud, front and center," Sergeant Dancer barked.

Seth smoothed nervous hands down his tunic. He'd been foolish to think a harden soldier like Dancer wasn't used to being around rangers. Casting a last look at Riley, he hurried through the panting young men and stopped at attention beside the wagon.

"You bone-heads will run one lap around Lea. It shouldn't be too difficult for you to find your way back to the citadel. Just follow this road all the way around. McCloud here will lead the troop, while I see to the supply ships on the docks. Those goods and ammunition won't see themselves into the citadel's storage." Sergeant Dancer slapped the side of the wagon and it lurched forward. "Don't be all day about it, McCloud. I don't want to ruin my luncheon by coming after you."

"Yes, Sergeant."

Seth took his place at the head of the troop and started them off again. Beta Three followed his lead without argument, falling back into the same steady rhythm. The mid-morning bustle of Lea began to clog the streets, but the city's inhabitants stayed to the sidewalks and let them pass.

The sweet smells of fresh bread and cooking meats wafted toward them from the market place. Stomach growling, he hurried them past the entrance. Seth kept them at a steady pace around the outskirts of town. Soon they passed the elaborate stone statuary and sign denoting North Burrough Park - their halfway mark. It was a pleasant community, not the most elegant part of town, but it was home to many of Lea's shopkeepers and craftsmen.

The next neighborhood was bordered by the brick backs of several buildings. Soldiers policed the row and the massive rubble pile separating North Burrough Park from the next neighborhood. Harrow. This was the thieves' district. It appeared not even the army would send its men into those rough streets.

Seth quickened the pace a bit as they ran past unfriendly eyes staring at them through darkened windows. Animosity. Greed. Bloodlust. They radiated in the air about Harrow. The light of good had been completely eradicated from its body. Evil longed to stretch its foul fingers into the row to grab them.

He gave a great sigh of relief when the southern tip of Lea's wall came into view. They'd be turning soon for a friendlier part of the city. Around the southern-most point of Lea they'd run, through more neighborhoods until they finally reached the gates of their new home.

Protect the innocent.

The Jalora's power grabbed hold of his body. Urgency flooded his being in a wave of irresistible impulse. He turned from his course and headed down a large row. Missing cobblestones and rubbish slowed his pace.

Tory caught his arm and pulled him to a halt. "Wrong way, Mate. This is Hedgewick Row. You don't want to go down there."

Seth shook off the mortal's grip. Seeing Tory with ancient eyes, this young man reminded them of another though the memory was out of reach. Concern. Comradery. Loyalty. Here was a friend. Someone to trust.

Riley, red-faced from puffing in air, skidded to a stop beside them. "What is it?"

Two Territorysmen followed the Lion's Squire while the rest of the troop stayed back on the main row. Fearless and skilled, they too were valuable allies. The Jalora eased away its power, giving Seth control of their shared voice.

Trust in your faithful, Lion.

"Someone's in trouble." Seth held Riley's gaze until he knew his squire understood.

"Let him go," Riley said. "We'll follow with the troop as quickly as we can."

"We will?" Tory threw up his hands. "Have you gone mad, Mate? Hedgewick Row runs right into the center of Harrow district, the meanest, thief-ridden part of town. Sergeant Dancer wasn't kidding."

Ignoring his warning, Seth ran Hedgewick Row and around the corner toward the rundown buildings. Evil's oppressive body descended upon him. It pushed against Seth, trying to throw him out of its kingdom. The Spirit of the Lion Ring burst through the leather hiding his ring. It surrounded Seth in a protective orb of pure light. Rolling away in fetid clumps of darkness, evil withdrew.

Deeper and deeper into the maze of rows and alleys he ran, drawn by the power of the Jalora. Then he saw them through the retreating mass. A group of thieves surrounded a carriage precariously tilting to one side. Armed with chains and bludgeons, they circled the disabled vehicle. One of the villains climbed up the canvas top. A shimmer of lacey fabric whipped the air sending him plummeting to the ground. The canvas top came down with a loud tear, revealing the band's true prize. Two women - wealthy if Seth had to guess - huddled together at the center of the carriage. The eldest swung her umbrella at two more thieves trying to reach inside. Her daughter clutched desperately at her mother's skirt in fits of hysteria.

A lone sword withstood the attack. It was the driver of the carriage. Gray hair clung to his head in thin wet strands. Blood flowed heavy from a wound along his arm. His opponent, a baldheaded swordsman with a few missing teeth, leered as he came in for the final blow.

Seth spun around looking for anything he could use as a weapon. Settling on a broken handle of a digging tool, he charged into the band of thieves. Striking at their legs and lower backs, he forced a path through to the driver.

"Give me your sword." Seth reached for the hilt. "You can no longer lift it."

"Take it with my thanks," he said, handing Seth the weapon.

Silence had fallen over the band of thieves. Greed. Lust. Murder. The sick sensations swelled in the alley, crawling up the walls of the buildings about them. In the distorted colors of hateful emotions, a single tendril of warning reached across the distance. Deception.

"Leave now and I will let you live."

The Harrow thieves looked at each other for a moment in surprise, then began to laugh. They were here for treasures and no more. Other men, out of place among the thieves, had come into the alley to kill.

"Very generous, my fine young cadet," one of the thieves shouted. "We'll be taking the pretty bird. You can keep the old bat. She won't bring much in trade."

"Greed and lechery have taken your souls. I see no redemption. Punish the Guilty," Seth and the Jalora said, raising their voices above the noise of hate and chaos. "There will be no mercy."

Running boots thundered down the alley toward them. Bludgeons slammed against the walls of the buildings, surrounding them with violent echoes. The thieves shuffled nervously. Anxious murmurs circled about their numbers. Beta Three had arrived.

"For our comrade and the honor of Beta Three!"

Riley shook a rusty pipe above his head and flew at the band of thieves. Echoing his battle cry, the cadets followed. They'd been creative in their selection of weapons, picking up what they could along the way.

The fight between cadet and thief reached them quickly. Flying fists and bludgeons pressed against the carriage, making a chasm of bodies between the men with swords and Seth. He couldn't see them through the tangled limbs.

Then he noticed the bald thief standing on the corner of a connecting alley, well away from the battle. Seth pushed through the fighters, charging toward the man. Warnings of a trap echoed in his mind, but still his feet moved forward. The Jalora's anger hadn't faded.

"Here kitty, kitty," he mouthed.

How did he know Seth's identity? Aunt Charlotte, Tymon, and Rodrigo were the only ones who knew they traveled to Lea. The Jalora's magic kept his identity hidden. Evil had its own tricks it would seem.

The bald thief grinned as Seth broke free of the fray. He darted into the alley and out of sight. Seth stopped at the corner, peering into the small space. Deception. Greed. Murder. Their hues were stronger here. He gripped the hilt of his borrowed sword tighter and took a step into the trap. Ten armed men stood in a half circle behind their leader. They were mercenaries, not the ragged bunch of Harrow thieves who'd circled the carriage. The unfortunate women had been pawns in a trap meant for him.

"Here you are at long last, Lion," he said. "This time you won't escape."

"I'm not running." Seth eyed the ten armed men. "I made you a promise."

He took his first stance and summoned the death mask. The ancient power swelled about his body in terrible fury. These beasts were vicious animals, killing for pleasure. Now some of these animals sensed their death. They screamed as the magic of the Death Mask drew their gaze into its cold silvery depths.

Punish the guilty.

Joined in will and body, Seth and the Jalora targeted their leader. Sweat rained down his baldhead. Frozen in the grip of the Death Mask's magic, he whimpered. Then the thief's eyes grew wide. He gave a final cry of defiance and leapt on Seth. The Spirit of the Lion Ring lashed out, slicing his body. Pieces of flesh fell to the ground in a gruesome heap.

"Mercy!" others cried.

Their pleas were met with the cold indifference of an eternal consciousness. They were vermin, unfit to live in the light of good. Seth and the Jalora's unstoppable sword thrusted and sliced through the guilty until the Spirit of the Lion Ring's bloodlust was sated.

The Ancient Power withdrew. Cold struck his face again, shaking him out of the sensation of battle. He had no remorse as he looked upon the gruesome bodies. Justice had been dispensed. Would they have shown kindness or mercy to the innocent women in the carriage? Seth spat upon the stone next to their bodies and turned from them.

Mercy makes the difference between a man of honor and a common killer, his mother's words whispered in his mind.

Seth gripped his hand in a tight fist. They didn't deserve mercy or remorse. It wasn't as if it were up to him at any rate. He shared his body with the Jalora. Sometimes the Spirit of the Lion Ring came to him. Other times the cold emotionless magic of the Death Mask. They all had a say in his actions. Didn't they?

"Watch your back, Lion!"

A hooded figure leapt out of the shadows. His sword came down swiftly upon another thief who'd come dangerously close to striking Seth's back. The dark green stone of his Heart of the Warrior Ring glowed with angry power as he threw back the hood. A familiar curly head shook with dismay as he prodded the body with the toe of his boot.

"Jason?" Seth cried, looking down at the coyote's head staring at him from within the dark green stone. "You're a ranger?"

"Hard to believe, I know." He winked at Seth.

"I didn't think rangers could lie. You said you were a constable."

"No, you assumed I was a constable." Jason grinned and sheathed his sword. "Listen to me, Seth. I think you can guess these men aren't typical thieves from Harrow. I've been watching them. They're mercenaries from the north. These devils have been paid to find and kill you."

"Is Julian D'Antoiné's hand upon my death warrant?"

"I'm not absolutely certain. The name 'Gorman' is spoken frequently among these villains, but I'm not sure who he is." Jason looked past Seth's shoulder suddenly. "Wolf commands I remain hidden. Promise you'll keep me out of the accounts of your battle today."

"Wolf? When did you see him? Is he all right?"

"He is with friends." Jason hurried into the shadows. "Stay out of Lea. It isn't safe, especially for you."

Remaining hidden in the citadel wasn't a promise he could keep. He had his duty to the army. Both he and Riley must obey their orders no matter which direction they pointed. Sergeant Dancer would see to it.

Chapter Thirty-Nine

THE BATTLE for carriage and country had ended when Seth stepped back into the row. His friends had won the day. Sweeping the row, the cadets took up what weapons they could find. They were showing good sense. This was evil's territory. They may need to defend themselves again before reaching the main row of Lea.

"The villains have been removed," Tory said with a mock bow. "All right, Mate? Looks like someone scored a hit on your leg."

A long red line stretched along the front of his left thigh. Someone had hit their mark. Seeing the wound brought its stinging sensation to his attention. He rubbed irritably at it with a hiss.

"I'll be fine," he said. "Well done. Sergeant Dancer would be proud."

A rumble of confident laughter swelled from the cadets as they cheered. Fierce grins stretched across their faces as they stood victorious over the unconscious bodies of their opponents.

"Listen, Mate. We're attracting a crowd above our heads. This is their backyard, Seth. One troop of cadets against the entire district? I don't like the odds." Tory waved a thumb toward the carriage. "Her ladyship says she won't leave her blooming packages behind."

"I'll speak to her. Tell the cadets to bind our prisoners. We'll take them with us."

"Logan already has some of the men on it. Handy man with knots. Right. Well, I'll tell them to get a move on."

Following the steady streams of cursing, Seth joined the driver underneath the wagon. Splinters of broken wheel covered the cobblestone. It was the bent axle, however, which posed the greatest problem. This carriage wasn't going anywhere.

"Is everyone all right?" Seth asked when bouncy ringlets dangled over the back of the carriage just above his head.

"Thanks to you, Sir. This is my mother, Lady Philippa Lambert, and I'm Fanny Lambert." The young lady smiled, holding her hand out.

"Seth McCloud," he said, quickly wiping his bloodied hands on the side of his trousers. "And Cadet Beta Three at your service, my lady. We'll escort you back to the citadel."

"See here, young man. You seem to be the leader of these cadets. My brother-in-law, Lord Lambert, entrusted me with the planning of his daughter's wedding. I am not leaving Alicia's wedding trove behind for these common thieves."

"Be still, you pain in my rump. You're the reason we're in this mess." The driver threw down a piece of wheel. "Haven't you noticed the street has become quiet and unfriendly eyes watch our every move? Let us leave the packages and escape with our lives."

"How dare you speak to me in such a manner?" she said. "If my brother-in-law were here, you wouldn't dare."

"I say we leave her." The driver rolled his eyes. "My Lord Tad the Falcon would be eternally grateful to you."

More rangers. Did they all know each other? Seth grimaced and held his hand toward the carriage. Lady Philippa grew pale with rage, but cast an eye toward the buildings. She took his hand at last and climbed down from the carriage. Fanny followed her, smiling again as she took Seth's hand.

A few howls bounced against the walls and fell to the row around them. Shutters slammed against their frames. Harrow was stirring. They must leave quickly before the unfriendly inhabitants regrouped for another attack.

"You see, Mama. We should have waited for Greg."

Near tears, the young lady pinched at her brown ringlets. The strands of hair twisted and spilled down upon the pale-yellow dress she wore. Fanny didn't seem to notice the fingers of her white gloves had torn beyond repair.

"Quiet Fanny. The whole town is a maze. Anyone could have turned a map the wrong way and led us off to who knows where."

"Anyone, or a rattled old cow like her?" the driver muttered. "I'll be glad to see the back side of this place and return home to Ghent."

"Alicia's my cousin," Fanny told Seth. "She'd understand if we left her things. I know she would."

An unwelcome and humiliating blush burned on his cheeks. Seth had troubles enough building up the courage to speak to his own class of girl on Marianna. Here were two ladies of wealth not used to hearing the practical. He was beginning to appreciate Aunt Charlotte's strong and confident wisdom.

You are my servant, Lion. The Jalora told him firmly. *Your behavior must be above reproach. This lady is not for you. Many a lion have I had to discipline for being overly fond of the chase. You, it would seem, have adopted the Islander modesty. I cannot have my Lion blushing like a school girl when he sees a pretty face. Take a calming breath. Good. Now look at her.*

Seth turned once more to look upon Fanny Lambert. She and her mother stood behind a thick wall of ice. Their thoughts and words could no longer touch him. He was standing in a pool of calm objectivity. Looking upon them through the clarity of the ice wall, he saw their dependence upon those who protected and shelter them. Independence and free will were foreign in their world of duty and social standing. Seth pitied them. It would be innocents such as these who would suffer greatly in the coming months.

Amery darted by them, sweeping down to pick up an abandoned bludgeon before one of the other cadets could snap it up. He brandished the weapon with a pleased smile. His uniform stretched across his muscular frame. Here was a warrior, quick and deadly. Accounts of the twins' travels and hunts were full of danger. Still, Seth hated to ask of him what he must.

"Damage to the carriage is beyond our ability to repair here, Amery. You must run back to the citadel for help. Go back the way we came, my friend. Take Aubrey with you in case there's trouble on the road."

"We will see you soon." Amery slapped Seth on the back with a grin. "Come on, Aubrey. We're taking a little run."

The other cadets were busy ripping strips of fabric from the thieves' garments. They began tying up their prisoners and forcing them to their feet. Riley pushed his bound captive into the center and came to join Seth. His eyes were on the Claybanks as they disappeared into the maze of streets.

Lady Lambert slapped her umbrella on the ragged carriage top. "Young man, are you certain you can trust those barbarians?"

Then balls of fire flew from the windows, showering the row with a curtain of flames. Seth smelled the strong stench of lantern oil and burning dung. The fire would last a long time and effectively cut them off from their escape route.

"Do you think Amery and Aubrey made it to the main row?" Riley asked.

Seth stretched out his power, but fire and hate blocked it. "I hope so."

The Jalora remained silent. It was up to him to find a way out and keep the ladies and his companions safe. How many mercenaries were hidden in Harrow, waiting for their chance to kill the Lion? He'd run right into their kill trap and had brought Beta Three with him.

"We've overstayed our welcome, Beta Three. Time to leave," Seth told them. "The ladies and our injured on the inside. Cadets, form a protective circle around them with prisoners in the front."

He joined Tory beside the line of criminals. Nimble fingers pulled tightly on the bands of fabric binding his unlucky captive. Tory slapped the thief on the back of the head when he squealed.

"Do you know another way out of Harrow?" Seth asked.

"I saw a map the rangers were using to search for the lost cadet three years ago. If we can find Hedgewick Row again, it will take us to the guard gate at the edge of North Burrough." Tory pushed the prisoner into the waiting grip of another cadet. "Mind you, this is all from memory."

"You're the best hope we have. Let's go."

Seth took up position beside Tory at the head of their group. Riley pushed through the cadets to join them. He nodded to Seth. Then they took their first steps deeper into the belly of Evil. Silent and on edge, his friends held their weapons before them. Anxious eyes darted from the windows above them to the shadows in the row.

Shouts of triumph filled the space behind them. The Harrow thieves had reached their abandoned carriage. Ripping. Banging. Pounding. Their greedy hands ravaged the wedding trove.

"The devils couldn't wait until we were out of site!" Lady Lambert shook her battered umbrella.

"Let's hope those packages keep them busy until we're safely out of this district," Riley said.

"The quickest way out of Harrow lies down Hedgewick Row to the east. We'll have to go through North Burrough. It's a good long walk to the main gate of the citadel." Tory leaned in close to save his words for Seth and Riley's ears. "A guard gate runs across Hedgewick at the border of North Burrough. It's not always manned during the day. We may find ourselves trapped against a metal blockade."

Howls of bloodlust echoed against the walls behind them. The thieves had finished with their spoils and were hungry for more. Sudden cries of pain rolled around the corner toward them. He well knew the sound of death. The villains were turning on each other. Greed drove them into a frenzy of violence. They'd soon tire of each other and set out to hunt other prey.

"We must keep moving," he said.

Frozen in their fear, the cadets huddled closer together. Even the prisoners were shaken at the outbreak of ruthless violence. One of them broke ranks and tried to run. Seth swung a fist at his head, knocking him back into his comrades.

"Don't be a fool. You're a dead man on your own." Seth lifted his voice, bringing the strength of the Jalora to his words. "Beta Three. We have a duty to protect the innocent. Weapons at the ready and hold the line. Now let's quicken the pace."

"You don't have to tell me twice, Mate."

Tory trotted along the row, passing several faintly marked signs. The howls of their relentless hounds followed in the stillness of the afternoon. More howls sounding from the row before them joined the baying. Tory stopped in the middle of the row, twisting about.

"Great gulls," Riley cried. "He's lost. Isn't he? Of all the woolie headed adventures, Seth McCloud, this takes the cake. We should have called the rangers before running into Harrow without decent weapons."

"Have a little faith in Tory," Seth said. "He'll find the way."

Banging bludgeons and more howls thundered behind them. The mob was getting closer. He regarded the mother and daughter who'd been used as bait in their trap. They must reach safety even at the expense of Seth's quest. He'd have to reveal his identity.

"I don't like the look in your eyes, Seth. Whatever you're planning, I'm coming with you."

Then a light touch rested on his arm. Fear. Helplessness. Trust. Fanny Lambert trembled beside him. Her hand gripped his right arm. Lady Philippa's fingers pressed into his other. It would seem a common fear removed any class barriers.

Fear can muddle memories, Lion.

Of course! He reached out with his power and touched Tory's memories. Rangers stood around a long table, their manner was tense and focused. They looked enormous to the boy peeking at them from behind the bar. Timid fingers smoothed at the map spread upon the table's surface after they'd gone. Using his friend's eyes, Seth found their position on the map. Pulling back the probe, he let out a breath of relief. Tory had been on the right path after all.

"Does Hurley's mean anything to you, Tory?" Seth asked.

"Say, he's the shifty broker at the corner of Hedgewick and..." Tory snapped his fingers with a grin. "This way! I've found our row. How'd you know about Hurley's?"

"You mentioned it earlier at the carriage," Riley interjected with a frown at Seth.

They passed another small row and turned left down a short block of buildings. Hedgewick Row stretched before them. Its cobblestone surface broke free of the imposing walls and ran past an open area. Evil's presence began to wane. A lightness settled upon his heart as they drew closer to a large steel gate stretching across the road. Armed men, constables from Lea, watched them approach.

"Tory Dawson?" one of them shouted through the steel rods. "What the devil are you doing in Harrow? I thought you had more sense!"

"As did I," Tory said with a wave. "You going to let us in? We've got presents for you."

"I don't recognize half this lot. You'd best see your prisoners into ranger hands." The constable nodded to the ladies. "Dragon's orders. They might be spies."

They stepped through the gates into a different Lea. The buildings were cleaner and a little more kept up as they walked. Proud. Hardworking. Perhaps not as honest as they should be. The people of North Burrough made up the back bone of Lea society. Seth was glad to be among them.

"Does your leg pain you, Cadet?" Fanny asked, her hand still glued to his arm.

"It stings, my lady, but it will heal soon enough."

Lady Philippa cast a wicked look at her daughter and asked in Geltic, "Why must you speak with him, Fanny? He is a commoner and no doubt Valdeonian."

"He's very handsome though."

Seth returned in Geltic, "My home is the Isle of Carlotta, my Lady."

"I meant no insult, young man. It is improper for you to be so familiar. We are kin to a gentleman well above your station."

"Well, that's gratitude for you," Riley murmured in Islic. "I'll just bet she'd change her mind if she knew you were the Crown Prince of Carlotta."

"And where did a cadet from Carlotta learn to speak Geltic fluently?" Lady Philippa asked.

Where indeed. No answer he could give would spare him from more awkward questions. He was saved from her interrogations as the group burst out into the afternoon sunlight. The Obsidian Citadel towered before them, shining like a beacon to their exhausted eyes.

"The Claybanks are coming and they've brought friends," Riley said.

A large wagon approached them from the north. Two identical heads leaned over the driver's seat. Amery waved quickly, then took to his seat again. Seth understood his uneasiness. Running beside the stable master's wagon, a small troop of rangers easily matched the pace of the horse.

"Thank the Heavens!" Lady Philippa cried. "It's Greg."

A golden head of hair towered above the others. The Phoenix ran at the front of his troop. Blazing blue eyes pierced the distance, scanning their bedraggled party. He'd taken on the appearance of the fierce predator bird living within his ring. Raw anger spanned the distance as his eyes fell upon Seth. Power touched his mind as Phoenix began insistent probing.

"Gregory Baldemar?" Tory asked Fanny, with a whistle. "The Phoenix is your cousin's fiancé? Have a care, Seth. His temper is legendary. Phoenix may not like you being friendly with his kinswomen."

Prisoners and cadets alike made a path for the blond ranger as he stopped before them. Phoenix' probing increased. Seth kept his block raised as the insistent touch tried to penetrate his mind.

"Greg! You came to meet us." Lady Philippa rushed forward. "We've been through a horrible ordeal. The villains have taken Alicia's wedding trove. How will we ever replace it?"

Her words went unheeded as the Phoenix' retracted his probe. His hand dropped down to the hilt of his sword. Fury. Concern. Indecision. They swirled about him in a frantic dance.

"Thank you, Cadet," Fanny said, releasing Seth's arm. "You saved our lives."

The heat of her hand upon his arm fell away and she hurried toward the ranger. Fanny fell against him, weeping rather unconvincingly Seth thought. Her tears broke the spell. Phoenix lifted her up into his own arms and held her. His attempts to comfort Fanny were almost tender.

"Your free afternoon is over, Ladies!" Sergeant Dancer barked. "Back to the citadel at double time."

"Hold, Cadet," Phoenix ordered.

He gently prodded Fanny into her mother's arms and marched toward them. The intensity of his gaze hadn't diminished. Seth lifted his chin, standing fast against it.

"You're coming with us into Harrow," Phoenix said.

"Justice has been done, Ranger." Seth took the sword out of his belt and let it drop to the ground.

"Where are they?" Phoenix kicked at the sword.

"In an alley across from the ruined carriage. I'm afraid there isn't much to salvage."

"Gecko. Mantis," Phoenix called to two of the rangers. "Escort the ladies and the prisoners back to the citadel. Take the wagon."

The other rangers formed a line behind Phoenix. He motioned them forward and off they went toward Harrow in a stream of ash.

"You've caused me some trouble, Ranger." Sergeant Dancer said beside him.

"You know?"

"How could I not know?" Dancer growled. "Do you think me a fool? You attract the wrong kind of attention. Ranger attention. Now you listen to me, anymore problems like this and I'll march you to the Dragon myself! If you want to stay hidden, that's your business, but don't expect me to treat you any different than the other cadets."

The sergeant's mustache bristled under his nose as he continued to stare in the direction the rangers had gone. Seth shifted uneasily as he waited. Sergeant Dancer was a man who'd always kept his promises to Beta Three. Seth believed his threats.

"Phoenix is in a foul mood. He doesn't seem to like you very much. Go to the infirmary for your leg. Tell the Doctor I said you must stay there at least until tomorrow afternoon. His temper may cool by then."

"Thank you, Sergeant."

The single ray of sunshine had retreated from the infirmary window. Seth lay awake on the cot, trying not to scratch off the ointment the healer had applied. His thoughts were fixed upon the thieves in the alley. The Jalora hadn't commanded him to chase after the villains. Why had he?

"The leg bothers you, Hopeful?" Phoenix said beside him.

Seth jumped in his blankets. He hadn't heard or sensed the ranger enter the room. Phoenix sat back easily in a chair beside his bed. Hair freshly washed, he wore a clean uniform and polished boots.

"Easy, I didn't come to kill you as your Sergeant or your friends suspect I would."

"Then why have you come, Sir?"

"To apologize. To thank you. To give you this." The ranger held out a silver box.

Seth ran his fingers over the beautiful surface. Inside the box, a dagger rested upon rich fabric. The image of the Phoenix had been etched within the blade. It was a fine weapon, expensive and well made.

"Thank you, Sir. I couldn't possibly keep it."

"Nonsense. It's the least I can do for your bravery today. Young Fanny told me of your tremendous courage. I'm overly protective of her sometimes. She was raised without a father and you've met her mother. Fanny was furious with me for suspecting the worst. I saw the ladies hanging off your arms and jumped to the wrong conclusion."

Seth shook his head and rubbed at the dagger. "I don't think such a fine lady would ever find me of much interest, Sir."

"You're wrong, Hopeful. My Lady Fanny speaks of little else. I'm afraid I couldn't condone her visiting you in the infirmary. You see, I know nothing about you. The name McCloud is a half-truth. Isn't it?"

"I'm not sure how to answer your question. You must trust me. I mean no ill intent." Seth smoothed at the blankets with sweaty palms. "Are you going to keep my secret?"

"I have so far…Cadet." The ranger winked at him and stood. "I'll leave you to your rest."

Phoenix hesitated by the door. "Don't let your mind worry about the alley. Sometimes it is difficult to see our duty done, but rest in the fact a higher wisdom guides our actions."

Seth stared at the door long after the ranger left. He'd let down his guard. Now there was no way to tell how much Phoenix had learned of what he was thinking. Seth lay back against his pillow with a sigh. He wished the higher wisdom the ranger spoke of would tell him what he needed to do next.

Chapter Forty

AN ANGRY DUST CLOUD rolled along the blue horizon. Many hooves stomped at the hot land, kicking up dried ground in their wake. The cloud was headed straight for San Lucida. Jorge crouched at the top of the ridge a few hundred yards from the opening of the canyon. Smoothing a hand along his torso, he rested it over the prickling power of the Regent Medallion.

"Could it be the Jackal?" Duarto asked.

"They came onboard ships in the night," Jorge said, dropping his hand. "These men arrive at midday like allies."

"Or men with nothing to fear," Duarto added with a scowl.

"Perhaps," Jorge said, giving his hunters a reassuring grin. "Let's get a closer look. Armed men, friend or foe, will cause panic among the people."

They followed the trail along the ridge upon quiet feet. His teachings of Pacarro Tribe traditions had turned field hands into silent warriors. His son was the most ardent pupil among them. Jorge's pride in Duarto was laced with sad regret. Weeks after the fall of Valdeon, Duarto continued to hate himself for not dying with his comrades.

Quick legs, now used to life in the wild, descended the rocky trail to reach the mouth of the canyon within minutes. Blending with the shadows among the rocks, Jorge and his hunters waited for the dust cloud to reach them.

Thundering hooves shook the ground as their deafening beats struck the row to San Lucida. Then dust parted. Gigantic horses pounded at a steady pace toward the canyon entrance. It was the San Marimosa Cavalry. His old friend, Alberto Mendoza, was at their head.

Dusty and stiff from the long ride, Alberto brought his men to a slow canter. Eyeing the canyon walls with care, the cavalry nervously drew closer. Archers aimed at the tops of the ridge. Cavalrymen held their muskets at the ready.

"You'll find no ambush in San Lucida, Alberto." Jorge stepped away from the rock wall only feet away from his friend's leg. "Well, not today at any rate."

"My eyes are glad to see you, Jorge." Alberto dismounted and embraced him warmly. "I wasn't sure what we would find in San Lucida."

"Your fortress was spared then?"

"The Jackal found us too stubborn," Alberto told him. "They gave up and sailed back to the east."

"Come, my friends. We have water for your horses and perhaps a little hope to share."

Hope and excitement filled the ruins of San Lucida. Seeing the legendary San Marimosa Cavalry ride triumphantly through their city gave even the weakest of them courage. Jorge delighted in his people's rare happiness. They danced and sang, following the cavalry until the horses reached the shores of Lake Lucida. Later in the evening, they feasted upon the dried meat Alberto had brought with him. For the first time in many days, every stomach was full.

"You said you had hope to share, Jorge."

Alberto poked the fire with a large stick. The flames danced within their stone pit, casting shadows upon the bodies of his officers. Features harden with war and loss, the cavalrymen waited with tentative interest for Jorge to speak. These men needed hope as much as Jorge needed to share it.

"The Orb of Valdeon pulses with the young Lion's heartbeat." Jorge grinned as stunned silence transformed into excited clamoring.

"Can this miracle be true?" Stephano, Captain of the San Marimosa Guard, came to sit beside his lord.

Jorge held up his hands to quiet them. "It is true. Cesar Santiago saw it with his own eyes."

Anxious ears listened as he told them Cesar's account of being summoned to the throne room and finding Xavier the Wolf standing before the Orb. More excited talk greeted the news of the Lion's return to the West. Alberto listened carefully and had him retell the story a second time as word spread among his troops.

"You've no idea the relief this news gives me." Alberto rubbed at his watering eyes. "I'd wondered after my son's fate. You've given us all hope, Jorge, but none more than I."

Alberto's son, Berto the Jaguar, was Wolf's second in the Sacred Guard. He was a talented ranger, devoted to his duty and to Wolf. Jorge had assumed he and the rest of the Lords of Valdeon were together in the East, protecting the Altar of Providence.

"What has happened to him, Alberto?"

"Fox arrived in San Marimosa the night Valdeon fell. He brought young Otter with him. They helped draw enemy fire away from the fortress. Berto joined them onboard the *Wind Chaser*. The last time I saw my son, he and his friends were sailing south to look for Tulio the Rabbit. We expected them back within a day, but they didn't return."

"Do you think they joined Wolf and the young Lion?" Duarto asked.

Alberto nodded with a smile. "Yes. It's what my heart tells me."

"What now, my lords?" Stephano asked. "Are we to send for aid from the Legion? Perhaps through the mountain pass?"

Jorge sighed and shook his head. "The mountain pass is closed to us. My hunters and I were searching for refugees when a burning Legion ship crashed in the narrow pathway. The Jackal have defeated the Legion Armada. I fear the rangers will have their hands full protecting Andara's other borders."

"We must get these people to safety. San Lucida can't shelter them for much longer," Stephano said across the fire. "We can't take them to San Marimosa."

Alberto turned away and stared down into the fire, ruthlessly poking the burning logs. He hadn't told them everything. The little light of hope was beginning to fade.

"San Marimosa has its own refugees, doesn't it?" Jorge asked. "And you fear the Jackal's return."

"We don't know why they left so suddenly. Our walls were close to falling under their cannon fire. I can't explain it." Alberto lifted his eyes to stare out across the hundreds of people crowding together beside their fires. "Refugees from all over southwest Valdeon came to San Marimosa looking for protection. They can't fit inside the walls. If we're hit again, many will die. I can't take these people with me, because I can't protect them either."

"Then there is no hope for the west?" Duarto asked.

"We have hope, my son," Jorge told him. "You must have faith. The Lion will return. I know it."

Burning power spread across Jorge's side. The Regent Medallion was active again. Warning him in times of peril, he'd become accustomed to the short bursts of pain. This time the burning crawled across his body with sharp fingers. It invaded his legs and arms until they were useless under his weight.

The power raced into his chest, digging deeper inside until it found his heart. A single scream ripped its way out of Jorge's throat as his body lifted into the air. Stars in a cloudless sky encompassed his vision. Then everything went dark. His conscious mind drifted in the nothingness.

A single dot of light appeared in the distance. It grew bigger and bigger as it approached. No. He was speeding toward it. Jorge tried raising his hands to block the brilliant glare from the dot, but he had no hands to lift. Suddenly he was in immersed dazzling white light as he stood in the gleaming atrium of the Palace of Kings. Rubbing at the front of his filthy hunting tunic, he couldn't quite make his hands obey. No matter. What would the king say if he came before the throne in such a state?

Something brushed against the back of his knees, propelling him forward. A massive Lion prowled along the tiles a few feet behind him. Its ethereal green eyes stared into his own, binding Jorge to its will.

Follow the Lion, Jorge Pacarro.

The Lion walked on silent paws farther into the light. Jorge's boots stomped down the atrium floor after the beast. He knew very well where they were headed. The golden doors of the throne room swung wide to greet him. Glowing with the white light of the young Lion's life force, the Altar of Providence waited. The awesome power of the Jalora was everywhere. It circled about him, holding his body in place.

I call you to service, Jorge Pacarro. A voice wrapped around him, piercing through his fear. *Lead the people and await the true King's return. This charge I give to you, Regent of Valdeon.*

"I am not worthy!"

The roar of the mighty Lion shook the foundations of the palace. Jorge screamed, covering his head with his arms. Would the beast devour him? The gruesome fate might be better than his future as Regent.

Something grabbed his arms, shaking at him. Jorge screamed louder, thrashing about against the creatures. More digits pressed into his legs and body. He struggled against them, but there were too many.

"Mercy!" Jorge cried. "I will obey! I swear it upon my very soul!"

"Father? It's Duarto. Wake. Come back to us in San Lucida."

San Lucida? Jorge sat up and opened his eyes. The brilliant light of the Jalora was still before him.

"I can't see!" Jorge clutched at the arms of his son. "The light…it has blinded me!"

"Father, what are you talking about?"

"By the Jalora!" Alberto said, gripping harder at Jorge's arm. "Look! There upon his chest. The Regent Medallion."

Jorge brought his trembling hands to the thick chain hanging about his neck. His fingers followed it down to a large medallion. Jorge ran his finger tip along the engraving there. The Altar of Providence burst from its golden surface.

"The Lion and the Jalora called me to service, but I am not worthy of this."

"The Jalora thinks you are, Father."

"What did the Jalora say, my lord regent?" Alberto asked.

"It commanded I lead the people until the return of our true king," Jorge said, laying back down.

Blurry images were beginning to appear inside the white. Jorge breathed a little easier. His vision had not been taken from him. Dear sweet Erthe Mother, what was he to do? He was a Pacarro tribesman, not a great statesman. How would he ever unite the scattered people of Valdeon? No. It was an impossible task for a mere man. Only their true king could perform such a miracle. The Lion would return one day and Jorge would be ready to serve him. Until then, he must keep the people strong in their hope.

Chapter Forty-One

Julian knelt beside the small door leading into Lord Gorman's room. It had taken several hours of persuading to convince the wretched laundry woman to divulge her secret. Marcellus, in his exuberance, maintained a child-like sense of playfulness as he'd questioned her. She'd had a bizarre sense of loyalty, but finally told them of the secret entrance into the Jackal General's chambers. Lord Gorman would have to find someone else to do his laundry in the future.

Pushing the small door open, he stopped when he heard voices. Lord Gorman's grinding tones were immediately recognizable. The woman's, however, was soft and melodic like crystal bells. Curious, he crawled through the space and came to crouch behind a pillar. A pool of water, suspended sideways in the air, floated before Gorman's seated form. It was perfectly tranquil, unlike the rough waters of the pool Uther had conjured. The angelic form of a woman shimmered within its depths. She was an Ancient, one of the timeless people across the sea - the Luminawni.

"Must you wear such a hideous mask, dearest?"

Pale hair wrapped around a golden tiara. Strands fell to her elegant shoulders and framed perfect porcelain features. Eternal youth smoothed her skin and made her body supple. It was her air, however, which told of a certain wounded nobility.

"You know very well I must, Mother. My father insists. Besides, it gives me certain advantages upon the battlefield."

"You are not on the battlefield now, my son."

"Am I not?"

Gorman was part Luminawni? This was ill news. They were immortals, impossible to kill. And yet Gorman's father, Uther, wasn't Luminawni. Perhaps the savage blood inside of Gorman would prove his undoing?

"Our time is short and I will not be drawn into another debate with you," she said, a hair's breadth from leaning through the waters. "Mark me. Uther has given you a half-truth, my son. Andara is much more important than a mere strategic location. It is a means to win the war and all of Erthe."

"I don't understand, Mother."

"I was there a century ago when the Jalora put the Lion Ring upon Mikel D'Antoiné's finger. Rohin and I helped create the Altar of Providence." His mother's eyes grew fierce. "Long have I waited for this chance, my son. I am sister to Rohin, Emperor of the Luminawni. I wasn't meant to be tied to a beast. As my son, it is you who should wear the crown of Andara as its emperor."

Gorman stood up from his chair and leaned against its arm. He appeared bored, as if he'd sat through this conversation many times. His mother seemed not to notice. Her eyes blazed with an emotion Julian understood well - ambition.

"The man who sits upon the Lion Throne holds Erthe in his hand. The Jalora and the Sarcion are equally matched in power and territory now, but if the Lion reaches his full potential, the Jalora will hold sway. The Sarcion will do anything to keep this from happening. Destroy the Lion Ring and take the crown for your own, then you will hold sway over both the Jalora and the Sarcion. They will give you anything you ask in exchange for your loyalty. Then we can be rid of Uther forever. I will be welcomed once more in the halls of my homeland."

"You forget one thing, my mother. If I kill Father, you will be weakened. Your wedding vows bond your life forces together."

"My brother will save me. He won't let me die. I may be diminished, but it will be worth it for you to take the throne, Gorman. Then we can both be rid of Uther."

He turned away from his mother, yanking upon the invisible chains of her love. Julian knew too well those bonds. Leo had tried to win his affection. It had been gratifying when his father had finally accepted the hatred Julian held for him.

"I will think on these things while I'm taking Andara."

Gorman moved away from his chair, but Julian's eyes were still transfixed upon the porcelain angel of doom within the pool. Her eyes still sparkled with fierce ambition. She finally let her hand drop. The watery magic disappeared.

"I wonder if she could ever fathom how much I want to be rid of them both?" Gorman said at his ear.

"You see, Julian. I understand you better than you think."

Gorman grabbed Julian by the nap of the neck and threw him against the wall. He hit painfully on his injured arm. Dropping to the floor, he tipped over upon his side. Julian lie still for a moment, waiting for the pin pricks of light to fade from his eyes.

"Yes, well, at least I had the courage to kill my father rather than beg for scraps at his table."

Gorman picked him up as if he were a child's toy and suspended him well above the floor. A knock at the door stayed Gorman's fist. Squeezing a hand tightly about Julian's neck, Gorman ignored the next two knocks. Then the door swung open. A feral growl escaped through the grill upon Gorman's mask. He dropped Julian and turned to face the Dirge and its keeper. Two Changeling had followed them in. Their black eyes sparkled in amusement when they caught sight of Julian.

"Pray your news is important enough to warrant breaking into my chambers unannounced!"

"We bring news from Lea, my lord," the Jackal handler reported. "Xavier the Wolf still lives. His friends have hidden him."

"I gave you ten Dirge! How could you bumbling fools lose him?"

Wolf. It would appear the ranger was as much a foil to the Jackal as he was to Julian. A begrudging sense of pride flickered momentarily in Julian's heart. He'd be proud of such a son of Valdeon if he didn't hate the man so much.

"He crushed my brethren to dust!" the Dirge moaned in its barely understandable tongue. "You underestimate this ranger."

"You dare speak to me, puppet!"

Gorman stretched out his hand. Power, lurid and hungry, engulfed the once human thing. The Sarcion constricted its power like a marsh snake, crushing the Dirge. It writhed with pain, but didn't plead for its life. Perhaps somewhere in the deep recesses of its mind, the human being still existed and was desperate for release from its horrible mistake.

"Dispose of the body." Gorman let his hand drop. "Remember this day. Do not fail me again."

Julian slipped around the wall to follow the creature's handler as he began to drag its body outside. Perhaps Gorman had worked out his ill will upon the creature? Either way, it was a good time to leave his presence and begin adjusting his plans. He crept toward the door, but a solid fist grabbed his collar and threw him down.

"I want you to mark this day as well, Julian bastard prince. The moment my father is convinced you are no longer of use, your life is mine to take. I despise you, worm. And your stench is unbearable.

"Hold him down."

The Changelings grabbed Julian and pinned his rotting arm to the ground. Gorman pulled his blade and sliced it through bone and flesh. Quicksilver fire burned through his body. Empty air filled the space where his arm had once been. Then a strange absence muddled his mind. The parting was unbearable. Julian screamed and clutched at his bloody stump.

Then an odd pressure pushed at the skin and bone of his arm. Gray skin covering a long bone and flesh sprouted from his severed limb. It grew, stopping only when it was the same length as his good arm. Long black nails jutted with a pop from his fingertips.

"Well, hello cousin!" one of the Changelings laughed. "You are a surprise!"

Gorman burst into laughter. "Julian, you truly are a bastard. And now we know by how much. A half-breed Changeling. Your sire must have tried for years until he found a willing brood mare."

Julian screamed as he stared at the gray flesh. Running from the room, he clutched the arm against his torso. The Jalora had cursed him. It had said he was to live with the truth he'd run away from for so long. Was it truth or was this yet another trick?

Black eyes and sharp teeth met him as he raced around the corner. It was yet another Changeling. There seemed to be more arriving each day. Soon the entire palace would be filled with them.

"Greetings, Cousin." The Changeling grinned, exposing its teeth. "Lord Gorman leaves soon for the northern shores of Andara. He must prepare for the invasion. He commands you stay here in the safety of your chambers. But he doesn't understand our need to seek out mischief, does he, Cousin? I recognize your hate. You seek the boy king. Perhaps your family can help? A Changeling king would be very powerful."

"No! I want nothing of you. I am Julian D'Antoiné, son of Edmund D'Antoiné, King of Valdeon. I am the rightful heir to the throne!"

"Then you don't know?"

Julian stared into those dark eyes sparkling with anticipation. "Will you tell me or make me suffer?"

"Oh now, Cousin. We are on the same side." It pointed to Julian's arm. "By blood, I will tell you all. The Jalora has chosen its Regent. The Medallion's power has awakened and the atrium shines brightly with the news. Our spies in the west speak of a great warrior - Jorge Pacarro. He has enticed the Jalora's favor."

"That barbarian! What can he do?"

"Much now he has the medallion's power. You will come around, Cousin, and when you do, your family will be waiting."

Julian ran blindly down the corridor toward his own chambers. They'd see who ruled Valdeon once he had the Lion Ring upon his finger. He had to find the boy and now he knew where to look. If Wolf was in Lea, then certainly he'd be nurse maid to the young Lion again. They were probably hiding in the citadel, weeping about their ill fortunes. How he hated them both.

Chapter Forty-Two

SETH SHIFTED uncomfortably in his ill-fitting dress uniform. He'd been hastily washed, dressed, and prodded out of the infirmary despite the doctor's order for bed rest. A nervous young corporal ordered him to report to Commandant Sharp's office. Impatient with Seth's stiff-legged pace, he'd fussed and fretted until they'd reached their destination.

UR Army Headquarters hung three stories over the main entrance of the citadel. Sun poured through the many windows lining the stone walls. Several desks formed a narrow walkway. Heads lifted in mild interest from the massive amounts of paperwork as Seth and the corporal passed.

The corporal ushered him into a large office at the end of the line of desks. Shelves of ledgers stood against the obsidian walls. Their plain spines gave the room an oppressive feel. Breaking the solid line of ledgers, a closed door stood at the back of the room.

"Cadet McCloud for the commandant, Lieutenant Finley."

"You took longer than you should have, Corporal. I'm sure the commandant will want to discuss your delay when he's finished. Now go about your duties."

"Yes, Sir."

Ranger ears captured the corporal's muttered curses as he left the room. He and his fellow soldiers shared a few colorful descriptions of the lieutenant out among the busy desks. The commandant's aid seemed to enjoy the power of his position a bit too much.

"You'll have to do a better job of standing at attention, Cadet." Lieutenant Finley smirked as he took in Seth's untidy uniform and wet head.

He was a spindly man with sickly skin and thinning gray hair. The sour expression he wore told of his unwarranted arrogance. Greed and pettiness vibrated off him in obnoxious hues.

"Yesterday you were the hero. Today you're the linguist. Is there anything you can't do, Cadet McCloud?" Finley leaned back in his chair, fiddling absently with his letter opener. "Better go in. He's been waiting for you."

Seth opened the door to the commandant's office and stood at attention before a great wooden desk loaded with papers. Commandant Sharp didn't look up as he entered. Engrossed in a parchment he was intently reading, his finger moved purposefully down the paper. Frustration. Anger. Fear. Seth was shaken by the intensity of his anxiety. Something had happened and it meant danger for the United Realm.

Flicking a wet strand of hair off his face, he swiftly put his arm back down before the commandant could see him break attention. He needn't have bothered. The man's balding head remained buried in the parchment he was examining. Maps spilled over the desk's edge. All of them appeared to be drawings of the territories to the north from what Seth could see.

"Well?" Commandant Sharp said, finally acknowledging him. "Are you McCloud?"

"Yes, Sir. I mean, Cadet McCloud reporting for duty."

"Where the devil have you been? We've been waiting for over an hour. Well, never mind. I have two visitors from the Buell countries in the next room. They don't speak the common tongue." The Commandant slapped the parchment down on his desk. "Their timing couldn't be worse. The only linguist in the entire UR who speaks Lydec has gone gallivanting off to parts unknown. Do you speak their language?"

Commandant Sharp popped up from his chair and marched around the desk without waiting for a response. In truth, Seth had no idea whether he could speak Lydec or not. He'd always been a quick study when it came to languages, but he'd never heard a word of Lydec uttered on Marianna.

He followed the commandant through another door nested between a shelf and a sickly-looking plant. Two men sat at the long oak table positioned in the center of the room. They were dressed in what appeared to be their traditional outfits. Bright red tassels covered tan vests and trousers. Bits of yellow embroidery made patterns around the edges of their vests. Similar in design, their outfits were different enough to distinguish each country. The men's emotions, however, mirrored each other exactly. Neither men trusted the other or the commandant.

West and East Buell speak the same language and have the same traditions. They were one people until civil war tore them apart. It was a silly squabble, but the Buellanders are a fiery race. Win their trust, Lion. They bring important news.

Then the Lion Ring tingled under its leather hiding place. Memories from Lions past filled his mind. Several of his ancestors had fought battles in the mountains of the Buells. Others had simply spent time among their people.

"I would ask the representative from West Buell to speak first, for his is the right of Age," Seth said in the Lydec tongue.

"You know our customs, Cadet. Very well, then you know once an agreement has been made it must be kept. If the agreement is broken, restitution must be made."

"We broke no agreement," his Eastern counterpart growled. "You accuse us falsely. We want compensation for the insult."

Seth raised his hands. "I invoke the right of mediation on behalf of the Commandant. Would the Western delegate please tell us what agreement was broken?"

"East Buell agreed to let our wagons of goods travel unmolested through their country when the sea grows too rough in autumn. They broke this agreement and attacked our caravan, taking our valuables and killing our people. We have right to compensation."

"Liar! They attacked their own caravan to trick us into paying."

A storm of angry voices rose again. The Western Bueller leapt across the table, his hands forming a tight grip upon the Eastern Bueller's throat. Seth pulled him off while Commandant Sharp held his rival at bay.

"I don't know what the devil you're saying, McCloud, but this is only making it worse!"

"I'll try again, Sir," Seth pushed the Western Bueller into a chair. "Do you have proof of the attack?"

The Western Bueller huffed and waved at a hard shell of armor leaning against his pack beside the wall. A painted Jackal growled from the armor's metal surface. Seth let his hands fall away from the man's body. He stared into the brutal symbol haunting his dreams each night.

Commandant Sharp seemed equally unnerved as he ran tentative fingers over the image. "Jalora protect us."

"You have seen this symbol before, Commandant?" the Eastern Bueller asked.

"You speak the common tongue?"

"It is our custom only to speak Lydec in times of ceremony."

"Yes, well very helpful." The Commandant grabbed a piece of paper and wrote a hasty note, handing it to Seth when he finished. "Go straight down the corridor past the officers' barracks and you'll see the Obsidian Gates. A bell hangs outside the door. Ring it and hand this parchment to the man who answers. Don't try to go in. It's forbidden. If you get lost, just ask for the rangers."

Seth saluted and hurried out the door. Lieutenant Finley staggered backward. He'd been eavesdropping on their conversation. Surprise. Anxiety. Greed. It was an odd mix of emotions. Seth hurried past him. He'd no time for another mystery right now.

"Ranger territory, eh?" Finley leaned against his desk with a smug smile. "Well, well. Aren't we moving up in the world/ Don't try to go through those black gates. One Zap and the orbs will kill you. Wouldn't that be a shame."

He laughed as Seth raced out of the office and into the hall. Setting aside the man's odd behavior, he concentrated on his own problem. How was he to keep his identity hidden now? He'd certainly never planned to walk straight up to the gate and knock.

A light touch upon his body brought Seth back to the business at hand. Magic. Its presence wrapped about him even before he turned the corner and saw the Obsidian Gates. Two orbs floated in midair on either side, twisting and scanning every angle. They stopped suddenly. All their intent focused upon him as he approached.

The Valdeonian man's horrific death by their power was forever in his memories. He was about to walk into range of the killing magic armed only with a note. Wait. Where was the bell? Seth ran a hand through his wet curls, giving them a good tug. Taking a tentative step forward, he waited for the angry zap of power. Instead, unspoken words formed in his mind.

Welcome, Bearer of the Lion Ring.

They knew him. Seth shook his head. Of course, they did. Standing between the two magical orbs, he looked more closely at the surface of the gates. The engravings, handles, and dimensions appeared to be the same as the gates in the arena. He squeezed the note mercilessly in frustration. Which ones hid the Book of Ancients?

Block, Lion! The time is not right.

Suddenly, the gates swung open and the orbs swept aside. For a moment, the image of a man Seth knew well stood in the center of the foyer. Edmund the Leo, his father, gazed out upon the gate opening.

An older, distinguished ranger marched into the hall. Immense power radiated from his body. Seth's attention was drawn to the brilliant white light surrounding his ring. The image of a white dragon burst from the dark purple stone. Cardinal Dragon, head of the Jalora Legion, plucked the note from Seth's hand. He marched quickly toward the Commandant's office without reading it.

Dragon stopped at the door, pressing a hand against the wood as Seth pulled on it. "I don't know why you're hiding, Hopeful, but your game has just come to an end. Panic and despair hangs over the streets of Andara. Every ranger is needed to keep order. You will take up your duties as a protector of the people."

Then he pulled the door open and stepped through without another word. Commandant Sharp, his aid, and the Buellanders bowed in deep respect as the Dragon came among them. The doors closed, leaving Seth shaken. The head of the Jalora Legion knew about his presence within the citadel, but did he know his identity? Time would tell.

Dragon doesn't guide your steps, Lion. I do. Isn't there something else occupying your mind? A clue perhaps?

The Jalora was right. Now was the perfect time to pass through the gates without being noticed. Leo's statue might very well give him a clue to finding the

Book of Ancients and some insight into his father's past.

Magic stretched back out to surround him as he stood before the gates. He was vaguely aware the orbs had stopped their spinning to regard him. Reaching out a trembling hand, he pulled upon the handles. The magic left him and turned outward to guard the hall once more.

Beautiful wooden walls and marbled floors greeted him as he entered. The large hall looked deserted. He moved with light footsteps, scanning portraits and busts of rangers. A plaque hanging above the portraits announced he was in the Hall of Heroes. It was a memorial to ranger heroes from the past and present.

Standing in the middle of the corridor was the life-size bronze statue of Leo. Seth hurried to the base of his father's statue and read the inscription: *Edmund 'Leo' D'Antoiné, Rank: Bishop. Hero of the Portsmeth and North Marsh border wars.*

His father had been a hero, someone the rangers obviously respected. If Leo had been a trusted and honored member of the Jalora Legion, then why had he suddenly changed his mind about sending Seth to the Obsidian Citadel?

He touched the cold bronze cheek. "I wish we had more time together. Sleep well."

"I suspected you were either a Lord of Valdeon or one of the Twenty-Two Altar Guard. Don't worry. You have my word. I'm a friend."

Phoenix stood quietly in the corner of the hall. His intense blue eyes took in the grief threatening to spill from Seth's eyes. The ranger nodded and smiled sadly.

"I knew Edmund the Leo. He was my mentor and a good friend. Leo took the time to encourage me when I was just an apprentice. I hope one day to be the kind of King he was. Maybe one of my subjects will love me enough to risk punishment just to see my statue. Don't worry, I won't tell Dragon. Come. The way is clear. Hurry now, before you're seen."

Phoenix winked at him and closed the gates. Seth stood staring at their black depths for a long time before moving back toward the infirmary. His father had been a king? He smoothed at the Lion Ring under his glove. The king of beasts, it was called. So, Leo had been the King of Valdeon and his mother had been a princess of Tslavia. Now he understood why his hunters were so intent upon his death. Such blind hatred festered in the ugliness of ignorance. It had been carefully nurtured in the nurseries of Valdeon and Tslavia for centuries. How could he ever overcome such deep seeded hate?

Chapter Forty-Three

"LEO WAS THE KING of Valdeon?" Riley plopped down on his cot in the barracks. "I can't believe it."

"Neither can I," Seth said, leaning his leg against Riley's cot.

Leo must have been very powerful as both ranger and king. He obviously had equally powerful enemies. His murderous son, Julian, may have arranged their father's murder, but who had been brazen enough to help him? These Jackal and their gruesome assassins, the Dirge, must have had an ally on Andarian shores well before they spoke to his half-brother.

"Good to see you back on your feet." Tory slapped Seth on the back. "Now what can't we believe, Mate?"

"The rangers are kings and princes," Riley said quickly.

Tory ran his fingers through his straight, straw-colored hair and flopped down on his cot across from them. Reaching under his mattress, he pulled out a bag of rock candy. Tory tossed a piece to Seth, Riley, and the Claybanks as they came into the barracks.

"Of course, they are, Mate. Only gentry can be rangers. Those rings of theirs won't pick commoners like you or me."

"How do you know so much about them?" Amery asked.

"They all romp about in Dad's pub. I know just about everything there is to know about them."

"Aye?" Riley snorted, giving Seth a quick grin. "Then tell me about the bishop ranger who was supposed to have gone missing? Leo something or other."

Tory sat up, staring at Riley with an open mouth. "Come, even on an island in the ocean you must recognize the Leo? Better known as Edmund D'Antoiné the King of Valdeon."

"We know little of southlanders in North Pointe," Amery said, plucking another candy from his bag. "He was special, this ranger from Valdeon?"

"Indeed, he was." Tory shook his head with a frown. "It was a great shame the day Leo disappeared. He was a kind man as I remember it. Used to give me a few coins every time he came to Dad's pub. You won't see one of those other bishops come down among the people."

Seth turned away, pretending to fuss about with his duffle. The memories of his own short time with Leo flooded his heart. Haunting memories of the hot blood pumping out of his father's body and onto his hands shared space in his nightmares with the Jackal.

Tory said with a wicked grin. "I know where they train, gents. I can take you to see if you're keen to know about them. If you dare set foot in Ranger Territory."

Aubrey frowned. "You know Legion HQ is off limits to us."

"Too afraid, Claybank? You can stay here with the other girlies."

"Claybanks are not afraid of anything," Amery stormed. "We will go if Seth goes, too."

"What about it, Seth?" Tory asked, warming to the idea. "We could sneak out of barracks right after lights out. The rangers will be sure to be doing something more interesting than sleeping. We could sneak a peek and be back before the sergeant misses us."

Riley gave him a warning look, but said nothing. It was a stupid risk. Tory might be exaggerating again, but Seth was out of ideas and no closer to finding the Book of Ancients. He nodded.

"Now you're talking," Tory said with a triumphant grin at Amery.

Aubrey smacked his brother in the back of the head and sunk down sullenly on his cot. Seth took to his own cot. Lights out was a few minutes away. They'd have to be careful. Sergeant Dancer had ears sharper than a rabbit.

Several minutes later, they crept through the snoring cadets and out into the dim corridors of the citadel. Utter silence met them. Cold and cave-like, the citadel was sleeping. Seth brushed his hands against the walls. They warmed at his touch.

"You're the one who insists on remaining hidden. Honestly." Riley pulled Seth's hand away as the walls began to glow. "This is madness! What if we're caught?"

"I was given a clue, Riley. Perhaps the mystery can only be answered in Legion Headquarters. And don't roll your eyes. I know perfectly well you've said as much before."

Tory turned a sharp corner and immediately took a set of stairs descending to the first floor. He stopped at the bottom and stuck his head out into the army's empty mess hall. Waving them forward, he hurried through the hall. Large double doors waited against the back wall. Tory held open the doors. Residual odors of fish, bread, and other food lingered. They'd arrived in the kitchens.

"A female friend of mine who works with me in the kitchens tells me there is a separate door for Jalora Legion diners."

Aubrey frowned at Tory. "Has she ever actually been inside?"

"No, but the other fellow I stole her from is one of the kitchen crew who serves the Legion. He hands the trays to the squires. Trust me. The door is there."

Large ovens, empty and cold during the night, made massive islands in the middle of spotless floors. Bowls of resting dough sat upon the counter tops. Waiting for skilled hands, they were destined to be breakfast.

"Found it. I told you it would be here, Claybank." Tory crouched beside a small door just large enough for a man to crawl through. "What are these lines boxing in the door?"

Tory shrugged and grabbed the knob. He twisted it quietly, but it didn't move.

"Locked," Riley said, with a grin. "Too bad, guess we'll have to call it off."

"It's a good thing I'm handy with locks, Logan."

Tory's fingers flew around the ancient lock. Mumbling in frustration, he kept wiggling and twisting his pick tools. The small hairs on Seth's arms prickled as magic touched them. Using his sight, he took in the door and walls. Tory, focused on the lock, couldn't see the two circles of light powering up on either side of the door. Now he understood why there were lines upon the floor. They were a warning. Magic, angry, and deadly, filled the kitchen.

These ancient guardians will not allow intruders, Lion. Make no mistake. It will kill your comrades.

Seth thrust his hand toward Tory's quick working fingers to stop him. The probing magic of the orbs suddenly stopped and the door clicked open.

"Why did they opened the door?" Seth asked the Jalora within his thoughts.

They open for you, my Lion. A Lord of Valdeon may bring guests within Legion Headquarters, but it isn't advised. Rangers stay apart from common men for good reason.

Pushing inside quickly, Seth made certain the orbs had gone before his friends could follow. Legion Headquarters was a different world than the obsidian walls housing the UR Army. Elaborately carved wooden paneling covered the walls of what appeared to be a central junction or hall. Beautiful paintings and fine statuary stood upon white marbled floors. It was the most beautiful place he'd ever seen. The Jalora's presence was everywhere. In the wall. In the floors. This, he realized, was one of its strongholds.

"I've heard tales from those who've had a peek through the door, but I never expected to see anything like this!" Tory told them, pointing upward. "Look at the ceiling, gents!"

Animals hovered above their heads, forever captured in paint. The artist's hand had captured every detail, from the smallest feather to the largest claw. They were incredible. None, however, matched the fierce beauty of the massive lion at their center. Its mane spanned across the entire center panel of the painting. Large ethereal eyes seemed to stare right down into Seth's soul. Here in full color was the Lion Spirit of the ring.

"Someone is coming," Amery hissed.

Boots made measured stomps upon the white stone. They were coming closer, with no signs of slowing. The Claybanks tried to push back into the kitchen, but Tory had shut it behind them. Seth looked desperately around the many corridors opening into the hall. If they were caught, his identity would be exposed. The punishment would be worse for his friends.

"Down here," Seth said, racing as quietly as he could toward a pair of double doors.

He stretched out the Jalora into the room as they ran. It was empty, but something within reached out to welcome his touch. Seth hesitated at the door, not certain if it was such a good idea to go in now.

His friends pushed at his back as the footsteps came closer. They raced inside and Seth soundlessly closed the door behind them. Pressing his back against the door, he finally noticed they were surrounded by hundreds of shelves filled with books. A library. He walked farther into the room, staring at the shelves. His quest was close to being fulfilled. The Book of Ancients must be somewhere in this library. Where else would it be, but behind magic doors in the very center of the Legion?

"Seth," Tory called. "They've gone. Will you look at books all day or are we here to see the rangers?"

Reluctantly, he stopped his searching. He'd have to come back tonight after everyone was asleep. The Jalora had instructed him to find and open the book, but he wasn't sure what would happen once the magic was released. It might not be safe for his friends.

Seth tore his eyes away from the books and joined his friends before the double doors. Several plaques hung above the frame representing the many countries of Andara. Animals - Spirits of the Heart of the Warrior Rings - had been painted in their respective country. Some countries contained more Animals than others. One plaque, much larger than the rest, hung in the center.

"Valdeon," Seth whispered.

Thirty-one animals stood proudly within the painted surface. The Lion was at their head. Eight creatures were just beneath its mane, standing out above the rest. Then he remembered Phoenix' words in the Halls of Heroes. These must be the Lords of Valdeon. The remaining animals must symbolize the twenty-two of Valdeon.

Riley came to stand by his shoulder. "Let's go, Cadet."

They stepped back into the hall. Seth closed the doors of the library. His deep feeling of regret and disappointment was echoed by the magic he'd left behind. Soon he'd return to find the book and complete his quest. And then? He had no idea.

"I think we've seen enough, don't you?" Riley moved back in the direction of the little door.

"Yes, I've seen what I wanted to see." Seth moved to join him.

He had to get his friends back through the door for their own sakes. They'd been lucky to avoid detection, but sooner or later a ranger would sense their presence. The rest of his friends began to follow.

"Do you hear that?" Tory twirled on the white floor like a hound with a scent.

The familiar sounds of sword play came from down the hall to their left. Another set of double doors hung within the paneled walls. Two crossed swords were painted in the wood. It must be a training room of some sort.

"Let's sneak a look." Tory tapped him on the shoulder and pointed at stairs leading to what might have been an observation balcony. "When will we get the chance again?"

Tory darted up the stairs before they could stop him. He waved his friends to follow. Seth shrugged at Riley and hurried up the stairs. Tory did have a point. This was a rare opportunity to see what may be in store for him.

He kneeled on the floor of the observation balcony next to Tory. Sword dummies, much more sophisticated than Leo's or the army's dummies, stood in three rows below them. Two young rangers moved through them, spinning their wooden foe at incredible speeds. One of the rangers stepped away with an angry cry. A long red gash dripped along his arm. Someone had fastened steel blades on the arms of the dummy.

"Look who it is," Riley said, pointing at the other end of the arena.

An open area remained at the end farthest from them in the perfectly formed circular room. Phoenix stood facing a large group of rangers. He was dressed in white loose-fitting clothes, as were his students. The ranger raised his sword and gave the word. His students began sparring each other with moves made in perfect unison.

"Do you know who the Phoenix is, I mean besides being a ranger?" Seth asked.

"Of course, I do." Tory grinned and shook his head. "Like I told you in North Burrough. That is Gregory Baldemar, the Crown Prince of Heidelbrecht. He is a second level Deacon. Phoenix is one of the best swordsman in the Legion. Be very glad he didn't want to fight you during the wager on sign up day."

Seth stared back down at the blond ranger. He was showing one of the students a move with the sword. Each move was executed with precision. He'd hate to cross blades with the Phoenix and was very glad he escaped the man's rage.

"He's a tricky one." Riley chewed on his lip irritably.

"Somebody's holding a grudge," Tory sang low. "His temper is legendary, Logan, I'll admit it. Doesn't do to make him angry."

Amery clapped Seth on the back. "Good thing Seth was with us."

"Yes, he likes Seth for some reason," Riley said. "The Phoenix and I share a mutual dislike."

Seth turned his attention back down to the class. They'd stopped sparring and had turned their attention back to the Phoenix. The blond ranger had a commanding presence about him. His students clearly respected him and were anxious for his word.

"You are ready to begin learning how to call the J'Morta, the Death Mask. Let us begin by using the horde's cry we learned yesterday," Phoenix ordered.

A ranger and his squire are protected from the Horde's Cry. Others are not.

Seth turned to his friends. "Cover your ears and head for the door, quickly!"

His warning came too late. The screech of hundreds of voices echoed through the training room and up to the observation deck. It spoke of death for enemies of the Jalora. The Lion's Roar rumbled low in his throat, trying to join with the voices. Taking deep breaths, he forced it down again.

Tory, Amery, and Aubrey clutched at their ears and fell to the ground in terror. Riley, pale and shaking, was still mobile. Seth gripped his arm, extending the Jalora's power to calm his squire.

"Help me get them to the kitchens."

Riley pulled Tory to his feet, while Seth coaxed and pulled at the Claybank twins. They stopped screaming once they made it down the stairs of the observatory. He pulled his friends toward the kitchens, while Riley pushed them. They burst through the door and Seth quickly locked it again behind them.

"By the Erthe Mother, what was that?" Amery asked.

"Something you must never explore again," Seth told him.

Tory looked at him with a white face. "Again? I wouldn't go back inside for anything."

"Good. You must swear to me you won't. We've just experienced the reason the rangers are separate from the rest of the army."

"What goes on here?" Sergeant Dancer barked behind them.

Tory's lie was quick, if not convincing. "McCloud and the others were helping me finish a few kitchen chores, Sergeant."

"Well, how convenient." Sergeant Dancer folded his arms with a malicious grin. "We have some late-night arrivals coming in soon. They'll need a hot meal."

"More cadets?" Tory asked.

"No such luck," Sergeant Dancer said. "Dragon has called the representatives of all the nations of the United Realms to the citadel. He's making a plea for aid."

"I can't imagine the Dragon pleading to anyone." Tory rubbed at his head.

"Mind your business," the sergeant snapped. "Dawson, Claybanks. You'll be in the kitchens helping. Logan, you're needed in the infirmary. And McCloud. You've got guard duty tonight."

"What now?" Riley asked low as they followed Sergeant Dancer down the corridor toward the infirmary.

"I must go back to the Legion Library," Seth told him. "The book is waiting for me there. I could feel its magic calling."

"Great gulls, Seth. It's too dangerous."

"I'll have you to watch my back. You're coming with me, Squire."

Chapter Forty-Four

SETH CLUTCHED the long wooden pike and stood at attention. The Sergeant of the Guard, a middle-aged man with a two-day beard, eyed him with an appraising frown. It was miserably cold and threatening snow. Clearly, the sergeant didn't appreciate being stuck out in the open training a cadet on the nuances of guard duty.

"First time to pull the duty, McCloud?"

"Yes, Sergeant."

"Of course, it is. Wet nose runts. All I'm getting lately. Listen up. We're on the top of a mountain. All you've got to do is walk along this ledge and keep your eyes open. You see something move, issue the challenge. Got it? We don't have time to teach you the finer art of guard duty tonight."

"Yes, Sergeant."

He wasn't about to ask what happened if the challenge flushed someone out of the shadows. His eyes drifted up to a single lantern swinging slowly at the true top of the mountain several hundred feet above them. Watching its lonely beam reaching out toward the south, Seth's heart became heavy, as if he'd lost more than he'd realized.

"You'll never stand guard up there, runt. Only the Lords of Valdeon walk those docks." The sergeant gave him a hard tap on the head with his fist. "Pay attention. I'm only going to go over your instructions once."

A group of four UR Soldiers huddled together warming their hands beside a fire barrel. Puffs of escaping breath billowed around the soldiers as they stomped their feet to keep warm. They didn't look pleased to share his fate.

"His rotten luck he pulled the midnight duty," one of them grunted between stomps.

"Keep that tongue from wagging or you'll be standing midnight guard alone for a week."

"Yes, Sergeant."

The soldier gave him a black look and turned back to the fire. Pulling his cloak tighter about his body, he spat into the stone. It would appear the Sergeant of the Guard was hated by cadet and soldier alike.

"You see the dark patch of wall over there, Cadet?" The Sergeant pointed into the blackest part of the long stretch of wall. "It's your patrol for the next four hours. The last cadet fell asleep on duty and got a real nasty surprise when he woke up in the infirmary."

The other soldiers chuckled. Seth could imagine what they had done to the luckless young man. They'd get their own nasty surprise if they tried any mischief on him. He turned with as much dignity as he could muster and moved away into the dark.

His stretch of wall had no fire barrel or torches at all. Seth did his first pass and turned to walk back again. The soldiers continued to warm themselves, passing around a bottle of what was probably rum once the Sergeant had gone. Seth shook his head. Would they be so lazy if they'd seen the enemy threatening Andara?

The wall was too high above the battlement to see any of the town, but merriment drifted upon the breeze to spill over the barrier. It seemed Lea never slept, especially now there were so many visitors coming to prepare for talks of war. His imagination wandered to thoughts of wonderful food and tasty drink among the taverns below. Perhaps a little dancing as well. It was torture standing guard on the West End.

Such thoughts wouldn't help him through his patrol. He resumed his lonely walk along the battlements. Bed would feel good after a night walking in the cold. Sleep. The very thought of it made his eyelids grow heavy. He slapped his cheeks, trying to chase the sleepiness away. If it took every ounce of his will, he'd not give those thugs a chance to catch him off guard.

A small scraping noise sounded in the darkness on the other side of the wall. Was it a bird or a bat, perhaps? Seth carefully reached out with his senses. Four men were climbing up the side of the wall. How were they scaling the smooth stone of Obsidian?

He flattened his body against the wall close beside what he hoped was their entrance onto the battlements. The first man lifted his body onto the top of the wall and swiveled until his feet dangled over the deck. He jumped, landing silently upon the battlements. Cloaked and hooded, his features and clothing were hidden. Something about him seemed familiar, but Seth couldn't be sure if he were friend or foe. He rushed at the man, sweeping the pike's handle at the back of his knees. The man fell to the ground with a surprised grunt. Seth put the steel point to his neck.

"Hold, intruder or you'll find yourself pinned to the battlement."

A pair of sparkling gray eyes stared back at him. They belonged to an old face with many small battle scars. The worn cheeks were framed with gray hair clinging to his wrinkled neck.

"A cadet. I must be losing my wit with age. No. A hopeful. Well, not much better."

"Never underestimate your opponent's skill," Seth told him. "And that goes for you gentlemen, too."

He swung his pike and struck out at the two men sneaking up on his back. The end of the pike caught one man in the nose and struck the other in the stomach. One of the men growled and pulled his sword. Seth stared at the blade. His pike would be no match for its steel. The element of surprise was gone.

"Stand down, Rangers."

Phoenix stood perfectly balanced upon the wall. He jumped onto the battlement and walked slowly toward them. The pit of Seth's stomach twisted and gurgled. Rangers. Not only had he attacked his superior officers, but they could have easily killed him in the exchange. He lowered the pike and stood at attention.

"On your feet, Tiger." Phoenix held a hand out to help the man on the ground.

The older ranger got to his feet with another disgruntled sigh. "I think I've endured enough humiliation tonight, Hopeful. You will keep this little brawl to yourself. Understood?"

"Yes, Sir."

"You have talent, Hopeful. Good move," Tiger said. "It isn't easy to catch a ranger by surprise. Next time, make sure you have a plan in case your opponent rolls right back up again onto his feet. Come on you two. I need a drink to take the night chill out of these bones."

"We will be coming and going from the citadel in the same fashion tomorrow night, Cadet." Phoenix chuckled, watching his men leave the battlements through a hidden door.

Seth smiled. "I will be off duty tomorrow night, Sir."

"Good. We must avoid being seen. It is of utmost importance." His jovial smile faded. "Strange men haunt the shadows of Lea. They're dangerous enemies who search for something, but their intent stays hidden from us."

This was ill news. Had the mercenaries grown bolder, leaving the shadows of Harrow? Or worse, had the Dirge found his scent? Would they dare be so bold this close to Legion headquarters? His memory flashed to the encounter with Dragonfly. The Dirge hadn't feared the ranger then.

"You trust me then, Cadet? Is it because I am a ranger or despite the fact?"

Seth pointed to the Phoenix ring upon the ranger's left hand. "The Jalora will not allow you to lie, Sir."

The fiery bird flapped its wings and stretched out a long neck toward Seth's left hand. It knew the power waiting beneath his glove. He hesitated for a moment. Phoenix seemed willing, almost anxious to help him. Should he confide in the ranger? Tell him his identity and about his quest? Seth was close to finding the Book of Ancients, but what then? His enemies were closing in quickly. Perhaps it was time to trust someone. Seth looked down at the half glove covering the Lion Ring.

"I sense your need and your fear, Hopeful." Phoenix gripped Seth's shoulder. "You can trust me. I swear it upon the Jalora. Have I not proven my friendship by now?"

"I do need your help, Ranger, and your protection."

Fast-moving boots pounded on the stone behind them. Seth turned hurriedly and stepped forward to meet the UR soldiers. Their noses and eyes were red from drink. Though the rangers had been silent, their prolonged power on the battlements must have gotten more attention than he'd supposed.

One of the guards stuck a finger at Seth's chest. "Who was you talking too, snot nose?"

Seth looked over his shoulder to find Phoenix gone. He tried to swallow the rising panic their encounter had caused in him. Squeezing the pike handle, he mastered his fear and disappointment.

The guard shoved Seth with a curse. "Answer me."

The Jalora's fury flared at the insult. Seth clamped down hard on his emotions, trying to calm the Jalora. He couldn't lie, but he could not tell the truth either. What could he possibly tell these men to satisfy their anger?

"Do you see anyone?"

"You've got too much brass to suit me, boy. Maybe we ought to give you a little lesson in manners."

Phoenix came out of the shadows. "You'd be making a career mistake, soldier. Line up for Inspection!"

The command of his voice made Seth jump as well. The pale, shaken soldiers did as they were told while Phoenix walked toward the alarm bell.

"Please, Deacon. We was just breakin' in the boy on his first time with guard duty."

Phoenix looked at Seth with raised eyebrows. "First time on guard duty, eh? I'll have to let our friends know." He put his hands behind his back and appeared to be reconsidering the alarm. "Very well. I won't report you this time, but leave the cadet alone. He was the only one of you doing his duty. Don't argue. I've been watching you warm your hands and drink."

The soldiers saluted Phoenix and made a hasty retreat to their own posts. A rough hand grabbed Seth's arm, pulling him along. Stale breath, heavy with rum, struck the flesh of his ear.

"You ain't stayin with him to tell more lies."

Seth looked over his shoulder. Phoenix stared after him in the dark. His blond hair was the only part of his body visible in the night. He stayed for a moment, then disappeared into the shadows once more.

None of the guard returned to the darkened stretch of wall. While Seth was given another, better illuminated stretch of stone to guard, he was still grateful when his duty was over. Half expecting to run into Phoenix on his return to barracks, he was a bit disappointed and a bit relieved. He plopped down into bed, his mind a whirl. Had he almost made a mistake telling the ranger about himself or would he at last find some answers? The weight of his secret grew a little heavier each day.

His thoughts turned to the strangers prowling around the streets of Lea. He wasn't sure if these men had followed him here or not. They could be after something or someone else. What if they were after him? Was he putting others in danger while he hid behind the black walls of the citadel? Perhaps he should march down to Legion headquarters in the morning and ask to see Phoenix.

Sleep is what you need, Lion. Put your mind at ease. The time is not right for you to come out of hiding. I will reveal you to the rangers when I choose. Never Fear. I will put my plans into action. The people of Valdeon are not as defeated as the Jackal believe them to be.

"It will be as you say," Seth whispered, his words already drifting away as he shut his eyes in sleep.

Chapter Forty-Five

JORGE WIPED at the sweat dripping onto his eyelashes. He adjusted his grip on the pole carrying their kill back toward San Lucida. The deer's emaciated body would hardly be worth the effort in a normal hunting season. Times were hard. They were lucky to find even this meager carcass. It had taken them the better part of yesterday to reach their hunting ground and most of the afternoon to return.

They pushed out of the trees and onto the empty road leading to the canyon entrance. Its rim rose over the tree tops to strike blue sky. His experienced eye looked for the guards he'd placed among the crevices and other hiding spots. He whistled the signal. No answer came.

Jorge brought his hunters to a stop. Whistling the signal again, he waited in empty stillness.

Dried branches snapped to their right. Mario burst through the trees holding a hand to his bloodied head. Bruises and scratches covered his face. Defiant anger mixed with the wounds.

"Thank the Jalora! You've returned at last, my lord."

"Yes, and with a little meat." Jorge slipped his hand off the pole and gripped Mario's arm. "What is it? Something's happened."

"A stranger came among us yesterday, my lord. He's taken over the town, demanding money and food from the people. Several of us tried to stop him, but he has a brute squad. We couldn't defeat them. I managed to escape, but my attempts to find your trail failed."

"Is he a Jackal?" Duarto asked, fury burning in his eyes.

"No," Mario said, spitting on the ground. "The beast is Valdeonian. I've heard tales of these men before the Fall. Tabor is a river rat from one of the slums on the Constantina River. He robbed cargo vessels before the Jackal invaded. Now he's moved on to more vulnerable prey."

"How can a man turn on his own people in their greatest hour of need?" Duarto asked. "He takes when they have nothing. How can he do such a horrible thing?"

In his time as a squire to his ranger, Jorge had seen a great many ugly things. The worst instincts often rose to the surface in men and women without honor. He'd seen law abiding citizens murder and rob their neighbors when disaster had struck their towns. Fear was a powerful motivator. The rangers had been on hand to set things right again and put a stop to such mischief, but there were no rangers left in Valdeon. It was up to him to protect the people from their own.

"Let's go ask him, shall we? Hide the meat, Neto. Join us as soon as you are able."

Jorge pushed the pole off his shoulder and sprinted toward the opening of the canyon. This man Tabor and his squad hadn't placed any guard in the canyons as far as Jorge could tell. They were overly confident or simply foolish. It would be their undoing.

"What will you do, Father?" Duarto hurried alongside him as Jorge marched through the canyon.

"I suppose I must reason with him."

"Tabor is a killer, my lord," Mario cried, his legs rushing as fast as they could to keep up. "He won't listen to reason."

They stayed close to the walls of the canyon, moving as quickly as they dared. Jorge stopped them at the edge of the city. No guards. Were these men complete fools? Mario tapped him on the arm and pointed toward the old city center and the camp. Jorge nodded and led them through the piles of rubble.

Chaos had visited while he was away. Carefully built shelters were smashed and torn. All the fire pits were destroyed. The hospital tent had been pulled down, leaving the injured and sick out in the open air.

Tabor stood amidst the chaos. He was a brutish man with legs the size of tree trunks and a body to match. His hair had been shaved close to his head, exposing a jagged scar from the top of his skull down the side of his face. He was every bit as ugly as his nature implied.

"I want every scrap of food in this pile now, or I'll start beating people again." He slapped at the nearest woman, missing her by inches. "Your protector has abandoned you. I'm owner of this city now. Everything in it belongs to me, including you worthless lot."

Jorge stepped out of the rubble and continued at a steady pace toward the would-be usurper. Duarto and the hunters followed a few paces behind. His Pacarro senses heard their elevated heart rates and the rapid whisk of air moving through their gritted teeth. They were angry, but would their rage be enough to turn hunters into warriors?

Tabor, alerted by the sudden hush, turned to face the parting crowd. Appraising eyes regarded Jorge, sizing him up and determining if he were another predator or victim. This man was used to being top predator. It showed in the hard lines upon his face. He wouldn't back down easily.

"What have we here? Rat balls. They're just farmers," Tabor said, lifting his fist upward. "Take their weapons."

Fifteen armed men stepped out of the rubble around Tabor. Their rough faces were covered in scars and hate. They looked better fed than his own men. The Erthe Mother only knew how many cities they'd plundered on their way to San Lucida.

Lifting his voice in a Pacarro war cry, Jorge ran at full speed toward Tabor. Power engulfed his body as the Regent Medallion came to life. Pulling his hatchet, he threw it at one of the hoodlums coming to block him. The blade lodged deep into his forehead with a satisfying thud. Jorge yanked the hatchet from the man's skull as he passed, never losing momentum in his run toward Tabor.

Arrows zipped past his ears, striking their targets in the throat. Jorge jumped over the dead bodies with a wild cry. His hunters had joined the fight. Duarto appeared at his shoulder, matching Jorge's pace. His sword dripped with the lifeblood of their enemies. Strong and confident, his son's eyes glowed with the frenzy of battle. Jorge's blood burned with the same lust for revenge. He raised his hatchet, readying to strike the final blow against the brute who'd taken the last piece of dignity from the people of San Lucida.

Then Tabor grabbed an elderly woman from the crowd, holding her before him. "Drop your hatchet, savage devil."

"Let her go, Tabor! We warned you." Mario shook his makeshift club at them. "The Regent of Valdeon protects this village."

"A barbarian from a dead tribe has been made Regent?" Tabor let an ugly grin spread across his cracked lips. "Well, that's Valdeon for you. The barbarians have taken over. You, me, and the Jackal. We're the same. Each dog gets his own bone. What do you say to a deal?"

Jorge twisted the hatchet in his grip, his eyes never leaving the woman Tabor held in his power. "I don't share my bones."

Letting the hatchet loose again, his weapon hit the mark. Tabor growled, pushing the woman away from him. He kicked the hatchet from where it was lodged in his left foot. Dragging his wounded appendage behind him, he hurried off toward the canyon. Two of his loyal rats remained to follow in his bloodied wake.

"I'll be back with more men, Regent of nothing!" He shouted over his shoulder. "We would have taken what we wanted and left, but now I will see San Lucida burned to the ground!"

An arrow sliced across Tabor's face, drawing a thick line of blood. The tip pierced his nose and struck the chest of the man next to him. Tabor screamed, grabbing the pieces of his nose in a bloodied clump. Racing into the canyon, he left his wounded friend to die upon the cobblestones of the city.

"Pity I ran out of arrows," Neto said, jumping off a large piece of crumbled wall. "His face would look much better with a hole right between his eyebrows."

"You may get a second chance, my friend. Take two men and fetch our deer. The people could use something to raise their spirits." Jorge turned to Duarto. "Strip the bodies and gather any belongs of value. Then throw their bodies in the gorge with the others. I must see to the people. Idle hands make for idle minds."

Frightened murmurs filled the crowd about him. Whispers of treks to the coast and threats of surrender hung like an unwelcome rain cloud over the crowd. He ignored their talk. Full bellies and undisturbed sleep would ease such talk for now.

"Nightfall will be upon us before we know it," he said. "I want the hospital tent back up. Then start on the shelters."

"Yes, my lord," Mario said with a proud grin. "It will be as you say!"

Jorge retreated to the abandoned rubble of old San Lucida. The Regent Medallion still pulsed around his neck as if reminding everyone, including its bearer, it ruled Valdeon. Political power came with the golden medallion, but the burden he must bear was not worth the esteem of his followers. Each day the responsibility of his impossible task weighed a bit more upon his heart. How could he keep them safe in such a cruel new world?

"You carry a heavy burden, Jorge Pacarro."

His hand flew to the hatchet as he spun around to face the intruder. A ranger stood among the stones of his old life. Hands pulled away the hood, revealing a long-forgotten face. Esteban the Hawk, brother to their dead king, stared unabashedly at the gold medallion resting upon Jorge's chest.

"I came looking for Cesar Santiago, but instead I find the Regent of Valdeon."

Hawk lifted his eyes slowly. The exploratory gaze swept methodically across Jorge's features, scrutinizing every inch of his face. Hawk's emotionless expression revealed nothing.

"I am at a loss for words, Hawk Prince."

Jorge kept his hand upon the handle of his hatchet. The last time his eyes beheld Esteban, Leo had given him the nasty scar upon his face for plotting to take the throne. Hawk had disappeared years ago. Seeing him now left Jorge strangely unsettled and confused.

"You don't trust me, My Lord Pacarro." Hawk moved forward at a speed Jorge's eyes couldn't match. "I've come to warn you. The Jackal know about the Regent Medallion. They'll come in force to find its bearer. You must leave San Lucida. I'm afraid you have no choice but to trust me."

Valdeon's conquerors knew about the medallion? How? Julian had told them, of course. The black-hearted cur would do anything to take the throne, including snatching away the last hope of his people.

"I can't leave these refugees. You've seen what it's like for them."

"Take them with you, my lord regent. The Jackal blocked the mountain pass into Tslavia in the hopes of isolating our people. They don't, however, know about the cave system on the west side of the Constantina. I've arranged to have food and other supplies stored there for you. There will be enough for everyone."

"You are very generous, Highness."

Those caves weren't well-known or seldom explored due to their dangerous twists and turns. Hawk did have a point. They would certainly house all the refugees of San Lucida. Yet, warning voices echoed in Jorge's mind. Why was Hawk helping them? He'd shown no interest in Valdeon for many years. Where had he been all this time? How did he come to be in Valdeon when all passage to and from had been blocked by the Jackal?

"Look for my sign at the cave entrance ten miles west of the Constantina. I would leave as soon as possible. You don't have much time."

"You aren't staying?"

"I go to join the young Lion," Hawk said, this time his eyes glistening. "He will be a strong ranger."

"You've seen him then?" Jorge stepped forward, fingering the medallion restlessly. "Is he safe?"

"I last felt his presence in the woods of the Commonwealth. The boy escaped me, but I know where he's headed. He has no idea of the storm he's about to enter." Hawk stared into a future only he could see. "Soon we'll be together. I'll mold him into what he's meant to be. The D'Antoiné family line will be great again." Hawk pulled on his hood. "Fare thee well, Regent of Valdeon. Mark me. Don't get used to the title. The Lion will return and take his rightful place."

"Yes, of course."

The Hawk Prince of Valdeon disappeared into the growing shadows. Jorge watched the darkness creep closer, shaken by the fervor in Hawk's voice. Esteban sounded as if he would use the young Lion, rather than aid him. Was he about to abandon yet another sacred duty? He smoothed at the medallion resting heavily upon his chest. Jorge could give no aid or no warning to his future king. His duty now was to look after their people until the Lion returned. Hawk and his plans would have to be foiled by someone else.

His thoughts drifted to Wolf. "Erthe Mother, guide Xavier the Wolf's path."

Chapter Forty-Six

THE HARROW DISTRICT in Lea remained the den of violent iniquity Julian remembered. Gloomy rows filled with thieves and cutthroats watched them with salivating jaws as they passed. Their hunger for his soiled finery may have concerned him in the past, but he'd seen much worse than these human hoodlums in his own home. Harrow was paradise compared to the devastation of San Leonora.

Resentment came unbidden to Julian's temper, threatening to skew his reasoning. He knew perfectly well the Legion couldn't reach San Leonora. Seeing others happy and safe still grated on his nerves. They had no idea what hell would come knocking upon their doors soon.

"According to your new friends, this is the house," Marcellus said, stopping before a rundown brick brownstone in the center of several equally filthy homes.

The Changelings weren't exactly his friends. He clenched the gray-skinned fist hiding under his glove. They claimed to be family by Julian's unknown sire. The very thought was repugnant, but he could no longer dismiss it as a lie. So be it. If his Changeling cousins insisted on helping him, he'd turn their lust for power to his advantage.

A large black bird landed on the street lamp above them. It let out a plaintive caw, darting the feathered head up and down. Julian took a tight grip on his impatience. His Changeling escort had promised to stay aboard ship. Their compulsion for mischief outweighed any promise to kin it would seem.

"You'd better pray Lord Gorman hasn't discovered your absence from Valdeon, Brother." Zoya rested a hand upon the dagger she kept hidden under her skirts.

"Time with the Jackal has robbed you of any feminine modesty." Julian slapped her hand away and tugged the skirt back into place. "Remind me why I brought you with us."

"You brought me along because you love me." She smoothed at his arm and rested her head against his chest. "And I threatened to alert my Jackal friends if you didn't, Brother mine."

A musket's barrel jutted at them from the circle of a dim street lamp. Its owner was a lanky man with a line of bronze rings piercing his ears. He was a mercenary. Gone were the loose-fitting trousers and brown cloak of his kind. Posing as a city dweller, he'd been forced to wear the snug-fitting clothing customary in Lea.

"Seeing the sights, are we? What's your business here?"

"I'm certain Lord Gorman wouldn't appreciate us discussing our business out in the street for all ears to hear, how 'bout you?" Julian folded his arms, looking bored.

Gorman's name aroused the reaction he'd hoped. The mercenary lowered his musket and hurried to knock three times upon the door. It flew open and they were ushered inside by another uncomfortable mercenary in ill-fitting clothes. The stale odor of sweat and drink struck Julian as he entered.

They were shown into a small parlor. It was littered with dishes and empty bottles. Several mercenaries, some wounded, sat around the room eating and drinking. Others were cleaning their weapons. None of them seemed overjoyed to see representatives from Gorman's camp.

A familiar face met his gaze. It was Cutter, or what was left of him. Patches of scar tissue checkered the strands of blond hair. One of his ears, the right one, was missing. Teeth marks around the stub of his missing appendage told a tale of his lucky escape.

"Well, if it isn't my old friend, Julian. You didn't bring more Dirge with you?"

"Lord Gorman took his displeasure at your incompetence out upon the creature. He won't be sending anymore replacements." Julian came farther into the room and looked around with mock distaste. "I've been sent to see to the young Lion's capture."

"You think it will be easy, do you?" Cutter threw his bottle against the wall. "We almost had the boy, but there's a ranger looking after him. The bastard's been having a grand time killing off my men."

"Xavier the Wolf?" Zoya asked and shrugged when Julian shot her a warning glare.

"No. I caught a glimpse of him a few days ago. He isn't Valdeonian. Nobody seems to know who he is."

A man dressed in the tidy uniform of a UR officer eased into the room. He leaned against the wall beside the door and calmly began plucking imaginary bits from his uniform. Shooting a belligerent glare at Cutter, he cleared his throat.

"I keep telling you to watch the Phoenix. He's the Lion's Partisan after all," he said.

"And why should we trust your word?" Zoya asked.

"I get paid to provide accurate information from inside the citadel, my lady. The Phoenix leads night patrols around Lea. If anyone was to attack spies in the city, it would be him." The peevish little man turned to Julian. "I know the ranger's comings and goings, being the commandant's aid. Of course, if you're not interested in my ideas, I'll just go back to working alongside the Lion. He's in disguise as the citadel's linguist. I'm sure you'll figure out a way to reach him, Prince of Valdeon."

"Hold a moment," Julian said, grabbing his arm. "Do you mean to say you know exactly where the Lion is right now?"

"My name is Lieutenant Finley." The commandant's aid pulled out of his grip. "Of course, I do. He's in his bunk with the other cadets about now. Guard duty will be over. Thinks he's so clever, hiding as a common soldier. He couldn't fool the rangers and he didn't fool me. Somehow, he's hidden his Lion eyes. The rangers know he's a hopeful, but not his true identity."

Wasn't his half-breed brother clever? Perhaps the young Lion was too clever for his own sake. Flushing him out into the open would be much easier with this revolting extortionist in Julian's employ.

"You and I are going to be great friends, Lieutenant Finley. I could use a man like you once I have the Lion Ring upon my finger." Julian slapped a large gold coin into his palm. "Perhaps we'll plan a special surprise for my dear brother tomorrow night?"

"And what of the Lion's ranger protector? He's not going to let you anywhere near the boy." Cutter gritted his teeth, clearly not liking the commandant's aid's new position of trust.

"I remember the rangers have a favorite drinking spot, a tavern Leo frequented quite often," Julian said. "Phoenix is no stranger to the place. We catch him there unaware."

"An ambush." Cutter nodded slowly. "Yes. I look forward to paying him back for each life he's taken."

Julian shared a pleased grin with his sister. Soon the half-breed would be dead and the Lion Ring upon Julian's finger. Adding to his joy was the image of Gregory the Phoenix, one of his father's most fervent worshippers, cut down like a common drunk. This visit to Lea was proving to be memorable.

Chapter Forty-Seven

SETH CLUTCHED the note from Fanny Lambert. It was an odd thing to ask, meeting in the dark after midnight. He ran a hand through his hair. It would be easy to guess what Riley would say about such a meeting. His squire had taken a dislike to the Lambert ladies and suspected they wanted more from Seth than simple friendship. He tended to agree, but had no intention of probing the ladies. Dread of what he'd find in their minds terrified him more than a room full of Dirge.

Continuing his moderate pace within the darkened citadel, Seth gave a resigned sigh. Somehow, he'd have to explain why he didn't return her interest and that she must stop her pursuit of his affection. Yes. He would have to explain all this to Fanny without hurting her feelings. She was a nice girl. He suspected her mother had a hand in her behavior. How had a lady like Fanny known about such lonely hallways within the Citadel? He briefly wondered if she'd brought someone down here before him, but quickly banished the uncharitable thought. Seth couldn't leave her standing in the dark at midnight.

Movement under the glow of a single lantern drew him forward. Fanny was wearing an ornate cloak with the hood drawn over her head. Skirts swayed as she turned her back to look in the opposite direction within the shadowy space.

"My Lady?" Seth called as quietly as he could. "My Lady? Fanny?"

Seth reached to touch her shoulder and she spun around. Fanny looked up, triumph in her green eyes. No, not green. They were taking on a bottomless black hue. Teeth, long and sharp, poked out of her red lips. This wasn't Fanny Lambert. This was something else. Something evil.

A sharp sting poked at his arm. Tiny trickles of blood rushed down his skin toward his fingers. Seth pulled his arm away from the creature's touch.

"What are you?"

The creature grinned again. "I am your destruction, Lion."

Staggering away from the creature, he lifted his hand to grasp the hilt of a sword no longer there. He'd left it in the locker beside his cot. Fumbling fingers pressed against the cold stone, searching for a weapon. His arms fell uselessly at his side. Whatever poison or drug the creature had injected into his arm was beginning to invade his body.

Others crowded about him as darkness clouded his vision. He recognized their clothing. Mercenaries. They'd found him again and this time there would be no escape. Seth focused his mind with all the will he possessed. Then he reached out in a frantic call. The Jalora's power surrounded his unspoken words.

"Riley! Help me!"

Chapter Forty-Eight

RILEY FLAYED his arms and legs like a fish caught in a net. He struggled against the blankets wrapped tightly around his body. The cot tipped over. He landed face first on the obsidian stone. Eyes watering, he gingerly touched his nose. Nothing broken.

"Keep quiet down there!"

Receiving no sympathy from his barracks mates, Riley bit back an Islic curse and righted himself. Great gulls. What a dream! He shook his head, lifting the cot back on its legs. Any moment now, Seth would be giving him a hard time. He looked over at his friend's empty cot. It hadn't been slept in. A sick feeling settled into his gut. It hadn't been a dream. Seth was really in trouble.

Scrambling over the cot, he reached for his clothes. Riley began pulling on his trousers with all the grace of a woolie in mud. Easing open the lock and trunk, he withdrew his sword. Seth was in trouble, but where was he now? Riley pulled his boots on hurriedly, cursing when he realized he was trying to put the left boot on the right foot.

Riley! Hear me. Seth's voice called from the hall.

Stumbling forward, he bumped into several cots on his way toward the barracks door. He rammed his knee on the jamb and grumbled a muffled cry of pain.

"Quiet!" a cadet by the door growled.

Letting the justified insult slide, he tiptoed past the sergeant's chamber. Snores loud enough to shake the citadel rumbled behind Dancer's door. Riley's cot wasn't located in the freshest smelling part of the barracks. Now he understood things could always be worse. Saying a silent little prayer of thanks, he vowed never to complain about the location of his cot again.

The barracks door squeaked and groaned in the silence of the citadel. Wincing, he let it close again with a small click. Riley crept farther into the empty corridor. Blackness flooded over him. He'd been reckless forgetting a lantern. As if to underscore his foolhardiness, a beam of light fell across the floor in front of him.

"Where you headed, Mate?" Tory asked, holding the lantern with one hand and rubbing his eyes with the other. "Don't look so surprised. You aren't exactly what I'd call stealthy."

The Claybank brothers were behind him. Neither had bothered with a tunic. Weapons belts crisscrossed over the bare skin upon their chests. Metal glinted in short bursts under Tory's lantern light. They'd brought their hatchets.

"Seth's in trouble," he whispered. "I've got to go help him. You three go back to bed."

"We owe McCloud a debt," Amery told him firmly. "If he's in trouble, then we'll help you get him out again."

Riley rubbed at the back of his neck. He certainly hoped he wasn't making a complete fool of himself. Sneaking about the citadel in the middle of the night on his own was one thing. Taking his friends along, because he was hearing voices? Well, he'd never live it down.

"Fine. Follow me."

A strange tug pulled at his heart as if his very being was attached with an invisible chain to Seth. He didn't know if it were some sort of magic or a squire's instincts. Whatever it was, the tug seemed to know the right direction. He didn't question it. In his short time as a squire, he'd seen things capable of challenging a man's views of reality.

Hurry, Riley! I'm in trouble…

"It's bad," Riley told his friends. "Seth's in a bad way. We've got to hurry. No time for quiet paces."

"How do you know?" Tory asked.

"I just know."

The tug pulled him down the back stairs toward the kitchens. He hurried past the double doors of the mess hall with Tory and the Claybanks following. Passing several storage rooms, Riley took them farther around the outer layer of the citadel. Why in the green, green fields would Seth come down here? Had he taken a wrong turn?

"Hang on, Mate." Tory pulled him to a stop. "I recognize this place. We're almost to the delivery docks. Dad and I bring in ale once a week for the rangers. What would McCloud be doing down here? Are you sure you weren't dreaming?"

"It could be he pulled a second guard duty," Aubrey said with a shrug. "We could check with the sergeant."

"Wake Dancer in the middle of the night, because Logan had a bad dream?" Tory snorted and shook his head. "Do as you please. I'm going back to bed."

His friends turned and began to walk away. Tory put the beam on Riley, waiting for him to follow. Light touched a folded piece of paper upon the stone ground between them. Riley snatched it up and held the paper before him. It was a letter addressed to Seth from that hussy, Fanny Lambert. She and her mother may be rich, but they were no ladies.

"What is it?" Amery asked, coming to stand at his shoulder. "I cannot read what it says." He sniffed at the page. "It smells like a fancy woman."

"Well, well. Is that so? It's pretty romantic down here now I think of it," Tory said, wagging his eyebrows. "You sure McCloud wants to be disturbed?"

"Seth's not the romantic type." Riley tapped at the letter. "Something's not right about this."

Then a small projectile struck Riley's forehead. He rubbed at the sore spot where the small rock had hit him. Another rock followed soon after, striking him in the head again. This time the blow was much harder.

"Seth?" he called in a rasping whisper. "Where are you?"

Keeping their bodies close to the wall, they headed toward the rock thrower. The hall abruptly ended, thrusting them into a large warehouse with several open docks. The absence of workers gave the deserted warehouse a lonely feel.

A hand grabbed Riley and pulled him back behind a stack of crates. Boyd, the Coyote's squire, pressed a finger to his lips. Dressed in the same clothes he'd worn in the Grey Cliff Isles, Boyd didn't look the part of a Legion squire either.

"Still haven't learned to be cautious, eh?" Boyd whispered.

"Unhand him, devil," Tory cried, rushing into Boyd's hiding spot.

The Claybanks charged up behind him, brandishing their hatchets. They looked the picture of savage warriors to Riley. Boyd, on the other hand, didn't seem impressed in the slightest. Instead, he seemed to be struggling with a grin.

"Easy, Tory," Riley said. "He's a friend. What are you doing here, Boyd? Where's Coy…Jason?"

"He's close. I think your own friend needs attention right now. Follow me and try to be quiet."

Boyd led them through the maze of crates toward the end of the docks. He pointed at the lip of the nearest platform. A circle of men stood close together, staring with keen interest at something in their center. They stepped away from the object of their intense inspection. Seth lay on his side, gagged and bound. He wasn't moving.

Riley pulled his sword and began charging forward, but Boyd held him back. "Those men who've taken Seth are more dangerous than you know. Jason suspects they have an agent of the Sarcion with them." Boyd pointed as a woman in yellow came to stand at Seth's head. "You see. There it is."

"Fanny Lambert?" Riley gave Boyd a sour frown. "I know she's a pain in the backside, but evil?"

"Just watch."

The delicate face and small frame began to change as Fanny Lambert laughed. Long hair and sharp features grew from its head. Men's clothing took the place of silky fabric and lace. Standing dangerously close to his ranger was a creature of evil.

"What the devil is it?" Tory cried.

"It is a monster we must kill," Aubrey said, twisting his hatchet. "My Da told me tales of Changelings hiding in the woods, waiting to feast upon the innocent. I thought such nightmares were for naughty children."

"Your father showed wisdom in warning you," Boyd said. "We don't know what magic the Changeling possesses." He turned to Riley, gripping the collar of his tunic. "We're going to need help. You must fetch the Phoenix. Use the arena entrance a few left turns just beyond the docks. It's the closest."

"What?" Riley shook his head. "That blond giant isn't too keen on me. I doubt he'll help us."

"It is his duty to do so." Boyd pushed him forward. "Your friends and I will follow Seth. Look for my trail markers. Go now. Hurry!"

"Don't rush off without this, Mate." Tory shoved the lantern into his hand with a worried frown.

"And you'll need this, cadet." Boyd handed Tory a beat-up sword. "I took it off one of the mercenaries."

Riley darted back through the crates and headed in the direction Boyd had pointed. He found the turn quickly. Funny they hadn't noticed it before. Racing down the stone tunnel toward the interior of the citadel, he held the lantern before him like a shield against the dark. The sands of the arena glistened in the moonlight. He burst out of the stone body and onto the shifting floor. The arena was empty of men, movement, and magic.

"Where is the blasted thing?" Riley leaned over, gulping in air. "I don't have time to run up all those stairs. It's needed right here, right now."

Then he lifted his head. The Obsidian Gates hung within the black walls as if they'd always been right before him. Two orbs floated on either side of the gates, spinning furiously. Their magic struck his body. Closing his eyes, he thought of Seth in the clutches of the monster.

"Please don't kill me," he whispered.

Gritting his teeth, he took a tentative step toward the gates. Nothing happened. Hysterical laughter mixed with grateful prayers upon his lips. He hurried to the gates and began pounding on them. Nobody answered. According to Seth, a ranger attended the gates. It was nighttime after all. A guard wasn't really needed when they had the deadly orbs watching the entrance.

The handles opened easily under his grip. Stepping inside Legion Headquarters, he let the gates close slowly. The angry power of the orbs withdrew from his body and turned out toward the arena once more. He dropped his shaking hands, grateful to be recognized as a squire. Weeks they'd spent here, marching around the arena and sleeping in uncomfortable cots. If he'd known it was this easy to get inside the Obsidian Gates, they'd have been looking for Seth's dusty old book the first day.

A hand brushed against his shoulder. Riley jumped, reaching for his sword. The life-sized statue of Leo gave him a bronze grin. Seeing the likeness of his teacher's face brought the grief back like an angry wave. He turned away. His own Lion needed him to keep his head, or he'd share the same fate.

He hurried toward the door, passing a sign saying, *Hall of Heroes.* What in the green, green fields was at work here? Seth had told him he'd found the Hall of Heroes when he'd entered on the second floor of the citadel. Was this the same hall by some sort of magic? No time for such riddles now. He hurried through the far door and came out into a large hall. It was the same hall he and his friends had first entered when they'd snuck into Legion HQ from the kitchen.

Rangers filled the area, shouting orders and forming lines. Their emotionless faces gave no indication they noticed him creeping about. Tiny prickles of energy tingled along his neck and arms. The Jalora's power pulsed about the rangers. Its strength took the breath from his lungs. These men about him weren't like Leo at all. He'd pestered Seth for weeks to turn himself into the Legion, but he hadn't understood what it could mean for his ranger.

Riley pressed his back against the wall and made his way toward the steps to the observation deck. Easing carefully past a group of rangers, he climbed the stairs. He had to find Seth's blond giant friend. What if the Phoenix was away from the Citadel? What would he do?

Then he heard him. Phoenix' loud baritone shouted orders in his heavy Geltic accent. Golden curls bobbed above the crowd. Riley bounded down the stairs and headed toward the last spot he'd seen the Phoenix. Carefully making his way through the armed men, he came upon the ranger. Fierce eyes burned into him as Phoenix rested his gaze upon Riley.

"What are you doing here? Can't you see we have an emergency? A young hopeful is in trouble."

They knew about Seth being taken? Great gulls. Had his ranger called the entire Legion?

"Yes, Sir." Riley gripped the ranger's arm tightly. "I know."

"I don't have time for games, Squire. Tell me where he is."

Riley looked about him nervously. They were beginning to draw a crowd. The rangers began to part, snapping a salute as an older man confidently walked through their numbers. He had no weapons, though something about the ranger told Riley he may not need any.

The Phoenix straightened into a salute. Riley quickly followed suit. The older ranger raised his left hand to smooth at his neatly trimmed beard. A dark purple ring glistened upon his finger. The dragon within its depths snapped toward Riley angrily. Great gulls. Here was the famous, Dragon, leader of the Jalora Legion.

"Tell the men to stand down, bishop," he said, to one of the men following respectfully behind him. "The Hopeful has been found."

Riley stared up at the man like a gaping idiot. Dragon's eyes met his own, pulling Riley's mind into a steel grip of resolve. He tried to look away, but his will was no longer his own. Dragon had exposed his mind. Every secret, every emotion was his to explore. Then suddenly Riley's mind was released.

"Phoenix, take a troop of rangers and accompany the young man. Bring me the oddity. Alive if you can manage it."

"Yes, Dragon," Phoenix barked back reverently.

Shaken, Riley headed back toward the Hall of Heroes at a run. Several pairs of boots followed.

Two sets, Phoenix and his squire, stayed at his elbows. The Dragon remained in the hall. He was glad to be out of the cardinal's presence. What had the ranger seen in those hidden places within Riley's mind?

"Do you think the Dragon knows about Seth?"

"Of course, he knows!" the Phoenix grumbled. "He's the cardinal. Withholding information from my superiors. What am I doing? Your Hopeful is playing at intrigue and now he has involved me."

"That's not fair! Seth doesn't know the rules. He has no one to help him but me, and I don't know how."

The Phoenix regarded Riley for a moment. "What about the boy's father?"

"He's dead, Sir. Seth didn't know his father until a few months ago. In fact, we didn't know anything about rangers until Seth's dad came to Mariana. Rangers don't come out to the Grey Cliff Isles, you see."

"I understand now why he doesn't recognize the Phoenix Ring. The time for games has passed, Squire. He must reveal himself."

"I gave an oath to follow Seth. If he wants to remain disguised, then I must help him whether I think it mad or not."

Phoenix stayed silent, but there was a hard determination in his eyes. He wouldn't take no for an answer this time. Riley grimaced and ran harder. What in the world was he going to tell Seth?

Chapter Forty-Nine

THE JALORA'S FURY flooded the streets of Lea. Wolf was drowning in it. They'd arrived a few hours before, hoping to find the young Lion and then leave with him again before anyone noticed their presence. Evil, however, thwarted Wolf's plans.

Tulio motioned toward the open docks. Standing upon the platform was a monster from Andarian legend. Long tar-colored hair dripped across pale, gray skin. Soulless orbs, shared by its Dirge ally, smoldered with triumph. The Changeling grinned as it gazed down at the still form of the young Lion. Waving its gray fingers, the creature motioned its squad of mercenaries to lift Seth.

"They dare show such brazen disrespect?" Tulio's hand reached for the dagger he obsessively fiddled with every waking moment.

"Have a care, Rabbit," Wolf whispered low. "The Sarcion's agent stands within striking distance of the Lion. We must have a plan."

Movement took his attention away from the Changeling. Across the row, a familiar curly head popped in and out of the shadows. Coyote was taking a careful pace, unlike the group of young men following his squire along the docks. Dressed in cadet uniforms, the three were barely out of boyhood. More bang tail mischief.

He resisted the temptation to probe them. The Changeling might sense his power. Of course, it didn't take a ranger's skill to see the boys were there to rescue Seth. They must be in the same troop. Being barracks mates, they were ready to take the risk for their friend's sake. These young fools were about to walk right into a hornet's nest.

The Changeling walked at their head as the group moved down Lea's silent row toward Harrow. Wolf and Rabbit followed. They must rescue Seth before the mercenaries took him in their warren of thieves. It would be nearly impossible to find the Lion then unless Wolf used the power of the Right-Hand. Evil would be warned of his presence and burrow into their stronghold. He'd have to summon the entire Legion to flush the villains out again.

Then a small explosion in the row ahead of them sent an eruption of ale into the air. Confusion momentarily scattered the mercenaries. They abandoned Seth upon the cobblestones and rushed forward to investigate. Coyote stepped onto the wet stones to meet them. What was the young fool doing, marching out into the open with sword drawn? Then Wolf saw them. He cursed as Coyote's squire and the group of young men crept toward Seth's bound body. A towheaded cadet removed the gag from Seth's mouth. They spoke in rapid whispers as another of their number worked on his ropes.

The Changeling wasn't fooled by the diversion for long. It turned around, caught sight of the young men and pulled a jagged sword. Barking commands to its lackeys, the creature moved to attack. One of the cadets pulled a hatchet and took out the first man. His twin echoed the movement, taking down another. Pulling a beat up old sword, the towhead stood away from Seth, despite the Lion's pleas. He headed toward the grinning Changeling. Striking with a speed rivaling any master swordsman, the creature took him down with a single blow. He fell in an unconscious heap upon the ground.

Wolf leapt out of his hiding place as the Lion's power began to build. It pushed against the walls of the row. Cracks tore through the façade of the buildings, popping and ripping up the walls. He'd take out a city block if he weren't stopped. The young cadet had released a destructive force none of them could survive. It was fortunate they were surrounded by warehouses and not homes.

Then Seth threw his head back and the Lion's roar thundered out of his mouth in a terrible wave of power. Several things happened at once. Boyd threw himself at the twin cadets, pulling them to the ground. The mercenaries turned as one toward the noise and quickly met their end under the crushing blow of the roar. Coyote's body vanished in the wake of Seth's fury as the buildings fell.

Wolf covered his face as brick and mortar were torn off the buildings. Crates exploded into thousands of tiny projectiles. He fell to his knees as the very Erthe shook beneath them. This young Lion would be a powerful lord, if he didn't get himself and his friends killed first.

The deafening roar faded at last, but Seth's power continued to burn bright around his body. Wolf and Tulio approached him slowly. A black bird cawed above them, shifting agitatedly upon its perch atop the rubble. It fluttered its wings and then flew off toward Harrow.

"See to Coyote's squire and the cadets," he told Tulio. "And remember, Lord of Valdeon. Hide your fear from the Lion."

He slowly came to stand beside Seth's writhing body, projecting comfort and protection.

You must calm him quickly, Right-Hand. The power is taking him.

Wolf kneeled beside Seth and reached out with shaking fingers. He'd calmed the bear certainly, but the animal had been a mouse compared to the mighty power of the untamed Lion. Would Seth remember him? Would he accept his touch? The Jalora had called Wolf as Right-Hand. He doubted Seth even understood the role Wolf would play in his life.

Smoothing at the wet curls, he brushed them away from the young Lion's face. Seth's eyes were rolling wildly under clenched lids. The boy's entire body shook with barely contained power. Low growls warned the Lion's Roar would soon burst forth again, crushing everyone in the row and the buildings around them. Then he remembered little Gaspar. Their special lullaby was the only thing able to calm his temper and stop the attacks upon his breathing.

He brought the Voice of the Right-Hand to wrap around the Lion's body and started to sing,

"Sailboats made with candle wax, sailing to the shore line.

Wave your little arms, help them find you.
Carry my little one to the distant shores of dreamland
And back again to Papa's arms come morning."

Papa. Wolf's heart lurched as he thought of the last time he'd sung this same song to Gaspar. Seth's arms wrapped around Wolf's torso as if he understood the loss. Wolf sang the song again and again until the Lion's arms fell limp and his breath deepened into sleep.

"I've done it. I've calmed him."

He lifted his eyes looking for Tulio, instead he found thick mists blanketing a forest floor. What had happened? When had they left the city streets? No. They'd left more than Lea behind. This was the Realm of Dream and Mists. The Lion had taken him into a dimension between dream and reality.

Soft sobs drifted toward him. A tiny boy with curly hair stood among the eternal flora covering the ground. He appeared to be four or five years old. His little hands covered his eyes as the tears streamed down his cheeks. Glistening in the gentle light of a constant spring day, the Lion Ring gripped his tiny finger.

Awestruck, he stared unabashedly at the Lion Child Vessel. This tiny little boy represented the innocent part of Seth's heart. It would be inside this small body that the Jalora would live as it walked among them. He was witnessing the most sacred and vulnerable aspect of the Jalora. If a creature of evil harmed this innocent child, then Andara would certainly fall and the Sarcion would win.

Wolf stood up and went to the child. He knelt and gently took the boy's hands in his own. Amber-flecked eyes blinked back at him. There was no fear in those orbs, only innocent trust and pleading. He smoothed a fingertip along the crystal of the child's Lion Ring. Wolf gazed into the boy's eyes once more as understanding came to him.

"You worry for your friends, yes? They're only sleeping. Soon the rangers will come and take them to safety."

The little Lion smiled and threw his arms around Wolf's neck. Aware he was committing the worst sort of sacrilege, Wolf folded the tiny child in his arms. It felt like holding a happy dream or sunshine on a spring day.

It is time to return to my garden, Little Lion, the Jalora called. *You will see Wolf again soon. He is to take care of you.*

The little Lion gave Wolf a bright smile and then darted toward a soft white light at the edge of his vision. His little hand waved good-bye. He gifted Wolf with one last smile. Then the tiny hand pointed back toward the alley. Wolf turned and saw his body holding tightly to the earthly form of the young Lion. Something stronger than gravity pulled his spirit form back into his body. He groaned and opened his eyes.

"Wolf?" Rabbit's worried face came into view. "Are you well? I thought the Lion had drained your life away."

Coyote stood behind him, a bit bruised but otherwise unharmed. His clever green eyes, usually filled with mischief, now held fear and respect in them.

Wolf looked down at the adult's body in his arms. This Lion was indeed special, for only his pure heart could contain the Jalora as it walked among the world of men. He remembered the careful instruction his father had given him as third-in-command of the Sacred Guard. The Jalora Master was both dangerous and benevolent, vicious and kind. Wolf knew his role as third guardsman. He sighed and let the fear escape into the darkness. Only the Hawk, Right-Hand to the Master, was trained in the ways of the sacred vessel. Only he knew how to care for the tiny entity the Jalora used to inhabit its Lion. Such a precious soul needed the utmost care. Everything depended upon it.

You must learn how to care for my sacred vessel for yourself, as all the Right-Hands before you have done, Xavier the Wolf. Do not fear. The little Lion likes you.

"Help me carry him," Wolf told Rabbit. "Coyote. Hide your squire and then stand guard over these cadets until the rangers arrive. Keep yourself hidden. You know of the boarding house two streets away from the Rollicking Rover? Good. Come to us when the boys are safe."

"It will be as you say, Right-Hand." Coyote gave him an uncharacteristic bow and went to his squire.

Wolf staggered on his feet. He hadn't expected how much calming the Lion's power would drain his energy. Tulio caught him as he swayed. His young comrade's eyes were full of fear.

"Help me pick up our Lion," Wolf snapped. "You are a Lord of Valdeon. Remember your duty."

"Yes, Wolf."

Tulio hurried to Seth's side. Hesitating, he picked up the Lion and put him over his shoulder. He walked beside Wolf, making sure he had a strong arm to lean on.

"Let's get Seth to safety."

Chapter Fifty

WOLF'S POWER SCANNED the darkness like a hungry animal. North Burrough's eyes were upon them. One feral glare sent them diving back behind their window shades. Not slowing their pace, Wolf and Tulio left a false trail to confuse any who may have followed them. Exhausted, Wolf kept moving for the sake of the boy who swung limply over Tulio's shoulder.

It seemed hours before their tidy little boarding house came into view. The landlady, Mrs. Tully, opened the door for them. She nodded to Wolf, keeping her eyes carefully from the young Lion's body. Hidden beneath her widow's lace was the naked steel of a sword. Mrs. Tully's husband had been one of Leo's most devoted Lion Friends. She was no less loyal to the Lords of Valdeon.

Rabbit's squire threw open the doors to their rented room. He stepped back to make way for them and their precious cargo. Tulio rested the Lion upon his own cot and stepped back to regard him. The squire joined his lord, casting curious glances at their boy deliverer.

Wolf collapsed in a nearby chair with a grateful sigh. Would he ever grow used to the drain upon his life energy?

"He isn't what you expected."

"I thought he'd be something grand - a hero to lead us. Look at him. He can't be any older than I am. How is he to defeat the Jackal and win back Valdeon?"

"I don't know." Wolf sniffed hungrily, watching as Rabbit's squire went back to cooking the meal. "We must trust the Jalora."

Wolf closed his eyes, feeling a sense of peace for the first time in a long while. The Lion's presence was a warm pulse of energy beside him. He'd never experienced such a deep connection with Leo, though they'd known each other for many years. Seth and he would have a much different relationship. It would take some explaining for the young Lion to understand.

Urgent tapping on his shoulder roused Wolf from his brief nap. Rabbit pointed toward the bed as the Lion stirred. Seth sat up in bed to regard them. The Jalora had hidden the Lion eyes from the rest of the world, but nothing could hide the Master from his Right-Hand.

"The cadets are safe," Wolf told him. "A friend watches over them."

"I'm glad to see you, Wolf."

Seth eased off the bed onto his feet. His voice was steady, controlled. Inside, his mind and heart was a different matter. Their unique connection gave Wolf an intimate view inside the young Lion's thoughts and feelings. Right now, he was gauging Wolf and the others.

"I don't think any of us are safe, Lion, especially you. It was foolhardy to be roaming around the citadel after dark on your own." Wolf stood, keeping his hands away from the hilt of his sword. "We are all hunted by these creatures of evil and must remain hidden. Think. The Changeling and its followers wouldn't have gotten far inside the citadel without help. A spy lurks somewhere in the obsidian walls."

Those intense eyes moved from Wolf to rest upon Tulio. The amber fire clouded over with sorrow. Tulio took an uneasy step back from their intensity.

"I know your face."

"This is Tulio Cristobal, Bearer of the Rabbit Ring." Wolf gave Seth what he hoped was an encouraging smile. "You remember the vision the night Valdeon fell, yes?"

Seth nodded. "Many suffer because of the evil unleashed that night. I see the people in my dreams. Sometimes I can feel…." He let his hands drop. "Are the rest of the rangers safe as well?"

"Yes. I've sent them into hiding as commanded."

"What brings you and Rabbit to Lea?"

"You, Lion. We are here to protect you and to continue your training."

"You mean you're going to stay in Lea with me?"

Relief. Delight. They exuded from the Lion's body in happy waves. His excitement was contagious. Here was a good man, kind and humble with no guile Wolf could sense. His heart lurched as he remembered the tiny Lion Vessel. Such a gentle soul shouldn't have to face what he would in his lifetime. How to break such news to an innocent?

"Of course!" Wolf rested a hand on Tulio to keep him from backing away any farther. "Rabbit and I are members of the Sacred Guard. Didn't Leo tell you of Valdeon?"

"My father said he would take me to all the great cities of Valdeon and to the northern forests." Seth ran a hand through his curls. "He said the king would welcome me into his palace. I suppose he didn't know how to tell me who he was." Seth's sadness returned like an untreated sore. "We were to travel together, my father and I."

Wolf took a tentative step closer, strangely drawn by the Lion's pain. "I have much to teach you about your role as a Lord of Valdeon. First, we must discuss what it means to bear the Lion Ring."

"You mean the new covenant," Seth said, nodding. "Yes. I've learned my role well."

Wolf probed him gently. Seth had indeed been training in his role as Lion protector. Images of growling Lion warriors passed across Wolf's mind. Their strikes were designed to hurt rather than simply teach. Wolf didn't agree with such methods, but he didn't question. The Jalora had chosen how its Lion would be trained.

"Are you both here to help me on my quest?" Seth looked expectantly at them. "The Jalora says I'm to find the Book of Ancients behind the Obsidian Gates. It will seal our covenant. I finally have a clue to the book's whereabouts. It's somewhere in the Legion library. My squire and I plan to go back as soon as we are able. You could come with us."

"Have a care, Seth." Wolf crossed the remaining distance to grip his shoulders. "The book's power shouldn't be taken lightly. We must train you to control your power. Opening the book will announce your existence to every creature of evil upon Andara. Upon my word, when the time is right, I will stand by your side as you open the cover."

Seth's fingers fidgeted nervously with the hem of his sleeve. Here was the true test of Wolf's role as Right-Hand. Would Seth listen to his guidance or would he dismiss Wolf as a stranger. Trust in his Right-Hand was the key to keeping the Jalora Master safe.

"Very well, Wolf. Unless the Jalora commands otherwise, I will wait." He smiled at last. "It will be a relief to have your wisdom when the time comes to release the book's magic."

Spoken like a diplomatic lord. The young Lion offered Wolf respect while still leaving himself a way out. Yes. He would indeed be a great leader of men someday.

"Come, our meal is ready."

Wolf guided Seth toward the small table and took the chair beside him. Rabbit's squire placed a full bowl of stew before him with shaking hands. He gave Seth an awkward bow and hurried away to fill the other bowls.

"It smells delicious, Sir," Seth said to Rabbit's squire. "I haven't had a real Valdeonian meal since my last night with Dante. But, aren't you joining us?"

Valdeonian squires ate after their lords, as was custom. Leaving their names and identities behind, they neither spoke or slept until it suited their lord's pleasure. This new Lion didn't share the condescension of his family line. Wolf liked him even more for it. He'd never treated his own squire, Basilio, like an old pack.

Wolf ignored the squire's discomfort and said, "Fill your bowl and join us, squire. This is a happy occasion, yes?"

Rabbit's squire hurried to obey, nodding his thanks to Seth. They ate their meager meal in uncomfortable silence. The Lion was aware of the curious stares upon him and blushed frequently. None of them had expected the shy, tender-hearted boy sharing a meal with them now. Wolf remembered his wife then. Dulcina had a gentle heart, but there was a strength about her which guided their family through hard times. Perhaps this boy's strength of heart was what was needed to save them all.

A warning whistle pierced the night. Wolf lifted out of his chair and stood between Seth and the door in one fluid move. Rabbit darted about the room snuffing out the candles. At the same moment, his squire doused the fire. Wolf kept a tight hold on the Lion's shoulder as they waited in the darkness. A swish of fabric announced Rabbit's presence close beside them on Seth's other side.

"A patrol," Tulio whispered and looked at Seth. "A ranger patrol and it's headed this way."

Seth twisted under Wolf's grip and came to his feet. "No sign of them."

"You have the sight as a hopeful?" Rabbit asked.

"If you mean can I see in the dark and through walls, then yes."

Then the door opened in a narrow break, just enough to allow two men inside.

"Jason!" Seth moved forward to embrace his friend.

"I'm glad to see you're safe and in good company, Seth." Jason grinned as Seth shook Boyd's hand. "Wolf, I have news. A troop of rangers have found the cadets and are taking them to the infirmary along with the Lion's Squire. Phoenix leads them."

"We must remain cautious. It won't be long before the entire Legion is sent out looking." Wolf turned a worried frown to Seth. "My intent was to take you to a safe location. It would appear the Legion knows more about you than I'd anticipated."

Power, raw and angry, ripped through the air just outside the building. Wolf lifted his block and wrapped it around the Lion. Fear for the boy's safety came to Wolf's heart in surprising intensity.

"They're coming closer," Coyote said. "The Phoenix is a better tracker than I supposed."

"They'll find you, Sir." Seth tore his burning eyes from the street to capture Wolf's gaze. "Let me sneak out the back and circle round to them. You can remain hidden."

He knew the Lion was right. They needed time to change their plans. Secrecy was necessary to keep the citadel spy from knowing their next move. He didn't like letting Seth leave his side, but they had no choice.

"Go," Wolf told him.

Seth looked away uncomfortably and ran his fingers through untidy curls again. "Can I help you in some way?" He dove into his tunic and extended a coin purse to Wolf without hesitation. "It isn't much, but perhaps it will see you to safety."

Wolf traded surprised looks with Rabbit. Those coins were all the young Lion had in the world, except for the sword his father had given him. Now he was giving his money to them without any thought for his own comforts. This Lion was nothing like his father, or his greedy half-brother.

He closed his hands gently around the Lion's fingers. "You keep it, Seth, with my thanks."

The young Lion nodded and headed through the door Boyd held open for him. He hesitated. Indecision. Anxiety. Loneliness. They penetrated the wall of calm Seth raised around his body.

"How will I find you again, Sir?"

"I will come for you soon. We must start your training right away," Wolf told him. "In the meantime, be safe. Keep your friends close. And Seth. Everything will be all right now we're together."

The Lion nodded and disappeared through the door, leaving them to listen in silence. Shouts echoed along the walls. Phoenix' cry of relief could be heard in their little chambers. They held their breath, but there was no knock on the door. The Lion had kept his promise.

"What now?" Coyote asked.

He seemed as eager as Wolf to do something, anything except stay in the confines of the boarding house. Thoughts and plans swirled in Wolf's mind. It was pointless to continue to hide Seth from Dragon. The cardinal must have his suspicions about the boy's identity. Wolf would visit Legion HQ in the morning and request a ranger detail to guard them. Seth must be trained to control his power. They'd need a quiet place out of the city to let the Lion's Roar loose. He'd use his authority as Right-Hand to convince Dragon to let them leave Lea. It was no longer safe for Seth to remain in the city. One off-handed comment or harsh rebuke could push the boy's fury out of control.

"See if you can find the Changeling. Have a care, Coyote. The creature of evil's powers come from the Sarcion."

"And what of us, Wolf?" Tulio asked. "Are we to help search?"

"No, Rabbit. You and I are going for a walk in the woods." Wolf turned to Tulio's silent squire. "Pack our things and be prepared to leave in a hurry. We take the Lion away from Lea as soon as possible."

Making their way through the pre-dawn streets, Wolf and Tulio passed unseen through the gates of the city. Wolf slowed their run a few miles from Lea's border wall. Stepping into the evergreen boughs, he walked at a slower pace. These woods were thick with old growth. It would be difficult for anyone to creep through the brambles without being heard. A perfect place for the Lion to unleash his power.

Amid the woody tangles was an abandoned village. Decades had passed since its last resident fled for more lucrative pursuits in Lea. They'd fortify the village's remaining structures and begin Seth's training in the peace of the woods.

Rabbit threw a stray twig against a tree. His young face was masked with the sour countenance of the severely disappointed. Wolf walked silently beside his murmuring companion. Best to have it out now.

"Is there something wrong, Rabbit?"

"Why must he parade around as a cadet?" Tulio grumbled. "It is beneath the Lion."

"I served as a cadet in the San Rudalfo army when I was his age," Wolf said, hiding a grin. "The hard work of an ordinary foot soldier teaches a man lessons he cannot learn otherwise."

"I don't think those lessons will help him deliver Andara from the Jackal. How will he ever free Valdeon?"

"Was I such a poor teacher when I trained you, Rabbit?" Wolf asked softly.

"There is no better teacher in all of Andara."

"Then have a little faith, Rabbit. This Lion is special. I can feel it."

"I do have faith in you, Wolf."

"How life affirming. I may be moved to tears."

A blackbird dove over their heads and landed upon the ground several feet in front of them. Flapping its wings wildly, the bird began to twist and grow. Its form stretched upward until the Changeling's body was whole. Malicious black orbs glowed with an eerie light in the darkness.

"You'll meet your end this night, Right-Hand." The Changeling bared its jagged teeth and hissed. "Our brother, Julian, will be king. Your house will fade from memory."

Wolf pulled his sword, ready to split the thing of evil down the center of its black heart. Then the forest moved. Mercenaries flooded the small space under the green canopy. Tulio's back pressed against his as they made ready to fight for their lives.

Chapter Fifty-One

PHOENIX LEANED across the desk he'd confiscated from an unlucky lieutenant in UR Army Headquarters. The surface buckled as a tendril of his power escaped from the fists he pressed into the wood. Seth forced his feet to remain glued in their current location, dead center in the eye of the Phoenix's ferocity. Riley had the good fortune to be designated a position by the door next to Phoenix's squire.

"Your antics are over, Hopeful. I've played along and helped you when I could, because you are a Lord of Valdeon. It is my duty to do so. A new threat has come to Lea. I can no longer allow you to roam about on your own. You will tell me which ring of the Sacred Guard you bear. Then you will tell me where to find Edmund the Leo. Don't try to deny he is in Lea. I heard the Lion's Roar!"

His probe struck Seth's mind like a battering ram. Raising his block, Seth brought it to full power and quickly extended the protective force about Riley. Phoenix set his jaw into an angry grind and pushed harder.

"Stop this! Great gulls. You're supposed to be on the same side."

"Keep the Grey Cliff Islander wisdom to yourself, Logan." Phoenix yanked back his power and stood away from the desk with a grunt. "You won't tell me? Very well. I go to search Lea for the Leo. You will remain here."

He stormed past Seth and threw open the door. Sergeant Dancer stood at attention just outside. He gave the ranger a respectful salute. Curiosity. Fear. Anger. They hung about Dancer in sheets of bright color. His gaze drifted to Seth briefly and then fixed upon the Phoenix.

"Sergeant Dancer, these men are to be kept in the infirmary until my return. Under no circumstances are they to leave their beds. Do I make myself clear?"

"Yes, my lord. I'll see them to their beds personally." Sergeant Dancer kept his salute in place as Phoenix pushed past him in a flurry of ash.

Their sergeant raised his arm and pointed to the hall. Seth and Riley marched silently ahead of him, waiting for the rebuke. He'd warned Seth not to bring down any more ranger attention. Tonight was just the beginning. Now Phoenix was certain he was a Lord of Valdeon.

The infirmary doors were a welcome end to the uncomfortable silence of their march. Riley leapt on the handles and pulled the doors open. The Claybank twins were in their cots relaxing. Tory leaned against his pillows in the cot next to them. He was already bragging to the pretty nurses about his brush with death.

"Your friend is lucky his wound was a minor one," Sergeant Dancer said. "I hope tonight's adventure helps you to understand what I've been trying to teach you, McCloud. Troop mates stand with each other. Foolhardy mistakes impact everyone, not just the man making them." He leaned closer to Seth. "Remember this lesson above all else, Ranger. Now go to your cot or hold up the wall if it suits you. I have to arrange for a night guard."

Tory had been lucky. They all had. If not for Wolf, the Lion Ring would be in Jackal hands now. Wolf. The thought of his teacher cheered him a little. He'd come for Seth. It was a relief to have someone like Wolf to guide him. Contrary to the Jalora's command, Wolf had told him not to open the Book of Ancients. He wanted to prepare Seth first. It had been over two hours since they'd parted. Waiting for word from Wolf was draining his patience.

"Come on, Riley," Seth said, grabbing at the door handle. "We're wasting an opportunity."

"What are you talking about? Dancer won't be away long." Riley hurried to follow him. "We're supposed to be in our hospital beds until morning, or so says the Phoenix. I really don't want to scrub the citadel from top to bottom. Great gulls! He may have. something worse in mind."

"Bed will have to wait. You and I are going to the Legion Library."

"This is mad! We were lucky enough to escape once, now you want to go back inside?"

Seth put a hand over Riley's mouth and said in a low voice, "You will give us away before we can reach the door. I must get the Book of Ancients. Then we're going to join a friend who is taking us out of Lea."

His squire pushed Seth's hand away angrily. "What friend? I know all your friends, Seth."

"Wolf is here in Lea. He's come to take us somewhere safe, and to train me."

"Aye. And how does he suppose we leave the UR Army or the Legion without being court-martialed? Honestly, Seth. How do you know we can trust him?"

"He's proven himself as an ally on more than one occasion. Why can't you trust in his deeds?"

The stairway leading to the lower levels was close to the infirmary. Seth dove down them, taking the steps two at a time. His teacher had saved both their lives in Haven Bay. He'd saved Seth again tonight. Why did he feel so protective of a man who could clearly outfight any enemy on Andara? By the offended frown on Riley's face, he didn't understand either.

"I'm sorry I was short with you. Wolf is the only one who's willing to tell me the entire truth about what I am and what I'm supposed to be. He was about to tell me everything when Phoenix found the boarding house we were hiding in." Seth brushed a hand along the obsidian stone. "Wolf even knows what's inside the Book of Ancients and why its connected to the covenant. He warned me not to open it until I've completed my training."

Dim lights illuminated the empty halls of the lower level. Lingering smells of beef and bread hung in the air to guide their steps. Seth hurried to the kitchen doors. Soon the kitchens would be full of activity preparing for breakfast. They must find the book and be out of the citadel before anyone woke.

"Over there, Seth." Riley pointed past the great ovens.

The little door waited for them at the far wall. This time, Seth kneeled before the door without hesitation. Magic, inquisitive and insistent, touched at his arms and torso. He ignored its touch. Leaning his head against the door, he stretched out his power into the hall beyond. It was empty.

"What now, oh my ranger? We haven't got Tory here to pick the lock."

Seth gripped the knob and turned it slowly. The door popped open, framing a landscape of utter blackness. He eased quietly inside, waiting as Riley joined him. The door closed after them of its own accord. A small click echoed in the silence as the latch locked them in.

"Tory didn't really open the lock, did he?" Riley gripped his arm as he took a step forward. "Wait, Seth. I thought this Wolf fellow told you not to go looking for the book."

"He told me not to open the cover. Listen, I must find it before we leave. Bringing the Book of Ancients to Wolf is my best plan. It will be safer in his hands."

"Fine. You've made up your mind. I'll look for a candle or lantern in the kitchen," Riley told him.

"I'm sure they'll have something in the library. We don't want to run the risk of someone seeing the light."

"How are we to find our way?"

Seth sighed. "I can see in the dark, Riley."

He looked upon his friend's shocked face. Riley's lips turned up into a grin. Seth grabbed his arm and began to lead him toward the library doors. His squire was getting more pleasure from these new gifts than Seth was.

Silence followed them into the library. Rows of bookshelves formed a maze impossible to navigate in the dark. Seth guided Riley to a sideboard lining the wall. Several crystal lanterns were tucked neatly into cubbyholes. Parchment, pens, and ink filled other containers. This library was kept by a dedicated caretaker.

Riley lifted the shade on his lantern. The crystal's light glowed happily in his grip. He whistled as he lifted the lantern higher. Light struck the maze of shelves housing hundreds of volumes.

"Where do we start?" he asked.

Seth held the lantern up to the plaques above the door. "Valdeon. The Jalora's source of power on Andara. Let's split up. We have to find the book quickly."

Running his fingertips along the bindings, Seth scanned the titles. All the books were leather bound with gold inlay. How he would love to spend a few weeks just going through the volumes. Books written about the Dance of Death, basic swordplay, and strategies for defense of an outpost passed under his fingers.

Open the book, Lion.

Yes, but which one? Perhaps the Jalora was trying to tell him the Book of Ancients was hidden under a false title? He pulled out *Strategic Defenses for Rural Outposts,* by John the Stagg. He began skimming the pages. His fingers flipped faster and faster as he read. Seth shut the book with a boom. In just a few seconds, he'd been able to read the entire book and absorb every word.

"How is this possible?" Seth asked the Jalora. "I read the entire book in moments and am able to remember its contents exactly."

The Jalora's laughter filled the library. *Open the book, Lion!*

"Which one?" Seth asked, his own anxiety rising. "There are so many."

The book is not on this shelf.

"These volumes are in different languages," Riley called over the rows. "I can't read them, but they look big enough to be history books."

Seth hurried around the rows. He found Riley in the center of the library. Two thick books balanced precariously in one hand as he pulled a third off the shelf. Seth lifted one of the volumes from Riley's pile. They were histories of the Heart of the Warrior Rings from each country. Seth pressed his hand on the gold inlay, his curiosity piqued again.

"Good work, Riley. I don't see Valdeon though."

The history of Valdeon will not be on this shelf either. Find it!

He wanted to find the book, perhaps more than the Jalora did. They'd have to start from one end of the room and make their way to the other side, checking each volume. It would take hours they didn't have.

"Why would the rangers put a cage in a library?" Riley asked him, pointing toward the end of the rows.

The Jalora's excitement flooded his being in a swift wave. Seth, caught up in the current of its power, dropped the book back into Riley's hands. He ran to the corner with a cry of triumph. Mounted to the floor and ceiling, iron rod enclosed a golden pedestal. Resting upon its elegant surface was a massive book with a worn leather cover.

Open the book, Lion!

"What about Wolf? He told me not to open the book." Seth circled the cage, panting like a hungry beast.

Iron rod completely circled the pedestal. He couldn't see a gate or any other breaks in the cage's walls. Slamming a fist against the bars, Seth growled with frustration.

Open it!

"How do I enter?" Seth cried aloud.

"Hush! You'll wake the citadel!" Riley hissed.

Seth grabbed the iron bars and began to shake them.

"Are you mad? Stop it."

It was too late to stop. His fury burned out of control. Seth threw his head back as the Lion's Roar burst from his throat. The bars twisted and fell like dried twigs. He threw them aside with a feral growl and stomped over the ruined frame of the cage. Standing before the Book of Ancients, he slapped his hand down upon the cover. Then a brilliant white light shot out of the book to surround him. Its power held him firmly, pulling his body forward. He couldn't look away from the blinding light. Hundreds of voices called to him from the past, filling his mind until he thought he'd go mad.

Chapter Fifty-Two

WOLF TOOK the First Stance and continued to face down the Changeling. Tulio pressed against his back. Fifty pairs of human eyes glared at them from the trees. Fury. Grief. Greed. The Lion had killed their kin. These mercenaries were out for blood.

"The young kitten has drained you, Right-Hand." The Changeling grinned, swinging its blade playfully into the distance between them. "I wonder if you can still lift your blade tip from the ground."

"Attack me, creature of evil, and we'll see."

The Changeling's dagger-like grin widened. It yowled a sudden battle cry and flew forward. Wolf met its blade head on, knocking the steel away and slicing down across the creature's ribs. The Changeling screamed an angry cry and rolled out of the way as two mercenaries came at Wolf. His blade met their attack with a mighty blow, passing through bone and flesh. He swept his steel in a swift strike along their throats. Two gruesome heads rolled away from their lifeless bodies.

Tulio was holding his own at Wolf's back. Youth counterbalanced the toll taken by his horrible wounds suffered the night Valdeon fell. Rabbit was still weak. Wolf, drained by the Lion, wasn't much better off than his companion. They had to find the high ground before their strength failed.

Wolf reached deep within himself and grabbed hold of the gift his forbears had given him. Endurance. Their family maxim had seen him through many battles. None was more critical to the future of Andara than this night. He took the last of his strength and called the power of the Right-Hand.

"Die!"

The Voice ripped through flesh, tree, and rock, not stopping until its ravenous appetite had been sated. He sunk down on one knee as the power left him. Panting, he stared out across the destruction his voice had wrought. It seemed more powerful and more destructive after his contact with the Lion.

"You must get up," Tulio cried, trying to pull Wolf to his feet. "The mercenaries, those left, are forming another attack."

Then a ranger's battle cry thundered through the trees. He moved like a juggernaut through the remaining mercenaries. Bodies fell at his feet in bloodied piles. The Changeling, seeing the danger, disappeared in a flutter of black feathers. It flew over the tree tops, leaving its followers to face their deaths.

Esteban the Hawk stood amid the carnage. Blood dripped from his sword. The Hawk Prince ignored his victims. His eyes, bright with hatred, glared at Wolf kneeling upon the ground. Wolf stood up slowly, leaning on Tulio's arm. Their questionable savior continued to keep his body a rigid testament of his hatred. Wolf - like Hawk - kept his sword unsheathed.

"You've flown back to Lea, Hawk," Wolf said, keeping his block up. "Did Dragon welcome you with open arms or do you remain apart from the Legion?"

"I don't answer to you, Deacon." The ugly scar running down the side of his face grew pale. "You seem overly concerned with my business, Wolf. Guilt feelings perhaps? Or are you worried I will take back the allegiance of the Sacred Guard?"

Hawk finally turned his gaze toward the destruction the Voice had wrought. "So, it is true. The Lion has called to him his Right-Hand. I'd heard rumors of your presence in Lea. Then found the alley where the Lion lost control. His power still embraces your body." Hawk shook his head. "I intercepted a communication addressed to *The Right-Hand* headed for Heidelbrecht. Naturally, I took the message for my own. I'm surprised you didn't feel the call, Wolf, being the Master's Right-Hand. The young Lords of Valdeon have been summoned."

"Give me the message, Hawk."

"You don't deny it? First you turn the Lords of Valdeon against me, now you've tricked the boy into calling you, rather than his own blood." Hawk's eyes flashed with fury. "I can see it has become critical I beat the Marianna dung from his brain and fix it to the right frame of thinking."

"The right frame? Don't you mean your own agenda?"

"You have no idea of the sacrifices I've made for his sake. He will do as I say."

"The Jalora would never allow you to control him, Hawk Prince. It protects its Lion."

"It won't have a choice, Right-Hand, once you're dead."

Hawk raised his sword over his head. The madman was going to attempt to kill Wolf in cold blood. Esteban was a gifted swordsman who had all his strength available for the fight. They'd have to use every ounce of will left to defeat him. Then Hawk grunted. His eyes rolled backward and he dropped to the ground. Jason the Coyote wiped Hawk's blood from the hilt of his dagger. The madman was alive, but he'd have a headache when he woke.

"Somehow, I don't think Hawk's heart is in the right place," Coyote said. "Rest, Right-Hand. I'll find the message."

Coyote's nimble fingers searched through Hawk's clothes and belt. He pulled out a parchment and handed it to Wolf. The seal had been broken and torn away. He couldn't see any indications of who may have sent the summons. Wolf opened the parchment. The message was urgent and couldn't be ignored.

"What is it?" Tulio asked.

"Someone has called the Lords of Valdeon to Muellerton Outpost and signed my name. The others could be walking into a trap."

He must return to Muellerton in all haste. Someone was playing a dangerous game meant to trap the Sacred Guard. He didn't have time to fetch Seth. It might not be safe to do so at any rate. He'd have to trust Dragon to protect their Lion.

"What do we do with Hawk?" Coyote asked. "We can't let him loose to go after Seth."

"Tie him to a tree. Don't worry about being gentle. Coyote, I want you to go to Dragon. Tell him what Hawk has done and ask him to lock this madman in the brig until I return. Then find Seth and don't leave his side. Understand? Tell Phoenix I told him to help you guard Seth as well. Nobody gets near him until I return."

"Yes, Wolf. You have my word." Coyote finished tying up Hawk and stepped back. "Will the Lords of Valdeon be returning with you? Seth needs allies around him now."

"I don't know. I hope so." Wolf gave him a nod. "Be swift, Ranger. Come, Tulio. We must get to our ship. Time is against us."

Chapter Fifty-Three

Voices from the past, present, and future wailed in unison from beneath the cover of the book. Seth's mind fell into the vastness of their emotions. His body swayed as his mind's eye floated above it, observing mortality with detached interest. Mechanical fingers flipped the cover open.

Free after one hundred years of confinement, the book's magic burst from the page. It exploded at Seth in a wall of light. Blinded, he screamed and covered his eyes. The magic pierced his fingers. It would not be denied his complete and utter obedience. Scribble became letters. Letters became words. The language was unfamiliar, like nothing he'd seen before. Then his eyes and mind adjusted under the magic's will. The words upon the page became as familiar to Seth as the common tongue.

His fingers began to flip through the pages. The book spoke of an ancient race called the Luminawni who'd fought on the side of Good to save Valdeon. They were witness to the covenant his ancestor, Mikel D'Antoiné, made with the Jalora. These god-like beings forged the Heart of the Warrior Rings centuries ago. The Lion Ring upon his finger had been the first.

Time grows short. They will come soon.

Seth took his hands away as the pages began to flutter. Turning faster at the whim of an invisible hand, their movement exuded odors of parchment, dust, and history. Then the pages stopped at a section called simply, "The Lion." The last chapter in the Book of Ancients, this section appeared to be fewer than ten pages long.

Seven men - past bearers of the Lion Ring - were listed in the middle of the page.

Mikel D'Antoiné, the Lion

Paulo D'Antoiné, the Azure Lion

Marcus D'Antoiné, the Stone Lion

Samuel D'Antoiné, the Thunder Lion

Enrico D'Antoiné, the Granite Lion

Gustavo D'Antoiné, the Lion Claw

He swallowed hard. The last name on the short list was 'Seth D'Antoiné, Hopeful.'

Seth staggered back when the book flipped on its own to the last page. His name was written on the top, but the rest of the parchment was blank. What could this mean? Was the book waiting for him to write upon it?

The covenant has been agreed upon. By the book's magic we are bound together. My power has been restored and will strengthen as your skill grows. First, there is a task I must do which weighs heavy upon my heart. Cup your hands together, Lion.

Seth did as he was told. Energy tingled along his palms, sending shivers up his arms. A heaviness pressed against his skin. Silver circlets struggled to appear within his bowl of flesh. Their forms became solid and real. Resting in his cupped hands were Heart of the Warrior Rings - about twenty in all.

Many of my servants perished over the Forbidden Mountains as they attempted to aid Valdeon. Their sacrifice will not be forgotten. Put them in something and leave them for the Dragon. These rings must find their heirs.

"Seth! Can you hear me?" Riley cried. "Someone's coming!"

Go, Lion. It is done.

Seth staggered out of the cage through the section of the iron rod he'd ripped from its mounts in the floor and ceiling. The fancy metal had been twisted like fabric. Wolf had been right. He couldn't control his power. It was a blessing no one had tried to stop him reaching the book.

"Give me something to put these in," Seth said.

Riley hurried to the sideboard and grabbed a long box from the shelf. He dumped out the quills, scattering them all over the top of the counter. Extending his hands over the box Riley held, Seth gently put the twenty rings inside. He took the box and set it on top of the Book of Ancients. Dragon certainly wouldn't fail to notice them.

The double doors of the library flew open. Riley grabbed Seth's arm and pulled him behind the shelves. Pressing their bodies against the far wall, they waited for the rangers, like grouse in a bush.

"Stay out in the hall! Manitou. Falcon. Swan. You're with me."

"Yes, Dragon."

Lanterns bobbed along the rows of shelves. Their light cast eerie bars of pale yellow upon the ground.

Seth pushed his back harder against the cool of the wood paneling. The rangers were almost upon them. He raised an unsteady block to hide Riley and himself. What if Dragon sensed his presence? He concentrated harder. They must escape and find Wolf.

"The Book of Ancients has been opened!"

"Don't touch it!" Dragon warned. "Your death will come swiftly if you do. Only the Lion may handle the book."

Riley leaned forward beside him, trying to catch a look at the men between the rows of books. Seth pulled him back again with a frantic shake of his head. It didn't matter who they were. Curiosity had thrown him in enough danger this night.

"Can you read what it says?" another of them asked.

"No. I know someone who can, but it's not safe for our…friend in Lea. We must go to him."

"Do you think it wise, Sir? Look what the heir did." A tap rang out against the twisted metal. "Do we dare leave him on his own?"

"We have no choice. Split up and find the boy. He can't have gotten far. Put a discrete guard on the library. If he comes back, we will have him."

"Sir, what do we do with the heir once we've found him?"

"Warn the rangers to be cautious." Someone tapped at the iron rod again. "This new Lion will have to be housed in a cell on the lower levels of the citadel for all our safety."

"What is in the box on top of the book?"

The rings clinked together as someone lifted the box. A long pause stretched into the night.

"Hope."

Dragon's powerful presence left the library at last. The other rangers followed, taking their excitement and anxiety with them. Seth rested his head against the paneling with a groan. Mercenaries and Changelings were trying to kill him. Now the Jalora Legion was hunting him too. He wouldn't be sorry to have Lea at his back.

"What happened? Why did you open the book, Seth?"

"I had no choice. We have to get out of here and find Wolf." He pushed away from the wall and peered between the shelves. "I can't believe it. They want to trap and cage me. Now I understand why my father and Dante warned me to remain hidden."

"Aye, old Dragon did sound keen on catching you. Well, we can't go out through the double doors. Maybe there's a back way?"

They made their way along the wall, staying close to its paneled surface. No sign of a door or a window. This room was completely closed off from the rest of the citadel. Panic edged its way into his dwindling calm. What would they do? He couldn't surrender and he certainly wouldn't allow himself to be caged.

"Well, what do you think of this?"

Riley put his hand over a small square panel in the wall. A section whisked to the side, revealing a short hall. He waved Seth inside and stepped in after. The wall closed with a whoosh behind them.

"How did you know about this passage way?"

Riley shrugged. "I remembered the symbol of the little man in the kitchen. It was right beside the entrance to Legion HQ. I figure it marks a squire's entrance. Had to be one in the library. Reading those dusty old books is thirsty work."

"You, Riley Logan, are as clever as they come."

Crystal lanterns came to life as they took a step down the passage. Ten paces more and they came to a door. The short hall must have been a buffer to block any sound from entering the peace of the quiet library. They had no trouble hearing the pandemonium on the other side of the door now. Shouts thundered through their wooden barrier. Doors crashed open with a series of booms as several boots ran up and down just on the outside of their hiding place.

Seth turned the handle and carefully opened the door a crack. Riley kneeled beside him to catch a look. Several men came out in their bare feet, rubbing their eyes. The more experienced among them had a sword gripped tightly in their hand.

"Curse the luck," Riley said after Seth carefully pushed the door closed. "This must be the squires' chambers."

Anger. Intense curiosity. Protection. They pulsed on the other side of the door. One of the rangers had come down the hall. Seth renewed his concentration on his block. The constant effort was giving him a pounding headache.

"Back in your rooms, Squires!" the ranger ordered. "We have an intruder. It may not be safe for you in the halls. You are to remain in your chambers until further notice by the Dragon's command."

"An intruder, Sir?" a familiar voice asked.

"You heard me. Go back inside and bolt the door."

The ranger's power moved farther down the corridor. Seth waited until he guessed the man was far enough away. Opening the door, he poked his head out into the corridor. The squires were shuffling back inside their rooms in a tidy line. Donny, Dragonfly's squire, remained outside. His fingers fiddled nervously with his bed jacket.

Seth plunged out into the hall moving with all the speed he possessed. He grabbed the young squire and pulled him into their hiding place before Donny could utter a cry. Thrashing about wildly, he jabbed at Seth's torso with his elbow.

"Quiet, Donny! It's us. Seth and Riley."

He released his grip and let the young man stagger forward. Donny's eyes were wide as he turned to regard them. Confusion. Disbelief. Anxiety. They weren't difficult to read on such an honest face.

"You're the intruders?"

"We're in trouble, Donny. We need your help."

"What has happened, Sir? Why does the Legion search for you?"

Riley cursed and stalked angrily toward the stunned squire. "We've got no time for explanations, Donny. You owe me your brother's life and I'm calling in the debt! I need you to show us a way out of here."

"Very well. A debt is a debt." Donny clasped his hands together nervously. "I can take you back through the infirmary. It's not well guarded. I go there every day to visit Ronny."

Donny, bare foot and dressed in his bed jacket, guided them down the corridor in the direction the ranger had gone. He stopped suddenly and pressed his hand against the wall. It whooshed open revealing a narrow set of stairs. They ascended quietly in the midnight black about them.

Seth breathed a gulp of relief when they came to the landing. It was suffocating in these narrow passages. Donny peeked his head into the corridor. Satisfied they were alone, he beckoned them into the opening. Their nervous guide tiptoed forward, never stopping as the corridor twisted around corners to the right and left. Seth marveled how Donny or any squire could find their way in the obsidian maze.

They were about to make yet another right turn when Donny froze at the edge of the corner. He backed up, running his bare feet over Seth's boots. The jittery young squire put a warning finger to his lips.

"The Legion infirmary is just around this corner, but there's a ranger guarding the door." He groaned and tugged unhappily on the ties of his bed jacket. "I'm in so much trouble. It's the same ranger who sent me back to my chambers. Don't you see? He's going to think I've disobeyed a direct order."

Seth pushed Donny gently to the side and poked his head around the corner. One ranger stood guard before the doors of the Legion infirmary. He was a large man, muscular and tall. Brown wavy hair framed a stern face. His neatly trimmed mustache made a downward arch as he stared straight ahead.

Remember Sara De Quintaro?

Yes of course! He'd rescued her aboard the De Quintaro family ship as it was moored on Carlotta. A traitor had held her as hostage. Seth and the Jalora used their joined powers to make the girl sleep. She'd fallen out of her captor's arms, giving Seth enough time to strike him down.

"You would allow me to do this to a ranger?" Seth asked the Jalora in his thoughts.

It won't harm him. I want the Dragon to know how strong we are.

The Jalora had a reason for everything it did. Above all else, he must trust in its wisdom. He turned to the squires as the lights of the corridor began to dim. The Jalora formed a thick mist about Seth's body.

"Donny, I want you to wait here with Riley. When you're asked about what happened, you'll be able to say honestly you found the ranger laying on the floor."

"What's happening? I don't understand."

"You must trust me. Now stay here and don't move."

Seth stepped out into the corridor, walking silently toward the ranger. Fingers of mist reached out into the space before him as he walked. Moving with a speed rivaling Phoenix, the ranger twisted his body toward Seth and took the First Stance. His sword tip remained perfectly still a hair's breadth above the floor.

"Hold Intruder!"

Seth ignored the command and continued his slow walk forward. He must get closer to ensure his power was strong enough to reach the man. Hard features became clearer as he closed the distance between them.

A Heart of the Warrior Ring glowed in brilliant blue upon his finger. He was a Deacon like Phoenix.

"You're a Ranger?" he asked with a grunt. "By the long dead saints. Why do you sneak about like a rat?"

A Tslavian. Wonderful. He must be swift. What would a Tslavian do to an unarmed Valdeonian with no witnesses around? The cloud of mist grew thicker, blocking the ranger's visage entirely. Seth breathed deeply as the Jalora's power flooded his body.

"Sleep."

The ranger's unconscious body fell to the floor with a loud thump. Parting the mists, Seth hurried to the fallen man. A hideous creature growled at him from the depths of the ring. He recognized the monster - a gargoyle. Its image had been imprinted in the golden depths of a coin he'd found in the fields of Marianna. The coin had been meant as payment for his murder.

This ranger bore the monstrous symbol of the Von Wolkhursts, Tslavia's royal family. He was kin, though Seth suspected the man would deplore their familial tie. Standing over his helpless body, Seth bit down his growing anger. The Von Wolkhurst family had been party to annulling his parents' marriage. According to Aunt Charlotte, hatred had brought them and the D'Antoiné family together for a rare show of odious solidarity.

"You've bested the Gargoyle!" Donny bounded up behind him with Riley in tow.

"Calm down, Squire. He's sleeping not dead. I may live to regret the fact. Come, help me get him into the infirmary."

Donny opened the door while Riley and Seth dragged the tall man into the infirmary. Several empty beds lined the walls. Good. It would be hours before anyone thought to look for Gargoyle in an unoccupied infirmary. They lifted him on to the nearest bed and stood back to gaze upon his sleeping form. Seth didn't want to be in Lea when the Gargoyle woke up.

"He's a Deacon, Seth." Riley regarded him with a raised eyebrow.

"Yes, I know." Seth gave him a sour frown his friend could no longer see. "Remember, Donny. You found this ranger on the floor. It's not a lie."

"It's not the truth either, Hopeful. What have you been up to, Seth? The Jalora is unsettled this night."

Seth spun around, reaching for a sword he'd neglected to bring. The infirmary beds weren't completely empty. Dragonfly sat upright against his pillow. Anger. Worry. Confusion. Shock. Clearly, he didn't appreciate Seth dragging his younger brother into their intrigues.

"Sleep!"

Seth lashed out before he could stop his power. Dragonfly tilted precariously to the side of the mattress with a rumbling snore. Donny hurried forward, catching his brother before he fell off the bed. Accusations filled his trusting eyes.

"Ronny! How did you do that? You aren't a Bishop, are you?"

"Sleep!"

Donny's limp form fell across his brother's bed. Seth turned away from them and threw his body against the cool wall. Panic. It was poking at the Lion's Roar, daring it to come out. Freedom and feasting. He was smothering in its hunger.

"Are you mad? You can't put the entire Legion to sleep, Seth."

"We must get out of here now."

"Aye. Let me put these two aright. Go wait for me by the door at the far wall. It's a squire's entrance. Donny told me they bring cloth and food through there."

Riley helped him through the door and out into the empty corridors of the citadel. They didn't stop running until they were safely away from Legion Headquarters. Seth was breathing hard as he rested his head against the wall. What had he done in his panic? He should've waited for Wolf. Seth covered his face with a shaking hand.

"What did the book say, Seth?" Riley asked. "I'm your best friend. I know you better than anyone. Whatever it said upset you."

"It's a history of Andara. The last section was about the Lion." Overwhelmed, he couldn't share the rest, not even with Riley. "We must get out of the Citadel and Lea. Tory might be able to help us."

"Aye, Seth." Riley's face was troubled. "We'll need our weapons."

"You head for the UR infirmary. I'll fetch our things." Seth gave his shoulder a quick squeeze. "I'm glad you're with me, Riley. I don't know what I'd do without you."

"Let's hope you never have to find out."

Chapter Fifty-Four

SETH RAN his fingers along the rolled-up mattress resting atop the bed frame. Hours before, he'd woken up here and had dined with the Lords of Valdeon at their table. Wolf had promised to train him. Now the room was empty. Nothing - prints, smells, discarded possessions - betrayed visitors had recently occupied the space.

"Are you sure you have the right house, Seth?" Riley asked. "All the doors and windows have been boarded up."

"Yes. I'm positive. They were here. I was here with them." He clutched nervously at the hilt of his sword. "Something must have happened."

"Well, we can't stay here, Mate," Tory said. "Maybe Dad can help you find a way out of Lea. We can get a message to these friends of yours."

Seth nodded and reluctantly turned to leave. Tory was right. He couldn't stay here waiting for Wolf. If the ranger had to leave for some reason, he might not be able to come back to Lea. Seth must trust in Wolf's ability to find them again.

"Yes, of course. Take us to your father's pub."

Walking through the streets, they went unnoticed in the pre-dawn hours. Lea wasn't a city satisfied to sleep at night. Music and laughter poured out of the various drinking establishments lining the rows. Several happily inebriated patrons staggered from one pub to the next, singing in slurring tones. Others, Seth noted, had collapsed under the street lights of Lea.

Tory seemed used to the scenes of excessive merriment. He stepped over a drunken sot and continued up the row without a backward glance. Seth and the others followed. Riley brought up the rear of their company, prodding the Claybank twins who kept stopping to watch the merry bedlam.

"Here it is, Mates! The Rollicking Rover." Tory stopped in the center of the row, gesturing toward a dingy looking pub. "Home!"

Tory frequently bragged about his Dad's pub. His stories suggested a grand inn with a stylish common room. Reality's cold truth was lost on Tory and the Claybanks. Grinning with thirsty excitement, they hurried up the short steps toward the entrance.

"Not exactly Paddy's Pub, is it? Maybe things look better on the inside?" Riley whispered to Seth.

"Come on, I'm thirsty!" Amery called.

Tory banged the doors open with flourish. Seth and his friends entered behind him. The Rollicking Rover didn't look much better on the inside, but the smells coming from the kitchens were appetizing. This pub was a comfortable escape from Lea's fast-paced city lifestyle. Its patrons seemed to agree. Lively chatter filled the relaxed common room.

They navigated through the crowd toward the long bar. The publican, a balding man of middle years, poured ale and other liquors with the speed of a magician. He placed them on the bar in reach of several waiting barmaids. They smiled at the young cadets. One of them gave Tory a kiss on the cheek as she passed.

"Tory, my lad," the publican said. "What the devil are you doing here? The army hasn't given you leave yet, surely?"

"These are my friends, Dad. Seth, Riley, Amery, and Aubrey." Tory leaned against the bar. "Listen, Dad. We're in a bit of a spot. Seth needs to get out of Lea quick. Are any of your cargo runners about?"

"I warned you, didn't I? The army isn't going to be lenient with your rascal ways, Tory. Tell me what trouble you're in."

"Ah Dad," Tory tilted his head with a grin. "The rangers are a bit upset with Seth. He just needs to lay low for a while until things settle down."

Mr. Dawson turned a parent's probing gaze on him. Seth stood a bit straighter, trying to look the innocent. A tingle of the familiar passed between them as their eyes met. The publican's bushy mustache wiggled with indecision. He ran a hand along his chubby red cheek.

"Coming here tonight wasn't the brightest of ideas then."

He motioned with his head toward the tables of the common room. Rangers peppered the pub. Some were drinking with friends. Others sat quietly on their own. Tory hadn't been exaggerating. This was a favorite haunt of the Legion.

"Go sit down. I'll send food and drink," he said. "Then we'll need to have a talk about your friend here."

A band of pretty barmaids loaded their table with drink and food. Each of them gave Tory a wink when they thought the other girls weren't looking. Seth decided he was best left in the dark as to Tory's relationship with his dad's staff.

Musicians climbed onto a makeshift stage close to their table. Guitars, drums, and a fiddle began the universal sounds of tuning. The music started, filling the common room with Andarian folk songs. The musicians were decent. Seth leaned back in his chair, daring to relax a bit under the spell of the cheery sound.

"Oh no," Tory murmured. "What's he doing here?"

Sergeant Dancer sat at the bar alone, sipping slowly on his tankard of ale. The cadets shrank down in their chairs. Dancer was the last person they wanted to see. Tory groaned and shook his head. Mr. Dawson had stopped filling glasses. Ignoring the impatient barmaids, he spoke with Dancer as if they were old friends.

"You didn't say your dad knew Sergeant Dancer." Amery took another long drink. "Do you think he follows us?"

"I wish someone knew for sure," Riley said, giving Seth a deliberate look.

The Jalora had remained oddly silent since they'd escaped Legion headquarters. He looked about slowly, avoiding eye contact with the rangers scattered about the room. They seemed to take no notice of him. Probing Mr. Dawson might draw their attention.

Several patrons around the common room suddenly stood as one. Making their way through the crowds, the armed men began tightening the snare on the table of rangers. They rushed forward as one. Throwing their hoods off, the rangers stood to meet them. Phoenix jumped on top of the table. He barked an order above the clamor. Other rangers positioned around the room came to cut at the back of their attacker's circle.

"Curse the luck!" Tory slammed a fist on their table. "Come to the back, Mates. This happens about twice a week."

Tory led the way, ducking under the counter. Riley and the Claybanks followed him behind the bar as they headed toward what Seth assumed was the back door. Taking a last look over his shoulder, Seth stopped before the counter. Phoenix's golden curls bounced over the heads of the patrons trying frantically to make the entrance. Three attackers thrust their blades at the ranger in coordinated strikes.

Protect your comrade, Lion.

Warning prickles of energy drew Seth's attention to the far corner. The assassin, hidden under a dark cloak, knelt in the open corner. His musket was pointed at Phoenix's heart. Engrossed in his battle with the three swordsmen, the ranger had no idea his death was approaching from the barrel of a coward.

Lifting his body upon the coils of smoke, Seth raced across the common room. He slammed down hard atop the man's musket. The loud boom sent the remaining patrons screaming toward the door. Its expelled bullet put a large hole in the floor of Mr. Dawson's pub.

The would-be assassin fell backward against the wall. His hood fell away, revealing distinct Valdeonian features. He glared at Seth. Hatred. Fear. Greed. The intensity of his emotions stabbed raw pain into Seth's being.

"Well, Half-breed," he spat. "The Wolf has let you roam loose like vermin. Prince Julian will thank me for exterminating you."

"Come ahead then, coward, if you have the courage." Seth drew his sword and took the First Stance.

The Valdeonian pulled his blade. He approached Seth in a slow methodical dance of his own. Sweeping his sword sideways, he tapped on Seth's blade with playful strikes. Was the man mad? Then he thrust his sword swiftly toward Seth's side. A dagger, held in his other hand, cut downward toward Seth's throat. He was forced to block with his left hand. The slice along his palm tore the glove asunder. Seth hissed with pain at the sharp cut. Underneath the rivulets of blood, the Lion Ring glowed in the smoky din of the common room.

"And there it is, the trinket everyone is making so much fuss over. My lord prince will pay well for its return once I cut it off your dead finger."

"Julian will bury you, traitor."

Spinning with furious speed, he did the Dance of Death. Rage found its mark when Seth's sword struck. The Valdeonian assassin's head rolled across the floor and into the musket hole. Breathing great gulps of fury, he looked out over the common room. Still bodies lay upon the ground beneath the tables. The rangers had fled the pub and so had his friends. One set of eyes, however, had born witness to his unmasking. Mr. Dawson stood behind the bar, his eyes fixed upon the Lion Ring's brilliant glow.

Shouts and whistles from the streets penetrated the pub. Military police. If they found him here, he'd be dragged back to the citadel in irons. He must leave Lea tonight, but where would he go?

"This way, Lion!" Mr. Dawson called.

Seth dove under the counter. Mr. Dawson held open a door leading into the kitchens. Cooked meats rested tantalizingly on the counters, waiting to be sliced. Abandoned by the cook, Mr. Dawson's livelihood was in danger of going to waste.

"Here," Tory's dad thrust a piece of meat into his hand. "Go west toward the gates. Hide until sunup and then circle back. I'll help you all I can. No, don't thank me. It's the least I can do for Leo's heir."

An alley waited outside the Rollicking Rover's back door. Seth stayed against the wall, taking great care to listen for signs of more Valdeonian traitors. He reached the edge of the alley and poked his head tentatively out into the row. A hand grabbed him, pulling him backward with steel arms. More hands lifted him into a waiting wagon.

"Well, Hopeful," Phoenix said. "It would seem we are destined to be friends. I owe you a life debt."

He released Seth with a warm laugh. Righting himself, Seth twisted around to face him. Several other rangers knelt within the bed of the wagon. They appeared to have won the day with no visible injuries he could see.

Then Phoenix's face turned hard as he caught up Seth's left hand. "I didn't want to believe you bore the Lion Ring! I prayed Leo had not fallen. What happened to Edmund D'Antoiné? Where did you get the Lion Ring? How is it the Jalora allows you to bear its covenant?"

Violent anger flickered in Phoenix's eyes. His hand squeezed harder and twisted Seth's wrist. The ranger's other hand held a knife to Seth's throat. Hope dwindled. He'd been wrong about the Phoenix. Looking around the wagon at the other rangers, he knew there would be no aid.

The Lion's Roar grumbled against their betrayal. "I was a fool to trust you, Ranger. Your word means nothing!"

"The Lion eyes!" one of the rangers cried.

The Phoenix and his troop shifted uneasily away from him. The knife lowered from his throat. Twisting free, Seth released the Lion's Roar as he jumped from the wagon. He didn't stop to see what havoc his power had dealt. Racing through the streets of Lea, he didn't look back. His senses told him, however, the rangers hadn't followed.

Chapter Fifty-Five

JULIAN PRESSED against the building, staying out of sight as the young Lion raced by. His amber eyes glowed in fiery rage as the Jalora's power surrounded him. He was dangerous, out of control. Now was not the time to confront his half-breed sibling.

"He's alone, my prince," Marcellus whispered, his eyes twitching wildly. "What challenge could a lone Hopeful be to three armed men?"

Julian scowled at his two companions, the albatross around his neck and the money hungry spy. Both were watching him. Marcellus bounced in his boots, anxious for the kill. The commandant's aid, their own secret spy, remained calm. Guessing a large sum of money was headed for his hand no doubt.

"Ask the wagon full of rangers about their luck holding the Lion while he swims in the Jalora's power."

Julian pointed at the ruined buckboard turned upon its side. The horses had bolted, freed by the raw power of the Lion's Roar. He must be patient a little while longer. There would be a time when the young Lion would find himself alone and Julian would be there waiting.

"Perhaps I might help?" the spy offered greedily.

"Yes, I thought you might have a few ideas," Julian said. "Come, I must prepare for the reunion with my long-lost brother."

He offered Lieutenant Finley his most convincing smile of goodwill. They left together to speak of murder, treachery, and the alliance such things would birth.

Chapter Fifty-Six

RUNNING BLINDLY along the rows of Lea, Seth had lost his sense of direction. Panic was driving him deeper into the city. He wasn't sure how to find his friends again or make it back to the Rollicking Rover. The Lion's Roar had dramatically weakened his strength. He couldn't run anymore. Slowing to a stop, he stood in the middle of the row completely lost.

"Great gulls!" Riley shouted behind him, hands resting upon his knees to catch his breath. "Didn't you hear me calling? What happened? We've been worried sick."

Tory and the Claybanks stood behind him gulping in the pre-dawn air. They looked down as one to his bleeding hand. The Lion Ring glowed in brilliant white upon his finger. Its light burned through the blood caking the crystal.

"You're a ranger? Why in all the world would you be a cadet in the UR Army?" Tory pointed at Seth's left hand. "That's the Lion Ring."

"Well spotted, Cadet. Why don't you shout it a little louder?" Riley grumbled and came to stand beside Seth. "Your eyes are back to normal."

"They blaze like fiero…fire!" Amery cried.

"Listen, Seth," Tory said, finally tearing his gaze from the Lion Ring. "If you're in trouble, we can help. We're your mates."

"He's in trouble all right." Sergeant Dancer marched up behind them with his sword drawn. "You sent the wagon flying at least five hundred feet! What were you thinking, Lion? Those rangers are going to be after you when they recover."

"How did you—" Seth began.

"Are you all mad? Let's get out of the street," Dancer said. "Why are your weapons still sheathed, Cadets? Be at the ready."

He took point at the head of their group, sprinting onto the sidewalk. The sergeant stopped before an empty building. Casting a quick glance up and down the row, he kicked open the door. Dancer moved inside for a quick look, then he ushered Seth and his friends into the building.

"Have you been following us all night?" Amery asked.

"I was called by the Lion's Roar." Dancer rolled up his left sleeve, revealing aged marks upon his forearm. "I didn't understand until tonight why the Dragon put you in my troop. Don't you see? He knew I was a Lion Friend."

Seth touched the pink welts upon the sergeant's skin. Images came into his mind of Leo unleashing his power upon Dancer. The act had been meant as a way of honoring the sergeant, according to his memories.

"My father gave you these markings. What do they mean?"

Sergeant Dancer's mustache twitched. He seemed at a loss for words. Then he knelt before Seth and took up the Lion Ring in his fingers. The sergeant put his lips to the ring and kissed it in homage.

"The markings mean I serve the Lion," Dancer told him. "Any time my lord needs me, I will answer his call. It is the greatest honor to be a Lion Friend. How is it you don't know of these things?"

Lion Friend. Yes. A special sensation permeated from the man. He recognized it now. Jason shared the same energy. He'd told Seth how the markings would bind them together as they sailed aboard the ship bound for Port City. Understanding was coming to Seth little by little. In his loyalty, Sergeant Dancer would risk his own life for Seth. All his friends would. It was time to tell them the entire truth. They had to understand the dangers.

Seth spoke of his mother's murder and Leo's arrival on Marianna. He warned them about the murderous Dirge. Heavy of heart, he also told them of his father's murder and Julian D'Antoiné's part in it. The Jalora's quest, he kept to himself.

"Julian and his evil allies have found me in Lea. They want the Lion Ring." Seth let out a long breath. "Phoenix knows I'm Leo's heir as well."

"That's good, isn't it? He can help you, Mate," Tory said.

"He put a knife to my throat when he saw the ring on my finger."

"I told you we couldn't trust that blond giant." Riley cursed in Islic.

Sergeant Dancer rubbed at his mustache. "I can't believe Phoenix threaten you. We live in mad times. Well, we must keep you safe from him and anyone else trying to find you until the Dragon returns."

"If there is trouble we are your men, Seth."

Amery took out his hatchet and beat it once against his breast. Pulling his own weapon, Aubrey joined his twin. Their courage went beyond the debt they believed they owed him. Here was true friendship.

Tory nodded. "Me as well, Mate."

Trust in your friends, Lion.

The Jalora's power wrapped around his body, sending their joined voices into the group. "You served the father, now will you serve his son, Lion Friend?"

"I swear it, my lord Lion." The sergeant bent his head in deep respect. "I would die for you."

The Lion's Roar came at Sergeant Dancer in a rush, wrapping around his forearm. It withdrew quickly, leaving the sergeant stunned. He looked at his left forearm. The skin had been crisscrossed by the mark of the Lion Spirit.

"And you three courageous young men. You have shown true friendship this day. Will you too serve us?"

Tory and the Claybanks dropped to their knees, bowing their heads. Seth and the Jalora let lose a short burst of the Lion's Roar. It struck the men, sending them to their backs upon the ground. The Jalora released Seth. Pleased, it withdrew from the men and left.

"By the green, green fields we're making enough noise to draw the Legion. Go keep watch while I bandage his hand," Riley ordered.

He took the pack from his shoulders with a grumble. The Lion Friends, much to Seth's surprise, immediately followed Riley's orders and took up position around the room. His squire didn't seem to notice. He pulled out bandages and ointment. Slapping them down on an abandoned chair, he grabbed Seth's left hand.

"You're angry, Squire," Seth said in Islic.

"Yes, Ranger I am angry! You made me promise to keep quiet about the Lion Ring and then you go blabbing about your identity to complete strangers. This isn't Haven Bay, Seth. Just because someone says he's your friend doesn't mean it's true. Take that blond-headed devil for instance."

Now they'd come to the real reason Riley Logan was so angry. He'd taken an immediate dislike to Gregory the Phoenix. His squire had shown wisdom there. Seth rested his free hand on Riley's shoulder. The tension in his body reluctantly subsided.

"I trust Tory and the twins too, Seth. I even trust Sergeant Dancer," he said, shaking his head. "But you need to be more careful. We are a very long way from Marianna and things are different here."

"I know, Riley. I'll try to be more cautious."

"No, you won't." Riley snorted.

"Are you done, Lion's Squire? Lea's day has begun. People are out and about," Sergeant Dancer told them. "We must move the Lion to a place of safety."

The floorboards squeaked behind him. Mr. Dawson stood silently in the middle of the room, musket clutched firmly in his hands. His eyes shifted to Seth. Grief. Fear and a strange joy floated around his body in mixing ribbons of color. Mr. Dawson lowered the weapon with a smile. Pulling up the sleeve of his left arm, the publican showed them the crisscross markings of a Lion Friend. Seth had somehow managed to double mark Mr. Dawson as well.

Sergeant Dancer rolled up his own left sleeve and held his arm out for the publican to see. "On behalf of our lord, I call you to service, Lion Friend. He needs a safe place to hold up until the Dragon returns."

Mr. Dawson gave the sergeant a respectful nod. "We can see him to the Rollicking Rover. He'll be safe under its roof."

"Why not just go find this Dragon?" Amery asked.

"Andara is a big place, Cadet. Where do you suggest we start looking?" Dancer shook his head. "No. We go to the Rollicking Rover."

"Are you certain you want to do this?" Seth asked, looking around the room at his friends. "It could mean you're punished."

"Stay close, Lion," Sergeant Dancer said. "Move out."

Chapter Fifty-Seven

SETH PICKED at the simple luncheon Mr. Dawson had provided them. He'd been staring at the same four walls all morning while his friends were busy being useful. Sergeant Dancer had positioned them around the Rollicking Rover, covering every view of the rows and alley with access to the pub. He had taken on the role as Seth's body guard, despite Riley's arguments.

"I can't understand why the rangers would risk angering the Jalora by locking me in a cage." He tossed the piece of cold chicken back on his plate.

"The world is being torn asunder, Lion. These are dark times. The Legion hasn't rallied around the Lords of Valdeon. Such a thing has never happened in the history of Andara. You and the rest of the Sacred Guard are in danger until the Lion Ring can be mastered." He ran his dagger's edge along the sharpening stone with a whisk. "I'd wager many yearn to wield its power."

"Yes, my father warned me. I wish I knew who I could trust. Is this Dragon any better than the Phoenix?"

"I don't know how to answer, Lion. He seems a good man, but then again so did the Phoenix." He sat next to Seth at their small table. "We must find a ranger you can trust. One who'll look after you until Wolf comes back. You're at a disadvantage not knowing about the Legion."

"I trust Jason Elder the Coyote and Dragonfly. They've proven to be my friends."

Sergeant Dancer nodded with a laugh. "I don't know Dragonfly personally, but Jason Coyote I've known since he was walking in nappies. He's a good man, but even he couldn't guide you through this nest of snakes, Lion. No, you'll need to go to the Dragon or the Lords of Valdeon for help." His face grew somber. "Wolf and the others are in hiding, aren't they? Why not find them? It is their duty to protect you."

"They can't reveal themselves. We made them swear." Seth pushed the plate away. "Wolf was ready to take me to safety, but I fear something has happened to draw him away."

He should've listened to Wolf's warnings. The ranger had been right. A maelstrom had descended upon him the moment Seth opened the Book of Ancients. If not for Riley and the Lion Friends, he'd be lost in a storm of violence and confusion.

"You've proven to be a trusted friend too, Sergeant. Thank you."

Sergeant Dancer patted tenderly at his left forearm. "These marks bind us together by the Jalora's magic, Lion. If you see these marks on another, know you can trust the soul who bears them."

"You're twice marked," Seth said with a smile. "It's special even among the Lion Friends, isn't it?"

"We are honored to serve the Lion who marked us, but serving his son as well? It is a great gift. None, outside the Lords of Valdeon, have more honor among the Lion Friends than the Lion's First Marked. He is a rare man indeed."

"First Marked," Seth said, thinking back to his escape from Larkspur. "Jason Coyote. He's my First Marked."

"I knew he was destined for greatness. Though he laughed at me every time I told him so. I'm glad you proved me right, Lion." Sergeant Dancer nodded with a proud grin. "I'd better see to the others. It's time to shift positions."

Mr. Dawson hurried into the room, two muskets in his hands. Fear. Resolve. Devotion. This Lion Friend was willing to risk everything he had for Seth's sake. The publican exchanged a somber look with Dancer and then handed him a musket. They moved to the edge of the window. Easing his head toward the glass for a quick look, Dancer flew back and pressed his body against the wall.

"The row is empty. All the surrounding businesses have closed."

Seth stood up and stretched his power out into the street. Raw power met his touch. They were coming in force. Every one of them was as equal to or stronger in power than Dragonfly. Two rangers shared the Phoenix's great strength.

He moved to the window, not bothering to hide. Phoenix stood alone in the row, covered by the protective magic of his Legion cloak. He returned Seth's hard look, but didn't make a move to come inside.

"Sergeant Dancer! Everyone has evacuated our row."

His friends flew into the room, stumbling over one another. Riley fell silent as he looked upon Seth standing at the window. His squire knew. Their escape plans were mute. Seth gave his friends a sad smile they could not see beneath the mask of indifferent magic. He must think of their safety now.

"You have put yourself at great risk for me," Seth told Mr. Dawson. "I must ask you to do me another great service. Give aid to the other Lion Friends. They will need a haven soon."

"The rangers feel safe coming here. They know it is the Leo who owns this pub, not I. And now it belongs to you, my young lord."

"My father trusted you enough to mark you, Sir. I think he would want you to have this pub."

Mr. Dawson sniffed and wiped at his eyes with the back of his hand. "Leo was a good man and a better friend. I thank you for the gifts. Anytime you need help, or board, you are welcome. Consider it your home in Lea."

"Here now, Mate," Tory said. "You speak as though we're about to be parted."

"I'm not giving up this easily. Out the back way!" Sergeant Dancer growled, pulling Seth's arm.

They raced down the stairs, behind the bar and through the kitchen. Stopping before the back door, Sergeant Dancer pulled it open a crack and peered outside. His hand shook on the handle. Closing the door, he pressed his forehead against the wood.

"Sergeant Dancer," Seth gripped his shoulder. "Swear to me you will look after the Lion Friends and my squire for me."

His Lion Friend nodded with a resigned sigh. The Legions gathered power was too strong to ignore. Sergeant Dancer had fought beside rangers long enough to recognize their presence.

"Seth?" Riley gripped his arm.

"It's no use, Riley. I count at least thirty rangers positioned around the pub. Some are as powerful as the Phoenix. You must stay inside no matter what happens. They'll try to take me by force."

"Now you listen to me, Seth McCloud," Riley growled. "I'm your squire. Where you go, I go."

"Very well, but don't give the rangers an excuse to hurt you."

Seth walked out the door slowly. It was pointless to try and escape now. They were watching him. He moved into the center of the street and stopped, keeping his hand away from the hilt of his sword. Riley and the Lion Friends, against his wishes, had followed.

"I can see you plainly, Ranger. No need to hide."

Phoenix pushed the hood back off his head. His cheek and forehead were bruised. A small cut drew red along the back of his hand. Minor injuries. Phoenix had been lucky. The Spirit of the Lion Ring hadn't been out for the kill last night.

"Does this mean you are ready to return peacefully with us to the citadel, Lion?"

"I'll gladly come with you, if the Dragon has returned."

"You will come with me now, Hopeful. Your games have gone on long enough."

Sergeant Dancer and the cadets surrounded Seth with their swords drawn. Phoenix remained still, ignoring

Seth's protectors. He showed no reaction as the door to the Rollicking Rover burst open. Mr. Dawson thrust out his musket barrel, aiming for the blond curls.

Dancer stepped between Seth and Phoenix, waving the tip of his blade at the ranger. "He's not going anywhere with you."

"You dare question a ranger and the Partisan, Sergeant?" Phoenix growled, his eyes sparking with fury.

"I do when he threatens the Lion with a dagger to the throat!"

Fury. Resentment. Shock. They burned about the Phoenix in furious waves of heat. He gave a deliberate nod. Streaks of ash burst into the street. Sergeant Dancer, Riley, Tory, and the Claybanks were on the ground in a lightening moment. Rangers surrounded them, weapons at the ready.

"Here now, you let me go! I'm the Lion's Squire," Riley shouted, trying to rise.

One of the rangers put a dagger to his throat and pressed until Riley dared not move. Rising like a giant wave, the Jalora's anger pushed against his control. Seth's breath came in great gulps of rage.

"Come quietly, Lion." Phoenix held out a pair of irons. "We don't want bloodshed."

Then another streak of ash slammed into Phoenix, sending him flying backward. The iron chains skidded across the row and under a hitching post. Jason Coyote stood in the space between Seth and the rangers, sword in hand.

"First you abandon your duties, and now you've struck a senior officer," Phoenix said, wiping the dirt from his uniform as he stood.

"I struck a traitor who held a dagger to our Lion's throat and then seeks to cage him while his Right-Hand is away." Coyote ignored the sharp intakes of breath from the rangers. "Know this. I serve the Lion."

Phoenix pulled his own weapon and stalked toward Coyote. His Lion Friend was outmatched. He'd be killed for Seth's sake. He had to do something to save Jason and his other Lion Friends.

Then the Lion's hunger broke free. Their roar shatter the windows on either side of the row. Doors flew inward. Exterior walls cracked. The very stones under their feet buckled, throwing the rangers and their prisoners off balance.

"You dare place violent hands upon the Lion Friends!" the joined voices of Seth and the Jalora growled. "Release them now or face my wrath!"

The rangers dropped their daggers and backed away. Riley and his Lion Friends backed away too. Seth breathed in their fear, feeding upon the emotions circling about him. The Spirit of the Lion Ring wanted to feed, to crush their bones into dust. No. He mustn't harm these men, or his friends. Seth's knees gave way as the power took him further on the verge of madness. He fell onto the stone. Struggling against the power, he cried out in pain as it bound him like a steel band.

Chapter Fifty-Eight

RILEY PRESSED against the wall of invisible energy separating him from his ranger. Seth writhed on the ground, throwing his arms about wildly. His eyelids blinked rapidly over white orbs. A terrible fit of some sort had taken his friend.

"What have you done to him, you blond giant?"

"I haven't done anything, Logan."

Phoenix held his hands before him, palms pressing against some invisible structure. The ranger reached upward until he couldn't lift his hands any higher. Failing to find some sort of opening, he took a step back.

"Lion's squire, you'd better move as well. It isn't safe," Coyote said, eyes locked on Seth's struggling form. "The Lion's power may kill you."

Phoenix suddenly flew at Coyote while his attention was on Riley. He struck the ranger's head with the hilt of his sword. Ignoring Boyd's cries of outrage, he pushed past Coyote's squire as if he were nothing. Phoenix stared down at the unconscious Coyote. Murder was in his eyes.

"Bind him," Phoenix ordered at last. "Take him to the brig."

"How dare you," Boyd growled. "He is a Lion Friend and the Right-Hand's man. You have no authority."

"Your ranger struck a superior officer."

Sergeant Dancer pushed forward to stand with Boyd. "He was defending his lord against a cowardly traitor! You've struck the Lion's First Marked. I hope the Right-Hand doesn't spare you with a painless death."

"Death?" Riley asked.

"It's treason to hurt or threaten a Lion Friend, Squire." Sergeant Dancer lifted the sleeve of his left arm. "These marks aren't given lightly by our lord. They are a badge of honor, respected by all who see them. And none are more honored among us than the Lion's First Marked."

Phoenix still held his weapon, fist squeezing until his knuckles were white. Sergeant Dancer didn't seem like a man who'd back down either. What could a handful of Seth's friends do against thirty rangers? If Riley didn't step in, someone was going to get hurt.

Riley hurried to stand in the space between Dancer and the Phoenix. He sheathed his weapon slowly, easing his hands into the air. He may not understand this world he and Seth had entered, but one thing he knew well. These rangers had a code they lived by. Honor was everything to them.

"I'm the Lion's Squire," he said, eyeing each of the rangers pointedly. "We all know it's against the Jalora Code to harm another ranger's squire. Know this. If you try to harm the Lion Friends, then you'll have to kill me. I don't think the Jalora will take too kindly to such treachery, do you? I call upon every ranger within reach of my words for protection against the Phoenix."

The rangers grew uncomfortable, awkwardly looking at each other and then to the Phoenix. He'd put them in a tough position against their commander, but Riley didn't care just then. He'd do anything to keep Seth and his friends safe.

"Don't be a fool, Logan." Phoenix sheathed his weapon with a loud clunk. "It isn't I who'd strike first. Why do you think I knocked the Coyote out? Use your head, or is there too much woolie dung between your ears?"

"Why don't you explain it to me," a voice said behind them. "I also have trouble understanding the words of a traitor?"

Fausto De Quintaro stood behind the group of rangers, sword held firmly in his hands. Valdeonian soldiers streamed into the row, circling the rangers in an angry swarm. Arturo, his son, was at their head. Lord De Quintaro's army had grown considerably since they'd last met on Carlotta.

"My father's beard," Tory cried. "The Raven has come back to Lea."

"Who is he, this Raven?" Amery asked.

"He's one of the Lords of Valdeon," Sergeant Dancer said, with a fierce grin. "Or at least he was. His son bears the Raven Ring now. Still, My Lord De Quintaro is a powerful man."

"But is he a friend to Seth?" Aubrey asked.

"Yes, I think so," Riley said. "Seth saved the lives of his family when spies tried to harm them. He owes Seth."

Lord De Quintaro stood in the row before Phoenix, unafraid and full of confidence. He seemed to give the other rangers no notice, focusing instead on their commander. Lifting his chin with a noble air of dignity Riley couldn't imagine ever possessing, the Valdeonian lord whisked his sword toward them.

"Release the Lion's Squire and the Lion Friends." Lord De Quintaro pointed toward their center. "You will relinquish the Lion to us. We see to his safety now."

"And where do you think you would take him, My Lord De Quintaro?" Phoenix asked. "San Leonora perhaps?"

"The Lion will ride at the head of his armies. He will bring us victory against the Jackal."

"You can't take him to Valdeon!" Riley cried. "Leo said it was too dangerous."

"The Lion must return to the safety of the Legion. You can see as well as I the power has taken him. He can't control it. Only within the walls of the citadel will he be subdued. He's much too powerful to roam wild on his own."

Subdued? Riley didn't like it one bit. Seth wouldn't be happy locked in a cage. No one would. The two men stared each other down. Both wanted Seth for their own purposes, though he couldn't guess Phoenix's reasons.

"Forgive the insult, My Lord De Quintaro. You are no longer a Lord of Valdeon. I am the Partisan and will say what is best for the boy." Phoenix rested his hand upon the hilt of his sword to emphasize the point.

"I should entrust the Crown Prince of Valdeon to you?" Lord De Quintaro spat. "I heard the Lion Friend. You lay threatening hands upon our lord."

Crown Prince? Great gulls. Riley exchanged stunned looks with Tory and the Claybanks. He'd known Leo was a king, but it hadn't occurred to him Seth was in line to rule. Honestly, how many thrones was he expected to sit upon? Well, these Valdeonians were serious about taking Seth back with them. Bloodshed seemed certain and this time he wouldn't be able to stop it.

"You have no say in this!" Phoenix pulled his blade. "I take my orders from the Wolf."

"Xavier the Wolf is third," another Valdeonian voice boomed behind them. "I am second as the Lion's Right-Hand."

Riley recognized the hard lines of his features and the horrible scar running down the length of his face. Esteban the Hawk had found them at last. He was a severe wind descending upon them at the worst possible time.

"Now, who is this?" Amery whispered.

"Seth's uncle. He's the last person I wanted to see."

"Did he say Right-Hand?" Tory put a palm to his forehead. "Do you mean to say I've swapped dirty socks with the next Jalora Master?"

"Disgusting." Riley wrinkled his nose. "Seth will always be Seth no matter what they call him."

"Fools. What were you thinking coming at the Lion in anger? I ought to whip the flesh from your backs for this!"

The rangers bowed before Hawk. Their emotions were hidden by the Jalora's power, but their hesitant salutes communicated more than a sour frown. Fausto De Quintaro's opinion of the Hawk Prince was showing plainly upon his face. Dislike and mistrust. Seth shared his opinion of Esteban D'Antoiné. Riley hadn't been around Hawk enough to know the man, but he trusted Seth's instincts.

Hawk came to stand before Phoenix. His hand whipped in an ash blur to slap Gregory Baldemar hard across the face. A small cut dripped with blood from his lip where the Hawk Ring had torn it.

"On your knees before me, Partisan!"

Phoenix did as he was told, shaking with fury. If ever a man wanted to kill another, it was Gregory Baldemar. Riley didn't care for the Phoenix, but he took no delight in seeing the ranger humiliated in front of his men.

"Can I trust you to bring the Lion Friends to the citadel?" Hawk asked. "Or will you let your temper sway you from your duty once again?"

"I will bring them, Bishop," Phoenix managed to say between gritted teeth.

Hawk turned to Fausto De Quintaro. "What a coincidence. The lackey of Xavier De Vincente meets the Wolf's best friend in an abandoned row over the body of the helpless Lion. Charming. Were you planning to help Wolf seize the throne once he was dead?"

Arturo pulled his sword and charged at Hawk. Lord De Quintaro grabbed his hot-headed son, pulling him protectively to his back. Great gulls. First Arturo attacked Seth, and then he challenged someone who clearly wouldn't have issue with killing him. What would happen to the young fool without his father to keep him in check?

"How dare you, Hawk Prince! I serve the Lion faithfully and have always done so. Can you say the same?"

"Then I call you to service, My Lord De Quintaro. Have your men take the Lion to his chambers in the citadel. Any deviation will result in your execution. Don't give me an excuse to kill you, Fausto."

Hawk turned his back on Lord De Quintaro as he would a beggar on the street and moved to kneel beside Seth. Somehow, he'd managed to pass through the Jalora's power where Phoenix had failed. Seth seemed to sense the cruel energy of his uncle close to him. His body erupted again in spasms of writhing as a threatening growl escaped his lips.

"Your games have come to an end, Nephew."

Hawk slammed his fist down on Seth's jaw, snapping his head to the side. Seth's writhing stopped abruptly and he became limp upon the stone. The tremendous energy dissipated at last.

"What do you think you're about, hitting him while he can't defend himself!" Riley marched forward toward the cold-hearted beast claiming to be Seth's kin.

Hawk flew at Riley, lifting him up by the tunic. Suddenly, Riley went sailing across the row and slammed hard against the wall of the Rollicking Rover. He gasped for the air roughly knocked from his body. A whirlwind of ash came at him with blinding speed.

The Hawk's sword tip was at his throat, breaking the skin as Riley gulped for air.

"How dare you question me, insect!"

Riley couldn't look away from those dark eyes filled with deadly intent. His face was stone-cold except for the scar stretching across the left side of his face. It blotched in strips of pink and sickly white.

"This young fool shares the same taste as my hapless brother." Hawk spat upon the ground as if he'd tasted rotten flesh. "He goes so far as to choose a woolie farmer from Marianna. Know this bumpkin. If you ever speak directly to me again, I will cut you in half. I had no qualms about killing my own incompetent squire, do you think I would have any misgivings about squashing a dung beetle born from the feces of farm animals?"

Every ounce of self-worth drained from Riley's being. He was nothing to this venomous Prince of Valdeon. Something behind those words, spoken in disdain, had found the very heart of Riley's soul. What had he been playing at, following Seth and pretending to be a gentleman?

"The Lion is very fond of his squire." Fausto De Quintaro broke in quickly. "They've been best friends since youth. If you hurt this boy, the Lion will turn against you, or perhaps even kill you."

"I'm certain I can convince him otherwise."

The Hawk dropped Riley with a grunt of distaste and sheathed his sword quickly. He spun away, ash cloak billowing behind him. Marching back toward Seth, he began barking orders at the shaken rangers.

"Phoenix!" Hawk bellowed over his shoulder. "You may rise now."

Murder was in the air as Phoenix got to his feet. His glare firmly fixed upon Hawk's back, the ranger clenched trembling fists before him. Fausto took Riley's arm, drawing him toward the blond-headed giant. The Valdeonian seemed to have had a change of heart toward the Heidelbrecht prince.

"Do not take what the Hawk said to heart, Lion's Squire," Fausto said. "I've seen your courage on Carlotta. You do your ranger credit."

"Thank you, Sir. You saved my life."

"The three of us - you, Phoenix, and I - share something in common now," he said, resting a reassuring hand upon the ranger's arm. "We all hate the Hawk."

Riley nodded. Seth's uncle was a hard one. Who knew why he wanted his nephew confined? Phoenix at least was no longer a threat. He'd been after the same thing they were - getting Seth to the Dragon.

"Now you understand, Logan," Phoenix told him, wiping at his cut lip. "I also serve the Lion. Maybe you'll remember that before you open your mouth again. Let's move out!"

Chapter Fifty-Nine

Some of the rangers bound Coyote's unconscious body and chained him to Boyd. They shoved the other Lion Friends beside the bound men. Sergeant Dancer and Tory picked up Coyote's shoulders while the others took his legs. Phoenix ordered a ranger guard to watch the prisoners, but made no offer to help carry Seth or Jason. He ordered the rest of the rangers to clear their path toward the citadel.

Lord De Quintaro had intervened when the rangers came for Riley. He'd been adamant about ensuring the Lion's care was seen to properly by his squire. Hawk, who'd been listening to their argument, said nothing. Instead, he strutted to the head of their precession like an old rooster in the yard.

Several of the Valdeonian soldiers lifted Seth with an unsettling reverence. They gently placed him on the makeshift litter they'd made from confiscated wood once belonging to the Rollicking Rover. The Valdeonians stepped forward as one when Hawk gave the order to march. They lifted their voices, singing in the Valic tongue. Each stomp of a boot on stone punctuated the beat of their song.

"They sing of the first Lion's courage," Lord De Quintaro said. "It is a warning to evil. Do not challenge the Jalora and its Lion."

"Aye. Let's hope evil listens. I thought things would be better once Seth opened the book." Riley scowled at the men who were hoping to use the Lion's power. "I wish Seth had never opened it."

"Book?" Lord De Quintaro asked, grabbing at Riley's arm. "Our Lion has opened the Book of Ancients?"

"Aye. Those rangers have been in a state since Seth ripped down the bars of its cage and opened the cover."

Excited murmuring spread like a grass fire through the Valdeonian soldiers. They were speaking too quickly for Riley to understand their words. This book certainly caused a stir every time it was mentioned.

"We must be more careful with our lord's secrets. Did the Lion say what was written?" Lord De Quintaro asked.

"Aye, he said his name had been written at the bottom of a short list of Lions. Why?"

"*And the stars rained down upon the land the night he was born*," he recited.

"Say, now how did you know?"

"We must teach you about your ranger, Lion's Squire. It is a line from a prophecy called 'The Sign of The Coming'. The Sacred Guard uses these omens to prepare for a new Jalora Master."

Riley looked to the group of tall Valdeonians carrying Seth. He understood a little better now why they were being so reverent with his unconscious body.

His best friend was about to be more than a ranger or a king. Would he remember his true self - Seth McCloud from Marianna? Riley slapped a fist upon his leg. What a mutton-headed question. Seth would never stop being Seth. He wasn't the type to let things go to his head.

"So, how does it go? The prophecy I mean," Riley asked.

The skies thunder the moment he is made and the stars fall from the heavens at his birth.

His strength of heart shall be a fortress to those without comfort.

His kindness shall know no bounds.

He shall be known as 'Lord' by his allies he draws to him with ease.

Many will know him when what was lost is found as the Creed of the Guardian shines

The Lion Child Vessel declares his naming as the Sacred Guard draws near.

Crimson circles the ring of the Lion until his mighty roar at last is heard.

This marks the coming of the Red heart."

Seth's curly head bounced gently as they carried him down the row. It wouldn't matter what some old prophecy said. Seth wouldn't like them making a fuss or treating him differently. And his uncle! The heartless creature needed to be knocked on his backside.

"I thought rangers couldn't lie." Riley glared at Hawk's stiff shoulders. "Seth's uncle claims he's this Right-Hand person, but Seth and Coyote both say it's Wolf." He shook his head. "I wish Wolf would have taken us away with him when he left Lea. No telling where he is now, but you can be sure he wouldn't stand for Hawk treating Seth like this."

"Wolf is the Right-Hand? Well, Squire, you've just lifted my heart," Lord De Quintaro said with a grin. "The Bearer of the Hawk Ring has always been Right-Hand to the Master. Perhaps Esteban can't accept he has been passed over and actually believes he is second?"

"You mean he's mad?" Riley whistled low.

"Overly ambitious would be more likely. He may plan to challenge Wolf."

Great gulls. Now they had an even bigger problem. How would they warn the Right-Hand if the ranger was in hiding?

"I suppose I need to find a way to warn Wolf." Riley rubbed at the back of his neck. "He saved our lives on Marianna and again here in Lea. It's the least I can do."

"You let me worry about Xavier the Wolf, my young friend." Lord De Quintaro grinned and patted him on the back. "I will see him to safety."

The massive gates of the citadel stood closed for the first time since they'd arrived in Lea. UR soldiers guarded each tiered level of the battlements. Standing at twenty paces apart, it must have taken every UR soldier and cadet to circle all the way around the citadel.

"Open the gates in the name of the Lion!" Hawk boomed.

Immediately, the two massive wooden gates groaned upon their metal hinges as they began to slowly open. Hawk moved their precession under the archway without stopping. The soldiers stationed at the gate whispered and gaped as Seth's litter passed. Hawk didn't stop to appease their curiosity. Riley recognized a few of the soldiers, but didn't greet them. He kept close pace behind Lord De Quintaro, shuddering as he was swallowed once more by the mouth of the citadel.

"Take the Lion to his chambers, My Lord De Quintaro," Hawk said, stopping at the center of the arena. "I will send someone to call for him when it's time."

"What of the Lion Friends, Sir?" Phoenix asked.

Hawk glared at the still form of Jason Elder and put a hand to the back of his head. The murderous look wasn't lost on his squire. Boyd pulled against his bonds, trying to stand between his ranger and the Hawk.

"Lock Coyote and the others in one of the barracks. Make sure it is heavily guarded," Hawk said at last. "They will give the Lion extra incentive to stay put. You, Deacon, will stay with me."

Phoenix's eyes blazed with revulsion as he followed Seth's uncle toward the Obsidian Gates. Lord De Quintaro and his men carried Seth after them, leaving Riley and the Lion Friends standing in a group of rangers.

"Come Lion Friends," a dark-haired ranger ordered. "We will see to your comfort, never fear."

"Let's go," Sergeant Dancer told them evenly.

The Lion Friends followed the ranger as he led them toward the steps of the UR barracks. Coyote's limp body swung between them.

"Not you, Lion's Squire."

An older man marched across the sand toward him. The metal tiger on his collar shimmered against the black uniform. Keen eyes looked Riley up and down with an appraising scan.

"The name is Arthur. I'm Squire to the White Tiger. Follow me."

"Remember who chose you, Riley Logan!" Boyd gave Riley a last look before following the others up the stairs.

"Come along, Lion's Squire. We don't have all day to stand here throwing kisses."

Arthur turned on his heels and began walking toward a solid stretch of wall not far from the Obsidian Gates. Riley hurried to follow him. Where else would he go? Hawk and the Legion had Seth. The Lion Friends were being held prisoner. He was on his own with no plan.

"Where are they taking Seth, Sir?" Riley asked, catching up to walk beside the squire.

"They prepare the Lion for his naming." Arthur frowned at him. "I guessed you were from the Grey Cliff Isles the moment I lay eyes upon you. Well, I have a job ahead of me training you for service."

"I was trained under the best, White Tiger's Squire." Riley bristled. "Dante De Vincente taught me everything I need to know."

"Arthur is good enough for me." He stopped before the stone wall and put his fists upon his hips. "What was Dante thinking, letting the Leo choose a woolie farmer as squire to his Heir. Probably thought it was a grand joke. You won't last a day with those fancy Valdeonian squires, boy. Now, come on!"

He pressed a hand upon the slight image of a little man carved in the stone. Great gulls. Another squire's entrance into Legion Headquarters! He'd passed this rock a million times, or so it seemed, while Sergeant Dancer had them jogging about. The stone slid open and Arthur stepped inside. Riley followed him, still trying to hold down his temper. Dante had thought Riley was a good squire. It hadn't been a joke. He'd spend his days proving he was just as good as any squire in the corps. It didn't matter what Hawk or anyone else thought. Seth had chosen him. They'd be together again soon, and when they were, he'd take Seth out of this citadel to freedom.

Chapter Sixty

Tunics and trousers of varying sizes were stacked on perfectly ordered shelves. Boots, high sheen glistening under the crystal lanterns, stood at attention on more shelves at the opposite end of the supply room. Riley sniffed at the scent of rich leather. No hand-me-down uniforms or boots for the rangers, it would seem.

"Here, take these packs." Arthur thrusted two empty knapsacks into Riley's arms. "Think of your ranger first. Having your own pack always at the ready just makes good sense. Nothing out of place, do you understand?"

"Aye, Sir. It's been my habit since we left Marianna."

Arthur ignored his churlish remark, taking two olive drab tunics and two pairs of matching trousers from the shelves. White Tiger's squire shoved them into Riley's arms. He fingered the fabric. It may have been plain, but the cloth was rich in texture.

"The uniform of an Apprentice." Arthur dropped a pair of boots and several pairs of socks into Riley's outstretched arms. "Someone will take the Lion's other uniform and boots up to him."

"I can take care of my own ranger."

"Put those things down on the counter. You'll need both hands for this."

A long ash cloak hung lightly upon Arthur's arm. Riley took it reverently. Seth's ranger cloak. Whisper thin, the patterns of the fabric played with his eyes. He found he couldn't focus on it for long. Magic. It had to be.

Arthur tapped on the countertop, breaking the spell. He placed a tin plate, an empty water skin, utensils, and a small medical kit on top of the clothing. Stepping back, he folded his arms and gave Riley a grunt filled with challenge.

"Show me how quickly you can pack the kit, Squire."

Riley gave him a defiant nod and dove at the pack. He flew through the exercise, remembering the careful instruction Dante had drilled into him. The position of each item had to be just so to adjust the weight evenly on Seth's back. Metal was not to touch metal. A ranger cut through air and across land like a ghost. It wouldn't do for him to clank.

"Very good, Lion's Squire. I can see touches of Dante in the arranging. Let's see your healing pouch."

Riley handed him his sack of herbs and medicines. He had to admit he was a little pleased as Arthur complimented him on his collection. The rare herbs he'd found on Carlotta had raised an appreciative eyebrow, as well. Tymon had showed him a great many uses for the herbs. The lessons were given out of necessity by the unfriendly Tslavian. Riley, for his part, had paid close attention, but he'd refused to thank the man.

Satisfied at last with Riley's packing skills, Arthur went to a large cabinet tucked between the boot and uniform shelves. He took a key from his tunic and opened the lock with a loud click. Two pairs of boots waited in the otherwise empty cabinet. Arthur handed them to Riley. They looked a perfect fit.

"Well, I'm going to have to guess," he said and closed the cabinet door.

Pulling the cabinet open again, Arthur nodded appreciatively and stepped aside. Three uniforms and a cloak hung neatly inside. Each tunic had a tiny lion upon the collar. Great gulls! He'd just seen real magic at work, unless Arthur was putting him on and someone was behind the cabinet passing supplies into the room. Not wanting to appear the fool, he decided not to mention it.

"Why is my uniform different than yours?" Riley asked, fingering the tan vest and black trousers.

"You advance in the Legion as your ranger advances," Arthur told him. "You don't get a uniform like mine until your Lion leaves Apprenticeship in a few years. A Hopeful's squire is dressed all in tan, but I think your Lion is headed for Apprentice today. No use wasting a uniform. Come along, Lion's Squire. Don't dawdle."

Riley shouldered both packs, Seth's cloak, and his squire togs as he hurried to follow Arthur out of the storeroom. It was a short walk onto their next stop. Arthur ushered him into a room lined with large wooden tubs. Several squires were filling one of the giant tubs with hot water.

"Do you have them washing the rangers' clothes, Sir?"

"No, Squire." He pushed Riley toward the steaming tub. "They've filled the bath for you."

"Great gulls! You mean to say you want me to sit like a cooked rabbit in a stew pot? The whole idea is indecent!"

Arthur bellowed with laughter as Riley dropped the packs on a nearby bench and raised his fists before him. Two squires dressed in black uniforms grabbed him and started pulling off his traveling clothes.

"Come now, Lion's Squire." Arthur wiped the tears of laughter from his eyes. "If you will not wash yourself we must bathe you for the sake of our noses. What would your Lion say if he could see you right now?"

Riley threw every Islic curse he'd ever heard at the two squires as they dropped him in the hot bath. Strong, determined hands scrubbed at his hair with sickening sweet soap. A horsehair brush began to sweep along his skin. He pushed the brush away as it headed down his back.

"I am a man full grown!" Riley hissed, grabbing the soap and brush. "I can scrub myself!"

The three chuckling squires supervised his every move, as if they didn't trust him to clean himself properly. Riley sat with his arms folded in the soapy water once he had finished. Great gulls. He smelled like he'd just taken a drunken roll in one of Aunt Charlotte's flower gardens.

"There now, Lion's Squire. That wasn't so bad," Arthur said. "Time for the unruly mop atop your head."

"Here now, what about my hair?"

"It needs cutting," one of the other squires said, pulling him out of the water while another covered him in a cloth.

They pushed Riley down on a stool and went about trimming his hair up over his ears. By the green, green fields, he just hoped they didn't make him look as ridiculous as Teb McKinney had when he came home from the citadel.

"Well done." Arthur nodded appreciatively at Riley. "You do your ranger credit as a proper squire now. Finish dressing. It's almost time for the Lion's Naming."

Riley pulled on the uniforms and laced up the tall boots. They fit perfectly, as if the clothes and boots had been made just for him. He wrapped the new cloak about his shoulders. It was a nice fabric and functional for a squire. He'd miss Leo's cloak though. It was a last bit of home.

Moving to stand before the glass, he caught sight of a young squire's reflection. His jaw was open and he was staring like an idiot. Riley closed his mouth with a pop and stood up straighter. He was a proper Jalora Legion Squire just as good as any of the rest. His hair was cut in a clean line just above his ears and fashioned in a stylish shape. They'd shaved him, ridding his chin of its red fuzz. Riley had to admit, he liked his new look.

"Here's your sword, Lion's Squire." One of his overeager bath attendants held out the blade. "It is a fine weapon."

"Valdeonian Steel," Riley told him, wrapping the belt about his waist. "Leo gave it to me."

"I hope your skills are worthy of such a sword," Arthur said. "It is a kingly gift."

"Aye. Leo wouldn't have given it to me if he hadn't taught me to use it first."

"Logan is to be taken to the stands and guarded along with the Lion Friends. Hawk's orders." Arthur spat with a curse. "If any would have tried to lock up the Lion's Squire or any Lion Friend in Leo's time, there'd have been hell to pay. Hawk has outgrown his britches now his good brother is gone."

It was a different sort of feeling, walking down the obsidian halls of Legion headquarters dressed in his squire's uniform. Sneaking about after midnight had been exciting, but here was the real thrill. Now he was a squire among squires.

"If you're done strutting about, Logan, we've come to the entrance."

Arthur opened the door, immediately triggering the power of the orbs. The magic swept over them. Sergeant Dancer, Tory, and the Claybanks were waiting for them at the edge of the orbs' power.

"Look at you, Riley Logan!" Tory gave him an appreciative whistle. "You look like a real squire!"

"And so, he is," Arthur said. "Now I must leave you. We deploy soon and I must prepare the White Tiger. These men will see to your safety."

Several UR soldiers marched forward, circling around their group. One of them shoved Aubrey into the circle. Arthur had his sword out in a moment, touching the tip of his blade at the soldier's throat.

"Touch the Lion's Squire or the Lion Friends again and I'll cut a smile across your throat! They are under the protection of the Jalora Legion. Remember?"

"Yes, Sir!" the soldiers saluted quickly.

Arthur gave a quick nod to Riley. Then he passed through the doors back into Legion headquarters. He regretted seeing White Tiger's Squire go. Arthur had been the first man, other than Dante of course, to treat him like a real squire. By the green, green fields. He'd live up to it.

"Well?" Riley barked, enjoying their startled looks. "Take us to the arena and be quick about it!"

"Yes, Sir!"

Sergeant Dancer gave Riley a savage grin. He stood aside, motioning Riley to lead the way. Maybe he'd get used to his title after all. Stepping forward with his head held high, Riley grinned as the rest fell in behind the Lion's Squire.

Chapter Sixty-One

SETH RUBBED a cheek against the plush pillow. It smelled of exotic spices and citrus. Rubbing at his sleepy lids, he yawned and stretched. Leo had let him sleep late this morning. They'd have to double their efforts if they were going to get the north field harvested before dark.

"Father? Has Dante finished the breakfast?"

"Awake at last, my prince?" someone asked in Valic.

He opened his eyes to find himself surrounded by several Valdeonian faces against a backdrop of expensive cherry-paneled walls. Swords drawn and muskets loaded, the soldiers had been guarding his bed as he slept. Fausto De Quintaro sheathed his sword. He'd taken the position closest to Seth's head. Perhaps the most dangerous, considering the Lion Spirit's untamed fury.

Leo and their happy time on the Marianna farm was simply a drifting memory. He'd awakened into a world of rich satin linens sown in hues of blood red and gold. The bed he slept in had room enough for three cadets, with room left over to spread out.

The Valdeonian men fell to their knees the moment Seth sat up. Each of them looked up at him with watering eyes. Hope. Reverence. Devotion. They swam about the room in overwhelming colors. Rubbing at his chest, Seth fingered the new nightshirt. Someone had bathed him and dressed him in rich bedclothes. The image of a golden lion was stitched in the pocket. He didn't deserve all this lavish fussing.

"Lord De Quintaro? Yours is a face I hadn't expected to see. How is your family?"

"They remain safely hidden, my prince." He smiled, rising to his feet. "Your aunt is a clever woman, but even she couldn't hide her travels to Andara. Merchant tubs are no match for Valdeonian war ships. We guessed you were here and waited to find you alone."

Aunt Charlotte had journeyed to the mainland? It must have been for an important purpose. She wasn't comfortable away from her cottage. A long trip at her advancing years must've been doubly hard.

"Am I at an inn then?"

"No, these are the Lion's royal chambers." Lord De Quintaro smiled. "Your chambers."

Seth bolted up off the bed. "Are we in Valdeon?"

He looked out of the window down at the city of Lea, stretching out in the afternoon sun. They were still in the citadel, but at a much greater height than he'd been before. Then he remembered the lone flag waving from the top of the mountain fortress. It waited for the distant ships from Valdeon. He was in the chambers of the Sacred Guard.

"Send for his Highness' attendants," Lord De Quintaro ordered.

Attendants? Riley wouldn't like the term one bit. He reached out gently with his power, trying to locate his friend. The familiar energy patterns were absent. Several strangers had taken his place.

"Where is my squire and the Lion Friends?"

"Hawk has them." Dislike dripped from Lord De Quintaro's words. "He knew you would not leave without Riley Logan. Your friends are safe, Lion. Never fear."

Seth nodded, turning his attention back to the room. He took a tight grip on his anger as the Lion Spirit's power burned within his heart. These men were not at fault. They too had fallen victim to Hawk's power.

Then a large portrait mounted on the far wall caught his attention. His father was at its center with two young boys surrounding him. Rips in the center of the painting obscured a likeness once there. He walked over to the portrait and stood before it.

"Are these my brothers, Sir?" he asked.

"Hector is the eldest, the youngest sitting upon your father's knee is Claudio." Lord De Quintaro's voice hardened. "And the demon in the middle is Julian."

Seth reached out to touch the ruined pieces. Leo's residual emotions still clung to the fabric from the day he'd damaged the painting. Hurt. Rage. Loss. Seth pulled the shreds back into place and held them to look at the little boy's face. Here was the devil who'd orchestrated their father's murder.

"Why would a son turn against his father?" Seth gently tore the pieces away, leaving Leo and his two lost brothers intact. Julian's ruined pieces he let drop to the floor.

"He's brought the Dirge and the Jackal among us. For what? Power? I am hunted by day. The night is filled with their foul deeds haunting my dreams."

Seth turned away from the family he would never know. Moving to a little silver frame on his father's nightstand, he lifted it gently from the table. A man and woman had been sketched side by side. They looked happy.

"Your grandparents."

"Do you think they will let me keep this portrait of father and my brothers? And this one?" Seth asked.

"Of course, my prince. These are your chambers now."

His chambers? He looked down at the Lion Ring pulsing with his blood. Protector of the people. He'd accepted the role willingly. Using his strength and skill to save the people of Andara during such times was his life's purpose, but must he be King of Valdeon as well? He knew nothing of such things.

Three Valdeonian men dressed in red swept into the room and fell on their knees before him. He backed against the wall as they each touched their heads to his feet. Seth looked to Lord De Quintaro for explanation, but he didn't seem to find this unusual in the least.

"Good Morning." Seth rubbed at his curls.

"Yes, Highness, it is a very pleasant day." one of the them, the leader, quickly agreed. "A meal has been prepared. Does his highness wish to dine?"

"His highness's robe!" Lord De Quintaro gave him a wink. "I think we'll dine in the parlor, yes?"

Seth nodded. He held still while the servants wrapped the lush blood red robe about him and put the soft slippers upon his feet. Bowing deeply, they held open the door for them. Seth fidgeted with the belt of his robe. He didn't like all this bowing and scraping. One man shouldn't grovel before another. It wasn't right. Leo's blood was in his body by the hand of fate. He hadn't earned anyone's respect yet.

The door opened into a large room rivaling Aunt Charlotte's great hall. It was lavishly decorated in greens and blues. Sofas stretched before a massive fireplace. Arturo De Quintaro and several more soldiers stood on guard positioned around the parlor. Some fell immediately to their knees as he entered. Others were a little more hesitant. The swirling mix of mistrust and unease in the energy about their bodies made one thing clear. They were following Lord De Quintaro's leadership, not the new half-breed Lion.

He brought the ice walls about him, blocking out the resentment his Tslavian blood incited. Seth followed the attendants to a black leather chair and sat down. A feast lay before him. Hunger outweighed his discomfort at the many eyes upon him. Seth gulped down the meal in an ungentlemanly frenzy. Lord De Quintaro shared his vigor as he emptied his own plate.

"You've been patient with me, My Lord De Quintaro," Seth said. "Ask me the questions plaguing your thoughts."

"Why haven't the Sacred Guard joined you?" he asked. "It is their duty to protect the Lion."

"They can't, Sir. We - the Jalora and I - made them promise to hide in safety until it commands our return to Valdeon."

A rumbling of relieved murmurs circled about the room. Seth gently probed them. These men - expect Fausto - were uncertain if the Lords of Valdeon were dead or simply neglecting their duties. Some were still unsure if Wolf and his men had abandoned their people by choice.

"The others are safe. Wolf can tell you when he comes back. I'm not certain where he is right now." Seth noticed Lord De Quintaro's hopeful grin and remembered they were friends. "He's going to train me soon."

"It will make my heart glad to see my old friend again. Does he have his family with him?"

"You don't know then?" Seth looked around at the anxious faces. "San Rudalfo was hit hardest the night Valdeon fell. Wolf's city and home were burned to the ground. His wife and children were butchered. I'm sorry."

"Dulcina and the children are dead?" He fell back in his seat, hands covering his face. "Ah Wolf. Such a loss. How has he endured?"

A purposeful knock at the door brought Lord De Quintaro to his feet. Swords sang sharply as his men pulled their swords in unison. Seth stretched out his probe through the door. Two men stood on the other side. Seth gripped the Valdeonian lord's shoulder and nodded. Lord De Quintaro gave the order and one of his men swung the door open wide. Dragonfly and

Donny stood waiting. They were dressed in their finest uniforms.

"We request an audience with the Lion," Dragonfly said with a bow.

Seth sprinted forward to greet them and gripped Dragonfly's hand warmly. The ranger seemed not to notice the armed Valdeonians, focusing his words of greeting to Seth and Fausto De Quintaro. His squire - in comparison - looked extremely uncomfortable.

"I'm glad to see you out of bed and on your feet," Seth told him. "I want to apologize for the other night. I shouldn't have put the Sleep on you."

"You put the Sleep upon a ranger as a Hopeful?" Fausto De Quintaro grinned, his pride permeated about the room on the faces of his men.

"Not just me, My Lord De Quintaro." Dragonfly grinned. "Seth also put the Sleep upon the Gargoyle."

"The Valdeonian blood outmatches the Tslavian inside our Lion's heart!"

Tension seeped from the room to be replaced by laughter.

"I should thank you, Lion. The Jalora has sped up my healing." Dragonfly stood at attention once again. "I must be about my duty. It is time for the Lion's Naming. We have come to accompany him."

The Jalora hadn't commanded he join the Legion or be named. Wolf should be with him at such a time at any rate. Hawk was behind this rush to get the Lion under the Legion's control. Of course, Seth had to do what they wanted now. His uncle had Riley.

"You will be tested. Listen to the Jalora's guidance," Fausto told him. "I am pleased your countrymen are here to witness this day."

Dragonfly motioned and Donny came to hand the nearest servant a dull olive uniform. The attendants ushered Seth back into the bed chamber. One of the men brushed his hair with a golden horsehair brush, while the other painstakingly shaved him. They would not let him dress himself in the uniform or pull on the fine sturdy boots. Seth let them have their way. They seemed so eager to please him.

"You will have a better view in the bleachers, My Lord De Quintaro. Would you show him, Donny?" Dragonfly asked when Seth joined them. "I will escort the Lion to the arena."

"My thanks to you, Ranger." Fausto returned the bow.

"For the honor of your countrymen, Lion." The Valdeonian men cheered as they followed Lord De Quintaro into the hall.

"I feel the fool for not seeing the resemblance." Dragonfly pointed up at a portrait of his father. "He was a good man and a noble ranger. Let us hope your name brings honor to your country as his service did."

"And if it doesn't? What if I don't pass the naming test?"

Dragonfly frowned. "Then you will never leave the arena."

Chapter Sixty-Two

DECADES OF POWER descended upon Seth as he followed Dragonfly into the obsidian corridor. Eight doors stood across the hall from the Lion's chambers. Animals peered out at him from their golden crests: Hawk, Wolf, Jaguar, Fox, Raven, Ferret, Otter, and Rabbit. The Sacred Guard of Valdeon.

"The top floor of the citadel is reserved for the Lords of Valdeon," Dragonfly said. "It is an honor to be walking with the Lion in this place. Not many are afforded the opportunity."

They descended a short staircase and came to a landing with three sets of doors. Orbs bobbed on the other side of each door, waiting to strike like vipers at any who touched the surface.

Do not fear the Orbs, Lion. Your ancestor and I created them. They bow to our will, for their lord has returned to his fortress at long last.

He lifted the Lion Ring, watching his lifeblood rise and fall from the crystal's stone belly. It had rested upon the last Jalora Master's finger as he built the Obsidian Citadel. Would it really obey a half-breed who shared the blood of Valdeon's ancient enemy? Seth rested a hand on Dragonfly's shoulder and then took a step forward. Immediately the orbs calmed, resuming their gentle floating.

"We take the first door to get to the arena," Seth told Dragonfly. "The others lead to Legion headquarters and the docks."

"You've calmed them. The orbs have been lashing out at everyone since the Book of Ancients was opened." Dragonfly, questions still swimming in his eyes, pushed open the door. "Come, Lion. They will be waiting."

Shadows cast dancing figures across the sands of the arena. Rangers and their squires lined the first rows in the bleachers suspended over their heads. Others joined them. Several men and women dressed in black ceremonial robes sat behind the solemn rangers.

"Delegates from the United Realms," Dragonfly said. "The Dragon summoned them here to request aid defending Andara's borders. This day isn't built upon coincidence. The Jalora's perfect wisdom has brought us to this moment, Lion. Hold this close as you fight today."

Perhaps it had. Someone hadn't accepted the invitation. Wolf's energy was missing from the spectators. Something must have happened to keep him away. Seth had to escape and search for him.

Then an intense wave of disapproval slapped at his mind. It wasn't difficult to find the stern force behind the blow. Esteban the Hawk stood against the railings at the very center of the section of seats. His dark eyes burned into Seth. He returned the stare, allowing his rage to show. Hawk had no right to hold Riley or the others. It was time to show his uncle that Seth was no longer the frightened and confused Marianna boy. He was the Lion now and would not be controlled.

Marching out onto the sand, he clutched at the hilt of his sword.

"Lion! Lion!"

Thunderous chanting shook the obsidian walls towering over the arena. Breaking the contest of wills with his uncle, Seth turned to the bleachers behind him. Fausto De Quintaro and his men filled the section. Riley and the Lion Friends were with them, joining in as the Valdeonians began to stomp their boots.

Focus on remaining calm. Remember what I have taught you.

Summoning the ice walls, Seth stood behind the clear surface. The chanting had faded. Emotions from the crowd stopped at the edge of the ice. Hawk's stern disapproval was a memory. He was at peace within the fortress of his own making.

"Go to the center of the arena," Dragonfly said, offering him a respectful bow. "I turn you over to capable hands."

Two rangers stood at the center of the arena. The first he recognized from the night he'd stood guard duty. It was the older ranger he'd managed to surprise upon the battlements. The second ranger was much younger and even more impatient. His mountain-sized body swayed as he shifted from one boot to the other. The head of a Bear swam within the dark yellow glow of his Heart of the Warrior Ring.

"Who comes before the Legion?" the older ranger asked, sending his words to the top of the bleachers.

"Seth D'Antoiné, heir of Edmund the Leo," he said, lifting his voice against those who would deny it. "I am the Bearer of the Lion Ring."

"Very well, Lion. You must prove your worth by defeating the Bear in combat." The older ranger nodded to the large young man. "Make ready."

Bear pulled his weapon and took the First Stance. His eyes were locked upon Seth. Determination. Hope. Anxiousness. The large apprentice hid his self-doubt and anxiety well.

He is a powerful opponent. Do not underestimate the Bear.

Fighting this ranger seemed an unnecessary formality, like some ritual that only served to draw blood for the pleasure of others. Everyone, even Riley, was caught up in the pageantry. Seth pulled his sword with a sigh. He had no choice if he wanted to see his friends free again.

"Begin!"

An expectant silence fell upon the arena as Seth and the Bear scrutinized each other. His opponent was powerfully built. Muscular shoulders supported a thick neck. Bear's broad chest pushed at the confines of his tunic with each eager breath. Indeed, his body resembled the beast whose name he bore.

Bear suddenly flew at him with full speed. Bone-jarring strikes hammered down upon Seth's blade as his opponent performed the Dance of Death. Blocking the blows, he endured the hammering on his weapon until the apprentice withdrew. He took the First Stance again with a perplexed look upon his face.

"Why do you not fight?" Bear asked, his deep grumbling voice matching the man. "Are you untrained?"

"You've learned the Fifth Stance, but nothing further?" Seth tightened his grip upon the hilt of his sword. "I will not draw your blood to please a crowd."

"By my father's beard! Who says you'll get the chance?"

Bear came at Seth in a rush. His movements were less sure. Seth ducked the blade and spun around the ranger, striking him on the back of the head with the hilt of his sword. Sweeping his blade in a quick arch, he disarmed the ranger. The sword fell into the sands of the arena with a small poof of dust.

The ranger staggered away from Seth, falling to his knees. Bear swayed, but didn't fall. Shaking his head in irritable jerks, the young man's eyes glowed with anger. He rolled across the sand and grabbed his sword. Lumbering to his feet, Bear lifted his weapon and held toward Seth in challenge.

A slow predatory smile stretched across Seth's face. The Lion Spirit had risen inside him and was feeding upon the ranger's rage. Bearer and Lion Spirit. They stood perfectly still, waiting for their hot-headed prey to stumbling into the snare. It would be easy. He was overeager to prove his worth to the rangers. Soon the mortal would rush at them. Then they would rip, tear, and finally devour his very soul.

Seth licked at the saliva pool at the edge of his lips. A slight quiver at the Bear's blade tip gave away his strike before he moved. Seth circled his blade around his opponent's weapon and pulled it from his hands. Bear's sword flew toward the bleachers. The ranger, with a cry of great fury, rushed at Seth with his bare hands.

Bloodlust filled Seth's body until he thought he'd vomit from its salty flavor. No. This wasn't right. The Bear was a servant of the Jalora. He mustn't kill a comrade. The Lion Spirit pressed at his control as Bear reached them. He grabbed the ranger's wrist and threw him to the ground.

"Enough! You are beaten. Control your impatience or it will control you."

The ranger stayed on his back. He held his hands up in submission. They were shaking violently. Seth didn't like the terror he saw swirling about the young man. He lowered his weapon and forced the bloodlust away.

Dragonfly and the older ranger approached Bear slowly. Their eyes remained fixed upon Seth. They each took one of Bear's arms and pulled him to his feet.

"Did you hear it? Did you see it?" Bear asked them. "A mighty lion of ice had me at its mercy. I thought I would be devoured. You spared my life."

"Ice lion? I don't understand." Seth sheathed his sword with an irritated thump. "Are you saying you saw the Spirit of the Lion Ring?"

"It means your naming has been accepted by the Jalora," the old ranger told him. "I am called White Tiger. And you are the Ice Lion."

Dragonfly gripped Bear's face, forcing him to break eye contact with Seth. "Go back to headquarters. Have your squire look at the bump on your head."

Bear saluted the rangers and then bowed low to Seth. "It has been my greatest honor to spar with you, Ice Lion."

Pride. Relief. Determination. They trailed after the Bear as he exited the arena. The ranger harbored no ill will Seth could detect. Rather, he seemed almost pleased to have lost.

"Those Valdeonians will bring down the citadel, Apprentice," White Tiger told Seth. "You'd better tell them your ranger name."

Proclaim your naming, Lion!

"I am called the Ice Lion!" Seth threw his head back and let loose the Lion's Roar.

"Ice Lion! Ice Lion!" The Valdeonians broke into frenzied cheering.

"Fastest testing I've ever seen," White Tiger said. "Let me see your ring."

Seth unwrapped the bandage on his hand. The Lion Ring's dark yellow light shimmered across the sands. Its brilliant glow cast shadows in the ridges of the old ranger's wrinkled face. An unbearable sadness was etched in his features.

"The Leo was our Bishop and my good friend." White Tiger rubbed away the grief from his eyes. "What happened to him?"

Seth regarded the old ranger for a long time before answering. Affection. Loyalty. Grief. He'd certainly felt a strong attachment to Leo, but could Edmund's son trust him? Seth had placed his trust in the Phoenix. It hadn't turned out well.

"He was murdered," Seth said finally.

A fire began to build within the old eyes. Shock. Anger. Revenge. Perhaps White Tiger was someone he could trust after all? Then the emotions faded as a band of will wrapped about his body. Duty. Honor. Integrity. They washed away the violent emotions of his grief.

"Welcome to the Jalora Legion, Apprentice. You will come with me to a containment area." White Tiger tapped on a pair of irons hanging from his waist. "Don't make me use these."

Chapter Sixty-Three

"YOU'LL WAIT in here, Apprentice," White Tiger said, stopping before a thick wooden door along the quiet corridors of the Legion headquarters.

He stepped aside, holding the door open. Seth frowned at the steel bars crossing a small opening in the door. Apparently new apprentices were to be taunted with a last small view of freedom. White Tiger slammed it shut again once Seth had stepped inside.

"Use this time to contemplate your new life with the Jalora, Ice Lion. I'll just lock this door so you stay put until he comes for you."

"Who?" Seth gripped at the bars.

"Your new Commander, of course." He folded his arms, staring through the bars. "I dare say the Dragon has gone after him. You should only be here for a few days."

"A few days! What of my squire and the Lion Friends?"

"They will be more comfortable than you are now, Apprentice. Enjoy your time in solitude."

Seth kicked the door as White Tiger's boot steps faded. They would see how long he stayed locked in this cell! Had they forgotten what he'd done to the cage in the library? He took a steadying breath and turned his attention to the tiny antechamber. Devoid of candles and furnishings, the antechamber contained one wide bench fashioned from the stone of the wall.

He plopped down on the bench under the only source of light in the room. A slight breeze crept in through the long thin window. Its fingers touched at his neck and shoulders. He rested his head in his hands, wondering how many other apprentices had done the same thing over the decades.

"You look so like him."

A tall figure stepped away from the shadows. His face and beard were the color of pitch. Two dark eyes filled with contempt bore into Seth like hot daggers. Evil wrapped about the man. Its presence was powerful and hungry.

"Who are you?" Seth pushed away from the bench and onto his feet.

"Come now, Brother." The intruder stepped under a ray of light. "Does your heart not recognize me? I certainly recognize you."

"Julian. How did you get in here without being seen by the rangers?"

"You share our father's limited intelligence as well as his looks," Julian said sneering. "What did you inherit from the Tslavic cow that bore you?"

Seth wrapped the ice walls about him quickly. The evil radiating off Julian, stretched its eager fingers toward him. Red and sickly green, the colors mixed in a nauseating film upon the air.

"You easily hurt our father with your words, Julian. I have no affection for you and no fear of your ill favor. Tell me what it is you want of me and leave."

Julian raised his eyebrows and tilted his head to regard Seth more closely. A rich laughter echoed about the walls of the tiny antechamber. His half-brother's smile spread between a well-groomed beard and mustache.

"Each son of Edmund D'Antoiné had a different mother. Did he tell you, half-breed? No?" Julian chuckled, an anticipatory glimmer in his eye. "Hector, the eldest, came from father's first wife. She died well before me though I have heard she was a decent enough queen. Rather dull about certain things, like our father's interest in my mother."

"Liar!" Seth growled, letting a crack form in the ice.

Julian began to walk languidly around the tiny chamber, running a gloved hand along the wall.

"My mother was in father's marriage bed less than a month after his first queen died. Mother was very ambitious you understand, though not completely stable." He sighed. "So, there we were, Hector and me. Neither of us the Lion's Heir. Looked over and disregarded like common cattle. Father married yet again. Then came sickly little Claudio. I'm not sure which of us he was ashamed of more."

The bitterness in Julian's voice spoke of a deep hurt. He'd endured his own tormentor growing up. Words of frustration cast upon a younger soul could sting. Yet, Seth couldn't imagine Leo to be guilty of such things.

"I'm sure Father never intentionally hurt you, Julian. He wasn't a cruel man."

"How do you know what he was like, half-breed?" Julian snapped. "Edmund must have fawned over you like some precious gift. You may have the Lion's eyes and our father's favor, but I will have his Lion Ring!"

"I'll never give you the ring."

"Of course, you won't, fool. I'll take it from your dead finger. Do you think I would give a second thought to ending you? I've culled the rest of our weak family. Now I am the last D'Antoiné left on Andara."

"Not the last." Seth drew his sword and took the First Stance.

Julian sprang at him with a savage growl. Evil reached out to grab him as their blades clashed. The Jalora's power flared in defiance, slapping away the touch. Julian twisted his body and moved out of his reach. Seth recognized the technique. They'd had the same teacher. The thought sickened him.

Dodging under Julian's thrust, Seth swiped at his torso as he passed. A long bloody gash seeped through Julian's tunic along the side of his ribs.

"First blood," Seth said. "Consider it payment for the pain you caused our father."

"You'll die swimming in your own blood just as he did, Half-breed." Julian grinned, sweeping his sword in great arcs through the space between them. "Did you take time to consider why Father - a Jalora Bishop - ran from me?"

Julian pounced upon Seth striking with several well-placed blows. Too late he understood his opponent had been gauging his skills. Julian's blade split skin along Seth's rib cage. He spun back around, planting a fist hit hard against his face. Seth dropped hard upon the stone floor. Stars blinked and shimmered before his eyes.

"You are no match for me, Half-breed," Julian said close to Seth's ear. "I will rule Valdeon and through it all of Andara! First, I need the Lion Ring. Give me your hand willingly and perhaps I'll make your death a quick one."

"I'm not beaten yet."

He pushed aside his pain. Staggering to his feet, Seth stood defiantly before his murderous brother. Blood dripped down his leg to pool upon the floor. He ignored the warm sensation, focusing instead on pulling all his strength about him.

"The Jalora rules Andara, Julian traitor prince!" Seth growled, lacing the Lion's Roar around his words.

Great fury filled the tiny antechamber as the Spirit of the Lion Ring came alive. It was ready to devour the treacherous soul before him. Seth wouldn't stop it this time. He braced himself as the Lion's Roar burst through the darkness to strike Julian in the chest. His half-brother flew against the wall with a bone-cracking smack. He rolled to the ground and landed in a heap.

Seth fell onto the stone bench, exhausted. It was over. He'd done it. Valdeon's traitor had been stopped. Then a hollow laughter hung about the room. Julian began to rise. No one should have been able to survive a direct hit from the Lion's Roar.

"Not very brotherly. Now it's my turn," Julian said.

"What goes on in there, Ice Lion? Julian. What treachery is this?" White Tiger shouted down the corridor. "Open this door! Quickly! You there. Go summon aid."

Julian spat a curse as a key rattled in the door lock. He raced toward the back of the room and stopped before a darkened section of wall. Gripping an ancient metal ring jutting from the stone, he pulled hard. Rock scraped against rock to reveal a passageway.

"Valdeon will be mine, Lion! You are a dead man when next we meet!"

Seth pushed away from the bench and raced after Julian. Slipping through the opening as the stone wall closed behind him, he stopped a moment to listen. Heavy boots slammed against stone as his quarry raced up the hidden stairway of the citadel. Gripping at his side, Seth pressed his fingers against the sticky wound. His own blood was flowing freely like Julian's upon the steps. He couldn't stop now, not when he had a chance to stop the butcher who had hurt so many innocent lives.

"This way, Prince of Valdeon!" a voice called above Seth.

Julian's entry into the citadel had been aided by a traitor. How many others were undermining the Legion's hold upon Andara? A heavy door banged just above him. Seth pushed his body up the last few steps. He burst out upon the battlements beside the airship port just as another door slammed to his right. A chilling winter wind struck his face, smacking away the frustrated disappointment. The traitor may have gotten away, but his true foe was still in reach. Julian limped toward a launch where a small crew of Valdeonian men were waiting for him. Other men rushed off the ship. They ran past Julian to block Seth's path. Mercenaries.

Ignoring the greedy villains, he kept his rage for his black-hearted sibling. "Julian! Face me and let us be done with this!"

"Kill him!" Julian shouted at the mercenaries.

Seth readied himself as the armed men stormed toward him. Julian was boarding the launch and starting the engine. He was getting away! The Lion's Roar rumbled deep in his throat, anxious for traitor's blood.

"You won't escape me, Julian!"

"I dare say my mercenary friends will keep you entertained, Brother." Julian threw a handful of coins at their feet. "What are you waiting for? Kill him! I'll give you ten times the price I promised."

Then the mercenaries slowed their lustful run toward him. Boots pounded behind Seth as a wave of Valdeonian soldiers charged across the battlements. Riley, Sergeant Dancer, Tory, and the Claybanks moved to surround Seth with their weapons drawn. Fausto De Quintaro and his men overtook the mercenaries in a savage wave.

"For the Lion! Death to the traitor prince!"

Julian pointed his sword at Seth in a final challenge. His launch lifted away from the docks and pointed toward the south. Seth let out a roar of fury as the little vessel jetted away from the citadel into the open skies. He raced with his friends to watch the little boat hover up toward the clouds.

"Hear me, Julian!" Seth and the Jalora cried as one. "Hear me Lea and all those who doubt the strength of the Legion! The Lion has returned! Gone is the old covenant. A new one has been forged. It is stronger than you can ever know. Doubt me not!"

They threw their head back and let a mighty roar of warning thunder into the skies over Lea. The Obsidian Citadel reverberated beneath them like the pounding of a gigantic drum.

We have much to do to prepare you, my Lion. The Jalora told him. *Soon we will journey from Lea to retrieve talismans, which will increase your strength.*

"What of Valdeon and those who suffer? I must stop Julian," Seth said within his mind.

You must fulfill your part of the covenant, Ice lion. Do not disobey my word. A sense of peace came over his heart as the Jalora touched his mind softly. *Trust in my wisdom, Seth. We must grow stronger before we can take back Andara.*

"Ice Lion! Ice Lion!" The Valdeonians lifted him onto their shoulders and brought him away from the edge of the battlements.

"You've sent Julian whimpering away in defeat, my lord!" Fausto cried with a shout of triumph. "We've given those mercenaries something to regret!"

His men let out a shout of victory. Seth drank in their joy. They had defeated the very men who had helped chase them away from Valdeon. Their confidence had been returned.

"Set him down!" Riley barked, pushing through the much taller Valdeonians. "I'll need to have a look at your wound." His squire ushered Seth toward a barrel after his feet touched the ground. "Your dark-hearted brother had a cut just like this."

"I drew first blood, Squire. Julian was returning the hit."

"His wound flowed deeper than yours, my lord Lion! Next time he will not be able to walk away." Fausto slapped Riley on the back and turned to his men. "Let us take the Lion back to his chambers."

Then a tingling sensation of power circled around the battlements. Rangers. They were prepared for a fight if he resisted. Not bothering to conceal themselves, the rangers circled their group. Appraising eyes took in the dead men, but discipline kept them from staring overly long at Seth.

"The Ice Lion must come with us." White Tiger walked calmly through the crowd of drawn swords. "Bishop Hawk wants to see you, Apprentice."

Several other rangers marched onto the battlements. They circled around the dead and cast appraising looks at Seth.

"The Hawk will have to wait!" Riley snapped, hatred swirling about his body. "I'm tending to his wounds just now."

Seth reached a probe around Riley. Violence. Resentment. Anger. He'd missed much when the power had taken him.

"And who says we will hand our Lord Lion over to the Legion?" Lord De Quintaro was saying. "He belongs with his people. They need him."

"He's in the Legion now, Fausto." White Tiger gripped the handle of his sword. "You know very well he must take his place."

The men about him were ready to fight each other and draw blood. His father had been right to warn him. These men and others - well intended or no - would try to use him for their own purposes.

"Put your weapons away." Seth stood, despite the hiss from his squire. "Are we not allies? Do we not fight for the same thing? It is the safety of all of Andara we must protect now."

He came to stand before Fausto. "I am a servant of the Jalora. It commands my path and has already set my course. I must fulfill the covenant before freeing Valdeon.

There are…things I must do. Please understand, my friend."

Fausto De Quintaro rested two hands upon Seth's shoulders and gave him a reassuring smile. "May the Jalora continue to guide your steps and protect you along the way. We are your men. You have given us back our purpose, Lion. We go where we can do the most good. I pray we met again upon the shores of our homeland."

"Safe journey to you, Lion Friend," Seth said, lifting Fausto's left sleeve.

"You will never have reason to regret marking me, my sovereign lord." Fausto stood up straight and nodded for his men to stand down.

Seth turned to White Tiger. "I will go with you, but you must allow My Lord De Quintaro and his men to have safe passage out of Lea."

"I give you my word. Rangers, see to the Lion's Squire and the Lion Friends as well." White Tiger ordered. "Never fear. They will be freed soon."

Seth nodded to Sergeant Dancer as the ranger circled about his friends. They'd better be released soon or he'd bring this citadel down about Hawk's ears. His uncle's absence from the battle with Julian had been alarmingly conspicuous.

"Come. The Hawk is waiting." White Tiger struggled to keep the distaste from his face.

Seth nodded slowly. Yes, he wanted to see Hawk as well. His uncle had a great deal of explaining to do.

Chapter Sixty-Four

SETH FOLLOWED White Tiger through the lavish office space. Legion headquarters contained the most elegant furniture he'd ever seen. Several rangers hurrying about suddenly stopped to regard Seth as he walked by. Ignoring their furtive interest, he focused on the confrontation ahead of him.

White Tiger steered them toward an office belonging to a *Bishop Falcon*. Hawk, it would seem, hadn't been honored with a space among the most powerful rangers in the Legion. White Tiger opened the door without knocking and saluted. Seated behind a rich wooden desk was Esteban the Hawk.

"The Ice Lion, Sir."

"Yes, so all of Lea heard," Hawk said. "Thank you, Ranger. You may go."

Hawk lifted his gaze from the parchment he'd been reading. Hard dark eyes took Seth in with calculating intensity. The pale pink scar flushed white as he pressed thin lips together. Though the skin tones may have been different, he took on the air of Pavel Sandor disguised as Fergus McCloud. A lecture was about to begin. Seth, however, was done listening to lectures.

"Where are you keeping the Lion Friends?"

"Rest assured, they will be released once you are safely on your way, Apprentice." He smoothed long fingers across the parchment. "You have been quite troublesome. I searched for you all night on Eastland Isle. Then I chased you in the forests of Tslavia. Not a pleasant experience if you're Valdeonian. Imagine my surprise to see you, the Crown Prince of Valdeon, rolling in muck with common peasants."

"I'd rather spend time with men I know I can trust than someone who uses the innocent to threaten and manipulate."

Hawk's jaw tensed. He appeared to struggle with a reply. Then his attention moved over Seth's shoulder to the door. He closed his eyes briefly. They were cold and filled with hatred when he opened them again.

"Come in, Phoenix. Don't dawdle outside the door."

The door opened slowly as the golden blond curls ducked inside. Phoenix stared at Seth with undisguised curiosity for a few seconds, then marched to stand before Hawk's desk. He saluted, though by the stiffness of his neck and shoulders, the ranger held no esteem for Hawk.

"Gregory Baldemar, you owe my nephew a life debt. You will repay it now." Hawk stood up, clasping his hands behind his back. "Phoenix's troop leaves for North Marsh within the hour, Nephew. You will be taken to the transport to join your new troop. I've arranged to have your things packed and placed onboard. Your Marianna squire awaits you on the battlements."

"And you imagine I'll go quietly? I have my own path to take."

"I can only guess what mad exploits you'd pursue next." His uncle leaned forward, smoothing his fingers across the desktop before him. "Use your head. If these murderers hunt you in Lea, why not escape to a place they can't follow? Go with the Phoenix and learn the skills you need to survive. Face this enemy when you are ready. You must trust me in this, Lion."

Seth gave the Hawk a bitter laugh. "Trust you? What reason has the Jalora Legion ever given me to trust any of you? My mother was murdered by a Tslavic assassin who tried to poison me as well. A ranger spared me from the assassin's vial, but only for his own purpose. He'd made a bargain with the killer and left me in his clutches away from my father. This I heard with my own ears."

"No ranger would do something so insidious." Phoenix broke attention to stare at Seth. "This villain must have been pretending to be a ranger, surely?"

"I had no choice," the Hawk said quietly.

Shock. Anger. Disgust. They pulsed about Phoenix in the rhythm of newly unearthed treachery. All pretense of respect or etiquette toward Hawk fell away. Raw fury emanated from his body. Seth, in contrast, was strangely numb. Had Esteban hated his brother so that he would deprive him of his family and his heir? What kind of cold-hearted people were the D'Antoiné family?

"How could you withhold Seth's existence from Edmund? Monster! Your silence has thrown Valdeon into war."

"So quick to judge me, are you Phoenix? I found Anne clutching at her tiny son, terrified I would harm him." A moment of sorrow was exposed in Esteban's countenance, then it quickly disappeared again under his hard mask. "She showed me her son's face. The eyes do not lie."

"Anne? Anne Von Wolkhurst? Leo married her?"

"Yes, the fool married her." Hawk sat heavily on the desk. "Anne made me swear to keep her location secret and Seth's birth from Edmund. I hated myself for keeping silent, especially with Pavel Sandor so close to them. What else was I to do? You know what happens to babes of Valdeonian and Tslavian blood. I had no choice but to make a bargain with Sandor. I would keep Edmund away if he would protect Seth."

"You could've taken me to my father after my mother died. Life with Sandor was unbearable. You abandoned me on Marianna with a killer."

"Emma was there to watch over you." Hawk sighed, squeezing his fists in unaccustomed impatience. "Please understand. Your father was a reckless man. He would have taken you to San Leonora and declared you as his heir. Even your father couldn't have stopped those who'd take you and stone you in the courtyard." The hard look Hawk fixed upon Seth froze him to the bone. "You agreed to bear the Lion Ring. Once it's placed upon your finger, you serve the Jalora. Your life no longer belongs to you. Now take up your place with the Phoenix. I will say no more."

"We must wait for the Dragon to return," Phoenix said.

Hawk turned in fury toward the ranger. "You dare question me after I spared your life? You threatened the Lion. Do you imagine any of the others would have allowed you to live after such treachery?"

A small cut Seth hadn't noticed earlier darkened the Prince of Heidelbrecht's lip. He reached a probe out quickly and withdrew it again. Hawk was a steel wall, but Phoenix had allowed him inside for a moment in his anger. Indeed, he had missed a great deal when the power took him. It was time he intervened or there would be bloodshed. Phoenix had helped him before he knew his identity. He supposedly he owed him such a favor.

"Phoenix was acting out of grief, Uncle. Would you judge his actions in such a time?"

"Are you saying I should forgive his violence and let the matter drop? You show a farmer's morality, Nephew."

"Give me your word, Uncle, when I leave you'll not hurt Phoenix or any of the Lion Friends. I'll promise to submit myself to the Legion. If you harm them, I'll disappear at the first opportunity."

Hawk's lip trembled, finally forming a derisive sneer. "A child's threat, but if it's your wish then very well."

"That is my command!" the joined voices of Seth and the Jalora ordered. "Do not oppose me in this. Never forget. You are not the Right-Hand."

The desk flew toward the far wall, carrying Hawk with it. Pinned behind the large piece of furniture, he stayed immobile. The scar upon his cheek burned red with his anger. Phoenix, pressing his back against the window, made no move to help the trapped ranger.

Seth threw them a salute and gripped the door handle. The Lion Spirit growled with hungry anticipation. It wanted revenge, but its bloodlust mustn't be sated this day. The safety of his friends must be considered. He turned to fix Hawk with one last glare.

"And, Uncle, if you ever touch my squire again, I'll kill you."

White Tiger and the others backed away as he marched through their numbers. The fury throbbed about him in unrestrained waves. He made no attempt to block it behind ice walls this time. No one followed as he made his way out onto the sunny battlements. Riley waited for him his face a mask of agitation. He began to bow awkwardly to Seth.

"If you bow and scrape to me, Riley Logan, I'll dunk you head first in a water barrel. I need my best friend beside me now."

"Aye. You'll never change, Seth." Riley grinned. "And glad I am too. So where are we headed?"

"We journey on our next quest."

"As long as it's not here mucking stables. Let's go."

Riley took his place two steps behind Seth. Then together, they moved out of the sunlight into the unknown future.

Chapter Sixty-Five

Wolf stared out at the thick forest surrounding Muellerton Outpost. Mists hung over the trees from a heavy rain. His eyes scanned for any signs of movement, whether it be friend or foe. He wondered for the thousandth time who could have possibly known about he and Tulio hiding here at the outpost. Hawk was a prime suspect, but he'd said he'd intercepted the message. Rangers, even fallen ones, couldn't lie.

"You'll wear out the floorboards, Wolf," Fox told him. "Let's go back to your chambers. The guards know to send our comrades inside."

He and Otter had arrived at the outpost a few hours before them. The naval rangers had hidden the *Wind Chaser* in the ravine close to where Charlotte Von Bohdan moored the ship she'd given Wolf. Leaving their squires onboard to guard the vessel, Fox and Otter hurried to Muellerton, expecting to find Wolf waiting.

"Very well," Wolf conceded. "Stay alert, Rangers. Someone has gone to a great deal of effort to make certain the Sacred Guard is in one place."

They made their way down from the battlement walls and across the courtyard. Wet droplets clung to his face and hair. He wiped them away with an irritable grunt. What bang tail mischief had befallen them now? Seth, at least, was safe in Dragon's care.

Wolf pushed open the door. Jaguar and Raven waited for them with swords drawn. Their boots and uniforms were caked with mud. Twigs and splotches of pine tar hung upon their legs. These rangers had traveled hard through the trees.

"This outpost's security is a little lacking, Sir." Jaguar sheathed his sword and saluted.

"Did you see anyone hiding within the trees?" Wolf's fears eased a bit. "Someone has laid a trap for us. We have to leave as soon as Ferret arrives."

"Do you think we should go after him?" Otter asked. "Rafael and I can take the *Wind Chaser* for a few rounds."

Then the door flew open and Lucio Santiago rushed inside. "It's an ambush! Look to the battlements."

Staying out of sight, Wolf peered through the window and across the courtyard. The Heidelbrecht patrol made scattered heaps along the battlements. No musket shots had been fired. No betraying arrows were visible. The guards had simply fallen unconscious.

Prickles of power rippled across his skin. Wolf twisted around, hand upon his hilt. A ranger filled the doorway. Had Hawk followed them and laid a trap for the Sacred Guard? He took the First Stance, focusing his will on defending his comrades from the power of a bishop.

Then a hand bearing a dark purple crystal pulled the hood off his head. Dragon greeted them with a slight smile. His white mustache trembled with self-satisfied glee. Several rangers waited outside the door. Seth wasn't among them. Wolf sheathed his sword with an angry growl.

"I can understand your frustration, Right-Hand. Unfortunately, this was the only means at my disposal to summon you." Dragon motioned at the men behind him. "Hurry, Rangers. Bring it inside quickly."

He moved out of the doorway, allowing Bishops Manitou, Falcon, and Swan inside. A small trunk on two long wooden poles hung between them. Ancient power pulsated through the wooden exterior. If his suspicions about its content were correct, these fools had taken a deadly risk removing the magical object from the citadel.

They took great care setting the trunk down upon the floorboards. Backing away, the bishops exuded relief. Dragon, ignoring their sentiment, came to stand beside the trunk. He lifted the latch with the tip of his sword and threw back the lid.

"The Book of Ancients." Wolf resisted smoothing his hand across the radiant pages. "When did he open it?"

"Not long ago. I boarded my ship to find you the very same hour." Dragon's intense eyes fell upon Wolf. "Do you know what it says?"

Read the words aloud, Right-Hand. I would have him know.

Wolf swallowed hard, fighting the urge to run as fast as he could to find Seth. *"The young Lion's name is Seth D'Antoiné, son of the Leo. The Ice Lion was tested in the arena of the Obsidian Citadel against a worthy opponent, the Bear. His identity was compromised after saving the life of fellow ranger and ancient ally, the Phoenix, giving the young Lion no choice but to test. The Lord of San Leonora won the day and was promoted to Senior Apprentice. His brother, Julian, ambushed the Ice Lion within the bowels of the citadel. Ice Lion fought the traitor, drawing first blood. Their battle was interrupted by two of the Jalora's servants. The traitor made his escape with Ice Lion on his heels. Agents of evil were waiting for them on the battlements, ready to cut down the wounded Lion. His faithful squire, the Lion Friends, and the brave men of Varianne came to his aid. They defeated the traitors, chasing Julian the bastard prince from Lea. The Lion was deployed into danger with his new battalion immediately afterward."*

"Who would dare breech protocol and deploy an Apprentice without my permission?" Dragon allowed an uncharacteristic show of temper through his calm façade. "I want the Lion at my side in the Citadel. He needs proper instruction. You gentlemen will be there as well, of course."

Dragon had his own plans for the young Lion. A Jalora Master who owed a mentor his favor would be a powerful ally. Wolf 's heart suffered a strange sort of grief for the man in whom he had once harbored no doubt. It would appear Charlotte Von Bohdan had been correct about Francis the Dragon.

"Evil has managed to fool all of us," Wolf said. "We have all abandoned the Lion the same night you sent us the summons."

"I only sent for you, Wolf. I didn't summon the rest of the Sacred Guard," Dragon said between gritted teeth. "I'd assumed they'd come to join the young Lion now the Book of Ancients has been opened."

Wolf slammed a fist against the wall. "Hawk! Somehow, he deceived me with a lie. Seth is his target and he's managed to get me out of the way. He intends to use the young Lion for his own gain. You, Francis the Dragon, have taken his Right-Hand from him out of vain curiosity. Now Hawk flies far afield with the next Jalora Master in his talons."

"Under the circumstances, I will forget your insubordination." Dragon slammed the lid shut once more. "Come, Bishops. We must return to the citadel and find out where young Ice Lion has gone!"

The bishops reluctantly resumed their grip upon the poles and lifted the sealed trunk. Manitou and Falcon cast worried glances at Wolf as they passed. Swan, in contrast, glared as if he were looking at a violent anarchist.

Dragon turned to the Lords of Valdeon. "Would you be kind enough to escort the Bishops back to our vessel, my lords? I would speak with Wolf for another moment."

Wolf nodded to Berto. His second saluted and ordered the guardsmen take up protective positions about the bishops. Their own opinions about the exchange between the Right-Hand and the cardinal were carefully repressed underneath a strict aura of duty.

"Oh, and my lords," Dragon called to them. "Be wary around Peter the Gargoyle. Your young Lion put the Sleep upon him. His anger has not yet diminished."

Long-forgotten laughter filled the chamber. It was a welcome release to the night's tension and came at the expense of Valdeon's greatest enemy. None were more boisterous than Rafael the Fox. His vicious glee was a reminder of the imminent probability of bloodshed should the two rangers meet. Both Fox and Gargoyle had lost their fathers in the last violent confrontation of their countries.

"Stand guard at our door, Fox," Wolf ordered.

Anger and hurt turned to understanding and acceptance as Fox closed the door. Trust still existed between them. He couldn't share the same with Dragon or his bishops any longer. A brief uncomfortable silence hung between them as he waited for the cardinal to speak.

"You don't seem surprised the boy can put a powerful Deacon to sleep as a mere Hopeful?" Dragon asked quietly. "You looked as if you expected the Book of Ancients to be opened as well. It's almost as if you've spent time with him. Is there anything else I should expect from this Ice Lion, Right-Hand?"

Wolf remained silent. Dragon, seeing he was not going to get a response, pulled a parchment from his tunic and handed it to Wolf. The ancient parchment crinkled in his hand. One side bore the seal of the Altar of Providence. The other side read, "For Lord Xavier De Vincente, the Right-Hand".

"I found it under the Book of Ancients. Only a Lion could have put it there."

He crossed the room without waiting for Wolf to open the parchment. An interesting move since Dragon had insisted upon knowing the minute details of the Legions protection of the Sacred Guard. Why had his curiosity been suddenly quelled?

"Cardinal," Wolf called to Dragon. "It may not be wise to take the Lion back to the citadel. Other things can sense when the Book of Ancients has been opened, not just the forces of good."

Dragon straightened, putting a hand behind his back. He gave Wolf a formal bow and opened the door quietly. Fox saluted as he left them. Wolf's world had become a bit more daunting now that he'd lost Dragon's unlimited goodwill.

The Lords of Valdeon returned a few moments later, flushed from their quick pace. Their expectant eyes burned into him. Hungry for answers, they shuffled anxiously. Yes. He'd give them answers. They may not like what he had to share. Wolf stared out into the trees at the fading light. Seth was headed into danger and didn't know it. Curse Hawk! Did his greed know no bounds?

"I have more to tell you. Hawk knows Seth the Ice Lion is to be our next Jalora Master. He discovered I am to be the Master's Right-Hand. In his mad hunger for power, Esteban tried to murder me in cold blood. If not for Coyote, his plans would have succeeded. He's used my absence as an opportunity to capture the Lion and send him off to heaven knows where."

"Esteban was never one to give up easily," Jaguar spat. "We'll be ready for his tricks."

"Go to your rest. We can do nothing more tonight," Wolf told them, though he didn't imagine he would sleep a wink.

"Shouldn't we go look for Ice Lion?" Lucio asked.

"Don't be foolish," Jaguar told him, rolling out his kit. "Wolf will know where he's going soon. The Right-Hand will always find the Master."

Twilight flickered along the tops of the trees. Peace had finally come to Muellerton. Wolf maneuvered through the sleeping rangers. He took a piece of tinder and set it aflame in the fire. Holding it over the ancient parchment, he ripped at the crest and quickly began to read before changing his mind again.

"Xavier the Wolf, much is asked of you during these difficult times. The Legion will succumb to treachery as the Hawk falls. You must take his place as Right-Hand until a new Hawk flies again. The Ice Lion is very special and must be guarded at all costs. He is the one great hope for Andara. His safety has been entrusted to you, Right-Hand. Do not fail. Best Regards, Gustavo D'Antoiné, the Lion Claw, Jalora Master."

Wolf closed his eyes as the heavy grip of fate clutched at his heart. A message from the grave written nearly one hundred years ago confirmed his greatest fear. No aid would help them face the dark times ahead. The Lords of Valdeon were the only hope Andara had left.

Embrace your fate, Right-Hand. You must be an example for those who also serve.

His gaze turned to the sleeping young men scattered about the floor. They felt hope now, but soon the reality of the road before them would sink in. The Jalora was right. He must be an example of strength and endurance as they set out upon their journey to find the Lion.

More signs will come, Right-Hand. What was once lost will be recovered by Ice Lion's hand. Soon he will call you at will.

Evil, too, will seek you out, and there'll be no place for you to hide. Remember the lessons of your ancestors.

"If you would have me serve this boy, then will you tell me where he is?"

The Jalora held him firmly in its power. *The Lion's ancient ally protects him as they journey to the north. Do not be too long, Right-Hand. The Phoenix is powerful, yes, but he cannot calm the Lion's fury. If you do not join Ice Lion soon, he will lose control, killing all who surround him. No one can fill the place of the Right-Hand, but you Xavier De Vincente.*

The Jalora left abruptly, releasing his body. Wolf leaned heavily upon the mantel. Its heat bit into his legs and torso. Yet his body took no warmth from the comforting fire.

"Is something wrong, Wolf?" Rabbit rubbed at his sleepy eyes.

"Go back to sleep." He tossed the parchment into the flames and watched it burn.

The End

People, Places, Things

People

Grey Cliff Isles

Cutter - Mercenary leader hired to kill Seth

D'Antoiné, Seth - Bearer of the Lion Ring

De Vincente, Dante - Leo's Squire

Emma - The McCloud's Housekeeper

Gunn, Sergeant - Head of the Marianna Militia

Leo - Valdeonian Warrior and Seth's Mentor
(see D'Antoiné, Edmund)

Logan, Andrew - Woolie Farmer, Riley's Brother

Logan, George - Woolie Farmer, Riley's Brother

Logan, Laura - Farmer's Wife

Logan, Michael - Woolie Farmer, Riley's Brother

Logan, Patrick - Woolie Farmer, Riley's Brother

Logan, Riley - Seth's Best Friend and Squire

Logan, Stephen - Woolie Farmer, Riley's Brother

Logan, Thomas - Woolie Farmer

Logan, Tom - Woolie Farmer, Riley's Brother

McBride, Stan - Haven Bay Youth

McCloud, Anne - Seth's Mother

McCloud, Fergus - Headmaster and Seth's Uncle

McDermott, Charlie - Haven Bay Youth

McFadden, Beatrice - Haven Bay Youth, Doctor's Daughter

McFadden, Doctor - The Isle of Marianna's Only Doctor

McKenzie, Alice - Haven Bay Youth

McKenzie, Danny - Woolie Farmer

McKenzie, Mike - Woolie Farmer

McKinney, Teb - Barkeep at Paddy's

McTavish, Angus - Owner of Haven Bay's Mercantile

McTavish, Constable - Haven Bay's Police Chief

Newcastle, Elder - Haven Bay's Elder

Newcastle, Jamie - Haven Bay Youth and Elder's Son

Paddy - Owner and Innkeeper of Paddy's Inn

Sandor, Pavel - Andara's Deadliest Assassin

Valdeon

Basilio - Squire to the Wolf

Benito - Chancellor of Valdeon

Bram - Framburg Healer and friend of Jorge

Cristiano, Felix - Usurper of San Angelica

Cristiano, Rafael the Fox - Member of the Sacred Guard, A Lord of Valdeon

Cristobal, Tulio the Rabbit - Member of the Sacred Guard, A Lord of Valdeon

D'Antoiné, Edmund the Leo - King and a Lord of Valdeon

D'Antoiné, Esteban the Hawk - Former Member of the Sacred Guard, A Lord of Valdeon

D'Antoiné, Julian - Prince of Valdeon

De Costa, Marcellus - Minion of Julian D'Antoiné

De Vincente, Danel - Son of Xavier

De Vincente, Dulcina - Wife of Xavier

De Vincente, Gaspar - Son of Xavier

De Vincente, Xavier the Wolf - Leader of the Sacred Guard, A Lord of Valdeon

De Quintaro, Arturo - Brother of Ernesto

De Quintaro, Ernesto the Raven - Member of the Sacred Guard, A Lord of Valdeon

De Quintaro, Fausto - Steward of Varianne, Former Lord of Valdeon

Hernandez, Inez - Jorge's daughter

Jalora - Embodiment of Good Upon the Erthe

Mendoza, Alberto - Steward of San Marimosa and Father to the Jaguar

Mendoza, Berto the Jaguar - Member of the Sacred Guard, A Lord of Valdeon

Mendoza, Stephano - Captain of the San Marimosa Guard, Cousin of Berto the Jaguar

Mendoza, Yuli the Otter - Member of the Sacred Guard, A Lord of Valdeon

Neto - Jorge Pacarro's lead farm hand

No Name, Zoya - Sister of Julian D'Antoiné

Orryo - Minion of Julian D'Antoiné

Pacarro, Donna - Jorge's wife

Pacarro, Duarto - Jorge's son

Pacarro, Jorge - Former Squire to Cesar Santiago and leader of the western refugees

Santiago, Cesar - Steward of San Lucida, Former Lord of Valdeon

Santiago, Lucio the Ferret - Member of the Sacred Guard, A Lord of Valdeon

Sarcion - Embodiment of Evil Upon the Erthe

Isle of Carlotta

Rodrigo - Mayor of Carlotta

Tymon - Aunt Charlotte's companion and protector

Von Bohdan, Charlotte - Seth's aunt and the Iron Queen of Carlotta

The Jalora Legion

Arthur - Squire to White Tiger

Baldemar, Gregory the Phoenix - Partisan of the Lion and Wolf's trusted ally

Boyd - The Coyote's squire

Donny - The Dragonfly's squire

Dragon, Francis (Cardinal) - Leader of the Jalora Legion

Dragonfly, Ronald (Acolyte) - Ranger and friend to Seth

Elder, Jason the Coyote - Seth's "First Marked" Lion Friend

Falcon, Tad Lambert (Bishop) - Member of the Bishops Council

Manitou, Burgess (Bishop) - Member of the Bishops Council

Roland - The Phoenix' squire

Swan, Percival (Bishop) - Member of the Bishops Council

Von Wolkhurst, Peter the Gargoyle - Crown Prince of Tslavia

White Tiger - Ranger and Phoenix' second-in-command

Lea and the United Realms

Dawson, Tory - Member of Cadet Beta Three. From Lea. Lion Friend

Claybank, Amery (Twin) - Member of Cadet Beta Three. From the Outpost Territories. Lion Friend

Claybank, Aubrey (Twin) - Member of Cadet Beta Three. From the Outpost Territories. Lion Friend

Dancer, Sergeant - Master Sergeant over Cadet Beta Three. Lion Friend

Finley, Lieutenant - Commandant Sharp's aid

Lambert, Lady Philippa - Sister-in-law of Bishop Tad (Falcon) Lambert, Lord of Ghent

Lambert, Fanny - Daughter to Lady Phillipa

Sharp, Commandant - Leader of the United Realm Army

Akutar

Changeling - Lord Gorman's Spy

The Dirge - Sarcion's Undead Assassins

Gorman - A Lord of Akutar, General of the Jackal Army

Uther - Emperor of Akutar

Whisper - Emissary of the Akutarian Emperor

The Realm of Dreams and Mist

D'Antoiné, Ignacio - Seth's ancestor and teacher

D'Antoiné, Hugo - Seth's ancestor and teacher

Places

The United Realms of Andara

Amity - Island in the Grey Cliff isles

Commonwealth - The Small Circular Space of Land Surrounding Lea, The UR Capitol

Eastland Isle - Located Off the West Coast of Andara

Estabelle - Located in Valdeon, Home of the Hawk

Fort L'Azure - Located in Valdeon, Home of the Rabbit

Fort La Val - Located in Valdeon, Home of the Otter

Ghent - Located in the Central Mainland Region

Grey Cliff Isles - Located Two Days from Andara's Mainland

Haven Bay - Town located on Marianna

Heidelbrecht - Located in northcentral Andara. Ancient ally of Valdeon

Horner - Island in the Grey Cliff Isles

Larkspur - Island in the Grey Cliff Isles

Lea - Located in the Center of the Commonwealth, Capitol of the UR

Marianna - Smallest Island in the Grey Cliff Isles

Muellerton, Heidelbrecht - Outpost where Wolf and Tulio are hidden

Obsidian Citadel - Located in Lea, Headquarters of the Jalora Legion

Palace of Kings - Located in San Leonora, Home of the Lion

Port City - Located on Eastland Isle, Major Airship Port

San Angelica - Located in Valdeon, Home of the Fox

San Leonora - Located in Valdeon, Home of the Lion

San Lucida - Located in Valdeon, Home of the Ferret

San Marimosa - Located in Valdeon, Home of the Jaguar

San Rudalfo - Located in Valdeon, Home of the Wolf

Temple Cave - Located in the Mountains on the Border of Valdeon and Tslavia, Place of Power

Tslavia - Located in the Central Mainland Region, Ancient Enemy of Valdeon

Valdeon - Located in the Southern Mainland Region, Realm of the Lion

Varianne - Located in Valdeon, Home of the Raven

Other Island Nations

Azure Isles - Located South of Andara's Mainland, Ruled by Raiders

Isle of Carlotta - Located Off the Coast of Valdeon

Cottage on the Cliff - Aunt Charlotte's mansion on Carlotta

Foreign Nations

Akutar - Located Far to the East of Andara's Mainland, Home of the Jackal

The Pearl Isles - Located Far to the West of Marianna, Home of the Luminawni

The Realm of Dreams and Mist

Created by the Jalora to model Otherworld, the Realm of Dreams and Mist is a place where time and reality are suspended. This is where the Jalora lives while it waits for the next Jalora Master.

Things

Altar of Providence - Stronghold of the Jalora on Andara. Consists of three parts: The Crown of Sorrows, The Lion's Seat and the Orb of Valdeon

Book of Ancients - Contains the history of Andara. Once opened by the Lion, its magic begins the transformation of the ring bearer into the Jalora Master

Crown of Sorrows - Crown of the King of Valdeon

Horde's Cry - Vocal weapon utilized by the Jalora Rangers to instill fear into their enemies. It makes one ranger sound like many

First Marked - See Lion Friend. This individual is the first person marked by a new Lion. They are honored and respected with almost as much reverence as the Lords of Valdeon

Lion Child Vessel - Captured at the very moment a bearer loses his innocence, this ethereal child is the vessel the Jalora uses to inhabit the Master's body as it walks among the world of men

Lion Friend - An individual who has either saved the Lion's life or has done a great service for him. They are marked by the Lion's power with three claw lines down the left forearm. It is considered treason to harm or threaten a Lion Friend

Lion's Guard - In the time of a Jalora Master, the Lords of Valdeon (Sacred Guard) are transformed into a special guard. Their only purpose is to protect the master. They are bound to him forever

Lion Ring - Symbol of the Contract Between the D'Antoiné Family and the Jalora

Lion's Roar - Mighty vocal weapon granted only to the bearer of the Lion Ring. Has the power to bring down mountains and devastate armies

Lion's Seat - Golden Throne of Valdeon

Orb of Valdeon - Conduit of the Jalora's Power to Andara's Ranger

Partisan to the Jalora Master - Traditional role of honor held by the bearer of the Phoenix Ring. The partisan holds a place of power in the Master's court and is considered a valued councilor to the throne

Regent Medallion - Made from the purest gold, the medallion contains the symbol of the Altar of Providence. Its magic grants the bearer power and ruling authority over Valdeon should there be no Lion upon the throne

Right-Hand - This special ranger is second only to the Jalora Master. He is bound by his very soul to protect the Lion and calm his temper when the power threatens to escape

Sign of the Coming - Prophecy which provide omens and signs a Jalora Master has been born

Voice of the Right-Hand - This vocal weapon is a rare and destructive gift used in service to the Jalora Master.

About The Author

C. R. Richards is the award-winning author of *The Mutant Casebook Series*. Her literary career began as a part-time columnist for a small entertainment newspaper. She wore several hats: food critic, entertainment reviewer and cranky editor. A lover of horror and dark fantasy stories, she enjoys telling tales of intrigue and adventure. Her most recent literary projects include the epic dark fantasy series, *Heart of The Warrior* and the novel length dark fantasy thriller, *Pariah*. She is an active member of Rocky Mountain Fiction Writers and Horror Writers Association.

For more information on the author's books and upcoming events, please visit her website:
www.crrichards.com

Other Books
by
C.R. Richards

THE LORDS OF VALDEON
(Heart of the Warrior Series - Book One)

THE OBSIDIAN GATES
(Heart of the Warrior Series - Book Two)

PARIAH

LOST MAN'S PARISH
(Short Fiction)

PHANTOM HARVEST
(The Mutant Casebook Series)

Did you enjoy the book?
Please leave a review and let me know.
I'd love to hear from you!

www.ingramcontent.com/pod-product-compliance
Lightning Source LLC
Chambersburg PA
CBHW030642120726
47905CB00001B/17